The *Miracle* on *Monhegan* Island

ALSO BY ELIZABETH KELLY

The Last Summer of the Camperdowns

Apologize, Apologize!

LIVERIGHT PUBLISHING CORPORATION

A Division of W. W. Norton & Company
Independent Publishers Since 1923
New York | London

ELIZABETH KELLY

The Miracle on Monhegan Island

A NOVEL

For information about permission to reproduce selections from this book,
write to Permissions, W. W. Norton & Company, Inc.,
500 Fifth Avenue, New York, NY 10110

For information about special discounts for bulk purchases, please contact
W. W. Norton Special Sales at specialsales@wwnorton.com or 800-233-4830

Manufacturing by Berryville Graphics
Book design by Ellen Cipriano
Production manager: Julia Druskin

ISBN 978-1-63149-179-5

Liveright Publishing Corporation
500 Fifth Avenue, New York, N.Y. 10110
www.wwnorton.com

W. W. Norton & Company Ltd.
Castle House, 75/76 Wells Street, London W1T 3QT

1 2 3 4 5 6 7 8 9 0

The Miracle on Monhegan Island is a novel. All of the characters are products of the author's imagination, and all of the settings, locales, and events have been invented by the author or are used fictitiously. Any resemblance to actual events, or to real persons, living or dead, is entirely coincidental.

For Caitlin

The *Miracle*
on
Monhegan
Island

"I am his Highness' dog at Kew;
Pray tell me, sir, whose dog are you?"

—ALEXANDER POPE

One

~~~~~~

May 1986

I disappeared from my life in the time it takes to buy a bottle of Yoo-hoo and a package of pork rinds. One moment I was curled up in the back of a cream-colored Mercedes Ponton sedan, sleeping the bespoke slumber of those destined for high thread counts, the next moment I was in an alien world of Naugahyde and errant springs, wondering what happened to all that buttery tan Italian leather.

Even before fear there's smell and this old car smelled like a thousand nights without mornings. I hardly had time to suppress my gag reflex when that old beater squealed out of the convenience store parking lot, fishtailing onto the main drag, and throwing me from the backseat onto a musty floor upholstered in stale onion rings, empty soda cans, and mildew.

"Go! Go! Get out of here!" the young guy who grabbed me was shouting, hotfooting it into the passenger seat, door flung open, jerky momentum slamming it shut. Bouncing in his seat, head swiveling this way and that, he hollered for the woman behind the wheel to drive faster as she gunned it for the nearest highway exit, carping and chewing all the way, her fist pounding the steering wheel.

Climbing back onto the seat, I huddled in the corner and focused on the backs of their heads. His hair swept the collar of his shirt in irregular black layers. Hers was a chemically tortured rack of what looked like lemon-yellow plastic fibers. He twisted in his seat, his profile visible, his skin white as snow.

Insides madly spinning, my mind playing hopscotch, I was trying to beat back panic when, in a sudden surge of recall, they came to me— my father's instructions about hiding your fears. Don't turn them into an opportunity for others to exploit or, worse, enjoy. Oh, but too late, I was leaking terror, holes springing up everywhere. Already I could feel the winnowing effects of too much water and not enough oxygen.

I started to pant.

Snow White bounced around to face me. "Don't be scared," he said, leaning over the back of the seat, big grin, hand outstretched, fingers wriggling playfully. "I'm not going to hurt you."

I had no reason to believe him, except that I wanted to, more than I had ever wanted anything, and with his bright complexion, high broad cheeks, and wide full mouth, he gave off a surprisingly mellow air of affability, creating an unexpected pocket of mildness amid the mayhem, a gently swinging hammock on a summer day strung between before and after.

Had he been a dog, he might have been a light-boned Landseer Newfoundland, black-and-white and friendly, improbably bordering on lovable, possessing a kind of elegant detachment—there was something about the eyes, though, they didn't match up—ice-blue and opaque, elliptical shape. This wasn't the brown-eyed family dog. He had cat's eyes—the only thing missing were the telltale bird feathers.

"It's okay, squirt," he said. "You're in good hands."

"*You're* nuts," the woman said. "What did you go and do that for? *This* is nuts. I don't need this, Spark."

"Relax," he said. "He's cute, right?"

"What are we going to do with him? Anybody ever tell you that you got a problem with impulse control?" she said, hoping to annoy him, but he laughed her off.

"You and my old man are going to get along great," he said.

I had a feeling he'd earned the name Spark—as hard as she tried to engage him, he wouldn't fight with her, just smiled and poked and teased, her exasperation the accelerant. She kept getting more worked up, cheeks flushed and glowing. I wanted to let her know she was wasting her time but it wouldn't have made any difference. She wasn't the brightest star in the night.

We drove for hours, dense evergreens on bleak monotonous loop, the wind rushing noisily into the car's interior through a half-open window that would neither roll up nor down, each mile taking me farther away from all that I knew, the speed with which it was happening magnifying the strangeness, until I felt myself becoming a foreign destination, exotic as some hothouse tropical, a green tree snake dangling from a leafy canopy, humid and unknown even to myself.

It grew dark and cool, the wind rocked the car and the woman's demands intensified.

"Let's just pull over and dump him by the side of the road," she— her name was Evie—argued.

"No . . . Think about what could happen to him . . . Jesus . . . What kind of a creepy suggestion is that?"

"Hey, I'm not the creep who took him, okay?" she said, voice growing shrill. "Let's just dump him and forget him. He'll be fine. Somebody will come along."

Powerless and striving to keep my imagination in check, I closed my eyes, buried beneath the crush of a devastating realization—the only thing between me and the blackness was the unknown heart of the man who stole me. At one point, the car slowed and pulled onto the shoulder, next to a quarry, foreboding crunch of gravel beneath the wheels. Evie turned off the ignition, climbed out and stood on the sunken tarmac, hands on her hips, yawning noisily.

Spark stepped outside and stretched. Bending down he picked something up and threw his arm high over his head. Silence, followed by the plunk of stone hitting water; the gurgle as it sank. He hollered something crazy-unintelligible into the night.

I coiled into a tight knot, pretended to be asleep and waited while they talked, their voices an indecipherable tumble, rising and falling. Finally, Spark opened the driver's-side door and slid in behind the wheel. The engine turned over. His turn to drive. I exhaled but not so you would notice. Retreating inside myself, I silently called out to the moon, my captive misery a visible glow on the midnight-blue surface of the water.

Even now, with all that's happened, I still turn to the moon in the small hope that someday it will call back to me.

At sunrise I awoke to the foggy chirrup of morning birds whose songs I didn't recognize and to the damp soupy scent of salt and seaweed, eelgrass and iodine, the briny smell of the Atlantic Ocean saturating the cool air. Within the car and beyond, it stunk of stranded shellfish and marine animals in pungent stages of life and death, decay and decomposition.

We were parked in a remote beachside picnic area somewhere in what I would discover was Maine, wooden tables gray and rotting, old tire swing hanging lopsided from a broken tree branch. Evie and Spark were passed out in the front seat, heads touching, bodies flung about like dirty laundry. Her fish-lips rippling, Evie was snoring, a low, rhythmic *phloof, phloof, phloof* sound—which had the somewhat cheering effect of making me think less about being killed and more about committing murder.

Hiding my face in the seat cushions, I thought about my parents, my family. It had been only hours but already I could barely remember what home smelled like. What it *didn't* smell like was unwashed hair and lawlessness—the latter composed of one part hangover, two parts cheap perfume, and a dash of incontinence.

I imagined myself walking up to the front door of my house, past the tended garden borders, fragrant violet clumps of lavender—that cloying musk—spilling into tall drifts of white cosmos, and climbing up the hand-cut limestone steps, the black lacquer door opening to reveal ebony-and-white checkerboard tiles in the entranceway, the walls a deep shade of coral, copper umbrella stand to the right, decades-old fern in an antique brass urn to the left, my mother and father there to greet me.

How long before memories fade? Before what was once in front of you becomes what's inside of you? Until who you were is only a remote story evoking a vague nostalgia.

Something I've learned: Not long.

I didn't happen by accident. There was no crude playing at all fours in my personal history. Like all that came before me, my parents, my grandparents, and their mothers and fathers, I am the product of an arranged marriage, part of an intricate historic design. In my family, making heads for children's ears was a strategic and purposeful endeavor.

Yet my origins are not without romance.

I am the chrysanthemum dog, the Chinese sleeve dog, the little lion, the holy dog presented to the imperial court by the Dalai Lama, the last surviving member of two great noble canine families—Zhou on my maternal side and Nuwa on my father's. Marco Polo himself recorded the perfumed presence of my forebears as they sat at the right hand of the Kublai Khan in his Peking palace. Prized and cosseted, insulated from the rough textures of ordinary life, my progenitors were tended to by eunuchs who bathed them in pearl-powdered waters, used violet-scented silk ribbons to tie their hair, and fed them a diet of fried magnolia and lotus flowers.

My ancestors drank kumiss from jade cups. Their portraits adorn ancient tapestries in museums and galleries around the world. Such privilege is not without its dangers. My family was all but wiped out when, in a violent concussion of love and hate, a eunuch poisoned most of them with ground glass rather than reveal the secrets of our bloodlines. Their gilt memories wind through my pedigree like gold tracery on a blue-glazed porcelain vase.

Then, common ownership by the many was forbidden; anyone caught outside the palace with one of my ascendants was put to death. Things are different today. Now, any shallow-ender can snap a collar on a Shih Tzu. Not an ideal situation, but what can you do? This is the way we live. I leave the self-pity to Pekingese. As even the dumbest dog will attest—that would be an Airedale, by the way—Pekingese are professional whiners and so grandiose. It's an absolute bore to listen to them go on about past glories.

I would rather sit through a Doberman's tedious accounts of war or listen to a Lab describe in drooling detail the best meal he ever had than listen to one more Pekingese name-drop their celebrated champions: Queen Victoria, P. G. Wodehouse, Sister Parish.

We know. *We know.*

My preference is to live in the world as it is, which, I have on good authority—my own—is no less interesting or challenging than it's ever been. It may surprise you to learn that dogs are living repositories of all that's gone before us; archival knowledge of the timeless world is in our DNA. We're born with full cosmic recall. The canine brain is an informal encyclopedia of recollection and received wisdom, for the most part anyway.

When it comes to the pug, however, think the Reader's Digest condensed edition.

For me, there wasn't a traditional coming-of-age trajectory, no bittersweet loss of innocence, no thorn-strewn path to enlightenment, nor cruelly acquired wisdom picked up in all the wrong places. Well, maybe a little, the odd thing, here and there.

Humans like to imagine knowledge is power, but to seek power is to lack knowledge so there goes that. I can't comment on Plato's theories about innatism as they apply to people, though I suspect he was on to something, but I can tell you that dogs do possess such intuitive knowledge, the difference being that we have unfiltered even casual access to it.

Why do you think we're so pleasure-loving? The dog doesn't exist who feels the need to ask: Who am I? Okay, maybe the odd schnauzer has pondered his identity but that's only because schnauzers generally can't remember their own names.

As I would come to learn that summer, humans spend so much of their lives anxiously coaxing skittish memories and obscure knowledge from their shadowy subconscious. Roll down the car window as it clips down a country road, stick your head outside, close your eyes and quit asking yourself how you should live your life; turn yourself over to the wind.

I was born on March 5, 1983. I am unusual in that I was spared the early trauma of separation that most dogs experience as puppies, wrenched from their mothers at eight weeks, never knowing their fathers. The only survivor in a litter of four, I grew up in the same house as my parents, with whom I spent the first three years of my life.

If adaptation is critical to survival, then my parents were notable pragmatists. My mother, Ting Ting, an American, took top honors at Westminster. My father, Alex, spent his first three years in Scotland before immigrating to the States. He won Best in Show at Crufts.

Prized for their beauty, and contribution to the breed, my parents put great stock in intellectual rigor and character development, which meant I grew up listening to stories about the heroic exploits of the grand dogs of myth and history, literature and science, though my father harbored bristling skepticism, bordering on snarling resentment, toward the latter.

While he respected the dogs who sacrificed their lives for Banting in his quest to make insulin, he viewed medical research with animals, especially the wholesale persecution of beagles—the canine version of Lennie Small—to be a stain on humanity's soul. Angered by the abuses of the Russian space program, he considered the death of Laika to be an unforgivable betrayal of trust between man and dog.

"Never put faith in anyone who loudly refers to the 'greater good,'" he told me. "It's how the wicked announce themselves."

The old boy had a real distaste and distrust for dogs in films and on TV. Acting, to him, enshrined vanity and exalted insincere performance, which, for a dog, is a mortal sin; inauthenticity, he argued, was a form of suicide. He held Lassie in particular contempt—a male dog pretending to be a female!

"What do you expect from a collie?" He said, having grown up with smooth, rough-coated, and bearded collies in Scotland, though he made grudging exception for the hardworking Border collie. Don't get him started on the subject of service dogs. Though he was a proponent of the classic expressions of friendship *freely given* between canines and humans, he was adamant that dogs be allowed to exercise personal choice. The sight of a listless and defeated guide dog in harness made him apoplectic. He considered it a form of indentured servitude, its incumbent loss of freedoms to him were "anti-dog."

My father took great pride in being a dog and although he loved individual people, and was devoted to our human family, he urged me to be realistic about humanity.

"Loveless beagles in sunless cages with their water tubes and their metal bowls, abandoned military dogs, discarded like jeeps on the field of battle—remember them. The Canadian Eskimo dogs murdered by the thousands over twenty years by the Royal Canadian Mounted Police, honor their sacrifice," he said, spouting editorial commentary with the same ease with which a canary sings.

Opinionated nature aside, my father, a liberal in social and political matters, was conservative in his domestic views and habits and cherished the traditional canine virtues of loyalty and faithfulness above all else. As a Scot, he idolized Greyfriars Bobby and talked about him with reverence and respect. He loved to tell us about his visit as a young dog to the statue commemorating his hero's vigilance.

It's hard to imagine either Martin or his wife Madelyn, the married couple who made up our human family, commanding such devotion. Martin was the son of a famous pop singer from the sixties. An only child, he inherited a considerable sum when his father died, which allowed him to indulge his weakness for antique cars, while Madelyn, a chocolatier, focused her limited attention span on raising show dogs. She had some success with Maltese, before moving on to Clumber spaniels, then she decided to raise Shih Tzu, but we too, proved to be an impulse.

They were good to us and kind, agreeable enough, if you enjoy baby talk and adult babble—wine was a preferred topic of conversation. I never could understand my father's inexplicable affection for Martin but how do you ever know another's heart? Romantic notions aside, canines are not particularly good judges of character. We're just more inclined than people to make the best of things, though I was less inclined than most.

My father was one kind of dog and I was another breed altogether.

His hero was Greyfriars Bobby, mine was Miles Davis. All I ever wanted to do was sound my own trumpet, chase cats, roll in carrion, piss in corners, and steal food from plates. When I was an adolescent I envied big dogs their access to toilet water. How I longed in secret to march alongside the dogs of war, to jump from planes, penetrate enemy lines, do something interesting with my life.

I wanted to sail the world and see its wonders from steerage, not first class. Sometimes I thought about running away but it would have broken my parents' hearts, a price of freedom I was unwilling to pay. Despite the example and early training of my father—his earnestness, his penchant for turning everything into a Sunday school lesson, his brown-eyed devotion to those he loved, embarrassed me—I vowed never to become one of those dogs curled up mournfully on a freshly dug grave waiting in vain to hear again the sound of my master's voice.

The experience of life has a way of teaching us what our parents can't.

As a dog I'm spared the stigma attached to personal circumstance—no one will ever fault me for lack of ambition, or laziness or poor judgment, nor will they celebrate me for my work ethic, or my brilliance, or exalt me for my pursuit of excellence. No one will ever revile me as the rich kid I was once, or bitterly lament my easy access to the keys of the kingdom. I'm spared the platitudes and the junk-thinking, the drivel about making your own luck.

Like my parents, I was intended for the international show ring, but a crooked tooth and controversial coat colour ended the dream, so I prepared myself, instead, for the indolence of the satin pillow— sounds good but it has its challenges, believe me—unless you're some- one who enjoys being compressed against the zeppelin-sized breasts of a cooing woman oozing Shalimar and cocoa bean.

(It could have been worse. I could have found myself earning an obedience degree or doing the merengue in a freestyle canine dance competition.)

Dogs have a saying: Where I am is where I find myself. Among canines, reinvention is always a possibility. In my case, life simply picked me up in one place and put me down in another; that's what happens when you weigh fifteen—all right, eighteen—pounds.

How can it be that the worst thing that ever happened to me was also the best thing? I think about my mother and father. I wonder what they would think of me. Would they know me at all? How it would astound them to see who I've become.

The first three years of my life I was called Lupine. I *know*, but it suited me then.

Now, I would tell you that my name has only ever been Ned.

You might be tempted to think that being a dog, I'm not equipped to tell this story, based as it is on human waywardness, that my illicit origins—I'm stolen goods, after all—in combination with the narrowness of my universe makes me unsophisticated, stunts my view of things, and inhibits my understanding of events and people and ideas.

You might be right—on the other hand, it's precise focus that yields rare discovery. There's no real genius in distraction. Open your mind and your heart and from the stoop of your porch you can chart the distance between heaven and hell.

Two

〰〰〰〰〰〰〰〰〰〰〰〰〰〰〰〰〰〰〰〰〰〰〰〰〰〰〰〰〰〰〰〰〰〰〰〰〰

Humming to himself and whistling, Spark carried me aboard the ferry, keeping me partly concealed in his jacket, his hand at rest on my head. Evie, who I'd begun to think of as an animated cold sore, cigarette dangling from her bottom lip, kept a sullen distance, all those big black birds circling overhead, the seagulls screaming, flying and falling, seal families sunning themselves on the rocks.

The water was rough—Evie, turning canned-pea green and moaning, throwing up over the side, the boat banging its head against the tumult, going up high and crashing down low in jarring sequence, spray from the waves soaking the upper deck—until finally we rocked, then rolled into the harbor at Monhegan Island.

It was the beginning of May 1986. I popped up to have a proper look around at the new world, and though I didn't know it at the time, it was all there, my second life laid out in front of me like a prophecy, the whole of my future contained in this isolated and intimate place.

"Let's go. What's the holdup?" Spark asked, extending his arm to Evie, who shoved her hands deep into her pockets, shook her head and refused to leave the ferry.

"This is the end of the line for me. I'm going back. I don't know why the hell I came this far."

Spark laughed. "Come on. Don't be like that . . ."

Was it just me or was he not sounding very persuasive?

"Forget it. I'm so over this. Five weeks I've wasted on you." Seemed Evie preferred another bout of seasickness to one more moment spent in Spark's company.

Spark shrugged, and squinted skyward. "Only five weeks? I would have said at least six. Suit yourself," he said, surprising her with the jauntiness of his indifference. "Sweet," he whispered in my ear. He swung around and, setting me down on the ground, started walking. I hesitated, watching the tail end of him. He stopped, glanced round, snapped his fingers and whistled. Still, I didn't move.

"Hey, up to you," he said. Pausing, he considered me for a minute. "Okay," he said, briefly meeting my eyes. "Good luck. See you around."

I observed him as he made his way up the steep incline, letting the distance between us build before I began to follow him. Catching up, I trotted out in front, nose to ground, sweeping the area for information.

"Glad you decided to join me," he said, seeming pleased. "Truth is, I could use a friend."

He wasn't the only one. Kneeling down, he called me over to him.

"Sorry, little guy," he said, rubbing my ears, "for . . . you know . . . my, uh, spontaneity . . . I'll make it up to you."

"Oh, will you look at this, then?"

I detected the remnants of an Irish accent. Spark closed his eyes, fortifying himself for the encounter to come. He stood up and turned around. "Mrs. Houton," he said. His eyes widened. "Tommy?"

"Hey, Spark. What's shaking?" Tommy, of indeterminate age, large and oval-shaped, was alarmingly smooth and white, like a giant egg come to life; all circumference and partitioned in the middle by a wide belt with an aggressively oversize buckle.

His mother—the hen!—gray-blond hair in a loose clutch at the back of her head, wearing a faded floral cotton dress and white apron, with big galoshes that came to mid-calf, was a creamier white offset by a rosy flush of pinpricks in her cheeks and her neck, a kind of bursting redness that created the impression of a peach with high blood pressure.

"It's obvious by the look of him how it's going," Mrs. Houton said, turning away from Tommy to address Spark. "No need to ask what you've been up to. You look about as low-down as a junkie's feet. You've got the map of the underworld tattooed all over your face. If your poor mother could see you now . . . I always used to say to anyone who'd listen, trouble will find that boy wherever he goes."

"Yes, you did say that," Spark said agreeably, eyes forecasting somewhere past the top of her head.

"It wasn't that long ago your mother and I caught you teaching my Tommy how to smoke cigarettes at White Head . . ."

"I don't know. Twenty years seems like a pretty long time . . .".

"I saw you there, I spotted you hiding up in the branches of that tree. Tommy could have been killed. He has the vertigo. You didn't think I'd know enough to look up, did you? If I'd a got ahold of you I would have beat the blood out of you."

So that's what explained Tommy's pallor.

"Do you remember what you said to me, because I'll never forget it if I live to be a thousand . . ." Mrs. Houton's flush had expanded so now it rose up from the divide of her bosom to the widow's peak on her forehead.

"I hope you do, by the way, live to be a thousand . . ." Spark said, sneaking a glance over at Tommy, who looked down at his feet.

"You said—"

"I said: 'Ahoy, skunk! Get back in your hole!'"

Tommy laughed so loudly and unexpectedly at the memory that my tail temporarily lost its curl.

Mrs. Houton gasped. "This is what I'm talking about. Wherever you are trouble follows. I haven't heard Tommy laugh like that in . . ." She searched in vain for a number.

"Four years," Spark supplied. "Last time I was home was four years ago."

"Nowhere to run, nowhere to hide," Spark said when, halfway through what should have been a fifteen-minute walk, we were stopped next by a middle-aged man in a red plaid lumberjack shirt with long stringy hair and cartoon teeth standing in front of his weathered, cedar-shingled cottage. He was bent over, examining a lobster trap, but straightened up when he saw us.

"Whoa! Lock up your daughters. Spark Monahan, as I live and breathe, is that really you?" He scratched his head and laughed uneasily.

"I came to make peace, not love," Spark said. "Hi, Beans."

"Where've you been? What the hell have you been up to all this time?"

"Traveling mostly, picking up odd jobs here and there."

"Few scrapes with the law, too? Just what I heard, not saying it's true, mind you. Your father told me you'd fallen in with a bad crowd."

"No," Spark said, "that's an exaggeration. My old man worries too much and he has strong opinions." Spark paused and pointed to his eyes. "Filtered through a distorted lens."

"Then again, Hugh told me he had to pay your legal fees after you got in some mysterious jam down in Louisiana . . ."

"Have you ever driven through Louisiana?" Spark said. "Saint Peter would get charged with a felony in Louisiana."

"So you say . . . Anyway, it's been a while. Seems to me the last time you were home was when your mother died," Beans said, moving on to a different topic. "Hard to believe Ellen's been gone that long . . ."

Spark nodded. "Yup."

"Seems like yesterday. I'll never forget your father, the state he was in, summoning me to the house . . . Lord, the smell of all that blood . . . Tough on everyone. Her going out that way. Jesus, she pretty much exploded, when you think about it."

"Yeah . . . well . . . What are you going to do? Is there a good way to go?" Spark said, wincing at Beans' indelicate reveling, as I continued to explore.

"Oh, I don't know. Ask Nelson Rockefeller . . ." He laughed. "Are you still beating yourself up? 'Cause it would've happened irregardless, you know? Nobody blames you."

"I'm not so sure about that," Spark said, sounding vulnerable, pushing loose a clump of dirt with the tip of his running shoe.

"You mean Hugh? Aw, hell, you know your brother. That's not his style. He keeps his judgments to himself."

"I hadn't noticed."

"Say, he's doing good for himself, isn't he? Gosh, that boy can paint a picture! He painted me a lobster one time and damned if I didn't want to pop it into a pot of boiling water that's how real it looked. Anyway, he never said a nasty word about you and what happened to anyone that I've heard . . . Look here, there's nothing you could've done. Hughie knows that. The way I see it, the Lord spared you in his mercy. Thank God you weren't there. And as for the little fellow, I'll betcha he don't remember a thing about it. Praise the Lord. Awful business. Good thing your dad's a man of faith."

"Is that what he is?"

"Don't be a smart-ass . . . You know, you need to put that mouth of yours on lockdown, if you don't mind a suggestion." He pointed at Spark with his forefinger. "They broke the mold when they made your old man, and don't you forget it."

"You got that right." Spark said, though I got the impression they were coming at this thing from two different angles. "Believe me,

Beans, I'm not looking for any trouble." He held up his hands in front of his face as if he were surrendering to an invisible enemy. For all his bravado, I was forming the impression that Spark, pale and thin, was burnt out. He looked as if he'd been eating carnival food, subsisting for too long on cotton candy and corn dogs.

"Good. Your dad's got enough on his plate. I hope you're home to lend him support after this mess with the concert . . . a damn shame. I always say your father is a creative and spiritual genius, but the practical side got ahead of him."

"That's the propaganda anyway . . . Most of it generated by him. Maybe he's just too ambitious given his limited resources. The problem is he doesn't have the dough to back him up and then he gets himself into a jackpot—"

"Listen, pardon my French, but you don't know what the hell you're talking about. You weren't there that day. It was a miracle, what he pulled off. The music and the ocean, all those people, all those voices raised up to God. Why, it was as if the sky opened up and the Lord himself came down to lead the orchestra . . . It changed people's lives, I'm telling you . . . and then the damn bankers and the damn reporters and the damn politicians got to pissing all over it . . . "

"Sorry I missed it . . . a Woodstock for religious geriatrics isn't exactly my thing."

"Still with the mouth . . . Maybe we should talk about something else." Beans nodded in my direction. "Fancy-looking mutt you got there. Real nice little mover, isn't he? A regular daisy cutter."

"I hear the kid's been wanting a dog so . . . "

My ears perked up.

"Good. He's reaching a bad age. Maybe it'll keep him out of mischief during the teen years . . . he's got a look about him. Reminds me of someone else I once knew . . . I said to your father, 'That one is going to be a handful someday.'"

"Depends on what you mean by a handful," Spark said.

"I figure I mean the same thing everybody else means when they talk about someone being a pain in the ass," Beans said. Despite the thin veneer of friendliness, Spark and Beans were having what humans refer to as a testy exchange.

"Come on. Were you ever a kid? What's he supposed to do? Crochet? He's twelve years old . . . What the hell?" Spark was sounding defensive. Beans took another detour.

"All right, all right. Well, this little fellow's a real thoroughbred, anyway," Beans said, eyeing me closely. "Must have set you back a bit." He raised both eyebrows skeptically and looked at Spark. "Does Pastor Ragnar know you're bringing a dog with you?"

"I stopped asking my dad's permission a long time ago. I'm not worried. He likes dogs well enough." Spark pushed his hair off his forehead and ran his hand down the back of his head, wrapping his fingers around his neck as if something ached. "Guess I should be shoving off. Good to see you," he said, setting out, offering up a perfunctory wave of his hand.

"Hey, if you're looking for work I could use some help on the boat. May's a big month, if you remember," Beans said.

"Not something I'm likely to forget. Maybe, yeah, I might just take you up on it. Thanks."

"Jesus Christ," he muttered after we'd gone a little way. It wasn't the first time Spark, who seemed to feel about God the way Jane Goodall's kid must have felt about chimpanzees, was driven to take the Lord's name in vain. "Kill me now," he said under his breath, snapping a twig in half. He looked down at me. "You know what? This stuff about never being able to go home again . . . If only . . . The truth is you can never really leave. You're forever sixteen where you grew up."

We continued along the hilly path and I noticed his step had lost some of its spring, but then again, so had mine. He picked me up as the terrain grew more rugged and carried me the last stretch.

"You believe in God?" he asked me, staring into my face as he walked and talked, chatting away as if I were a buddy of long standing and it was the most natural question in the world to ask of a hijacked stranger. (Didn't matter to him that I was a dog, nor did I feel especially flattered by the attention. I had an idea Spark would engage an opossum if it made eye contact.) "When I was a kid, my dad used to make me go to his church every Sunday. He's a minister, invented his own religion, well, you'll meet him soon enough, and sometimes there'd be guest speakers and they'd talk about how their belief in God transformed them, turned them from bad to good, though you'd have to take their word for that . . . let's just say it wasn't usually an obvious transformation . . ."

"One time, this big fat guy showed up. He was huge, had to be three hundred pounds. He wasn't that old, in his early twenties. He starts right in: 'I was a drug addict. I was a thief. I was an alcoholic. I was promiscuous. I was a gambler . . .' So by now I'm dying inside and next time he says, 'I was . . .' I shout out, 'Orson Welles!' "

"See this," he said pointing to a faded vertical scar that ran from the bottom edge of his right nostril to the middle of his upper lip. "After the service, my old man took me to the church basement and let me have it. Split my lip, like he'd taken a box cutter to it. I needed eight stitches. Sounds weird but that's when I started to believe in God. I realized the universe is not an indifferent place. Somebody's keeping score. You've always got to pay up. There's nothing random about taking a shot to the head."

I wagged my tail for the first time in two days. I always did like a good story—my father was a great storyteller—and Spark had a million of them.

"I don't want to scare you about the guy. You've got to know when to push and when to pull when it comes to Pastor Ragnar," Spark said, lowering me back onto the ground. "You'll figure it out. Dealing with my old man's like an aerial walk. Only you're always working without a net. You're okay—unless you happen to trip."

We walked along the path until we came to a busy field, like something out of a kids' cartoon, flying insects and birds of all types taking off and landing everywhere around us. The wildflowers were blooming, and the tall grasses, purple and red, yellow and multiple shades of green, wavered in the wind. Soon the field of flowers gave way to the rocky shoreline and the panoramic ocean, the open sea, bubbling and spuming, roaring, overwhelming my senses, so everything I saw and heard and smelled conspired to make me blind and deaf and anosmic. So mighty was the effect, it was as if I'd come face to face with the metaphysical.

After a time, in the clearing mist, I was able to discern a storm-cloud gray house, slumped on one side, foundation crumbling, its cedar shakes curling and splitting. Looking as if it had been assembled from the gloaming, the old place was built on a foggy ridge of rock at Lobster Cove, on the southern tip of the island where it had stood for more than a century, facing down the open Atlantic.

At first, from a distance, the house seemed almost level with the shoreline, though as we grew closer I saw that it was set on higher ground and surrounded by massive boulders erected around a lumbering incline, as if nature had arranged a series of giant steps sloping incrementally downward to the water's edge, the waves rolling in, the house and the water dangerously intimate but mutually accepting, having carved an uneasy harmony out of all that wild proximity.

A depressive wraparound porch listed to the right, floorboards giving way. Moss grew thick over the roof, new growth sprouting, lime-green shoots poking through tangled clumps of brown roots, and a profuse ivy entangled the entire structure, the place so overwhelmed by vegetation it appeared to be something that had taken root in the ground, was itself alive and growing, nature having already begun its steady ruthless reclamation.

Bizarrely, the front door was painted a confounding van Gogh-yellow.

Worn and sagging, yet there was something in the house's demeanor suggesting a durable New England esthetic. On the one hand—that yellow door!—bold and unapologetic; on the other hand, dark and irritable, secretive, like the charismatic conundrum of a plainspoken friend concealing a mysterious past. With its brilliant slash of color, the house projected a kind of schizophrenia, managing to be both light and dark at the same time, as if the sun had taken up with the moon.

Wind shook the cracked window glass and lashed the spruce groves, waves battering the rocks, foamy arcs of spray adorning the shingles in a slick layer of seawater and salt.

With a shiver from the damp cool air, Spark cleared the steps in a couple of bounds. I bumped alongside him, navigated the broken boards, then sidestepped holes in the porch where the wood had collapsed. A screenless door, freed from its hinges, was propped up alongside the yellow door, which Spark reached out and opened.

Coming slowly up behind him, I peeked between his legs, which narrowly framed a good-sized living room, wider than it was long, cherry-chocolate wood paneling on its walls; the wide-planked floors, scuffed and scraped, still retained their honey-red pine hue. It felt vaguely nautical, like the living quarters of a vintage yacht that had known better days. An old sofa upholstered in faded cobalt-blue fabric sagged in the middle of the room in front of an open hearth. Two Mission-style chairs, in dark wood, with pumpkin-colored leather seats and backs, held positions on either side of the fireplace.

Books—there were books everywhere, in antique cases, in stacks on the floor, piled on occasional tables. Religious icons, too. Books and paintings. Canvases, some vivid, others muted, some watercolor, others in oil, took up every inch of wall space, dominating even the galley-style kitchen at the edge of the living room. The out-of-date refrigerator and stove were a rich retro shade of turquoise, defiantly tropical, as if someone had been forced to buy appliances when what they really wanted was a parrot. Old wooden stairs, chipped and sloping, decorated in hand-painted flowers and birds, creaked up to a second-floor loft. Another set of stairs visible beyond an open door on the main floor led to a separate upper level.

Down the hallway beyond the door I could see a couple of additional smaller rooms. Sunlight burned through the narrow crack in the living room's floor-length curtains, though the tall and wide kitchen windows were bare, the ocean swallowing the view. The overall effect was simultaneously deliberate and accidental. Not one thing about the place was modern or streamlined, everything was irregular, not a clean line in sight—particles of dust floated in the amber light, everything filtered through a burnished prism.

Steam rose from a pot of water boiling noisily on the stove. Spark and I both looked up at the sound of footsteps on the loft staircase. The young man with the russet hair who appeared at the top of the steps stopped his brisk descent mid-flight when he saw us. He managed to look both surprised and not surprised, which would turn out to be his default expression.

Spotting me, ignoring Spark, he paused at the bottom of the stairs to gently call me over to him. Bending down, extending his hand, he patted my head and scratched my ears and spoke softly to me, and then he stood up, walked into the kitchen, pulled a bowl from a cupboard and filled it with water.

"I'll bet you could eat something," he said as I gratefully gulped the water. He opened the refrigerator and pulled out some leftover chicken, which he chopped up and served to me on a sandwich plate. It was only then I realized how hungry I was.

Blue jeans stained with oil paint, his scent was all over the paintings on the walls. I knew from the conversation with Beans that Spark and Hugh were brothers, though I didn't need to be told—I could smell it on them, their blood connection—and despite the differences in their coloring and some minor physical details, they suggested a variation on the same theme, as if they had come off the assembly line, only one was issued in silver, the other in gold.

I guessed they were in their twenties, though I found out later that Spark, the older of the two brothers, was thirty-one, while Hugh was two years younger. Tall and slim, Hugh, had a heart-shaped face, wide mouth like a bow, slightly aquiline nose, fair complexion that matched his red-brown hair—a color not unlike my own—carelessly chopped, as if he'd lunged at it with a pair of dull scissors, uneven bangs a jagged fringe over his almond-shaped eyes, a few shades lighter than his hair.

"When's the last time he ate anything?" Hugh asked Spark, who shrugged and said I was fine, don't worry, he'd been taking care of me.

"Oh, it's obvious *you've* been taking care of him, all right," Hugh said.

"Good to see you, too, Hughie," Spark said.

"He's not just an ordinary mutt," Hugh said as I ate and listened, my good opinion of him solidifying. "Where did you get him? Snatch him from someone's yard or did you grab him from the backseat of a parked car?"

Ha! This ought to be interesting.

"No, but thanks for always thinking the worst . . . If you really want to know, I did odd jobs for this wealthy older woman in Vermont."

"Odd jobs? So that's what they call it in Vermont . . ."

"She couldn't keep him." Spark carried on as if he hadn't heard his brother. "She was sick or something, I don't know, needed to go to a nursing home, something like that. She asked me if I wanted him. Naturally, I thought of the kid . . ."

Hugh chuckled. "Now I know you're lying."

Spark tried to ignore the dig though it hit its mark. "What are you doing here? I heard about your show in New York . . . Congratulations, by the way."

"What the hell do you think I'm doing here? I go back and forth. I try to spend the summers here and the fall . . . and the winter . . . Truth is, I'm here pretty much all the time. Am I just going to walk away and leave Hally alone to fend for himself with Pop?"

Another jab. Things were heating up nicely when the yellow door blew open on a sudden gust of wind and banged against the wall. A boy rode into the room on a funnel of sea air, and a caravan of familiar jostling smells—fresh grass, brine, tree bark, something sweet. He smelled like Ivory Snow by way of a fishing boat.

If Spark and Hugh were tall and narrow silver birches, then Hally, twelve, almost thirteen, was a pawpaw tree, shorter, rounder, with broad shoulders and a narrow waist. Exotic by way of scrappy, he had blue-green eyes, golden hair, wide mouth turned up at the edges, and ample lips. A subtle but evident gap between his two top front teeth only added to his singular appearance. Despite his glossy cocker-spaniel's friendliness, those eyes had a familiar feline flicker.

"Hey," he said, stunned to see Spark. He fumbled for something else to say.

"Jesus, when did you grow up?" Spark said as Hally transferred his glance to Hugh.

"That's what kids do. It's been four years, Spark," Hugh said.

"Well, you look good," Spark said as he dropped stiffly down onto the sofa's edge. "Life treating you okay?"

"Yeah, sure." Rubbing his hands together, looking for a way to gather his thoughts, Hally bent down to first loosen, then tie up his running shoes, which is when I made my move and stepped out from behind the sofa.

"Whose dog?"

"Yours," Spark said.

"Mine?" he said. "He's mine." He wheeled around to face Hugh. "I can keep him, right?'

"Yeah . . ." Hugh said. "Sure. You can keep him."

"What are you asking him for?" Spark said. "I already said he was yours."

Typical human arrogance—they were under the impression this was all their decision. Lying down, head in my paws, I weighed my options and held my ground, resisting all entreaties.

"I think he wants to think about it," Hally said. "I get it. You don't even know me, do you?"

"Dogs don't care about things like that," Spark said. I was beginning to realize Spark enjoyed pretending to be obtuse. "You're good to him. You feed him. Throw him a bone, he's happy, that's it."

"How would you know?" Hally said. He got down on the floor, his gaze meeting mine at eye level. "You're thinking about it, aren't you?" he said. "It's okay. I'd want to think about it, too, if I were you."

"What's his name?" Hally asked Spark.

"Skippy," he said, to my horror.

Hally made a face. "It doesn't suit him."

"He's yours now. Call him whatever you want," Spark said.

Hally thought for a moment. "Ned," he said.

"It's a good name," Hugh said.

"I guess you've never heard of Buddy?" Spark said.

I got up, stretched fore and aft, and walked over to Hally. I sat down next to him and put my paw on his knee. I was quickly learning to be a pragmatist. You've got to start somewhere. Anyway, I liked him. Liked my new unpolished doorstop of a name, too, had a certain plain and solid quality conspicuously lacking in Lupine.

Hally stroked my head. "What kind of dog is he?" he asked Spark, who looked momentarily flummoxed.

"The woman told me but I forget. It'll come to me."

"He's a Shih Tzu," Hugh said. "Ruthie had one. He ran the joint."

"Whatever happened to Ruthie?" Spark asked.

"You might say, *you* happened to Ruthie. This . . . my life interrupted"—Hugh spread wide his arms—"happened to Ruthie. Strange thing about most adult women, they aren't interested in a guy who spends months at a time sleeping in his boyhood bedroom."

"I told you she was a hopeless traditionalist."

"You stole him, didn't you?" Hally said, turning the topic back to me. "The dog."

"No, but if you think I did, then maybe you should register your outrage by giving him back."

"What about Gramp?" Hally said. "What if he says no?"

"You leave him to me," Hugh said.

"Where is the old man, anyway?" Spark asked, jumping up from the sofa and heading into the kitchen.

"He's in Augusta for a couple of days. Dealing with the fall-out from this concert debacle," Hugh said. "Looks like you've got a reprieve." He smirked.

"I don't need a reprieve. I came here to see the kid and to help out for the summer . . ." Spark said, opening the refrigerator, peering inside.

"Would you guys please stop calling me 'the kid'?" Hally said, exasperated.

"Sure, kid," Spark said. "How's Pop doing? I read something about him not paying the performers, mishandling the proceeds from the concert, something like that, anyway. I'm a little fuzzy on the details." Spark had this inattentive throwaway delivery, a fake carelessness, his nonchalance something he'd cultivated to conceal the sharp angles of his intelligence.

"He didn't steal from anyone," Hally said. "He would never do anything like that."

"Believe me, at this point, I wish he had," Hugh said.

"Oh yeah?" Spark said, drinking from the milk carton. "I'm shocked."

"Do you mind?" Hugh said, opening a cupboard door and handing Spark a glass.

"Lots of people got in free by sneaking onto the island," Hally explained. "He didn't have things set up right, with the security and ticket takers and stuff, but it wasn't his fault. He tried to do everything by himself. He was operating on a shoestring but he didn't let anybody know. Right, Hugh?"

"There's a surprise," Spark said, wiping his mouth with the back of his hand. "In other words, he misrepresented his backing. What'd he do? Put a buck in a bank account and call it a company? I'm right, aren't I?"

"What's so wrong about that?" Hally said. "The concert was important. He doesn't do stuff for money like everybody else does."

Hally was only a child and yet he already possessed a sophisticated level of contempt for money and its pursuit. I had never met people like the Monahans of Monhegan, with their complicated relationship to money and profit. They despised its accumulation, wrestled with its necessity, and acted as if it was a sin to make money the reason for work. Yet theirs were mostly rarefied interests, and in many ways they lived as freely and recklessly as if they had all the money in the world.

The takeaway was if you can't be rich, your next best choice is to be broke. It's what's in between that gets you in trouble.

"You're telling me?" Spark said. "Pop always made it clear his precious beliefs took precedence over everything else. Remember, Hugh, how he used to say: 'You kids will starve to death before I will ever turn my back on—fill in the blank, the cause of the day. He expected us to view dying for his principles as a privilege. Every day was like the Franklin Expedition."

"Who are you trying to kid, Spark? You came home because you're broke and you're desperate and you have nowhere else to go," Hugh said. "Just what we need around here."

"Got any peanut butter?" Spark said, biting into an apple.

Later that night, I followed Hally up the stairs and into his bedroom. He picked me up and put me on his bed. "You can sleep here," he said, "with me. It's pretty comfortable." He lay back and rested his head on a pillow and patted the spot next to him. I curled up alongside him and looked into his eyes.

"I know my dad stole you," he said. "I'm sorry. I am. I hope you don't miss your family too much. I'd give you back but I don't know where you belong." He sat up on his elbows and stared down at me. "Want to hear something bad? Another part of me is glad I don't know where you belong because I don't want to give you back. I'm even a bit happy he took you."

He lay back down again. "I guess I am like my dad after all."

Outside the keening wind clamored, crawling up the side of the house, scratching against the windows. I closed my eyes and was awakened from my doze by a long, low moan that came from deep inside of me. I had dreamed all I loved was taken away and I awoke with a cry only to discover it was true. Strangely, the hollow ache of reality felt less acute than the sharp sorrow of the dream. Hally's warm hand rested on my neck as he offered up drowsy words of comfort.

From downstairs I could hear Spark and Hugh talking, their conversation winding furtively upward to the bedroom, like a back staircase.

"I don't see how he can dig himself out of this one," Hugh said, voice registering defeat. "He won't concede a thing but everywhere you look it's bad. Got to admit, I'm feeling a little trapped. I mean, I can't just abandon them, and I don't want to . . . I'll never leave them in the lurch."

"I'll stick around and help out, Hugh. You've done enough. Beans offered me a job on the boat. I'll tell him I'll take it."

"Spark . . . Look, stay or go, it's up to you. Just don't say you're staying if you don't mean it."

"I mean it. I'm staying."

"That would be good . . . I could use the moral support if nothing else."

Hugh was sounding positively buoyed at the thought of having Spark around—apparently, like his brother, he had grown adept at concealing his real feelings, though not for long.

"It's only money. You never know," Spark said.

Eyes drooping, I drifted off, hoping to dream a different dream.

Three

～～～～～～～～～～～～～～～～～～～～～～～～～～～～～～～～～

"Catch!" Spark said the next morning. He was slumped down in one of the worn armchairs in the living room, looking over at me in the opposite chair, while I sank deeper into the leather, watching still and indifferent as the ball landed inches from my front paws.

"Bring it here," Spark said, snapping his fingers, trying to compel obedience.

Fat chance.

"Come on, Ned, You going to punish me forever? You should thank me. You've got a fantastic setup here. That guy driving the Mercedes looked like a gilded wiener."

The gilded wiener to whom he referred, would be Martin "Yoo-hoo" Robinette. Hmm. Say what you will about him, Spark had a predatory talent for instantly sussing out character.

"The way I see it, I rescued you from a lifetime of stale affluence and soul-sucking privilege. Be a good dog and bring me the ball."

Spark and I obviously had sharply differing views of what constituted a good dog. Bored by his entreaties, and hearing Hugh and Hally on the deck at the back of the house, I jumped down to the floor and walked to the kitchen door where I stopped and waited, loudly sniffing at the threshold.

Spark got up from the chair to let me out. "You want to see your new buddies?" he asked me with exaggerated friendliness, apparently unaware that it took more than a round of fake enthusiasm in high register to recruit my goodwill.

Hearing laughter outside, I wagged slightly the tip of my tail.

"Good boy."

Good boy yourself, Sparky.

Spark stared down at me, eyes narrowing as I pretended to ignore his scrutiny.

"You are one cool cat, Ned," he said finally as he held wide the door.

"Ned!" Hally got down on his knees, his arms thrown open as I stepped out onto the deck and surveyed him from a distance. He straightened up. "I think he's mad because we didn't take him with us for the walk. I was afraid he might run away," he explained to Spark.

"Where the hell's he going to go?" Spark said, bringing up the rear. "He's a dog in the middle of the Atlantic Ocean. He's got limited options."

"We'll take him with us next time," Hugh said. "He's got plenty of walks in his future, haven't you, Ned? I'm going to make bacon and eggs before I head into the studio. Anybody care to join me?"

"I do," Hally said.

"Does that invitation include me?" Spark said.

"You want some or not?" Hugh said.

Hally picked me up and carried me over to the kitchen table where he pulled out a chair, sat down, and deposited me on the seat of the chair next to him. "Ned wants bacon and eggs, too," he said.

Spark sat down at the head of the table. "I've been thinking I'll stay in the guest cabin."

"Think again," Hugh said, grease in the pan popping and crackling. "Pop had Chip and Arche Wallace and some other guys from the church help him fix it up so we could rent it out and make a little extra money. My idea."

"Your idea?" Spark said.

"An experiment with initiative. There's a family arriving tomorrow. The dad's a botanist, doing research on indigenous spring plants on the island. It's a business-family holiday combo."

"They'll be right up our noses," Spark said. "Why so desperate? You've got dough, right?"

"I'm not Picasso. I've had a few successful shows. I'm trying to get ready for another one and the circumstances aren't exactly ideal. Pop's sitting on a ton of debt. I should be able to put a dent in things over time if everything works out . . . Anyway, what the hell? Why am I explaining myself to you? I can't believe your nerve. All you've ever contributed to this family are headaches."

"The bacon's burning," Hally said.

"How many times have we gotta go through this?" Spark countered. "All I did was sign up for a regular life. You know the part where kids grow up, become adults, and leave home? Oh no, wait, I forgot, you didn't get that memo. You're too busy being a martyr and permanently auditioning for the role of the good son. Great news, you got the part! As for him," he gestured over at Hally, who was pouring salt on the table in separate neat little piles and appearing not to react, though I could hear his heart pounding in his chest, "I wanted to take him with me from the start but Mom wouldn't hear of it."

"To do what? Train him to be the Artful Dodger? Don't blame this on Mom." Hugh's voice took on a dangerous edge. He reached over and flipped off the front element of the stove.

"Come on, you guys," Hally said. "Please . . ."

"Go ahead. Say it," Spark said. "You've been dying to tell me off since the moment I walked in the door. Get it over with."

"Stop it," Hally implored but they ignored him.

"What do you mean? Get it over with? You think this is something I just need to get out of my system? You left a terminally ill woman in the final stages of cancer alone with an eight-year-old boy. You knew better, Spark. She dropped dead right in front of him."

"Look. She was fine when I left. She was fine with me going. She was the one who said to go, leave. They were playing cards. I made them supper. Grilled cheese. Milk shakes. They were eating and playing cards. They were talking. They were laughing."

"Yeah, it was a scene right out of a Rockwell painting, I know."

"For Christ's sake, Hugh, you think I wouldn't change it if I could?" Spark's voice wavered with anguish.

"Okay, okay, not now, all right?" Hugh hissed, reacting to Spark's distress and nodding pointedly at Hally, who was looking down at his empty plate. Spark stared at Hugh in frustration, hands extended in a silent but easily interpreted question: Does Hally blame me?

Hugh frowned and shrugged.

"Please don't fight," Hally interrupted, looking up, twisting the fingers of his hands together. "You're getting Ned upset."

Spark and Hugh looked away, both riveted on something lurking beyond the kitchen window, as if they had heard the same imaginary noise. I climbed out of my chair and onto Hally's lap. He wrapped his arms around me and held me close. "It's okay," he said.

The Monahan brothers were a volatile pair, or so it seemed. In the short time I'd known them, they were always hopped up on some aroused feeling—tossing emotional hand grenades from one to the other—but Hally's tenderness softened them, unnerved them.

Hugh was the first to speak. "Bacon and eggs are ready," he said.

Spark took him aside. "How much does he remember?"

"I don't know. He never talks about it. I don't exactly feel like grilling him on the subject."

〰〰〰

"That's a good-looking sailboat," Spark said later that afternoon, sidling up to Hally, who was sitting on the ground at the side of the house, amid the tall grass and the short grass and the rocks and the weeds. "Wow, you've got a whole marina here," he said appreciatively, indicating a small hand-dug pond with several old-fashioned wooden replica boats bobbing on the water's surface. "Where'd this come from?"

"Hugh and I made it," Hally said, focused on his boat. He was repairing one of the sails.

"You must have put tons of work into it," Spark said.

"I'm not a little kid, you don't need to pretend to be so enthusiastic. It's just something we did. It's no big deal."

"I'm not pretending anything . . ." Spark stopped and tried to regroup. "Cool colors," he said, crouching alongside him, admiring Hally's collection.

"Hugh painted them."

"He did a good job. Maybe I could take you sailing sometime," Spark said, hesitating a little.

"Hughie, too," Hally said, not hesitating at all.

"Yeah, sure, Hugh can come."

I looked up at the sound of two men approaching, one younger, one older, both of them dressed in matching work pants and long-sleeved shirts. They were coming from the direction of the guest cottage. The younger one, broadly grinning, spoke first: "Hey, chief, how's it going?"

"Fine, well," Spark said, looking both pained and amused, standing up to greet them, his hand extended.

"Keepin' you out of trouble?"

"Yup. Always."

"That's too bad . . . I heard a rumor you were back home. It hasn't been the same around here without you. Oh gosh, I see you're getting reacquainted," said the young man, who along with his father turned out to be the aforementioned Chip and Arche Wallace. "This one," he said, rubbing the top of Hally's head, "this one's got a heart o' gold."

"Who's this then?" Arche asked, pointing toward me.

Hally wasn't forthcoming so Spark chimed in. "This is Ned. I got him for Hally."

"That's one way of putting it," Hally mumbled.

"Oh, that dog, he's a beauty, all right. He's got a heart o' gold, just look at him." Appearing delighted to be alive, Chip wore a permanent openmouthed smile, gaping front teeth taking up the bottom half of his face. "I'll bet you were livin' the dream, weren't you? Spark? People'd say to me, 'What do you think ol' Spark's up to?' 'Livin' the dream,' I'd say right back."

"Yeah, well, I think I just woke up," Spark said as Chip threw his head forward, and doubled over at the waist, overcome with laughter. "Where does he come up with this stuff?" he said, searching his father's and Hally's faces for the answer, Hally looking unimpressed. Straightening up finally, Chip asked Spark if he intended to stay.

"If Hally wants me to," Spark said as Hally stood up, sailboat in hand.

"Do whatever you want," he said, walking toward the house. "I don't care. Makes no difference to me."

"Isn't he something?" Chip said. "I'm telling you . . . that boy's—"

"—got a heart of gold, I know," Spark said, watching Hally disappear into the house.

Four

~~~~~~

The first time we saw them they were standing on the rocks, watching the waves roll in. The boy, about eleven, was wearing a T-shirt and hooded jacket, but was naked from the waist down. His sister, thirteen or fourteen, was in her bra and underpants. The mother wore a bright pink, skirted bathing suit and the father was in long plaid shorts, a white dress shirt with sleeves rolled to the elbow and on his head he had an Australian slouch hat.

Worse, they had a French bulldog, which in the canine world is the equivalent of that guy who bums smokes, belches the theme song to *Rocky*, and thinks that pepperoni sticks are a palate cleanser between courses. It's a private joke among dogs that Frenchies are fashion accessories for the privileged. If only they knew! They might as well walk around with Stanley Kowalski at the end of a leash.

Immediately dubbed the Sex Family by Hally, he watched fascinated from the deck as farther down the beach the boy lay facedown on the rocky ground while his sister piled stones in a vertical spire on his bare ass and the bulldog snuffling with nose to the ground, scavenged for seagull droppings.

"Hally! Stop staring," Hugh commanded to no avail. "And for the millionth time, don't call them the Sex Family. Their name is Wrendle."

"What's the big deal? I can't take an interest in people now?" Hally asked, eyes wide, as Hugh looked on skeptically and Spark yawned and pretended to be inattentive.

"Oh, please, do you think I was born yesterday?" Hugh said.

"That kid's got to be a bonky," Hally said, reaching for the binoculars.

"Hal!" Hugh spoke sharply. "There are more respectful ways to refer to people who have intellectual challenges."

"The problem is you have to be mentally competent yourself to know what they are," Spark said, coming to, jabbing Hally in the ribs with the sharp stick of his habitual slander.

"Now what are they doing?" Hally said, before hoisting himself onto the flat surface of the railing where he sat down, feet dangling. I stood on my hind legs and stretched. He pulled me up alongside him and pointed.

"Hal, you are just hell-bent on getting into trouble with that family," Hugh said.

"Jeez, now the girl is getting a piggyback ride from her dad! In her underwear! What's the deal?"

"Maybe they're just close, a loving family. I hear they do exist," Hugh said, lying down on the chaise longue, and opening his sketchbook. Hugh was always drawing. Sometimes I'd see his fingers moving in the air, as he sketched away in his imagination. "Anyway, they're entitled to their privacy and they aren't doing anything wrong as far as I can see, so let them enjoy their holiday without your prying little eyes following their every move."

"Counting the days until these nutjobs leave," Spark said, stripping off his T-shirt and lying on his back on the floor of the deck, hands covering his eyes, protecting against the warm spring sun. I tried not to stare at the faded pink diagonal scar extending upward from just above his waist on his right front side to just beneath his chest where it curved behind his back.

"Can't come soon enough," Hugh agreed, all his good intentions collapsing.

"It's your fault for renting to a family of perverts," Hally said.

"What was I supposed to do? Submit them to a round of psychological testing?" Hugh said.

"Next time call in a demonologist to screen potential renters," Spark said.

"They seemed okay over the phone," Hugh said.

"What happened to you?" Hally asked Spark, overcome finally by curiosity.

"You mean this?" Spark said, sitting up on his elbows, pointing to his scar. "Appendix."

"Anybody want something to drink?" Hugh asked.

Later that afternoon, Spark quietly disappeared. He was gone for a couple of hours and when he came back he announced he'd run into the Sex Family on one of the hiking trails. He introduced himself and they told him they were lost so he led them back home.

"So? I can't believe I'm asking but what do you think?" Hugh said as Hally and I looked on from where we sat on the living room sofa.

"They're nuts but they're harmless enough. Turns out nakedness is an avocation for them. They live in some nudist colony—sorry, community—in upper New York State. Being half-dressed most of the time represents a real compromise for them, a form of 'social conformity and oppression they're struggling with,' the woman explained to me . . ."

"Antiheroes! You must have felt right at home," Hugh said.

". . . So no need to alert the zookeepers . . ." Spark looked momentarily deflated. "Why does life have to be so disappointing? They could win a contest for being the people you'd least like to see naked . . ."

"I still think they're nutty," Hally said.

"Who said they weren't nutty? Everybody's nuts," Spark said, flopping down next to us on the sofa, stretching his legs, kicking off his sandals, sending them flying across the room, deliberately pushing Hally into a corner with his bare feet. "It's only a matter of degree."

Hugh looked up from the work he was doing in the middle of the living room, stretching a canvas. "I'm trying to decide whether you're the most reliable person when it comes to evaluating anyone's mental health."

"Are you kidding? Nobody knows from crazy like me."

Hally, imprisoned against the sofa's armrest, laughed as Spark, sitting up, put his right palm flat on the top of Hally's head and used it as a platform to leverage himself off the sofa. Hugh's grin faded and he resumed work on the canvas. He'd seemed more relaxed around Spark, was starting to enjoy having him around, but something about this conversation had made him uncomfortable.

"You want to bring me one of those?" Hugh said, glancing up, then back down, as Spark reached into the fridge for a beer.

"Catch," Spark said, simultaneously tossing the bottle of beer, causing Hally to duck and Hugh to lunge, and almost miss, grabbing the bottle in midair as it sailed halfway across the room.

"Jesus, Spark," Hugh said. "Mature."

Hally, grimacing, watched Spark neatly remove the cap from a bottle of beer, with his teeth. I admit, Spark was growing on me—criminal types (for that's how I viewed Spark in those early days) were not without their charms, I thought, or maybe I was experiencing a form of traumatic bonding.

"What do you do anyway? Do you have a job? How do you live?"

"I work with my hands," Spark said, glint in his eyes, as Hugh looked at him disapprovingly.

"I'm not a baby," Hally said. "I know what you're implying."

"Oh, okay, I'll speak more frankly then in deference to your worldliness. I bed wealthy women for money."

"For Pete's sake, Spark," Hugh said.

"You do not," Hally said coolly, blush creeping up his neck.

"You're right. I do it for free."

"Why do you want to make people think you're a creep? It's like you do reverse bragging all the time."

"Excellent point," Hugh said with enthusiasm, pointing at Hally, glaring at Spark. "Do you get what's going on here? Impressionable kid. Paternal role model. Good example. See the connections? You want to cool it?"

"Don't worry, Hugh," Hally said. "I know what he's doing. He's trying to shock me and avoid answering my questions."

"Okay, you want to know if I have a job? I've had plenty of jobs. I don't have a job right now. Among the many things I've done: I worked in construction. I sold vacuum cleaners. I sold cameras in a camera store. I typed out labels in a pharmacy. I stocked shelves in a grocery store. I painted houses. I busted my ass on a sod farm. Worked the harvest on a tobacco farm. I worked in a racing stable taking care of the horses. That was my favorite. I've worked on more stinking fishing boats than I care to remember."

"Did you even *go* to school?" Hally asked.

"Your dad went to college for a couple of years. He dropped out when you were born," Hugh said, coming to Spark's defense.

"It's all right, Hugh, I don't need an advocate," Spark said.

"What did you study?" Hally said, demanding proof.

"Animal husbandry," Spark said, "with particular emphasis on marsupials."

"He majored in English literature, with a minor in Latin," Hugh said as Hally looked incredulous. "I can't figure out who's joking and who's telling the truth," he said.

"Trust me," Hugh said.

"Say something in Latin," Hally said to Spark. He still wasn't convinced.

"Semper ubi sub ubi."

"It never gets old for you, does it, Spark?" Hugh said.

"Don't you want to make something of your life?" Hally, unamused, said to his father.

Spark set his beer down on the table in front of him. "I'm here, aren't I?"

It was nearing sunset, the sky a watercolor wash of blue and gray, when I trotted alongside Hally back to the wildflower meadow where he had been spray-painting his bike. I was touring the area around him, nose to the ground, the flattened grass and damp earth a smorgasbord of smells, rodents, rabbits, birds. My head shot up in response to someone's not-quite-soundless approach.

The Sex Family girl was making her way through the tall grass, a bouquet of wildflowers clutched in her hand, arm at her side, tips of the flowers almost dragging on the ground. She bent down to pick something up, dishwater blond hair falling down over her face. She straightened back up and I finally got a good look at her. You could stare at that girl for a thousand years, study her under a microscope, do her makeup, paint her portrait, you could marry her and sleep next to her in bed for the rest of your life and still not be able to pick her out of a lineup—it was my first experience of face blindness. She didn't even have a distinctive body smell of her own. Inhaling her was like stepping into a stadium of indistinguishable odors.

"Hi," she said as Hally looked up, hand at his forehead, squinting against the piercing rays of the setting sun.

"Hi," he said.

"It speaks," she said. "What are you doing?" She was wearing a short cotton nightgown, though it was a chilly night.

"Painting my bike."

"What color?"

He held up his hand, his palm red.

"Can I help?" She was twirling her bouquet, a perverse coquette with dark circles beneath her eyes. I drank her in. Something off about this girl; she left an aftertaste, like milk about to turn.

"You can watch if you want to. It's getting dark. I'm almost finished," Hally said unenthusiastically.

She walked over and sat down beside him, introducing herself as Loretta-Christine.

"I'm Hally." It was a reluctant admission. He got up and moved farther away, sitting down on a patch of sand and grass.

"Weird name," she said, laughing. "My new pally, Hally. You live at the gray house, right?"

"Yup."

"My family's renting a cottage from you guys."

"I figured that out on my own."

She stared over at the house. "Your house gives me the creeps. Why's it so run-down? Are you poor or weird or both?"

Hally sighed and ignored her, which only seemed to incite her.

"My father says your family is broke and that your grandfather is a crook who stole a bunch of money from people who came to some lame God concert he put on."

"That's not true," Hally said. "What does your father know about it?"

"He's a professor. He knows everything about everything . . . anyway, who cares? So, are you a God boy like your grandfather?"

"No," Hally shot back defensively. "I don't even like God all that much."

"What? Who says they don't like God? Who do you like? The devil? Why do you go to church every Sunday, then, if you don't like God?"

"I mean . . . I don't care about God," Hally said, fumbling. "Anyway, who says I go to church every Sunday?"

"I've seen you," she said. "Your good clothes don't even fit you. Your shirt is too big and your pants are too small. My mother said it's obvious you got your Sunday outfit from the Sally Ann."

"I don't care about clothes," Hally mumbled, his desperation growing.

"You don't care about much, do you?" she said. "Your dog looks like an ewok. Why does he keep staring at me?"

"Maybe he thinks you're a Wookiee," Hally said.

"Princess Leia more like it . . . I hate this stupid boring island," she said suddenly. "How do you stand it here? Rocks everywhere. It's like Alcatraz. You can't even go swimming. Stupid currents. Stupid cold. Worst vacation ever."

"What do you want me to do about it?" Hally said.

She kept on talking for the next half hour or so, her tone growing more challenging and rude, but strangely intimate, too, as if she and Hally had known each other for a long time.

"Why do you live with your grandfather and your uncle? It's weird. Why don't you live with your parents? Don't they want you? Do you even have parents?"

"I have a dad," Hally said quietly.

"Oh yeah, that guy. He seems kind of cool to be *your* dad. My dad says your dad is like some kind of criminal. He said for me to stay away from him. He said it figures that a Holy Roller like your grandfather would have a good-for-nothing son."

"I've gotta go," Hally announced finally, his face barely visible in the deepening darkness.

She got up and moved over to where he was and sat down beside him in the grass.

"Don't. Not yet," she said. "You're cute. I've seen you spying on me."

"Huh?" Hally said. I could smell his mounting apprehension—it radiated from him in sticky waves, as if he were applying a layer of warm licorice to his skin.

She leaned over and kissed him.

"What are you doing?" he said, leaping up, scrambling backward. Spontaneously, I jumped at her ankles, nipping, barking.

"What does it look like I'm doing? Ow. Get lost, mutt," she said, kicking out at me.

"I've really gotta go," Hally said. It was almost comical, his embarrassment lighting up the surrounding darkness, and before she replied he took off, me dashing along beside him.

Something about this girl, this family that she embodied—for all that they bared to the world, they were cloaked in a strange purposefulness.

"Hey, wait!" She called after him. "It's not like I was going to go all the way with you. Why are you running away? You'll be sorry," she said, and then she laughed her eerie little laugh.

You better believe Hally ran! I had to transform myself into another creature altogether, had to practically sprout wings, to keep up with him, that's how fast he was flying, his feet leaving a vapor trail. I felt like a saluki chasing down a rabbit, my stumpy little legs growing longer, leaner, and more elegant with every bound.

When we got back to the house Hally picked me up, opened the back door a crack, and with a decisive plop, deposited me inside the kitchen. "Stay, here, Neddy," he said. In disbelief, I watched from the door as he dissolved into the darkness. Leave me behind! Devastating. I may even have cried a little—a dog's emotions are never far from the surface, constantly gurgling, roiling, erupting. (Why do you think cats annoy dogs so much with their sangfroid? They make us feel like schlubs.)

An hour later, still sulking, my mind operating on a narrow single track, I saw two flashlights wavering in the blackness, heard three voices, a man, a woman, and a boy, her parents and her brother I guessed, calling for Loretta-Christine.

The wind shifted, whistling. High overhead an owl hooted.

"Hally? Is that you?" Hugh said, looking up from the art book he was reading in the living room as Hally banged the kitchen door, me running ahead, gaining enough momentum to leap forward and hurl myself into Hugh's lap. He gave a sharp intake of air when I landed.

"Ned! Take it easy." He looked over at Hally. "What were you up to?"

"Nothing. Just hanging out."

I heard footsteps coming down the stairs leading to the second floor. "Out playing spin the bottle with the girl next door?" Spark teased.

"No! Jesus," Hally said.

Hugh gave him the once-over. "What's wrong? Hally . . . you weren't spying on the Sex Family, were you?"

"No! Quit calling them the Sex Family," Hally said as he fled the room and bounded up the stairs. Hugh set down his book, perplexed expression on his face. He looked into my eyes, then over at Spark. "Go figure," he said.

The next morning we awoke to the sound of loud knocking on the yellow door. Jumping down off the bed, I was first on the scene, and waited silently for the others—I leave the reflexive barking to Keeshonden—the stale intermingled scent of coffee, sugar, and warmed-over lard coming from outside, powerful enough to break down the door. Hugh, who wore his off-white robe over a pair of purple-and-yellow plaid boxers, appeared first, greeting the two uniformed officers on the veranda. Spark used to kid him that his propensity for wearing whimsical socks and underwear confirmed his status as an artist.

"Looking for Hugh Monahan. Would that be you?" the older and more heavyset of the men inquired. He looked like a dump truck masquerading as a middle-aged man.

"How may I help you?" Hugh responded, brisk and formal, a little bit contrived, as if he were brushing lint from a morning coat instead of being caught out in his underwear. Spark came up behind him, pulling his T-shirt over his head and ironing his wrinkled shorts with the palms of his hands. He ran his fingers through his hair.

"My name is Rudy Guerin. I'm from the Lincoln County Sheriff's Office. This is my deputy Bert Connor." About his hirsute sidekick, he may as well have added that he moonlighted as a mustache and sideburns. "Sorry to disturb you on a Sunday morning, though I guess it's not all that early. Must be eleven o'clock by now," he said, smiling vaguely, trying in his stilted way to be personable.

"I didn't know it was a crime to sleep in," Spark said.

"May we come inside?" the sheriff asked.

"Yes, of course. Is this about my father? Has something happened?" Hugh led them into the living room.

"No, no, please, everyone's fine," the sheriff said with an outward thrust of his arms that was supposed to be reassuring.

"I know your father, belong to his church," the deputy said. "Been committed to Cludo right from the get-go. Everything makes sense with Cludo. Wonderful man, your father. He opened my eyes to the true nature of things. I tell my wife, we'll be reading about Pastor Ragnar one day, mark my words. He's going to be a big man someday. This concert episode is his personal Calvary. I told him myself, 'You will rise again.'"

"Like yeast," Spark said.

"Oh. You must be the older boy . . ." The deputy's tone was instantly transformed—as if he were stepping out of one costume and into another. He made *older boy* sound like a euphemism for *chimpanzee on the loose*.

"We're looking for Hally Monahan. Is he here?" he asked, back to business, in an excess of strained politeness, his labored precision manufactured as a clip-on tie.

"Hally's out . . . went to play basketball. He left the house an hour or so ago," Hugh said, exchanging a confused glance with Spark.

"What do you want with Hally?" Spark asked.

"We just want to talk to him," the sheriff said. "Your name?"

"Spark, uh . . . Jamie Monahan. I'm Hally's dad."

"Oh, I understood . . ." The sheriff didn't finish his thought but looked over at his deputy.

"Spark's been away. I'm Hally's uncle. I've helped take care of him the last few years since my mother died. Is there something wrong? Why don't we all sit down?"

"Thank you," the sheriff said with real feeling, sweat pooling on his forehead and creating a widening soggy circle on his stomach, armchair straining beneath his heft. "Damned hot for May . . . Well, I'll get right to the point." He flicked a drop of perspiration from the end of his nose. "We've had a criminal complaint filed against Hally by the Wrendle family. Ring a bell?"

"What family is this?" Hugh said, frazzled.

"Your tenants?" the deputy reminded him.

"Oh, the Wrendles!" Hugh said, recognizing the name at last.

"They're staying at your guest house, I believe, a family of four including a teenage girl and a younger brother. There was a break-in at the cottage last night. Money was taken, around five hundred dollars from a dresser drawer, and a number of plant specimens and valuable research notes are missing.

"The girl says Hally's been peeping in her window watching her and when she confronted him about it last night in the wildflower meadow, he tried to kiss her. She rebuffed him and he said she'd be sorry," the sheriff continued. "Apparently, now, her necklace is missing as well, a family heirloom, a religious medal, something of the nature. When she didn't come home as expected her parents got worried and went out to look for her sometime around nine or so last night . . . That's when your boy entered the house and the damage and the theft occurred."

"They're saying Hally did this?" If Hugh had been a champagne cork, he would have put a dent in the old tin ceiling overhead. "Whoa! Whoa! Wait a minute." He was fully animated now, as the implication of the allegations began to take root. "Hally isn't even thirteen years old for Christ's sake. A thief? A peeping Tom? That's crazy. There's no way. Where's the proof?"

The sheriff was obviously accustomed to this particular drama and the ways in which it tended to play out. His flat aspect was in contrived contrast to Hugh's volatility—his mien so low-key, a coma would have represented an upgrade in his condition.

"I understand this is a shock and you're upset. Please try to understand our position." He held up his hand and, using his fingers, patiently began to outline his civic duties. "We receive a complaint of a serious nature. We have to act on it. We need to ask questions, gather information, and then try to make a determination as to exactly what's taken place, whether a crime has been committed or not. At this stage, all we want to do is talk to Hally."

"Not without a lawyer you're not," Spark said, calm counterpoint to Hugh.

The deputy reacted as if someone had set his foot on fire. "Why involve a lawyer if your son has done nothing wrong? If he's innocent, then he has nothing to worry about." He paused for effect, unaware of how clumsily he was telegraphing his intentions. "If your first response is to call a lawyer, I have to ask myself, why?"

"Bullshit and you know it," Spark said. "Being innocent only means that he needs even more protection from all your good intentions."

I bit into a piece of kindling and started chewing.

All of us looked up simultaneously in the direction of the kitchen door, which rattled open and then banged shut, a thin wave of cooler sea air surging into the living room. Hally appeared to the sound of a basketball being dribbled on hardwood. Seeing the officers, he came to an abrupt stop, and caught off guard, dropped the ball, which bounced, one, two, three times before landing at the feet of the sheriff.

"Hi," Hally said, pausing at the edge of the room. "Is something wrong?"

"The girl staying at the guest cottage says you've been spying on her through her window. She says you broke into the cottage and stole money and a necklace. She says you tried to kiss her and when she wouldn't let you, you threatened her," Hugh said.

"What? The Sex Family girl?" Hally said, astonished, as the officers, reacting to his stunning tone-deafness, simultaneously first sat back and then forward in their seats, a pair of landlocked synchronized swimmers.

"Hally!" Hugh sputtered as Spark blinked, briefly shut his eyes, and, leaning back deeply into the chair cushion, linked the fingers of both hands behind the back of his head, a net to break the impact of his silent plummet.

"What did you call her, young fella?" the sheriff asked Hally. "'The Sex Family girl,' did you say? Answer me, son."

Hally nodded. "It's just a stupid name we gave them because they hardly wear any clothes . . . Well, I gave them . . . It's a joke, that's all. Did I say something wrong?"

"It's never wrong to tell the truth," the deputy, the situation's self-appointed moral arbiter, pronounced as even the sheriff, giving his head a subtle weary shake, looked as if he had just bitten into an aspirin.

"Yes, Bert, yes, quite right," he said, clearing his throat. "Tell me, Hally, where were you last night from eight to ten?"

"This can't be happening," Hugh said.

"Hally, don't say anything," Spark said.

"I don't mind. I can tell them," Hally said. Clear-eyed and straight-forward, if a little pale beneath the camouflage of an island tan, Hally said he worked on his bike for a while. "I was just hanging out with my dog, Ned," he added, "then I went for a walk."

Spark walked over to the farthest corner of the room, where he sat down cross-legged on an old pine chest, leaning forward, intently focused on Hally, chin in hand, elbow supported by the crook of his leg. At the mention of my name, I jumped down from where I was sitting and ran over to Hally. Standing on my back legs, I extended my upper body until my paws, scraping against his shin, reached almost to his knees.

"I take it that's Ned," the sheriff said, amused. "It seems as if he's trying to corroborate your statement. Too bad dogs can't talk: they're privy to so many secrets and I trust they could be counted on to tell the truth."

Obviously this guy had never spent much time with a Tibetan spaniel.

I dropped down onto all fours, walked over to him, tail wagging, sat down in front of him and licked his hand, probably the most insincere gesture of my life. I smacked my lips. He tasted smoky and stale, like a discarded cigarette stub.

"Aren't you the cute one?" the sheriff said as I choked down my pride and performed the expected pirouette, twirling around on my stubby hind legs, hoping that Hally knew all that I was prepared to sacrifice to engender some good press for him. I surprised myself with how quickly the Monahans had become my world. Intensity and drama, it seemed, were a powerful emotional draw. Sometimes, in my former life, listening to Martin talk about bare spots on the lawn or the state of the gutter, or what he had eaten for lunch, I prayed for the power of human speech, if only to tell him I never wanted to hear another word about the oozing retro charms of the baked macaroni and cheese on the lunch menu at the club.

"Did you run into anybody?" The sheriff, smiling now that I'd warmed him up, asked Hally, who told him that he hadn't. "So then what did you do?"

"Just walked around, looked at the stars . . . thought about stuff," Hally said.

"Are you sure there isn't someone who can vouch for where you were?" The sheriff wanted to stick to the matter at hand.

"Who would he run into?" Spark interjected. "Liza Minnelli and Truman Capote on their way to Studio 54?"

"You got a lousy attitude, you know that?" the deputy said.

"Sorry, from now on I'll try to be more open-minded, like you," Spark said, triggering a rush of accusations from the deputy who bore down on Hally.

"The girl said you've been spying on her, peeking in her window at night, that you tried to kiss her . . . and when she said no, you said she'd be sorry . . ." the deputy said.

"Are you out of your mind?" Hugh was incredulous. "Look at him! He looks like he just fell off the back of a Campbell's Soup truck." Even the sheriff sneaked a doubtful glance in Hally's direction. I watched him making mental note of each freckle.

"What?" Hally said, gasping. "I never . . ." He looked around desperately, face crumpled. "You guys have got to believe me . . ."

"Why do we have to believe you? Why would the girl lie?" the deputy challenged him. "Who else would have done it? I've been doing this a long time. You can look as angelic as you want, you don't fool me."

Spark stared at the deputy, a mix of contempt and amusement on his face. "Back off, Barney Fife!" He pointed to Hally. "He'd pass out cold if a girl even looked at him. Why would he steal? He'd have to be a career criminal to be guilty of what you're accusing him of."

"Maybe he had help. Maybe somebody gave him ideas, put him up to it," the deputy said.

"So now it's a family operation? Is that what you're saying?" Spark demanded.

The deputy glanced over at a chair leaning into the corner on one wobbly leg and shrugged.

"It gives me no pleasure to say it but it's no secret the Monahans are having money problems. Let's be generous and call it a misguided attempt to help out his grandfather."

"No one in this family stole anything," Hugh said.

"All right. All right," the sheriff said, extending his arms out in front of him and making a tamping-down gesture with his flattened palms. He sighed. "Let's everyone take a deep breath. Did any one of you see or speak to the Wrendle girl at any time during the night?"

"No, I didn't," Hugh said.

Spark shook his head.

"What about you?" The sheriff glanced up from what he was writing, and concentrated his gaze on Hally. "What do you say?"

"Nope," Hally said.

"Tell Ned to stop giving me the third degree," Hally said. We were in his darkened bedroom. It was late. He was lying on his bed, beneath a white cotton sheet and I was standing on top of him, my front paws propped up on the high part of his chest, my face inches from his, doing my best impersonation of a single, raw, interrogation-room light shining into his eyes.

"Tell him yourself," Spark said, standing overhead looking down on the two of us.

"Look, Spark . . ." Hally tipped to one side, causing me to slide down onto the mattress, where I was temporarily pinned between his shoulder and the wall, and then he pulled himself into a sitting position, legs tucked up to his chin, his arms hugging his knees. I squeezed out from behind him and sat on his pillow. "I was going to tell you the truth if things got really bad."

"How much worse do they need to get? The police think you're a budding pervert who stole a whack of dough. How can I help you if I don't know what's going on? I don't believe you had any intention of telling the truth. The only reason you're coming clean now is because I saw you with her." Spark stared up at the ceiling and then down at Hally's smoky outline, the silvery light of the moon casting a shiny metallic glow around us.

"I was scared. I didn't know what to say. I didn't mean to lie. It just came out and then I was stuck with it. You've gotta believe me. I didn't do anything bad."

"That deputy is a total wingnut. You heard him. He thinks he's caught the Zodiac Killer."

Hally looked as if he was going to be sick.

"We told you to stay away from her. Jesus, Hally . . . What did you do to make her so mad?"

"Nothing! How is it my fault? She came after me! She just appeared in front of me in her weird way. She was watching me paint my bike. Then it got dark. We were just sitting around talking. I was listening, more like it. I said I had to go. Next thing I know, she kissed me."

"What? What did you do?"

"What do you mean, what did I do? I didn't know what to do . . . Give me a break, okay? I'm not the Fonz."

Growing up isolated on an island in an unusual family situation had given Hally a certain naïve, almost sweetly old-fashioned aspect that, in combination with the amount of time he spent in the company of adults, rendered him slightly out of sync with most of his peers and tended to make him seem both older and younger than he was.

"So then what happened?" Spark, who had instantly twigged to this lack of sophistication, asked him.

"So then I just stood there and . . . I kind of froze for a minute. The thing is, I don't even like her. I took off. I just started running. I kept on going until I got home. I dropped Ned off and then I went outside and walked around. I felt weird. I just wanted to be by myself."

Spark dropped down next to him on the bed, an improbable father and son reunion, the two of them lying side by side, hands behind their heads in similar fashion, staring up at the ceiling fan as it whirred. I was nestled in between them, my head resting on Hally's neck, listening to the steady pulse of his heart as they tried to figure out what to do next.

"Spark?" Hally spoke after a few minutes of silence. "I think I need to tell the police the truth."

"Let's not go crazy here. Just hang on. See what happens." Spark sat up and stared down at Hally. "What the hell? Why are we on the defensive and scrambling? Don't forget, you didn't do anything. I'll bet she stole the money from her parents and she's trying to pin it on you. You're the designated chump in her little scam."

"Why did Hughie have to rent out the guest house?" Hally moaned, back of his head flat against the pillow.

"I know," Spark said. "This is what happens when an artist tries to think like an accountant. It's going to be all right, kid. We'll figure it out."

"What about when Gramp finds out? What do I tell him?"

"Nothing. You tell him just what you told the cops."

"I don't know . . . I don't like lying, especially to him. He'll know. He's like a human lie detector."

Spark lay back down alongside him. "Okay. Technically it's a lie.

Here's the thing, though—it might as well be true. The lie, I mean. It's truer than what that girl is saying about you. Right?"

Even more animated than usual, Spark was developing his theory as he went along. "Are you supposed to get charged with something you didn't do because some crazy chick decides to tell a lie? Maybe one bad lie deserves another lie—a good lie—to make things right."

"That doesn't seem right," Hally said. "Besides the moral stuff, there's too many things that can go wrong. For one thing, what if I did do it and you just figured I didn't and you lied to protect me, thinking you were telling a good lie but really it's a bad lie?"

"Did you spy on that girl in her bedroom? Did you steal from the family?"

"No . . ."

"So then why are you making things complicated? This isn't something hypothetical. It's real. You didn't do it. You know you didn't do it. I know you didn't do it. The crazy girl knows you didn't do it. So, what the hell? Do the right thing and lie, if that's what it takes to get to the truth." Stretched out, with their heads almost touching, staring up at the stars as they glimmered in the clear black sky, framed by the skylight, they talked long into the night, me, with my eyes closed, struggling to stay awake, listening.

The most interesting conversation between Martin and Madelyn that I could recall was whether a tomato was a fruit or a vegetable.

"Thanks for believing me."

"Don't thank me. I've got the odd insight into these kinds of things."

"Honest to God, Spark, that girl scared me."

"Hey, you think I wasn't a chicken at your age? Especially around girls?" Spark said.

"Thanks for trying to make me feel better but I don't think you were ever scared of anything, especially girls," Hally said, making a

point so transparently true even Spark gave in and resisted the temp-
tation to argue.

"Why do I feel guilty when I didn't do anything wrong?"

"You're asking me?" Spark said. "You're talking to a guy who
never feels guilty, even when he did it."

"I don't believe you," Hally said. "Why do you pretend so much?"

"Because I'm a tragic and a melancholy figure," Spark said.

They stopped talking, things got quiet, the air itself seeming to
thicken and doze, Spark, idling with his eyes closed, Hally with his
eyes open.

"Who gets to choose? Who gets to decide what's a good lie and
what's a bad lie?" Hally asked, disturbing the silence.

"That's easy," Spark said. "Me."

Five

~~~~~~

The Church in the Clearing stood at the center of a long curved driveway at the end of a remote rural road on the mainland, a few miles and a ferry ride from home. Surrounded by a solemn semicircle of tall, slender, sparsely furnished spruce trees, it had been an old Methodist place of worship erected in 1800 on fieldstone footings and built of hand-hewn trunks and beams. Long abandoned, Pastor Ragnar picked it up when it was considered worthless and had made it home to his own idiosyncratic ministry.

Freed from the confines of the car, I looked around feeling as if I had stepped into an old sepia-toned photograph, nothing fresh about it, even the air seemed drab and toasted, burnt rather than warm. The building in front of me looked like what it was, an ancient and vaguely derelict country church, humble, in various states of start-and-stop repair, but sturdy, almost defiantly permanent.

A slanted roof with ancient cedar shingles formed a canopy over a wide-open porch with three sloping original wooden steps. Birds flew in and out of holes in the gutter where they'd made their nests, the ground littered with feathers and fuzz and string and straw. Natural pine double doors, stained with age, sagged partly open. The exterior clapboard was peeling and wan, the same shade as tea-stained linen. There were three tall meditative windows with multiple panes on either side of the outer building, their glass cracked in spots, forming a spidery network of visible arteries.

The old wooden floors, dark and worn, creaked as we stepped inside. A thousand smells accosted me the second I crossed the threshold, though the humans around me were oblivious. I looked up expecting to see the spectral outlines of pigeons and doves, oily colonies of bats tucked away in the rafters, expecting to hear noisy families of squirrels as they chewed away at the old and spongy wood.

Ghost scents from a century of rodent droppings and raccoon shit and bird crap made my head spin. Though the congregation had tried and were confident they'd succeeded, a battalion of church ladies down on their hands and knees and scrubbing with bleach and steel wool over several generations couldn't erase their invisible stain.

Handmade pews inhabited either side of the long aisle, their high backs blackened with sweat, a grimy patina left over from past legions of overheated summer worshippers. The altar consisted of a wooden table and wooden cross in identical shades of unpolished walnut.

In Pastor Ragnar's absence, Hugh, Spark, and Hally took me along on a visit to check up on things and get the church ready for the next service. Hugh immediately began to dust the altar and align the candle holders, gathering up the white linen to be laundered. "Here," he said, taking charge, handing Spark a broom.

"What am I supposed to do with this?" Spark said.

"Sweep the floor. Hally, will you please wipe down the pews?"

The side door creaked open and the church caretaker, Mr. Herman, trundled in, wearing faded overalls and a train engineer's hat. He was a railway enthusiast in his sixties who spent most of his time at the local station, greeting arrivals and departures. Out of charity,

Pastor Ragnar kept him on for years past his expiry date. Most days, he merely wandered the property and thought about riding the rails. "Spark?" he said, narrowing his eyes. "Is that you? Never thought to see you back here again. I'm surprised the church hasn't been struck by lightning."

"You never know. It's still early in the day," Spark said. "Always good to see you, Mr. Herman."

"Hmmm . . . hello, Hugh, and there's young Hallelujah . . . say, could I interest you in a high-protein snack?" Mr. Herman said, pulling a worm from his overalls pocket. He held back his head and dangled it wriggling over his open lips and then, straightening up, he grinned over at them. "Remember, boys? Spark? Hugh?"

"Haunts my dreams," Spark said to a man who liked to say he'd been eating worms since the year God invented masking tape.

"How did I wind up with a stupid name like Hallelujah, anyway?" Hally asked as he worked alongside Spark, who was taking a fairly casual approach to his assignment. "You don't exactly seem like the religious type," Hally commented to Spark. He paused. "What about my mother? Was she religious?"

"Be happy," Hugh said from the front of the church, as Spark uncharacteristically fumbled for an answer. "You owe me. Pop's first choice was Melchizedek. I had to promise to go to church six Sundays running to get him to change his mind."

"I didn't think he could change his mind without first getting permission from a burning bush," Spark cracked.

"I still don't get it. Why did Gramp get to name me?"

"Your mom and I needed stuff when we got our own place. Pop gave us a secondhand washing machine in exchange for naming his firstborn grandson," Spark said, sweeping debris into a dustpan.

"What would he have gotten if he'd thrown in a dryer, too?" Hally asked.

"Your soul," Spark said.

"You guys got married?" Hally asked, sounding surprised.

"I didn't say that," Spark said tersely. "Hey, what do I do with this stuff?" Spark stopped and spoke to Hugh, who pretended to be annoyed. "What do you think you do with it? You throw it in the garbage in the kitchen."

"What was she like?" Hally wouldn't be dissuaded from his line of questioning.

"Who?" Spark asked, a stalling tactic.

"My mom. I mean, Gram told me she was rich being a Mac-Namara and stuff. She said she was an Irish Catholic . . ."

"She was born here in America. Just like Hugh and me," Spark said impatiently.

". . . She said they worship idols and commit all the sins they want and then just go to confession and start all over."

"That's a distortion," Hugh said, joining Hally to inspect his work. "Gram brought all her old-world tribalism with her when she came to America."

"You think?" Spark said. He didn't appear to be enjoying the conversation.

"Gram said we had the same color eyes, my mom and me. Is that true?"

"Yeah, I guess," Spark said. "I can't remember. You must have seen her picture, right? There were some kicking around."

"I think Mom threw them out . . . after . . ." Hugh stopped himself from finishing.

"After what?" Hally said.

"After your mom and dad split up."

"Gram said my mom was a wacko," Hally said.

Hugh glanced over at Spark, who used the stubby tip of the broom to push a small pile of dirt into the aisle before he finally spoke: "That is what is known as Yankee-by-way-of-Ulster plain talk."

"Whatever that means," Hally said.

Spark stopped sweeping and faced Hally directly. "What do you want me to say? Your mother was beautiful. She was smart. She was funny. She was gutsy. When she left it broke your grandmother's heart and made her say things, not all of them reliable. Anyway, all of this stuff happened a long time ago." Eager to end the conversation, Spark looked pleadingly to Hugh for help.

"Your mom was a great girl," Hugh said. "I think about her a lot. You remind me of her, Hal. The best part of her."

Hally plopped down onto the pew seat, rag in his hand. "You never answered my question," he said to Spark.

"What question?"

"Did my mother believe in God? Was she religious?"

Spark ran his hands through his hair and rubbed his palms together. "Yeah, I guess. It's not something we talked a lot about. She was a pretty devout Catholic, though she kept spiritual things to herself. She went to Mass regularly. Why do you care so much?"

"No reason. Just wondering."

"Look, Hal." Spark leaned the broom against a pew. "Let it go, okay? You want to know about your mom. Fine. I get it. I'm just not the guy to talk to about it. I don't have much to say on the subject. I'm sorry. That's just the way it is."

"Hold on, Spark . . . I think it's only natural for you, Hal, to be curious about your mom. You're getting older, you want to know all about her, including how she may have felt about religion," Hugh said, striving for calm, trying to be understanding, attempting to soothe both parties. "After all, religion has been a huge part of all of our lives. It's a daily presence."

"Sometimes it feels as if my whole life is about God and religion and being good and noticing what everybody else is doing and whether it's good or bad." Hally stood up and resumed cleaning. "When I grow up I'm going to be an atheist."

"I've got news for you, kid, that's just another form of religion," Spark said, less agitated, bending down and picking up a stray piece of paper— a photo of Pastor Ragnar on it, printed alongside some typewritten church announcements— and folding it into an airplane.

"You think I didn't feel the same way as you when I was a kid?" Hugh said. "There are worse ways to be raised than to consider what's right or wrong."

"Think of it as piano lessons for the soul," Spark said. "Something you hate now but will be grateful for when you get older."

"You mean like you?" Hally said.

"Leave me out of this. We're talking about you."

"Okay. Let's talk about me then," an exasperated Hally challenged his father. "I don't care what you say. You're not the only one with feelings. I have feelings, too. Why did you guys break up? What happened to my mom? How did she die? Why didn't you take care of me like a real dad? How did I wind up here?"

"Talk to him, Spark," Hugh urged.

Spark considered for a moment before replying. "Your mom got sick and she died . . ."

"What do you mean sick?"

"Meningitis," Spark said.

"It's the first time I've heard that . . ." Hally said.

"You want to listen to what I have to say or not?" Spark ignored Hugh's steady stare. "I was a kid. I couldn't take care of you properly. The MacNamaras were a cold, entitled, and privileged family . . . Nobody wanted to see you with them. Gram and Gramp stepped in to make sure that didn't happen. That's about it."

"Hally, you've done all right," Hugh couldn't resist adding his own two cents. "Gram was nuts about you and despite this current mess, you should be proud of your grandfather. He's got a big following. He's pastor to a number of important people including the governor and that congress woman, what's her name . . . Lots of people think he has the potential to become an important religious figure in this country . . ."

"Just ask him, he'll tell you," Spark said, relieved to be talking about something else. "Jesus, Hugh, you make him sound like the CEO of a corporation. Isn't ambition beside the point when it comes to Christian ministry?"

"Here we go," Hugh said.

"Because every time anyone mentions his name you feel obliged to deliver a sermon defending him. The guy's not perfect, all right?"

"You're telling me. I don't have a normal family and then I wind up with some weird Bible-thumper name," Hally interjected, bringing the conversation full circle.

"What are you complaining about? It's a joy-of-life name. You're like an exaltation! Hallelujah!" Spark cupped his hand around his mouth and shouted it out into the silence.

"Would you rather be called Sheldon? He named me after the most loserly apostle, James the Less, so what does that tell you?"

"That Pop was unusually prescient," Hugh said.

"You should have been called Manessah," Hally said to Spark, as he moved out ahead of him, rubbing a particularly resistant mark on the outside of the pew.

"Why do you say that?" Hugh asked him.

"Because Manessah sacrificed his son to a pagan god to win his favor," Hally said.

"Not his favor, kid," Spark said, sending his paper airplane soaring. "His washing machine."

Later that night, we were alone in bed when Hally opened the door to his nightstand and pulled out a paperback. Opening it up, he retrieved a snapshot of a smiling girl with golden hair, sixteen, maybe seventeen years old. She had a slight gap between her two front teeth.

"My mom," Hally said, showing me. I had thought he resembled Spark but I was wrong. He turned over the photo and read aloud the inscription on back, written in blue ink with youthful flourish—a circle rather than a dot drawn over the *i*—stumbling over the pronunciation: "Flora MacNamara at the Grotto of Massabielle in Lourdes . . . or however you say it."

He looked at me. "You're the only one who knows I have this. I found it at the bottom of Gram's picture drawer." He stared at the photo, tenderly outlining her face with the tip of his finger, as if he were tracing the route of a private journey on a map. It seemed Hally had found his way in secret to his mother.

"I don't think she looks bad, do you? Gram said she was a bad person. How does a bad person look? How do you tell anyway?"

The tip of my tail wagged in response, an innocuous way of being agreeable and noncommittal at the same time.

"Gram said I need to be vigilant and watch for signs I'm starting to be like my mom, whatever that means. She gave me three questions to ask myself: Are you sleeping okay? Are you eating what you should? Are you feeling anxious all the time? Yes, yes, no," he said, ticking off the answers, seeming slightly relieved.

Hally threw back the covers and, standing on the end of the bed, spent a few moments looking at himself in the wall mirror over his dresser. Sighing, he lay back down, slid the picture between the pages, shut the book, and returned it to its hiding place. He leaned over and reached under his mattress and when he withdrew his hand he was clutching a silver necklace, tiny medallion hanging from its delicate chain, an image of the Virgin Mary engraved on its surface. I recognized it immediately as the missing necklace belonging to the Sex Family girl.

"It's the miraculous medal, Ned," Hally said. "It was my mother's.

Don't ask me how I got it. We have so many problems in this family. It seems like we need a miracle and nothing else is working. I've been praying to the Virgin Mary—she seems like the nicest member of that family—but I don't want anyone to know.

"Gramp wouldn't like it, for one. Spark would only make fun of me and Hugh would just get that worried look on his face." Hally sighed and snapped out the light.

It was a black night, no stars, and there was a wind off the ocean blowing in through the open window, agitating the curtains, the scent of wild lupines in the air. In the darkness I could hear Hally's fervent whispered prayer. I shivered. The evenings were cool on Monhegan Island.

The next morning, looking for a distraction, and at Hugh's urging, we all set out on a hike. I paced myself. Walks on Monhegan tended to be an uphill climb. The wariness between Hugh and especially Hally and Spark was still present but they were gradually growing more accustomed to one another and moments of tension, though persistent, were relieved by occasional pleasant intervals of a more relaxed nature.

After an hour of walking the trail, we wound up at Black Head, a cliff that soared one hundred and fifty feet above the ocean. Hugh disappeared temporarily to take some photos. He liked the way the light hit the water's surface. "Gives me a great idea for a painting," he said. He was hard at work on a new collection for his New York show in the fall; he had been working on it for months, and was excited at how everything was coming together.

"This was your mom's favorite place," Spark said quietly to Hally when we were alone. Seemed he was trying to make some amends for yesterday at the church. "She always claimed on a clear day she could see all the way to Spain from here."

"I never looked that hard before," Hally said. "Can you? See Spain, I mean?"

"No," Spark said, bending down to remove a burr lodged in my paw.

"How did you and my mom meet?" Hally asked, shy and tentative, but eager for information and taking advantage of Spark's rare bout of openness on the subject.

"When I was a kid, around your age, the MacNamara house was pretty much empty all year round. Hugh and I thought it was haunted. The MacNamaras had owned Tutela Heights for generations but the family had stopped coming."

"Like now?"

"Nah. Now it's gone to hell. In those days, there was a caretaker who lived in the house and maintained it. He kept it up. When your grandfather MacNamara inherited the place he opened it up again and he and your grandmother and your mother used to come for the summer.

"We were the same age, seventeen, when we met."

"Did you like each other right away?"

"You might say that." Spark scraped the sole of his foot on tree bark, as if he were trying to remove something that wouldn't budge.

"Did her parents hate you? Gram said they did."

"Yeah, they did."

"Why?"

"Classic stuff. The MacNamaras are a prominent family. I had no money. No prospects. Pastor Ragnar had the kind of notoriety they didn't appreciate. Then there was my de facto older brother, Cludo, the gangster religion. In fairness to them, I wasn't exactly a dream come true from any parent's standpoint. My parents weren't thrilled with her either so it achieved its own bizarre harmony."

"Why didn't they like her?"

"Because she came from money, because she was socially prominent. It's called reverse snobbery."

Hally frowned, mulling it over. "That's stupid."

"Yeah, lot of that going around."

We stood staring out over the immense ocean, wild and deep blue, touch of sadness in the air, no one speaking.

"I shouldn't tell you this . . ." Spark said. He had no talent for melancholy. "What the hell?" He pointed to a lone tree surrounded by rock and beach roses. "You were conceived right there, on a starry night, beneath that tree, on a socially equalizing bed of club moss."

"Yuck, jeez, I don't want to hear about that," Hally said, embarrassed but amused, too, squirming, maybe even a little bit delighted. Hally reminded me of every American cocker spaniel I'd ever met.

"Don't tell Hugh I said anything . . . Okay? Sorry. Forgot what it's like to be a kid . . ."

"When did you become an adult?" Hally teased. "What's club moss anyway?"

"Lycopedium. Little feet of the fox—that's what your grandmother used to call it. Spreads like crazy. You can grind the spores—it makes a yellow dust that's flammable—and use the paste to create flash powder. Makes this impressive fireball but it's easy to control. You just have to be careful not to breathe it in. Magicians use it. It's what they use to make fireworks, too.

"It makes a big splash but in the end it's a whole lot of nothing. Fun, though," Spark added. "I learned how to make it when I was a kid. I singed my eyebrows first time I did it."

"Didn't that scare you off?"

"Who needs eyebrows? They're like the appendix of the face."

"Gram told me you cut off your eyelashes once with a pair of scissors. She said everybody used to say your eyelashes were so long they made you look like a girl . . . so you decided to cut them off."

"I did. Here's the thing, though, you can cut them off till the cows come home but you can't stop them from growing back."

It was a clear day. Blue sky. No clouds. Hally looked out over the ocean and beyond.

"I think I can see Spain," he said, squinting. Spark followed his gaze.

"Nope," he said, "you can't."

Six

Everyone called him Pastor Ragnar. Even his sons sometimes referred to him as Pastor Ragnar. I started to think of it as his given name, a portentous compound like Alexander Graham or George Bernard.

His mother was born in Norway, but grew up in Canada. His father immigrated to North America from Northern Ireland in his teens and lived on and off in the U.S., eventually moving to Canada for a time. Mindful of his father's Irish-Scandinavian roots, Spark used to describe him with canny precision as a "belligerent reindeer."

Hugh and Spark's Irish grandfather started out as Church of Ireland but once in America he took a short detour to become an Episcopalian minister—called Anglican in Canada—as did his son, Ragnar, though in the latter's case, not for long.

"I realized almost immediately I had no vocation for being a dilute Catholic," he said, explaining in that edgy, dispassionate way he had, the spiritual crisis that sent him around the world in search of a religion and a philosophy big enough to hold him. He was gone for two years, abandoning the care of his wife, Ellen, and two baby boys, to her parents.

Once home, dark hair curling to his shoulders, and with a loan from his father-in-law, he bought an old, ruined church, which he called the Church in the Clearing, on the outskirts of Boothbay Harbor, an hour or so by ferry from Monhegan, and set up a kind of spiritual chop-shop, tearing apart the world's religions, stealing shiny thoughts, dismantling philosophies, stripping canons, looking for salvage, reimagining and repurposing all those old parts.

He was an ambitious man, in possession of a fierce pacing intellect released finally from its cage. Now he needed an ideology to package and a fate to fulfill. He founded his own religion, which evolved over time into an eccentric manifestation of his idiosyncratic views on theology, faith, philosophy, psychology, politics, life, death, and the culture. He oversaw a large, woolly flock of noisy, unwittingly compliant bleaters who teetered and tottered between wild-haired tribe and earnest social-service organization, occupying the murky middle ground somewhere between Jonestown and the La Leche League.

In those early days of his ministry, in his combustible eagerness to be heard, he took up essay writing, attracting some notice for his views from the secular press, in particular for a piece that appeared in *The Christian Scientist Monitor,* called "God, the Angry Guy Next Door," which laid out the preliminaries of his growing view of the deity as an essentially human male in middle age with too much time and power on his hands, kind of like the typical grouchy dad who loves his kids, will do anything for them, but is subject to unreasonable, obscure, and punitive flashes of rage.

Also has a talent for irritability, irrational expectations, and unpredictable behavior—imagine Pastor Ragnar with a magic wand.

"He fucks you up, your Heavenly Father . . ." His lede was a paraphrase of Larkin.

"Why the infantile need to see God as perfect?" he wrote. "God gives us the example of our own lives to better facilitate our understanding of our relationship to Him. As small children we idolize our parents, imagining them to be infallible. Once we're old enough to see their flaws, we spend the rest of our lives blaming them for the state of the world in which we find ourselves. So it is with God. While all of nature tells us different, when the entire history of humankind testifies otherwise, still we cling to the childlike notion that God is incapable of error.

"God, evidence suggests, is the reckless face of humanity reflected back at us, in equal measures both good and wicked.

"Satan isn't a separate entity with whom God wrestles for power. Satan is the devil within Himself that He wrestles to control—not eliminate entirely, but only manage, this is the critical distinction. Made in His likeness, so then do we simultaneously battle and embrace the demon within. Humanity represents the way in which God plays out the duality of his nature. We, each one of us, are God's own struggle made manifest.

"A loving but flawed father, God, temperamental and idiosyncratic, has His favorites, and he makes his preferences felt. Not fair, perhaps, but it benefits no one to pretend otherwise. It's worth reminding ourselves that being among the chosen isn't always all it's cracked up to be, either, but comes with its own excruciating torments."

Interesting twist. Pastor Ragnar was remaking God in *his* own image and likeness.

On the strength of the article he wrote a book that was picked up by a small press, a personal manifesto with a pop-theological bent, written in what he described as an inspired trance over four months. It was called "The All-Too Human Face of God" and opened with a quote from Chaucer ". . . If gold were to rust, what then will iron do?"

In his custom fit designed to accommodate, promote even, a vividly flawed deity, Pastor Ragnar expressed the view that in keeping with his declaration that He made us in His own image and likeness, God was declaring to humanity that while he was all-powerful and all-knowing, He was also all-too-human, an imperfect being with a talent for beauty and ugliness, kindness and cruelty, impulse, regret, and eccentricity.

Like all tough, mercurial, and powerful A-Types, God was prone to unreasoning anger and violence and in the classic tradition of the unchecked bastard with an army and a kingdom at his disposal, had a "soft" son, who could never do anything right, short of hanging from a cross to appease the old man's endless preposterous demands.

In essence, Pastor Ragnar advanced the takeaway view that the distance between good and bad is a short walk.

Asserting his premise that God was imperfect and unpredictable, occasionally even unstable, Pastor Ragner laid down in detail his own religious-ethical doctrine, which he called Cludo (derived from the Latin word meaning to conclude, which in his case meant case closed), and which he subsequently deconstructed to its two essential branches: Defectivus (Imperfect), which articulated in detail the theoretical aspects of Cludo, and Peccavi (I have sinned), which outlined ways to execute the ideas embodied in Defectivus.

Despite its endless complications, Cludo boiled down to one basic idea—set yourself free or as Spark used to say, "Embrace your inner demon." Give up "project goodness," as Pastor Ragnar dubbed it, and acknowledge individual imperfections as a reminder of the flawed deity that lives within each of us, even as Satan exists within God, rather than as a separate foe with a tropical zip code.

His ideas propelled him onto the national stage and attracted a small but enthusiastic following and the church enjoyed steady growth over the years, though the ministry, and subsequently the family, was plagued by money worries.

Spark had no problem using the C-word to describe what was both contained and uncontained in an old derelict church on an old abandoned road.

"It's a cult," he said.

"That's an uneducated observation," Hugh said, taking issue. "If anything, Pop encourages discussion and dissent, deplores isolationism, discourages rule-making."

"Part of the con," Spark said.

"Do you ever plan to evolve beyond your own cult of adolescence?" Hugh said, exasperated by what he termed his brother's "teenage cynicism," though the better I got to know him, the more Spark's love-hate for his father seemed like something organic, circulating within him like his blood.

Hugh liked to tell the story that his mother told him about the first time Spark, as an infant, saw Pastor Ragnar. He began to cry, prompted by some secret terror. That meeting set the template, father and son in protracted conflict with their own DNA, the war of the cellular worlds. Pastor Ragnar had given life to his nemesis, creating an unusually dense and murky family dynamic, as if Lex Luthor had to sit across from a young Superman at Thanksgiving dinner.

A couple of days after the visit from the sheriff and his deputy, I finally met Pastor Ragnar. The kitchen door swung open and this great black cloak of a man stepped inside. I yelped as he crunched down with his gleaming ebony brogue on my front paw. Startled, he knelt down and then stood back up again, holding me in his arms.

"This is a surprise. Where did you come from?"

Something inside cautioned me against wagging my tail, instead I met his gaze head-on, avoiding any sort of supplication. Intuitively, I recognized, this was not a man to whom you willingly gave the advantage, psychological or otherwise.

Inhaling the crosscurrents around him, I could smell it on him, his drawing power, the black-hole talent he had for sucking people into his orbit. Primitive but somehow refined, a graceful animal, he gave off this scent, like a worn leather saddle on an overheated horse, though it's possible I was confusing personal magnetism with his signature cologne. Equipage by Hermès.

Not for sissies.

More intriguing than the usual overheated messianics with flecks of dried spittle in the corners of their mouths, Pastor Ragnar, fifty-six (looked younger), was just shy of six feet, trim but muscular. He had glossy black hair of medium length about which he was leading-man vain. He always wore it the same way with part between the middle and the side, tapered sides and back shorter than the top, which was longer and combed over. The overall effect was a poor man's Errol Flynn. He had arctic blue eyes (same as Spark, who had inherited his father's coloring) and a challenging, almost rakish expression with full lips that conspired to be simultaneously sensual and pursed, as if he were a man who knew better than to be conceited but was reluctant to deny himself the voluptuous pleasures of vanity.

Ragnar Monahan was improbably handsome and not in any ordinary symmetrical sense of the word—he was uneven, imperfect, riveting. He made an intelligent, sophisticated impression, creating the intriguing effect of a man indifferent to the judgments of others, someone more at home sitting at the best table in the house than leaning hunched over a pulpit.

"Hally! Hugh!" Pastor Ragnar called out just before Hally came into the room. "Who is this guy?"

"His name is Ned," Hally said. "He's mine."

"Oh, is he? Since when? I don't recall making any decision about a dog."

"Please, Gramp, he's no trouble and I'll take care of him."

"Famous last words. Where did he come from?"

"Me," Spark said, entering the living room from the hallway. "I gave him the dog."

Pastor Ragnar displayed only mild surprise, though I could sense he was rocked by his older son's sudden appearance. "Jamie," he said, "this is unexpected. When did you get here?"

"A few days ago."

"Just passing through, are you?"

"That depends on you."

Pastor Ragnar handed me over to Hally. "This is your home. There's no statute of limitations on how long you can stay."

"I just thought . . . since Mom . . ." Spark said, voice thickening, wanting to get to the heart of the matter, but faltering. I looked on, surprised at the unexpectedly withering effect his father's presence had on Spark's characteristic jauntiness.

"Jamie," Pastor Ragnar said, walking toward him, giving him an antiseptic hug, "your mother would never forgive me if I were to turn my back on you. You're my son. End of story."

Hally gripped me tightly, his fingers digging into my shoulders. "Hughie said I can keep Ned," he said, seizing an exploitable moment.

Hugh was standing in the doorway leading to the back of the house. Pastor Ragnar, withdrawing awkwardly from Spark, nodded over at him. "Oh, he did, did he? Well, who am I to overrule your uncle and your father?"

"Thank you! Thank you, Gramp," Hally said. "You won't even know he's here, I promise."

"Anyone ever warn you about making promises you can't keep? Little dogs are notoriously hard to house-train," Pastor Ragnar said, loosening his tie and taking off his suit coat jacket, which he slid over the back of a kitchen chair.

Momentarily bristling at his untidy little insult, I reminded myself that only the facile make a habit of being offended.

"You've lost weight," Pastor Ragnar said, frowning, critically surveying Spark, who stood by the kitchen door, his hand lightly hovering around the knob as if he were poised for sudden flight.

"Maybe, a little," Spark answered.

"Should I be concerned? Are you ill?" Pastor Ragnar asked. "Is that why you've come home?"

"No, I'm fine."

"You don't look fine," Pastor Ragnar said. "You look terrible. No one has heard from you in almost a year. Hugh will tell you we've even discussed going to the police to track down your whereabouts. What have you been up to? Where have you been?" His indignation was gathering strength. "Did you not think we would be worried?"

"No. Why would I?" Spark said, sounding surprised. "It's not like you ever make an effort to contact me. Last time I saw you . . . well, we didn't exactly part on good terms."

"Your mother's funeral," Pastor Ragnar said.

Spark nodded, the door handle rattling as it rotated.

"Well, come on then. Tell us. What's the story? How did you live? Were you working?"

"Here and there, seasonal stuff, mostly. I traveled around, looking for jobs, seeing the country . . ."

"Getting into trouble . . . Hugh took care of that mess for you in Louisiana last summer just before you vanished . . ."

Hugh looked pained. "It was no big deal," he said, as Spark, no longer tense but resigned, his muscles softening, eyes hardening, prepared to settle into a familiar pattern of engagement with his father.

"Whatever you say, Pop," Spark said.

"Don't patronize me. After all you've done and not done? Then you come waltzing back home whenever you feel like it . . ."

"I knew this was a mistake," Spark said as things quickly degraded, stepping away from the door, the knob giving way, falling in a loud clunk to the floor as he reached for his jacket.

"No!" Hally said, springing from his chair, surprising Spark and looking imploringly at Hugh, who did not disappoint him but moved quickly. "I'll take that," he said as Spark, too drained to enact his usual defiance, compliantly handed him the jacket, which everyone in the room took to be a measure of his desperation.

"Pop, come on . . ." Hugh said. "Have a heart."

Pastor Ragnar sighed loudly. He was annoyed but outnumbered. "Listen, Spark. It's been a rough few days." Hally walked over and put his hand on his grandfather's forearm. "Gramp . . ." Pastor Ragnar, eyes half-closed, looked over at Spark. "Don't go. Stay. I want you to. Please." It was a formal appeal, more legalistic than heartfelt, but adequate to get the job done.

Hugh hung Spark's jacket back on the peg.

"How did it go?" Hugh said, shaking it off, trying to act as if nothing had occurred. Relieved but unfazed, he was a veteran of family crises.

"As expected," Pastor Ragnar answered, sounding tired. "No surprises."

"Sorry about what happened, Pop, the concert, I mean," Spark said, following Hugh's lead, pulling up a chair to the table.

"Thank you, Jamie. It was a great artistic triumph and that's the main thing. The rest is only money. We'll be fine." He sat down at the kitchen table, a heaviness in his manner. "You want to make me a cup of coffee, Hugh? It's been a long few days. It's not easy going up against a team of lawyers under your own steam. Anyway, it's done, over. I owe a pile of dough.

"This is one of the few times that it pays to be broke and possessionless. Thank heavens your mother insisted on putting the house in your names when she found out how ill she was, or we would have lost the place as part of the judgment."

"Does that mean everything belongs to Spark and Hugh?" Hally asked as he lowered me to the floor and I followed him into the living room where he sat down on the sofa and I leapt up next to him.

"That's what it means," Pastor Ragnar said, massaging his forehead with his thumb and forefinger. "Your grandmother's mother died when she was a young girl and then her father remarried and he left everything to his second wife, who shut out your grandmother after he died. The second wife's son from a previous marriage wound up with everything."

Hally nodded. "Oh, Gram already told me all about her step-brother. His name was Ewart and she said she hated him so much she used to put castor oil in his orange juice and one time she gave him a wiener the dog had swallowed and then threw back up again."

"Gram could be a little . . . irrepressible," Pastor Ragnar said with an uneasy smile. Maybe, I thought, his wife's death hadn't been an unmitigated tragedy. "In any event, Ellen wanted to make sure that our children, including you, Hally, would never suffer a similar abandonment. So it looks as if I need to behave myself if I don't want to wind up on the street."

"I don't get why Gram thought you would do something like that," Hally said.

"I wouldn't," Pastor Ragnar said. "I knew better, however, than to go up against your grandmother when she felt strongly on a subject."

"Was there a subject she didn't feel strongly about?" Spark said.

"It's our family home. It doesn't matter whose names are on the deed," Hugh said quietly. "What about the church?"

"The building isn't worth a dime but the land is a different story. The court's still waiting on the appraisals and we're fighting it but I don't see how we can hang on to the church. It's going to wind up being seized as part of the judgment, just a matter of time."

"We won't give up," Hugh said.

"No, we won't," Pastor Ragnar agreed, though he didn't sound convinced.

"You hungry, Pop?" Hugh asked. "I can heat something up for you."

"That would be wonderful, thank you," Pastor Ragnar said as

Hugh began to pull leftovers from the fridge. He attempted to start over with Spark. "You'll have to bring me up to speed on your life . . ."

"Yeah, sure thing," Spark said. He paused, the others looking at him expectantly. He grinned. "I guess that just about covers it."

"I'll bet . . ." Pastor Ragnar said with more than a little skepticism. "For another day, then, when we're both feeling up to it . . . So anything exciting happen when I was gone? Give me all the dirt."

"I can't help but worry," Hugh said. "What if they press charges?"

"Let not your hearts be troubled. Believe in God; believe also in me," Pastor Ragnar reassured him, tone sprouting wings. He had this manner—I never knew whether he was serious or kidding. He always sounded ironic whenever he quoted scripture, as if he were indulging in a private joke.

"I know," Hugh said. "I'm trying."

"This is quite a situation you've got yourself into, Hally," Pastor Ragnar said.

"I didn't do anything," Hally said.

"So you've said."

Pastor Ragnar looked for the least comfortable chair (wooden, armless), pulled it into the middle of the living room and sat down in front of Hugh, Spark, Hally, and me, all of us sitting side by side on the sofa. He turned his full attention to Hally. "Why do I feel you haven't told me everything about this little drama?"

Hally, eyes lowered, surprised everyone by instantly confessing to spending time with Loretta-Christine on the night in question.

"Was it the threat of torture?" Spark asked him, incredulous.

"Oh, Hal," Hugh said, looking dismayed. "Did you know about this?" he asked Spark accusingly. "You never said anything?"

"Never mind, you two . . . I thought as much," Pastor Ragnar said. He was sitting erect, shoulders a pair of matching low-rises, impressive posture betraying his wartime stint in the army (Korea), gaze fixed on Hally. For a moment I felt as if it was a military inquiry and at any moment he was going to have the four of us shot by a firing squad.

"All right," he said abruptly. "Let's see how things shake out in the next day or so. The deputy sheriff is a member of my church," he said, smiling slightly, as if he were describing someone he'd bought at auction. "I'll have a little chat with him. One of those overzealous types easily deflated and redirected."

"The man's an idiot," Spark said as his father leaned forward, his confidential speaking manner making a "little chat" seem like a euphemism for fingernail extraction.

"In the meantime, you boys are not to discuss this with anyone, is that understood? No more casual conversations with the police either. What were you two thinking? Spark, I would have thought you, in particular, might know better."

"Thanks," Spark said, getting the message. "You do know I'm not John Wesley Harding?"

Pastor Ragnar sighed deeply. Sighing was practically a side occupation for him. "One of my congregants is a lawyer, a good one, he's been advising me about my own case, we'll have him step in and end this."

"I don't need a lawyer," Hally said. "I haven't done anything wrong."

"I minister to men sitting on death row who made the same proclamation . . . I'm not asking for your permission, Hally," Pastor Ragnar said.

"Maybe we should just put our faith in God," Spark said. He never could resist.

". . . Or you can continue putting your faith in sarcasm," Pastor Ragnar replied, standing up, heading for the door leading upstairs.

"Are you going to tell the police about . . . you know . . . what I told you about being with that girl?" Hally asked as Pastor Ragnar stopped and considered for a moment.

"I should tell them, however, I'm going to do everyone a favor and keep your little secret for the time being. It's only because I know you're innocent. This is the exception, not the rule. Understood?"

Hally nodded.

"No more convenient omissions, all right? You need to make a practice of telling the truth."

"I know," Hally said, seeming contrite, though Hally's conscience seemed to be a moving target.

"Isn't that exactly what you're doing?" Spark said. "Committing a 'convenient omission'?"

"Why can't you ever just let it go?" Hugh said, appearing to be suddenly exhausted.

Pastor Ragnar paused at the door. "Why, yes, Jamie, that's exactly what I'm doing. Good catch." He turned to face his older son. "Maybe you would be kind enough to pray for me, that I might do better in the future. Until then, I'm afraid you'll just have to bear with your imperfect father. In the meantime, welcome home."

Later, after everyone had gone to bed, I could hear Pastor Ragnar wandering around the house in the early hours of the morning, which I'd learn was the ordinary run of things. He wrote at night, developed his sermons, composed letters, worked on his new manuscript, a memoir of the spirit.

He would mumble to himself, sometimes escalating to a shout, a nearly violent exchange ensuing with someone unseen with whom he appeared to be arguing, his words regularly waking me up. I would lie there unmoving and listen, feeling troubled, knowing the others,

Hugh, Hally and Spark, were being held hostage to the same unsettling nightly ritual.

Pastor Ragnar rarely went to bed before three and even then hardly slept more than four or five hours. Hugh used to say it confirmed his status as a genius. "All the great men of history have only needed a few hours of shut-eye compared to the rest of us."

"Yeah, so I've heard," Spark said. "Guys like Pop are too important to sleep."

It was barely light when I registered the small thump of the kitchen door as it closed behind him. I climbed onto the open window ledge in the upstairs hallway and watched from above as he paced back and forth on the deck below, reading from his Bible, lips forming silent prayers.

He kept it up for a while, treading the same ground over and over, and then, closed Bible in hand, he walked over to the guest cottage and knocked on the door. After a few moments, the father answered wearing only his tiny briefs with a leopard-skin pattern and a pair of lopsided glasses. "Do you have any idea what time it is?" I heard him demand.

"I want you and your family out of here today," Pastor Ragnar said, voices carrying in the quiet.

"We've paid for a full stay . . . You can't evict us, especially since the problem originates with your grandson . . . thanks to him, my research is set back significantly. We aren't budging."

"Your money will be refunded, I assure you."

The Sex Family father was adamant they weren't going anywhere.

Pastor Ragnar leaned in to him. "If you and your family aren't out of here by noon today, I will give you every reason to regret your decision."

The Sex Family father, faltering beneath the shadow of a human baseball bat, considered for a moment. "All right. Frankly, I'll be delighted to get as far away from here as possible."

"Then we are of the same mind," Pastor Ragnar said, relaxing his stance. He turned around and began to walk away. "For heaven's sake put on some clothes," he remarked. "Consider it a public service."

⌇⌇⌇⌇⌇

"Where's Pop?" Spark asked Hugh. We were assembled around the breakfast table, the heavyweight aroma of peanut butter combining with acrid low notes of burnt toast.

"I don't know. I heard him leave the house early this morning," Hugh said.

"Another dark night of the soulless for Pastor Ragnar," Spark said.

"What are you up to today?" Hugh asked him.

"I want to talk to Beans about working on his lobster boat. I need to make some money."

Beans Tansy, who had greeted Spark and me on our arrival, lived alone in the small one-story cottage he shared with his twin brother until Beezy died in a boating accident five years earlier. Turned out he was a handyman as well as a fisherman and did odd jobs for Pastor Ragnar around the church, also acting as his de facto security man and driver. Apart from his devotion to Pastor Ragnar, who tended to attract and cultivate bizarre loyalties (for all his aspirations, Pastor Ragnar only ever truly relaxed in the company of men such as Beans, like a comic trying out new material in an out-of-the-way club in front of a well-lubricated audience), Tansy fancied himself an unofficial ambassador and amateur historian, waylaying unsuspecting tourists with a bottomless inventory of island folklore and facts.

Hissing, or more precisely, hi*th*ing—he was missing most of his teeth except for two lower canines that jutted from his underbite like some interspecies evolutionary marker—stinking of fish and liquor, he would launch himself from the steep inclines of rocky ledges or from behind the mossy camouflage of densely wooded tracts of forest at first sign of another human presence. "You're not from around here, are you?" he'd say, his chilling catchphrase.

Hally was reaching for another pancake when Spark asked him if Beans was still a favorite target of local boys.

"Yeah, kinda," Hally agreed, a bit warily, uncertain about what was behind Spark's line of inquiry. "Do we have any brown sugar?" he asked Hugh, who got up from his seat to retrieve some from the cabinet.

"I spent the best years of my life tormenting Beans," Spark said nostalgically from his spot at the table across from Hally.

"Did you get into trouble when you were a kid?" Hally asked.

"Isn't there enough trouble right at the moment? We don't need to dredge up the past to mine for more," Hugh said. "Beans may appear to be friendly enough, but he isn't the kind of guy you want to mess with."

"Um, Beans is just an old drunk," Spark said.

"A lunatic with a chip on his shoulder and a cabin full of guns, booze, and ammunition is not just an old drunk. You should know that better than anyone," Hugh admonished, addressing Spark, but all the while his eyes were fixed on Hally, whose uncontainable innermost thoughts gave him away, shimmering like the dull glow of a flashlight beneath bedcovers.

"Remember the time I broke into Beans' place and stole the bullets . . . ?" Spark said, chuckling at the memory.

"How could I forget?" Hugh said.

"What?" Hally said.

"The cabin was full of all this ammo. There were dozens of jars everywhere filled with bullets. I stole some and divided them into a couple of glass jars and then I tossed in a lit match . . ."

"Okay, enough," Hugh said. "Sometimes I wonder about you, Spark."

"What happened?" Hally said.

"Your uncle's right," Spark said, looking sheepish, surprising Hugh and me, too, for that matter. "Nothing happened. Big fizzle and dud. It was a dumb thing to do. I shouldn't have mentioned it. Just forget I said anything."

"You stay away from him, Hally," Hugh said, turning on the faucet, filling the sink with dishes and water, seeming preoccupied.

"You mean Spark?" Hally said, joking.

"Yeah, him, too," Hugh said.

Hally took a final bite of his pancake, tossing me what was left. He got up from the table and popped up onto the counter, where he sat, legs dangling carelessly.

"It'll be okay, Hugh," he said unexpectedly, intuiting Hugh was more upset than he was letting on. "I didn't do anything wrong."

"I know you didn't. Believe me, I do. I'll just be happy to put this behind us." Hugh leaned over and put his arm around Hally's shoulders. "Everything's going to be fine," he said. "Right?"

Spark nodded as Hally and Hugh looked to him for encouragement. He kept on nodding as he spoke. "Yeah," he said, knee rocking up and down. "You bet."

He looked back down at the newspaper spread open in front of him and it occurred to me that we were having the same thought—it's a perilous position when you find yourself seeking reassurance from Spark Monahan.

Hally must have been reading my mind. He looked at his father, then back over at his uncle. He slid down from the counter to the floor. "Where are you going?" Hugh asked.

"Nowhere," Hally said, seeming dispirited. "Outside."

"Why don't you invite some friends over? Toilet-paper the guest house. You could use the distraction," Spark said offhandedly, eyes still on the paper.

"My best friend moved away a couple of months ago," Hally said dejectedly.

"Oh well, so that's just one guy . . . there must be other kids you can hang around with," Spark said as Hugh drilled a hole in the back of his head.

"Not really. Some kids think I'm super religious or something because of Gramp or their parents think that he's head of a cult and they don't want their kids to get sucked in. Did you guys have that problem when you were kids?"

"Yeah," Hugh said, "I remember. It can be a tough one . . . I—" Before he finished speaking, Spark interrupted, "Nope. You're probably just sending out the wrong vibe . . . you're approaching these kids hat in hand," he said obliviously as Hugh stared at him in disbelief. "I'm sure that's not the case," he said firmly, walking over to the table, trying to send Spark a message.

"Did you have lots of friends when you were a kid?" Hally asked Spark.

"Sure, why wouldn't I?" Spark said cheerfully.

"Your dad attracted friends the way a dog attracts fleas—no offense, Ned," Hugh said as from my vantage point I could see him nudge Spark with his foot. "Maybe you'd like to go to Beans' place with your dad?"

"You want to come?" Spark said.

"I don't know. Maybe," Hally said, the prospect of being alone with Spark a daunting one.

"Up to you," Spark said as Hugh, exasperated, gave him another sharp shot.

"I'd really like you to come, though," Spark added, a bit woodenly, finally cluing in.

"Okay, if you want me to," Hally said. "Why don't you come, too, Hugh?"

"I've got work to do for my show," Hugh said. "It will be good for you two to have some time alone together."

"Can Neddy come?" Hally asked.

"Sure," Spark said, as relieved as Hally to have a third-party presence on their outing.

I followed Spark into the study when I heard Hally leave the house. Hugh immediately went after Spark. "What are you thinking? 'Oh, I had tons of friends, no end to the friends I had,'" he mimicked. "How can someone so smart be so dumb? You really don't get it, do you?" he said as Spark asked him what he was talking about.

Jogging back down the hallway and into the kitchen, I scratched at the door until Hugh, temporarily abandoning his lecture, let me outside. Once free, nose in the air, I shot after Hally, streaking toward the edge of the low-lying granite bluff, sun largely obscured by billowing gray clouds, seabirds swooping and diving, waves battering the boulders just below, the spray surging upward like a geyser, soaking him in its cold spatter. Slipping and sliding on the slick surface of the rocks, I slowed my pace and made tentative progress in his direction.

He was facing the ocean. Enshrined on all sides by that fierce setting he looked to be at the epicenter of one of those semi-hysterical religious paintings warehoused at the back of the closet in Pastor Ragnar's home office: Noah, presiding over the firmament, staff glowing like thunder-and-lightning-on-a-stick, commanding the winds and the seas and all the animals of the earth.

Roused by the roar of the waves, and the hollow whoosh of the wind, not for the first time, I was struck by the solitary experience of that aloof place where nothing was soft or giving, everything was hard and unyielding and slipperiness was the island's only concession to flexibility. No sand for sinking but one false step and you're swallowed up into the watery abyss. Facing down the Atlantic's mercurial temperament, the island, for all its spectacular beauty, sometimes felt less like a safe harbor and more like a penal colony with ducks.

"I don't think Spark likes me very much," Hally said. "I'm not his kind of kid."

Seven

⧗⧗⧗

"Do you think maybe Beans would let me work on the boat, too?" Hally asked Spark just before we arrived at Tansy's cottage.

Spark made a face. "I was your age when I started on the boats. You don't want to follow me into the mines. Maybe just come the odd day or so for a lark . . ."

"It's okay," Hally said. "I don't need to if you don't want me to."

"No, no, it's not that. I want to spend time with you," Spark said, sincere but dutiful, recalling Hugh's admonitions. "I just don't want you to wind up like me."

I looked up at both of them and wagged my tail, happy to be in their company, wishing they could be happier to be in each other's company, knowing how much they both wished for the same.

Hally looked down at me intently. "Do you think animals think about things?"

"I'm always being accused of anthropomorphizing animals, but what do we really know about what Ned's thinking?" Spark said, delighted to be expounding on a favorite topic—though this applied to most topics, I'd noticed. Pastor Ragnar once said Spark was just like the women back home in his father's little Irish village. "They get together on the porch and drink tea and talk and gossip by the hour and solve the problems of the world. They'd be perfectly content doing nothing else forever."

"Science nerds are just speculating when they talk about what animals think and feel so why can't I speculate however I want?"

Spark bent down to pick me up, including me, as if I were a part of the conversation.

"I don't know why we want to differentiate ourselves so much from other animals. I think I have more in common with Ned and the way he thinks than I have with most humans. I dare you to anthropomorphize Himmler! I think it's more challenging to anthropomorphize any number of human beings than it is dogs." Spark, not waiting for a reply, set me down and made a sudden right turn, ducking into a cul-de-sac of overgrowth, leaving Hally temporarily stranded, and me curious enough to bolt after him.

"Hang on for a second," Spark yelled. A few minutes later I trailed him back into view.

"You snuck off for a smoke," Hally said. "You know you're not allowed to smoke outside of town."

"I told you I don't smoke and you shouldn't either," Spark said, a spectacular lie—Spark's lies were circus performers. They wore feathers and crowns and sequins. They rode unicycles.

"Then what were you doing?" Hally kept at him.

"Didn't anyone ever tell you it's rude to ask personal questions?" Spark said as we climbed onto the porch and banged on the screen door. "Anybody home?" He peered through the rusty mesh and into the cabin's interior.

"Hello," he said, pulling open the door and motioning for us to follow him inside. "Beans?"

The cabin's interior was dingy and cluttered—we had to push our way through the debris, the trapped air oozing an oily consistency, reeking of Beans' bloodhound, Salamander, grime, cigarette smoke, and cat piss. The windows were unadorned and open to spring but there was no evidence of May inside Beans' cabin.

"Oh man, I don't believe it," Spark said, reaching for a miniature man made entirely from repurposed beer cans that sat on the top shelf of a dark cabinet covered in a scrawled veneer of black magic marker. "Do you have any idea how many times I stole this from Beans when I was a kid? We used to hide it in plain sight in crazy places all over the island. Drove him nuts. I can't believe he's still got it.

"When I think how I used to torture that guy . . ."

"Did you ever get in trouble from him?" Hally's eyes were shining.

"He used to chase my friends and me with his rifle. Shot at us more than once, too."

"Weren't you scared?"

"At that stage in my life, I had no higher aspiration than tormenting Beans and getting my head blown off for a piece of prison art. My obituary would have read: 'He died doing what he loved.'"

"What's changed?" Hally chirped.

"Hail and farewell, old friend . . ." Spark set the beer-can man back on his perch. "I feel as if I've just lost my innocence."

"You hear that?" Hally said.

Voices in lively conversation. I stood up on my hind legs and peeked through the smear of nose-and-paw prints on the glass windowpanes. Pastor Ragnar and Beans emerged from behind the house, walking side by side, Pastor Ragnar's hands linked behind his back as he talked, Beans listening reverentially. They stopped for a moment and Pastor Ragnar put his hand on Beans' shoulder in comforting fashion. Beans hugged him in return. The two men clasped hands for a moment and then resumed their walk.

"Looks like Beans is going to be your new grandmother," Spark said to Hally.

Beans had Salamander with him. For a dog with such an impressive sense of smell, Salamander stank so much he was a threat to the planet, a creeping dose of stagnant pond water, sunbaked roadkill, and human body odor. I enjoy the scent of decay and decomposition as much as any dog but I draw the line at organ tissue damage.

I sneezed in head-jerking fashion, trying to shake off the traveling stink show as he bounded across the yard, ahead of Beans and Pastor Ragnar, the offshore wind carrying his signature perfume into the cabin—Beans contributing his own rank atomized spray—and generously dispersing it like noxious pollen.

Spark walked toward the front door. "Coming?" he asked Hally.

"Yeah, I just need to use the bathroom first."

"Be careful what you touch. Don't get pregnant," Spark said.

I started to follow Spark but stopped at the door. He stepped outside and waving, called to Beans and Pastor Ragnar, Salamander braying at the sound of his voice. After a few minutes, Hally emerged and we were about to leave and join the others when he spotted several jars of ammunition sitting on a bench near the back door.

"Whoa," he said, coming to a full stop, his heart audibly clicking in renegade sequence like a safe being cracked open.

Impulsively, he grabbed one of the mason jars and emptied a handful of bullets into his pockets.

"Hally!" Spark hollered from outside the cabin where he was standing talking to Beans and Pastor Ragnar. Hally looked at me and put a finger to his lips.

"Hold on. I'm coming!" he shouted out to the others.

Laughing and breathless, leaping along an obstacle course strewn with rotting logs and jutting stumps, fairy houses, moist lowlands, and tangles of old growth, Hally collapsed beneath the canopy of the Cathedral Forest on a narrow footpath of pine needles, among the lime-green ferns and the white and red spruce in a grove of quaking and big-tooth aspen.

He was lying on his back, gasping and giddy, arms and legs out-stretched while I, panting and wriggling, climbed over and around him, pausing to lick a cheek or a hand, tap his forehead with my paw.

I watched as he pulled a small package of Pall Malls and some matches from his denim backpack.

"Yeah right, you don't smoke, not at all," he muttered. "Found these under his bed." He reached into the backpack and pulled out three empty glass jars.

Then he hopped up onto his feet, and with an unlit cigarette dangling from his bottom lip, began positioning the jars on the ruins of an old, waist-high stone wall, setting them apart from one another. Into each open jar he put a number of the bullets he'd stolen from Beans.

Striking a match, the tiny flame almost instantly extinguished by the wind, he cupped his hand around it and held it aloft over the first jar. A solitary seagull came in for a landing, settling near us on the low-hanging branch of a balsam tree, but he wasn't interested in us. He looked right past us, as if we didn't exist, his yellow eyes glinting, keenly fixed on whatever we might leave behind.

"Hally!" Spark's shrill voice cut through the smoky haze, the seared air smelling like a ground explosion of fireworks. Hally, hollow-eyed, weak-in-the-knees, slowly backed away from the scene. Spark whistled for me and called my name.

"Hal," Spark repeated, speaking softly as he came closer, extend-ing his arms as if he were trying to reassure a panicked animal.

"I'm sorry . . . I didn't know . . . I just wanted to see what would happen," Hally said, panting, his whole body trembling.

"I could have told you what would happen," Spark said, tone changing from concern to anger as he realized Hally was fine. "You could have been killed," he said, smear of bright red blood on his sleeve. "You could have killed someone else. Me. Pop. What were you thinking?"

"But you—"

"You're not me, okay? You and me. We're nothing alike."

"I just thought—"

"You weren't thinking. You know who's going to get blamed for this, don't you? This is just great. How the hell am I going to explain this one to your grandfather? To Hugh? Jesus Christ, Hal. I should never have come home."

Hally stared at Spark. "No. Don't say that," he said, and then he turned around and ran (took off like a bullet shot from a mason jar if immediate memory served), running as fast as he could and not looking back.

"Hally!" Spark lunged for him, missed and grabbed me before I could follow after him. There was wet blood on his fingers. "Shit," he said. "I'm sorry. Hally!" he shouted after him.

"Quiet, Neddy. Take it easy," Spark said, but I just kept on barking.

We watched Hally vanish down the darkening trail, tall trees overhead blocking the sunlight.

"Holy Christ!" Hugh said, pausing mid-step as he ran down the stairs from his studio. "What happened?"

Pastor Ragnar was standing in the middle of the living room. His face was white, his shirt stained red. He had his hand pressed against his left arm, cupping the area just above his elbow. His fingers, his hands, were covered in blood.

Arms around his shoulders, Spark led him to a chair and made him sit down as Beans and Salamander followed behind them, Beans slightly limping, Salamander leaving red footprints on the floor, charging at me as if I were to blame. I immediately went on the offensive, our noisy skirmish only adding to the chaos. Beans, hollering, pulled Salamander away. Encouraged by Hugh, I leapt up onto a kitchen chair and then onto the table, out of reach.

"I'll tell you what happened," Beans said, huffing and puffing from exertion, voice filled with self-righteous anger. "That kid done this to his own grandfather. Pastor Ragnar could have been killed. We all could have been murdered. Salamander! His paw! To say nothing of me."

"What are you talking about?" Hugh demanded.

"I've been shot, Hugh," Pastor Ragnar said, his voice registering supreme levels of annoyance combined with a low note of sarcasm.

"Shot!" Hugh said. "Pop!"

"Don't worry. I'll live. It's only a graze, highly survivable, no thanks to Hally. I managed to come through a war without injury but a chance meeting in the woods with my twelve-year-old grandson and I'm lucky to escape having my head blown off."

"Hally!" Hugh said, reduced to a series of exclamations. "What does Hally have to do with it?"

"He trespassed onto my place and stole some ammunition. Ask that damn dog there, he was with him," Beans said, and pointed at me. "Then he heads into the woods, puts the bullets in some jars, throws in a match, and boom, bang, Pastor Ragnar, Spark, and me and Salamander walk right into a firefight, bullets whizzing everywhichaway around us. I tripped and fell over a rock trying to escape." He rolled up his pant leg to reveal a bloody knee, little more than a glorified playground injury.

"Thank God above for sparing us. What if Pastor Ragnar got killed? I don't even want to think about it. I'm sure I'm only here now talking to you people because God has a plan for Pastor Ragnar's life and he wants me in on it somehow. He saved me for some special reason."

"Yes, Beans, quite right," Pastor Ragnar said tolerantly enough, though it was apparent he didn't believe a word of it.

"What about me?" Spark asked. "I was there, too, remember? What's God's special purpose for me?"

"Where's Hally now?" Hugh said, rushing to find the first aid kit, opening and shutting chaotic kitchen drawers. "Is he all right?"

"I don't know where he is. The last time I saw him he seemed full of life," Pastor Ragnar said as Hugh took a closer look at his arm, the wound superficial but messy.

"Pop, we should take you to a hospital, just to be safe," Hugh said.

"Why don't you think about that for a second, Hugh? Hally's on thin ice as it is. You really want to involve the authorities? I'm fine. It looks worse than it is. Clean it, disinfectant it, wrap it up, forget it. I don't need a doctor, though Hally may, by the time I'm through with him."

"You can have him after I'm finished with him," Beans said.

"Okay, that's enough," Spark said flatly, uncharacteristically subdued.

"Somebody needs to look at this," Hugh said. "I'm going to get Mrs. Houton over here."

"Oh no," Spark said, revived. "Let Pop die. It will be less painful for everyone."

Shivering, I pressed myself against the doorway, the wind lashing the trees and rattling the glass, the rapidly dropping temperature casting an unseasonable chill. Sounds of recorded music from the studio above drifting idly in the background. *The party's over.*

Dusk found us gathered in the living room. Pastor Ragnar and Beans, even Salamander, were all cleaned and patched up, under the humorless supervision of Mrs. Houton, with help from Hugh, who was now standing in the doorway, holding himself slightly apart, erect and rigid, as if he were wearing a brace to contain his emotions.

"I said to my Tommy, wherever Spark Monahan goes, trouble follows and look at this. Look what's happened! He's been home for a matter of days and already his father is practically murdered." Mrs. Houton, the surface of her skin aglow with redness, her sky-blue eyes snapping, wasn't exactly shy about expressing her views, Spark resigned to patiently listening, his expression bemused but a little long-suffering.

"I used to say to Ellen, 'That boy will sink this island before he's through.' She spoiled him, you know she did, Ragnar. Don't deny it. Oh, she complained all right, but there was nobody as cute and funny as Spark as far as she was concerned and she let him do whatever he wanted. I was always realistic about Tommy. I used to tell her, 'If that was my Tommy and he was up to some of Spark's tricks, I'd beat the blood out of him' . . ." She had just finished wrapping up Pastor Ragnar's arm. "You should be just fine," she said triumphantly, making him swallow a couple of aspirins. "After thirty years of nursing, I should know."

"You're being a little hard on Spark, don't you think?" Hugh said.

"I don't know about that," Pastor Ragnar said. "She makes some salient points."

"Well, of course I do!" Mrs. Houton said. "Everyone knows I'm not an idle talker. You know that better than anyone, Ragnar, after all these years. I only speak when I have something useful to say."

Hugh's mind was elsewhere. "I'm worried about Hally. He's probably wandering around in shock, afraid to come home," he said, looking over at Spark. "You think we should go look for him?"

"Yeah, I do," Spark said, rising to his feet.

Pastor Ragnar had taken up his favored position in front of the fireplace with his back to all, injured arm pressed to his side, his right leg bent at the knee, one black leather brogue on the pine floor, the other resting on the stone hearth, his whole demeanor falsely suggesting nonchalance, though he was so engaged he may as well have been plugged into a socket. He held up his hand. "Hold on, Spark. I want to get a couple of things straight before I talk to Hally. What have you to do with all of this? It's apparent you were involved."

"Alleluia! Finally," Mrs. Houton said, folding her arms around herself in a self-satisfied embrace.

Spark stared at him. "Me? You think I was behind this?"

Pastor Ragnar turned around and stared back at him. "I do."

I could smell his intensity, feel his emotion present in every heartbeat, though on the surface he was cold as a snake assessing his victim's potential for compression.

"I must have a death wish, then, because I walked into the same blaze of bullets that you did. You think I would deliberately endanger myself, you and my own kid?"

"Don't forget me!" Beans said.

"I thought I mentioned you first," Spark said.

"I'm not suggesting you orchestrated it, but of course that would be your first reaction. Make a mess, then be equally reckless in the way you put things straight. You've worked hard since you came home to create a certain impression on Hally . . . that you're some kind of romantic outlaw figure . . . He did it to impress you, can you at least admit that?"

"Pop, it's not fair to blame Spark. If anything, he discouraged Hally from doing something so stupid . . ." Hugh said as Spark looked at him gratefully. "It was a prank gone wrong."

"I'll say," Mrs. Houton said in a stage whisper to Beans. "He's set out for his own amusement to corrupt his own sweet boy, that's the long and short of it."

Pastor Ragnar, sensing he was on the wrong side of history, walked into the kitchen to pour a cup of tea. "Am I hallucinating or did he just give in?" Spark said as he and Hugh got ready to head out, the room growing dark. The red-gold sun dipped and made its final ascent, the sky streaked with pink and gray, charcoal and blue, its colors deepening, black edges advancing, black silhouettes of seabirds, hundreds of them, forming feathery points of connection on a flowing veil of blackness that stretched across the clouds. A threatening wind blew in through the open window, the curtains flapping manically. Hugh leapt forward, reaching to steady a vase on the windowsill filled with pink and orange poppies that was at risk of toppling.

"That's him! The little bastard! You rotten son-of-a-bitch . . . Sorry, Pastor Ragnar, it's just that . . . Look what you've done to me. To my dog! To the pastor!" Beans, breaking the silence, was on his feet and raving the moment Hally poked his head around the corner and stopped, stunned, in the door frame at first sight of his greeting party.

"Looking every inch the little Irish hooligan in training," Mrs. Houton said, mercury rising to unstable levels.

"This isn't the County Down," Spark said. "Jesus."

If anything, Hally looked as if he was going to pass out. Mouth open, he stood and stared, unable to speak. He didn't look right. Stepping into the room, he reached for the back of a chair, trying to steady himself. His hands were shaking.

"Hally, come on, you're creeping me out," Spark said. "What . . .?"

Hally abruptly fell to his knees and to everyone's utter astonishment, he bowed his head and with eyes shut tight he began to recite the Hail Mary.

Eight

At first, when Hally dropped to the floor, I assumed he was just a terrified kid throwing himself on the mercy of the court of stern adult judgment. No one in the family was exactly an apostle of understatement, so the theatrical entrance was consistent. Then the more cynical part of me thought that maybe praying was part of a panicked strategy (with self-entertaining features) that Hally had come up with to appease (titillate), his grandfather.

I narrowed my eyes, scrutinizing. If this was a hoax, Hally wasn't enjoying it much.

"Tell me again what happened. What did you see?" Pastor Ragnar kept his attention on Hally and persisted in his line of questioning, an ice pick thrusting away.

"He's already told you what he saw," Spark snapped. "Do you expect it to become more believable with repetition?"

"Again. Tell me again," Pastor Ragnar said. "Hally, start again and this time tell the whole truth. Leave nothing out."

Sitting on the sofa, speaking nervously as he began, Hally talked in a voice so quiet that Pastor Ragnar had to ask him to speak up as he described what happened to him after he fled from Cathedral Woods, winding up at Black Head.

"The birds were so loud. I'd never heard them so loud."

"What were you doing at Black Head?" Pastor Ragnar urged, holding forth from the living room's center.

"I don't know . . ." Hally stumbled. "I . . . well, after . . . what happened . . . I'm so sorry, Gramp . . ."

"I know you are. Carry on," Pastor Ragnar urged.

"I just didn't want to deal with you guys yet . . ."

"Obviously you were traumatized. Time enough to discuss and review all that later. Right at the moment I need to know what happened to you afterward," Pastor Ragnar said.

Hally, his breathing shaky, his eyes darting often to Spark, resumed his story. "There were hundreds of birds all making noise at once, screeching at me. Then I heard this swooshing noise, coming from the water below me. The waves were going crazy. There was so much foam; it was like the water was boiling. I went to the edge of the bluff and I looked down and I saw a humpback and her calf. I was watching them and the gray seals dive and resurface. The waves were huge."

"You shouldn't have been there at all today. You know better than to go to the highlands on a windy day like today." Hugh was reviewing all the things that could have gone wrong. "What were you thinking?"

"Are you his mother or his uncle?" Spark interrupted, a bit mindlessly, in what was more of a reflex than a real accusation.

"Never mind all that now," Pastor Ragnar said. "Carry on, Hally."

"I was going to leave. It was so wild, it was scary. I started toward the trail but I couldn't find it. It was weird; everywhere I turned was the wrong way. I couldn't figure out how I could get lost when I know my way so well." Hally paused and looked over at Spark, who was sitting on the chair across from him, listening.

"There was a huge flash of white, this kind of brilliant light. It hurt to look at it. I figured it must be lightning, there must be a storm coming and then the birds got quiet and even the waves got calm and it was quiet and all I could smell were beach roses, the smell was so strong, it felt like it was going to knock me down.

"So freaky. You could almost see it, the scent of the roses, coming up off the ground, rising up and covering everything like a mist or something. It was like it was raining. Then, I don't know why, I just felt this strong urge to look behind me. Something made me stop. I turned around.

"The air got so clear, and the water got so still, it was shining and from the top of the bluffs you could see all the way to Spain . . ."

Spark's head shot up. "Aw, come on . . . this is such horseshit."

". . . and then I heard them, like wind chimes. It was like the wind was playing this music"— he stopped and took in several deep gulps of air—"and that's when I saw her."

"Hally . . . who did you see?" Pastor Ragnar prodded.

"A lady," he said. "She was standing on the cliff. She was wearing a long white dress with this, whatever you call it . . . a blue sash thing and she was carrying a yellow rose. Her hair was long and dark."

"Could it have been some bohemian day-tripper? The place is crawling with them this year."

"Hugh, please . . . I'd like to hear this." Pastor Ragnar's face was open, his manner nonjudgmental but critical, as if he were being presented with an intriguing thesis by an unconventional grad student and wanted to hear every last word of her defense. "What did she say to you? This woman in a white dress? How did she identify herself?"

"She didn't," Hally said. "I knew who she was. I knew it was Mary."

"Jesus, Mary and Joseph," Mrs. Houton wailed, crossing herself.

"Give me a break!" Spark couldn't believe what he was hearing. "Oh wow, Hal."

"At least that's what I thought," Hally explained, "well, I was scared, too, but then she made me feel . . . I don't know exactly . . . not scared. That's how I knew; by the way she made me feel inside." Hally spoke tentatively, looking from face to face, practically begging for credibility.

"Hally, are you sure it wasn't DeeDee White?" Hugh asked.

"Who's DeeDee White?" Spark asked, Hugh explaining that she was a new year-round resident of the island, an eccentric dance and school teacher with a penchant for pale togas, fey notions, and ethereal wandering.

"It wasn't DeeDee White," Hally answered, anguish on his young face. "I wish it had been."

"Because it sure as hell sounds to me as if it was DeeDee White," Hugh persisted.

"Hally, cut the crap." Spark finally let loose. "Everyone knows what you did. You don't need to lie about it. So you get grounded for a few days. Do the crime, pay the time, that's the deal."

Pastor Ragnar had moved from his spot at the fireplace and was crouched down in front of Hally, staring into his eyes, listening attentively to every word he was saying. There was something mildly disturbing about it, as if he was trying to crawl into his head.

"Thank you for the jailhouse wisdom, Jamie . . . Don't listen to your father. You focus on me. What did this woman say?" Pastor Ragnar said.

"She told me to pray. She said to make penance for my sins and for the sins of the world. Her voice sounded like music. It wasn't music but it made you feel as if you were listening to a song."

"Christ," Hugh said, staring over at Hally, who sat with his head slightly bowed, unwilling to make eye contact with anyone. "Can this possibly get any worse?"

"I'm not lying," Hally said, looking up, voice more firm. "I know you think I am. You'll see. She'll be at Black Head again in three days and I'm supposed to meet her at the same spot . . .

"She said we should love one another. Nothing else matters. She said it was the most important thing we can do in our lives."

"Did you tell her about Hands Across America?" Spark said.

"You asked me what she said," Hally responded, flaring up. "It's easy to be a wise-ass when you're sitting here in the living room. Try it when you're at the edge of a cliff talking to a shining lady on a golden cloud."

"Hally!" Spark said. "What's wrong with you? Why are you saying such crazy things?"

"Don't say I'm crazy. I'm not crazy!" Hally, sinking deeper into the sofa, was growing more upset. I could feel him retreating into himself. It wouldn't be long before he shut down entirely, like an overwound mechanism.

Standing next to Spark, Hugh, unaware of his own escalating anxiety, kept telling everyone to calm down, an annoying tic that was having the opposite effect.

"And a child shall lead them," Mrs. Houton said. "To think I would be present at such a moment as this. Thank God and His goodness."

"You've heard of Fátima, you've heard about Lourdes, presumably," Pastor Ragnar said, addressing his sons. "The Virgin Mary has appeared on different occasions throughout history. It's not so outrageous. Have a little intellectual and spiritual curiosity, is that possible from you two? The default position shouldn't be to brand someone as crazy because they present us with something that's alien to our thinking or experience. Come on, boys," he snapped his fingers. "Let's not make this about our failure of imagination, all right?"

"Have you totally lost it, too?" Spark said. "I can't listen to any more. Why are you indulging this?"

"Be more respectful," Pastor Ragnar said as Spark got up to leave.

"For shame," Mrs. Houton said. "What else could we expect from the likes of you?"

"Don't go, Spark," Hally entreated, "please . . ." but Spark wouldn't be persuaded.

"Look, I'm sorry, kid, no offense, but I need a break before my head explodes."

"What about my cabin? The wrong done to me and my dog? Funny, how all that's been forgotten? Maybe that's the idea, here. Do you know you almost killed your grandfather, young man?" Beans said to Hally, who reacted as if he'd been slapped.

"I'm sorry. I didn't mean it," he said. "It was stupid. I never thought anything bad would happen."

"Sorry doesn't mean a tinker's damn to me. Who's going to compensate me for what I've been through? What about my emotional distress?"

"Enough. This, what's happening here, is far more important," Pastor Ragnar said, rising to his feet.

"Well, I know, Pastor Ragnar, but it's only that—"

"Send me the bill. I'll take care of you."

I watched Hugh's eyebrows soar in response. He looked like a man contemplating a future painting kids with big eyes on black velvet.

"Nothing for you to worry about. Now, go home and don't breathe a word of this to anyone," Pastor Ragnar said, turning his back as Beans mumbled something about being grateful and Hugh escorted him and Salamander and Salamander's companion stench to the door.

"How can I ever thank you, Clara?" Pastor Ragnar said, kissing Mrs. Houton on the cheek. "I know I can count on your discretion in this matter."

"Discretion is my middle name," she said, "especially in matters of the heart and soul."

Hally stood in the open doorway of the study looking at Spark, who was sitting alone at Pastor Ragnar's desk, toying with a paperweight, eyes averted. I sat at Spark's feet and stared up at him, wanting to know what was going on in his head. No one spoke.

Shooting someone with a mason jar isn't exactly an everyday occurrence for most people. Then again neither is a Marian apparition. Hally managed not only to shoot his own grandfather with a bullet fired from a glass jar but on the same day, he was also able to fit in a tongue-tied meet-and-greet with the Mother of God.

"Look," Spark said, breaking their impasse, pointing down at me. "You've disappointed Ned. Good going, kid." Spark, for all his talk, wasn't exactly a hard-liner.

Hally, relieved, walked over, bent down, and ruffled my ears.

"You're fine, aren't you, Ned? You believe me, don't you, Neddy?"

He leaned in and kissed me on the top of the head. He drew me near, my muzzle grazing his chin. I recognized the sweet spring fragrance of trampled grass.

I was trying, like everyone else, to digest recent events—isn't it strange how you can go along, day by day, each passing moment as predictable as porridge, the rituals and rhythms, the quiet conduct of your life engraved in a glass of orange juice, and then one morning you wake up and you're staring down a plate of scrambled eggs?

Like most of us do when faced with a crisis, dogs as well as human beings, I fell back on reflexes, familiar patterns and ideas. The easiest thing was to decide it was hokum. Spark was right. Hally was making up this cockamamie story to get himself out of a jam. If the adults in his life would just nod indifferently, turn on the TV set, and forget about it, by tomorrow morning he'd be back to putting too much brown sugar on his pancakes.

Operating on the working theory the Marian apparition was a fraud, I slipped away, went off to be by myself in the spare bedroom upstairs (a drastic step for a dog, typically such isolation is reserved for death or bath avoidance). Looking for a place to think, to work out all my problems, I crawled under the bed, wishing for all the world that my father would magically appear with some gratifying insight or advice, even a tediously instructional anecdote would have been welcome.

After only a few moments, the door opened and Pastor Ragnar and Hally entered, the door clicking shut behind them. Pastor Ragnar sat in the corner on a threadbare powder-blue slipcovered armchair while Hally took up a spot on the edge of the bed. I could hear him reach across the chenille bedspread for a pillow that he pulled onto his lap.

There was a moment of silence before Pastor Ragnar spoke, his voice low and quiet.

"It's been a difficult day. How are you feeling?"

"Not so good."

"Would you like to tell me about it?" Pastor Ragnar said, his tone sympathetic and subdued.

"I already told you about it."

"I want to hear more."

Hally's breathing was labored. I could hear the scraping sounds of his palms, rough and dry from constant exposure to sand and wind, rubbing together. "I don't know what . . ." His voice cracked with fatigue and emotion.

"Why don't I ask you a few questions, just the two of us, and you can answer them? You'll feel better, Hally," Pastor Ragnar said in the same soothing voice, so tranquilizing I could feel my eyes drooping.

"I guess."

"Were you trying to copy your father when you took the bullets and ignited them?"

"Uh . . . sort of . . . yeah. I just wanted to see what would happen. Spark wouldn't tell me," Hally said, his voice faint and growing fainter. "I'm sorry. I didn't mean for anyone to get hurt." The heel of his running shoe thumped rhythmically against the wooden leg of the headboard.

"I know. I'm proud of you for telling the truth. That wasn't so hard, was it?"

"Kind of . . . it was. I'm sorry. I am. I didn't know the bullets would go off. I thought at the worst they might just blow up the jars. I never meant for you to get shot."

"Of course you didn't. Anyway, it's just a scrape. Then what happened?"

"I ran. I didn't know what else to do . . . I know I shouldn't have run away . . ."

"Hally, why are you crying?" Pastor Ragnar said, soporific strains of his voice rocking the room like a cradle.

"I don't know . . . Is Spark still mad at me?"

"No, I don't think so."

"I feel bad."

"I think it's because you are a better boy inside than you imagine yourself to be," Pastor Ragnar said, applying layer after layer of palliatives. "After the . . . incident . . . Then what happened?"

"I went to Black Head. I don't even know how I got there. I was just there. I wanted to get away from everything, all the trouble and the blood . . . the bad stuff I'd done."

"Do you like Black Head? Do you go there when you're upset?"

"Sometimes I go there to be by myself."

"You must have been very upset by all that happened. Were you afraid you would get into trouble?"

"Yes, well, I already *knew* I was in trouble. I knew everything was my fault . . . I wish I—"

"Never mind all that now," Pastor Ragnar said, annoyance creeping into his carefully modulated voice. He regrouped.

"Black Head, that's where you say you saw the Virgin Mary?"

"I did see her. I already told you a million times."

"Hally, you've admitted what you did with the bullets so there's no more need for you to make up anything to protect yourself from getting into trouble. I can deal with Beans. Nothing bad is going to happen to you. I need to ask you something and I want you to tell me the truth just as you have been doing. Hally, did the Virgin Mary appear to you and speak to you at Black Head today?"

"Yes," Hally said. "I wish I were lying but I'm not."

"Why do you wish you were lying?"

"Because I don't want to be crazy!"

"You're not crazy. You mustn't think that. You aren't the first child to have this happen. The Virgin Mary appeared to children at Fátima and at Lourdes. She appeared in Belgium, in Mexico—all of these visitations are considered by the Catholic Church to be credible apparitions."

"I thought you always said the Catholic Church was crazy . . ."

"Well, about some things . . . that's beside the point . . . These children weren't crazy. You're special. Special to God."

"Why do I have to be special?"

"Because you are. My God. You are! You've been given a glimpse of infinity. Do you have any idea what this means? Most people can't see beyond their preoccupation with the price of small appliances. But you . . ." Pastor Ragnar's voice trembled as he struggled to compose himself. "All right, that's enough for the moment. You say she's planning to appear again on Tuesday, let's see what happens then. In the meantime, it's obvious to me that God has an important plan for your life."

"Oh no," Hally said. "I just want a regular plan for my life."

"There are no regular plans for life, don't you see? This is how we delude ourselves. Life is only regular when you settle for the ordinary at the expense of the extraordinary. Mystery, mystery, Hally, we live at the unknowable heart of a great mystery. It's not ours to unravel or to solve but only to embrace. If you open yourself up to it you will never be sentenced to the banality of certitude. Do you know how lucky that makes you?"

"I guess."

This was exhausting. These Monahans! I thought my father was intense.

"I've seen men knowingly give up their lives for others. I've seen men throw others into the line of fire to save themselves. These things resist explanation. It's the province of small minds to try . . . You leave it to me," Pastor Ragnar said, fully restored, in the manner of a man who felt he could deal with God on a direct basis and still come out ahead, as if God were a Beans Tansy but with straight white teeth, a good haircut, and wearing a bespoke suit.

"You believe me?" Hally asked tentatively, slightly incredulous.

Pastor Ragnar got up, walked over and sat down beside him on the bed. "Yes, I believe you. With my whole heart and soul I believe you. Even if the whole world denies you, I never will."

"Thank you, Gramp," Hally said. His gratitude was pathetic.

"I understand a little of what you're going through," Pastor Ragnar said, a note of hesitation in his voice. He seemed to be mulling something over in his head. He got up again and walked toward the window. "When I was seventeen I saw something . . . I was walking along a lonely rural road in the little Ontario town I grew up in. It was hot and I was tired. I stopped to rest under the shade of a tree.

"My mother was ill. She was dying and I was very upset. Day and night, I prayed for her recovery. Lying there in the breeze, I began to pray for her when I felt something . . . it was inside me but separate from me. I had this sensation of an inward spiraling, as if something or someone had come from someplace on high and was winnowing its way deep inside of me and I heard—in the sense that I felt—a voice distinct from my own inner voice.

"The separate presence communicated to me that my prayers were not going to work this time, as they had worked for me in the past. My mother was going to die. I should have been devastated but I felt such peace. I fell into a deep sleep and when I woke up the world around me seemed ablaze, vivified into a single pulsing entity that consumed me, even as I flowed into it. I felt a part of something greater than myself and that feeling filled me up. It was a transcendent and transformative moment." Pastor Ragnar stopped talking for a moment. When he resumed, he seemed almost surprised at what he had confessed.

"I've never told anyone else about that," he said. "I'm not as brave as you are, Hally."

"It's still hard not to think it's a bit crazy . . . Gram said— Ned!" Hally said, breaking off his own thought, as I crept out from under the bed and jumped up alongside him.

"Ah, Ned! Everywhere we look, there's Ned. Ned, as far as the eye can see," Pastor Ragnar said. "What did Gram say?"

"Nothing," Hally said. "It doesn't matter . . . Gramp, if I'm so special why did God make it so that girl lied to the police about me? What if no one believes me? What if I get arrested and have to go to jail?"

"Did you ask the Holy Mother about it?"

Hally nodded. "She said for me to have faith."

Pastor Ragnar walked over to the bed and reached out for Hally. At the same time he edged me out of the way so he could give him an unobstructed hug. "You let me take care of everything. Things will turn out fine, just wait and see. Together, you and I will see this through, all of it."

I sat back and took in the full canvas, a dimly lit portrait of Pastor Ragnar embracing his grandson, stroking his hair with one hand, the fingers of his other hand forming a V at the back of Hally's neck. Though I should have been warmed, I was seized by fear, as if by the throat, apprehended by the secret dangers of love and family.

Pastor Ragnar finally left Hally and me alone. Pulling me onto his lap, holding me close, he pressed my ear against his heart.

"Ned," he whispered, "I'm never going to do anything bad again."

He kissed me on the forehead and I licked his chin. Vowing to be a better person is a fearful declaration and usually means that someone is about to insist that everyone around them start eating fish on Friday. Human beings are at their most arrogant when morality strikes.

I don't know what happened to Hally that spring day on Monhegan Island—he was the same only he was different. It was like waking up after a bad storm and seeing the beachfront transformed, huge swaths of rock and sand gone, absorbed into the ocean, redistributed along the shoreline, everything different even as everything—the wind, the waves, the birds, the grasses that swayed—remained the same.

Later that night, though I was tired from the day's high drama, I stayed outside on the deck with Hugh and Spark, who were alone together in the dark, sitting across from each other in the old Adirondack chairs, illuminated only by a gray sweep of moonlight and fog. Hally had gone to bed. Pastor Ragnar was still awake, the light burning behind his door.

Shaking my head, I struggled to keep my eyes open—love and hate are alleged to be the greatest motivations but if there is a more powerful catalyst than eavesdropping I don't know what it is.

"Are you thinking what I'm thinking?" Hugh said, voice low.

"No," Spark said.

"I know you're worried, too," Hugh said. "We can't ignore the possibility. We always knew it could happen. What's wrong with saying it out loud? Voicing it won't make it come true."

"I'm not so sure about that."

"What if it's like Flory?" Hugh was saying. "He's had a lot to deal with. Mom's death. Your absence. The mess with the concert. You coming home unexpectedly. This family and their bogus accusations.

Can trauma, like Pop getting shot, trigger such a thing? If it's lying dormant, can you awaken it?"

Spark shook his head. "You make it sound like a sleeping dragon. I think he feels guilty and scared. He made everything up to get himself out of this shooting incident with Pop and Beans. He's got an active imagination and he went too far. Naturally he's going to go for something religious to try to grab the old man's attention, and it worked. It started out as a prank, typical kid stuff, took a wrong turn and now he's stuck with this nutty story and doesn't know how to get out of it . . . Hey, I've been there."

"Come on, Spark, we're not talking about you as a kid. Hally is different. If that were the case, the whole thing would have collapsed by now. He's not a member of the CIA. He couldn't sustain it," Hugh argued. "It's just . . ."

"What is it?"

"It's weird, that's all. I know Hally isn't perfect . . . but he's not a liar. Think about it. He would have had to be so committed to this deception, which is so out of character. Seems way too much like homework for him. Then, without so much as cracking a smile, he falls down on his knees, head bowed, praying aloud. In front of you, no less?"

"Hughie . . ."

"Wouldn't it be crazy . . . if? Well, I'm sure there is a reasonable explanation . . ."

"Where are you going with this?"

"Think about it, Spark. Humor me. Wouldn't it be absolutely insane, if Hally was telling the truth?"

"If Hally had come home and said he'd run into Neptune sunbathing naked on the rocks, would you believe that, too?"

"All right, I hear you," Hugh said, standing up, stretching, switching on the deck light. "But what the hell? It's better than the alternative. I don't want to think there's something wrong with him. I'd rather believe everything's possible except that."

"There's nothing wrong with Hally." Spark's fingers tapped against the armrest. "Keep the light off, will you?"

Slowly, I fell asleep to the hypnotic lash of wave against rock, the increasingly pale and fading voices of Spark and Hugh, their whispered words softening in the evening air, diminishing gradually, like a soothing series of notes on a string instrument as it recedes into the background, until you're no longer hearing the music but only feeling its stuporous effects.

On the deck that night, I imagined that I sat at the foot of a giant spruce in a dense woods and on every tree branch was a mason jar, each one lit up, luminous in the darkness, hundreds of clear glass jars poised like devotional candles in the vastness and silence of the Cathedral Forest, tiny flames flickering sideways in the cool night wind as I awaited the first of the explosions to come.

Nine

Pastor Ragnar was the first to give a name to whatever it was that Hally saw. The Miracle on Monhegan Island, he called it, and soon that's how it was known. Word got out and spread quickly: A twelve-year-old boy with sand in his hair and a gap in his front teeth claimed to have had a private audience with the Queen of the Heavens on an obscure island in Maine.

(Not so bizarre when you think about it. There's an audience on permanent standby for such things. Martin used to belong to a chain-mail-weaving club and frequented medieval fairs.)

The second time the Virgin Mary appeared, this time by appointment on May 13, 1986, there was a small group assembled to greet her, maybe a hundred people, most of them from Pastor Ragnar's church, the rest made up of touristy stragglers from the mainland and a flotilla of skeptical island stalwarts.

My trepidation grew at first sight of the assembled crowd, most of whom reminded me of what my father used to say when the occasion warranted, ". . . proof, Lupine, that not all the lemons are in the fruit store." All around me were chattering day-trippers in hiking boots and straw hats with cameras slung around their necks; a smattering of giddy teens, mostly girls in cutoff shorts, huddled together laughing and gossiping, collectively smirking when confronted by the disapproving stares of a strong-jawed contingent of habitually censorious churchgoing men and women.

The odd pair of nuns clacked their rosaries and kept their distance and a cluster of curious area reporters, breathing hard from the rugged climb, asked witless questions of people who were eager to talk but had nothing of value to say.

I watched fascinated as one lone woman knelt with bare knees on hard rock praying and crying. She wore ankle socks and penny loafers and clutched a statue of the Virgin Mary, and looked like a middle-aged schoolgirl pumped full of air.

Some people brought their dogs. They ran loose, weaving in and out of the assembled crowd, barking and chasing one another, bearing down on the seagulls, the birds taking off and landing, taking off and landing, crying out. With no desire to join the pack, I watched them from where I sat with Spark on an overturned log in a naturally sequestered area surrounded by large rocks and long grasses. Not my kind—the standard Rabelaisian convergence of four-legged brain stems—I felt about them the way humans must about the hooting-and-hollering party element that starts drunken food fights at open-air concerts.

Beans, behaving as if he were a tour guide, had been every bit as indiscreet as Pastor Ragnar had hoped he would be. He and Mrs. Houton blabbed to anyone who would listen—within hours of the initial apparition all of Monhegan knew about it. Then word began to circulate outward, escaping the island in concentrated concentric circles.

A woman arrived with her five daughters, members of Pastor Ragnar's congregation. The girls, who ranged in age from six to seventeen, were dressed in identical outfits, a miniature version of the mother's homemade sailor-girl tunic in red, white, and blue. They had on white socks and black patent leather Mary Janes and wore red ribbons in their hair and looked as if they subsisted on a diet of oatmeal and scripture. They called themselves the Tick-Tock Girls, a reference to the imminent end of days. The mother carried a guitar. She sat down on a vacant tree stump, the girls standing alongside her, organized in a straight horizontal line from tallest to shortest. The mother strummed away, rudimentary skill set immediately apparent and the girls began in earnest to sing "Shall We Meet Beyond the River?"

Hally arrived with Pastor Ragnar, their appearance generating a silence that buzzed. For a minute, shocked, I almost didn't recognize Hally; he looked so serious, pale despite his sunburned skin, preoccupied, set apart. I hadn't seen much of him since the apparition. He had been locked away in his room, not eating, not talking. I scratched at the door and he ignored me. "Go away, Ned," he said.

My heart slowed. He may have lost a little weight, too, otherwise why did he appear suddenly to be so thin and dark-eyed? Hally! Golden and shaggy, robust and hardy as a Shetland pony, he seemed almost fragile, as if he was recovering from a long illness. What was going on? I felt a pang of sadness tinged with panic.

Spark stood up to survey the crowd on the top of the cliff and in narrow pockets along the side trails. He acknowledged Hugh with a brief twist of his wrist, his arm over his head, his hand blocking the glare of the sun. Hugh waved back and then resumed painting. He was set up at a spot overlooking Pulpit Rock. Spark said before we left the house that morning that Hugh was hoping to persuade the Immaculate Conception to sit for a portrait.

We stood several yards from the edge of the bluff, separate from the crowd, the atmosphere bubbling and percolating, increasingly loud and festive, like the off-pitch steam whistle of a calliope, people popping up between the trees, silly as balloons.

I looked again for Hally but couldn't find him.

Pastor Ragnar, in creamy linen suit, took up his place at the highest point of the cliff, the part that extended out over the ocean and into the skyline, black birds, the same shiny color as his hair, circling round and round and calling out, their cries reverberating in the wind, silver spray from the waves ascending skyward and falling like light rain. He was acutely mindful of the many curious glances directed toward him, but in the studied manner of someone—a self-loving leading man aglow with false modesty—accustomed to scrutiny from strangers, was practiced in the art of seeming not to notice.

"Welcome, welcome!" He extended his arms as if he were providing a blessing to all assembled. "Do you know what matters about today? I'll tell you what matters: You're here. That's what matters. Chances are you don't even fully understand what brings you here. Faith. Belief, maybe. Curiosity, perhaps. The wish to be entertained. The desire to have your cynicism rewarded. You might be here for the spectacle, for the sheer sensation, showing up as you would for fireworks or for a public hanging. I suspect many of you, if you're being honest with yourselves, are here for reasons you're keeping secret, you're here because you want to elevate the conversation you have with yourselves and with the greater world. You're here because you long to lift up your experience of life, scrub off the daily dullness, polish away the accumulating darkness, until you expose the shimmering world, the hidden world, feel its magic, absorb the wonder, find sweet refuge from the twin tyrannies of materialism and ego that grip us.

"You're here because somewhere deep inside, in the concealed innermost part of you, you crave the sublime, you long for splendor."

The crowd responded enthusiastically.

"Open up. Lift up your hearts and your minds to God. Be your own great work of art. Honor the great mystery of life, the mystery that transcends human words and understanding.

"Words are useless on such a day. Words fail us. Such a day calls for the transcendence of music. Among us is one of New England's great opera stars. Evelyn Katarsos, an esteemed member of my congregation, a person I'm privileged to call my friend."

Everyone was oohing and aahing, clapping.

He was joined by a dark-haired middle-aged woman, whose name had generated applause and excitement from the onlookers and pouting resentment from the Tick-Tock Girls. Unaccompanied, she began to sing "Ave Maria," the power of her voice ringing out in what was beginning to feel like an elaborately orchestrated old-time circus, Pastor Ragnar at its dramatic center ring.

The thing is—it worked. Circuses work, the opera works. This was the arousal business, full of propaganda and emotional grandiosity and spectacle. Even I felt somehow thrilled and transported. As she sang, her classically trained voice, soaring like the girl on the flying trapeze, broke free from the constraints of refinement to become something wild and untamed, and for a moment I imagined everything was possible and anything could happen, Pastor Ragnar with whip in one hand, inverted stool in the other.

After she finished, he closed his eyes and held his arms up in a combination gesture of victory and surrender, clouds darkening behind him. "Hail Mary," he said, others in the crowd joining him, no Protestant before him so ready to evoke so iconic a Catholic prop, no Christian minister of any faith ever sounding more like a pagan god.

Only Spark seemed unmoved. Shaking his head, he pulled a dented pack of cigarettes and a matchbox from his jeans pocket. He attached a cigarette to his bottom lip and struck a match on the matchbox. The flame ignited and leaning away from the wind, he lit the cigarette and took a long deep drag. Up to then he had concealed his smoking from almost everyone but me.

Pastor Ragnar had barely finished praying aloud when a collective gasp rose up from the crowd. The woman next to me fell to the ground. Then others, too, began to tumble forward onto their knees. One of the little girls in the sailor dresses pointed skyward and called out:

"Look! The sun!"

I looked up along with everyone else.

The sky turned mauve and purple and seemed to wrap itself around the sun as if it were a gauzy sash and the sun appeared to spin, a giant silver orb, crystalline and shiny. Then the sky turned back to blue and the light from the sun was every shade of blue, sapphire, indigo, cobalt, and turquoise and the sun was surrounded by a halo of pink.

So I've been told. Honestly, I never saw a thing out of the ordinary but that puts me in the minority. Most of those gathered at Black Head that day described a sun dancing and twirling like a disco ball, a psychedelic sky—the only thing missing was John Travolta—a heavenly arc of blue, all of which was only a prelude to the main event.

Hally approached the edge of the bluff where he dropped to his knees and stared rapturously at absolutely nothing. He appeared to be talking to someone, someone I might be tempted to call his imaginary friend, but as more of the people around me began to collapse as if they'd been cut down by an invisible scythe, I wondered what they were seeing that I wasn't.

I looked over at Spark. A chorus of Hail Marys and Our Fathers and Glory Bes went up as men, women, and children trembled and stared, transfixed, as if they were in a trance.

"What the hell?" Spark said as I wagged my tail, happy to know I wasn't the only one destined to be left behind after the Rapture.

"What is wrong with you people?" he shouted, but no one heard except for Pastor Ragnar who was staring over at him, listening to him with such intense and narrow focus, it seemed to me as if they were the only two people present.

Many in attendance later reported feeling as if time had slowed, the minutes static and engorged as Hally knelt at the edge of the bluff. According to the testimony of a long list of witnesses, he could be seen listening, then speaking to an invisible presence, framed by a glowing mist and surrounded by white birds that swooped and glided and soared but never once flapped their wings.

After ten or fifteen minutes, Hally rose to his feet and was immediately engulfed by Pastor Ragnar and some members of the crowd, many of whom were crying or speechless, but who ran wanting to hear what the boy had heard, to touch him, to stand next to him, to reach for his hands, wrap themselves at his ankles.

Others continued to kneel and to pray. Some prayed aloud. Some prayed quietly to themselves.

"It's not real," Spark said, speaking to no one in particular.

"Maybe you're not real," someone shouted back.

"You're not allowed to smoke here," someone else hollered, confirmation that should God Himself ever decide to appear among us, there will be some hall monitor in the crowd who will seize the moment to lecture the person next to him about picking up after his dog.

The sound of elevated voices drew my attention back to the edge of the bluff.

"Blessed be the Lord!" a woman's voice rang out louder than all the rest. "The dog!" I turned around to see what dog she was referring to, figuring some Lab had run off with the Virgin Mary's cloak and then realized that everyone was staring at me.

A little girl shouted out: "The dog is blue! His eyes are pink!"

Magenta. They weren't pink, they were magenta, so Hugh said, and if there is one thing that Hugh knew about, it's color. My hair, normally a rich red-brown, was every shade of blue and my eyes, instead of their usual dark amber, were magenta. So people told me anyway. To me, I was the same old colors I had always been.

I glanced behind me. I saw Hally, trying to distance himself from the circus. He was looking out over the ocean, a solitary figure amid the acrobats, the hoopers and jugglers, the clowns, the girl in the trapeze, the dancing dogs, the lion tamer. Even from a distance I saw his cheeks damp with tears.

Pastor Ragnar approached him. He stunned me with what he did next—the lion tamer on his knees in front of his grandson. Oh, the theater! Hally leaned toward his grandfather, pleaded with him to get up, as others approached with their hands outstretched. The last time I could see them, Pastor Ragnar had his arms around Hally, shielding him from the same crowd of people he had summoned.

Spark, dismayed, stood still and separate at the lonely heart of it all.

Hugh came up behind him. "Wow," he said. "That was . . . I don't know what it was . . . Did you see . . . ?"

"For Christ's sake, Hugh . . . If you tell me you saw something . . ." Spark said.

"No, but Hally did," he said, though Spark was having none of it.

Hugh patted him on the back. "Just remember, what doesn't kill us—"

"Only makes us want to kill someone else," Spark said. Forgetting that he didn't smoke, he reached into his back pocket for another cigarette.

Later that evening, back at the house, Hugh patiently explained why the crowd saw me turn blue. He advised that it was as a result of something he'd once read about it. "It's a special effect of staring at the sun—a visual artifact, it's called."

The dancing sun, the sky of many colors, me appearing to turn blue, was all part of the same phenomenon and the rest was easily explained as a mass hallucination induced by religious fervor.

"Makes sense," Hugh said cheerfully. "There is always a rational explanation . . ." He was standing in the kitchen, looking into the living room, where we were assembled for a postmortem.

"Interesting information . . . thank you, Hugh," Pastor Ragnar said, standing in the middle of the room, addressing his younger son as if he were a grade-one teacher patiently acknowledging the class nerd. "Now, let's focus on what's really important here and that is what Hally saw," Pastor Ragnar said.

"What *did* you see, Hally?" Hugh asked gently.

"I don't want to talk about it anymore . . ." Hally said, sitting in the corner of the sofa.

"I know, but you must," Pastor Ragnar said. "What happened? What did she say to you?"

Hally stared at his hands in his lap. "She said the same as before, how important it is to pray and to ask God to forgive sinners, to ask forgiveness for our sins. To always love one another."

"Did she tell you to eat the peas on your plate, too?" Spark said, perched on the edge of a windowsill, strong breeze blowing his hair forward onto his face.

"Is that all she said?" Pastor Ragnar asked. "Did she have any special instructions for you besides telling you that you must pray?"

"She said I should never give in to doubt. She said that even if everyone in the world makes fun of me, I mustn't ever deny her. She told me I have to set an example of faith and love and hope so others may follow." He looked over at Spark.

"Jesus, Hal . . ." Spark said.

"I'm sorry," Hally said.

"What are you apologizing for?" Hugh said.

"This is what she said to you? You're certain?" Pastor Ragnar said, unable to conceal his excitement as Hally nodded unhappily.

"Why are you doing this?" Spark said. "It started with wanting to save your ass, right? You came up with an inventive way of doing it. It worked! Even crazy old Beans was down on his knees today. It all went right but it went wrong, too, didn't it? You didn't expect Pop to run with it, did you?"

"I'll pray for you, Spark," Hally said quietly.

"Hally! What are you doing? Stop this! You can end it. There's still time. A week from now no one will give a shit."

"Spark! You think you're helping him but you're not," Hugh said.

My father once told me that he had a special talent for detecting when human beings were lying. "Though they and the people around them remain quite unaware of it, humans give off the unmistakable odor of lupines when they lie. Purple lupines to be specific, smells like Grape Crush," he told me. "You can wipe the smile from your face. It may seem ludicrous, but it is quite true, I assure you."

"What if they believe what they're saying even though it's not true at all? Do they smell like bullshit?" I asked, thinking myself clever and willing to risk a sharp-toothed rebuke.

"No matter," my father told me, deliberately ignoring my wise-acre comment. "The body betrays the mind every time. Lupines, Lupine. Lupines." He laughed at his little joke.

Even then I suspected how easy it was to lie to yourself, to believe in something you know to be false, hoping, however subconsciously, that the power of your belief will make it true. The opposite is true as well, perhaps even more so. Who among us doesn't practice some form of denial?

Toy breeds are especially prone to self-delusion, imagining ourselves to be one-part Caucasian Ovcharka and the other part demigod. I once saw an affenpinscher face down a raging Bouvier—never met a Bouvier yet that wasn't a psychopath—armed only with a savage sense of confidence and a sparking molten core of self-belief. You must pick your spots, though. Hubris gets you precisely nowhere with a Turkish Akbash.

I tried to imagine what my father's attitude toward Hally's claim would be, though I had a good idea. Among dogs such manifestations are a more taken-for-granted phenomena, not—surprise!—exclusive to the human race. Though our saints aren't formally recognized—German shepherds aside, most dogs are unimpressed with authoritarian governing bodies—there is de facto acknowledgment among all dogs that certain among us have attained something akin to beatification.

Their names are well known among all breeds—the martyr Guinefort, of course, the only dog canonized by the Catholic Church. Greyfriars Bobby, no bombshell there. The heroes Balto and Togo, sled dogs whose courage prevented a diphtheria outbreak in Alaska. Barry the Saint Bernard in Switzerland credited with saving over forty lives, and Judy, a liver-and-white pointer, the only dog ever registered as a POW. A ship mascot during the Second World War, she was held by the Japanese in the Pacific and saved many Allied lives. She was eventually awarded the animal equivalent of the Victoria Cross by the British for her fearlessness.

Dogs have our own mystic caste. Great Danes are notorious ascetics, tediously dedicating themselves to austere lives of prayer, study, chanting, and self-abnegation, which is why they are assiduously avoided by the rest of us. No breed is more unwelcome at a dog park than those dreary monks.

The Irish wolfhound, on the other hand, was born mad drunk, singing off-key, hoarding obscure angers, wearing a toga and dancing at the rousing head of a conga line.

As for me, the closest I had ever come to a dark night of the soul was when that son-of-a-bitch Curly invaded my life. Curly, an Old English bulldog owned by Martin's uncle, was a mindless blitzkrieg of a dog—my parents and I nicknamed him Goering. He was an industrially obese, slobbering fart-machine with criminal tendencies who was dropped like a giant cartoon anvil into our corner of the planet.

Every time Martin's uncle visited he brought Curly with him, which meant my mother had to endure multiple attempts at rape while my father was isolated behind a closed bedroom door to prevent the inevitable resulting skirmishes.

My mother didn't take it lying down. She nearly tore off his ear after one especially unpleasant interaction. Curly was a sexual omnivore without boundaries—though I was only a puppy, I, too, had to fight off his brutish snuffling advances. I can still smell the rabbit shit on his breath. Fortunately, I was young and trim and agile and he was . . . not.

It's my great pleasure to report he died prematurely of a heart attack while trying to hump the long-suffering Siamese cat, Betty. Unlike human beings, dogs are not revisionists. We have no driving compulsion to romanticize or sentimentalize the dead, elevate their memories or reimagine their characters simply because they've jumped the queue and beat us to the inevitable.

When I say there was great rejoicing among my parents and I when we got the news of his humiliating death, be assured we spent not a single second trying to posthumously reinvent that oleaginous stormtrooper as Rin Tin Tin.

I stayed up long after everyone had retired to bed. I couldn't sleep—the things I'd seen and not seen, the claims and the counterclaims, the colliding opinions and allegations ran through my head, over and over in a confounding loop. In the end I was less preoccupied with what was true and what was false than I was with trying to figure out the point of it all from the perspective of the person at the heart of it, the Virgin Mary. I mean, why bother?

If she really did appear to Hally and all those other people, which I think we can agree is a fairly significant move on her part given her

apparent dislike of public appearances, then why didn't she say something more interesting? She told them to say the Rosary, and to pray
for their own souls and the souls of the sinful. The word penance came
up a lot. Okay, but as Spark said, tell us something we don't know. She
didn't say anything new, but repeated the same generic sort of stuff
that she had said to the kids at Fátima and Lourdes, sounding more
like the mayor of a small town during a zoning bylaw session than the
Queen of Heaven and Earth.

It was dark and quiet as I walked from the living room into the hallway, and then headed up the stairs to the second floor where the bed-
rooms were. Outside I could hear the insistent pummeling of wave
against rock, timeless natural ritual, while inside the only sound was
the grandfather clock as it chimed two o'clock. I kept walking. The
door to Pastor Ragnar's bedroom was open a crack, wide enough for
me to see and hear him and Hugh in whispered conversation.

"What exactly did you see out there today?" Hugh asked him.

"Enough, my boy," Pastor Ragnar said, patting him on the back.
"I saw enough."

I kept walking. I heard a soft muted sound coming from Hally's
room at the end of the upstairs corridor. When I reached his open
door I glanced inside and by the pure white light of the moon I saw
him down on the floor, kneeling, his head bowed, his fingers making a steeple on the mattress, his red-blond hair aglow like a candle,
miraculous medal in hand. He was praying: "Hail Mary, full of grace
/ The Lord is with thee / Blessed art thou among women . . . "

I stepped back into the shadows where he couldn't see me and I
listened as he prayed, the silver and white light from the moon spilling
out into the hallway and illuminating my wonder.

Ten

~~~~~~

We ran without stopping, galloped full tilt until I thought both our hearts would burst, me panting, him gasping for air, the two of us sprinting all the way to the big house called Tutela Heights, overcast and bleak, gloomy and gray as rain, high on a windy bluff overlooking the ocean. The house was cloaked in fog, thick and wet as a sponge, and took recognizable form only as we drew near.

I sat at Spark's feet when he finally stopped running as we surveyed the stark vacant house, left to fade from one season to the next, so now it resembled a part of the natural world, less a former home than a desolate rock bereft of feeling or memory or story to tell.

Spark stood and looked at the house for a long time, mournful foghorn on Manana Island sounding a dirge. Seditious curls of smoke from Spark's cigarette rose skyward, then quietly dispersed.

"Come on, Ned," he said finally. "Let's go."

"Hey, chief, how's it going?" I recognized Chip Wallace's voice. Spark shut his eyes as if he were trying to draw strength from blindness. He turned around, forced smile on his face. "Good," he said.

"Keeping you out of trouble?" Chip persisted.

"Yup," Spark said wearily, obeying the patterns of a lifetime.

"That's too bad," Chip said, binoculars in hand, telling Spark enthusiastically about the peregrine falcon he'd seen earlier, watched him as he dropped from the sky, talons extended and vanished with an unsuspecting herring gull. "Poor guy. Never knew what hit him. That falcon, though," he chortled, "he was livin' the dream!"

After a funereal walk along the rocky shoreline and trail, we wound up at Black Head, Spark standing in the same spot at the edge of the cliff where Hally had knelt only days earlier. He stayed there for a while, looking out over the ocean, straining to see the unseeable. Intensely focused, he startled when a sandpiper landed lightly next to him. Spark was a realist but he was human after all and even the most rational human being is only a piece of toast away from seeing the Sacred Heart of Jesus.

"To hell with it," he said finally as we made our way back home, skirting the shore at Lobster Cove, staying well above the tide line, wary of the slippery black rocks and the encroaching waves. It was so easy to slip and slide into the waiting water, so hard to get back onto shore. Spark had grown up on Monhegan and was used to navigating its uncertainties, intuiting its dangers.

"Jesus!" he said loudly. I turned my head and jumped out of the way, just in time. He was struggling to keep his balance, the toe of his shoe caught beneath a large outcropping of rock. He lost the fight and fell hard against a boulder. I heard the dull thud of bone against stone, his shin making first contact. He sucked in a loud breath and swore some more.

"Holy shit, that hurt!" It took him a few minutes before he was able to get to his feet. For some reason, though, once he was vertical, the painful fall had the effect of lightening his frame of mind. It jarred him. I could feel the instant change in him, almost as if nature had inflicted its own version of electric shock.

Dogs would describe Spark as a burier, whatever he was feeling, he carried around briefly and then dug a big hole, dropped it to the bottom and covered it over with layers of soil—unlike Hally, who wore everything vibrating on the surface of his skin, like a fresh tattoo.

"Bloody hell, Ned," he said. "What's wrong with this place and all these lousy rocks? You have to watch every step and every step you take is a treacherous one and there's no safe place to land anywhere."

"Maybe you need to fall down less," Hugh said later when he expressed the same thought to him.

Once back home, Spark, tired of being morose and finding Hugh alone out on the deck, kidded him about the novel he was reading—there was a gun on the cover and the title was a dirty scarlet scrawl, like a desperate message written in lipstick on a bathroom mirror in a dingy truck stop. "You might as well be reading a doughnut," he said as he pulled up a chair across from him. He paused, considering. "I've been thinking about our problems."

Hugh looked at him inquiringly.

"Maybe we should get Hally to ask the Virgin Mary if she'd float us a loan or at least give us a good tip on a racehorse." Spark reached over and took a bite out of a half-eaten oatmeal cookie I had my eye on, abandoned on the small patio table. I glared at him. He broke off a small piece and tossed it in my direction.

The sun, pale as lemonade, had a has-been quality, shining weakly, even the natural world in recovery mode—where were the birds, what happened to the wind?—tacit agreement in place to ignore the grotesquely obvious, set aside temporarily the madness that had beset the household and the island, even as the ocean waves kept up their steadying ritual, rolling back and forth.

The house, our house, for I had begun to think I had never lived anywhere else, had gone quiet since the apparitions. Where was all that buffeting talk? The entangling irreverence? The effortless judgments? The casual cruelties and unexpected kindnesses? The chatter, the banalities? Where were the proclamations? The ruthless conversational continuum banging away like wave against rock? It was as if everyone had been catapulted into an unknown world of enforced silence and were having trouble finding their way back home.

Spark said he always knew it would take an act of God to get the Monahans to shut up and listen. Well, maybe not all the Monahans. Pastor Ragnar had closed himself away in his study but I could still hear him talking to himself and in frequent muffled conversations with others on the phone. Though I couldn't make out what he was saying, I could feel its accumulating power, something building up inside that small room, like air pumped into a balloon, getting ready to pop.

As for the others, Hugh was in his studio painting to all hours, faint strains of recorded music filtering down the stairs. Hally rarely left his room, ignoring all entreaties, even mine.

"Hally," Hugh said, rapping on the door, "come on. You can't stay in there forever. It's not healthy."

Crack of the door as it opened. "Let him be," Pastor Ragnar said, sliding out into the hallway, surprising Hugh.

"Pop! I didn't know you were in there with him."

"We have things to talk about."

"Like what?" Spark said, appearing at the top of the stairs, drawn by the surprising sounds of human speech.

Pastor Ragnar waved him off. "If he wanted you to know, he'd tell you himself."

"What's the big secret? You two planning a coup to overthrow the pope?"

"This is beyond your spiritual pay grade, Jamie. Let it go," Pastor Ragnar said.

Pastor Ragnar was moving down the hallway and toward the stairs. He pushed past Spark, who stepped aside. Spark put a hand on his father's shoulder, all levity gone. "What are you up to?" He looked over at Hugh. "Do you know what's going on?"

Hugh shook his head.

"Whatever you've got planned, you leave the kid out of it," Spark said as Pastor Ragnar brushed away his hand and kept on going down the stairs.

"You think I would do anything to harm Hally?"

"Not intentionally. Just remember, he's not an opportunity, he's a boy. Sometimes your ambitions get in the way of your better judgment," Spark said.

"Speaking of ambition . . . Say hello to Beans—otherwise known as your future," Pastor Ragnar said from the bottom step before veering off into the living room.

"He didn't mean that the way it sounded, Spark," Hugh said, accustomed to apologizing on behalf of Pastor Ragnar.

"What the hell?" Spark said, hand on the railing. "He's right. The truth hurts."

Hugh reached out and tapped Spark's forearm. "You went to Tutela Heights."

"How'd you know that? Oh, wait, don't tell me, Chip. Does anybody around here mind their own business?"

"Come on, Spark. You really think it's such a good idea to churn up all this old stuff?"

"So now a guy can't indulge in a little nostalgia about where he almost bled to death?"

"Don't turn what happened into a punch line. It's not a joke."

"I get that part," Spark said as he walked past Hugh and headed for his room.

Romantic love isn't something that happens often among dogs. Typically, with purebreds, breeding is arranged between two dogs who have never met but are compelled by biology and commerce to perform as if they're planning a future family together. Occasionally, as with my parents, the dogs live out their lives as mates but that is a rare occurrence. When I was younger, there was some talk of breeding me with the goal of producing a puppy the family would adopt, a mini version of me with better teeth being the hope.

I was flattered but after careful thought decided I wouldn't participate, and when the time came and I was introduced to a young and flashy red-and-white Shih Tzu recommended as a good match for me by Madelyn, I showed no interest—completely ignored her, a triumph of restraint given the biological circumstances—which generated a great deal of lively discussion among my loved ones, both human and canine.

Martin announced to everyone that I was a eunuch, which was a hot one coming from him, and then he speculated tastelessly that I was asexual or sexually retarded.

"Maybe he's just hopelessly sexually inept," he said.

I scanned Madelyn's face for some kind of reaction to that last remark but in an amazing test of uxorial loyalty she betrayed nothing.

It's not that I didn't feel the desires and have the same basic needs and wants of every other living creature, only something inside me caused me to turn away from the conventions of my caste. I didn't fully understand my reluctance then, though I understand it better now.

"You surprise me, Lupine," my father said. "I never had you pegged as a Jesuit."

I felt the usual wisecrack rising up in my throat, but I bit it back because it occurred to me my father was a tiny bit right. I surprised myself. Jesuits adhere to a simple precept in their vocation—to help souls—a mission they're supposed to apply universally and with love.

Cosseted though I was during the first three years of my life, I always had an intuition something more awaited me. Not that I imagined myself as a creature of destiny, nothing so arrogant, but only that I harbored a sense that my experience of life wasn't going to be limited to the backseat of a collectible Mercedes sedan nor circumscribed by the shibboleths of the country club.

After I got over my initial shock and fear at being taken, I came to see, Spark hadn't stolen me from my life at all but he had come for me, the heartbreaking loss of my parents the toll I paid to get to where I was supposed to be, in a gray house on Monhegan Island surrounded by the only family of human souls that ever truly mattered to me.

That day, listening to Martin and Madelyn laugh and kid about my failure to perform, I felt, not for the first time, the profound limits of human insight and as I wandered off by myself to the sheltering consolation of an old apple tree, I endured, too, the deep sorrow that comes with being misunderstood.

The next morning, Pastor Ragnar left early for the mainland. Fingers snapping, humming briskly, black hair sleek and wet from the shower, he was practically crackling. So galvanized was he by recent events, I imagined him strapping on an outboard motor and powering himself across the ocean's surface fueled by excitement.

"Where's Gramp?"

Spark, sitting on the sofa in the living room, me next to him, swiveled around to look at Hally, who was reaching into the cupboard for a box of cereal, his back to his father. I clambered onto the top of the sofa.

"I don't know," Spark said. "He left a few hours ago to go inshore. I thought you might know what he's up to."

Hally shook his head. Spark told him that Hugh was gone, too. "Alone at last, just the three of us," he kidded. Getting no reaction, he pressed on. "Hugh took his sketchbook with him. Apparently the world can't survive without another painting of a yellow bird in a green tree."

Hally, in faded gray sweats, turned around to face him. "That's not a very nice thing to say."

"It's a joke."

"I thought jokes were supposed to be funny."

"So does that mean if it's funny it's a joke?"

Hally concentrated on pouring milk into his cereal. "I know you're laughing at me."

"I'm not laughing at you and so what if I was? None of us are made of spun gold, Hal."

"I saw her. All right? I wish I didn't, but I did. I'm not making it up. What do I have to do to make you believe me?"

"Quit trying. You can't make people believe what you believe just because it's what you want."

"But it's true!"

"You think truth's the sole criteria for belief? You've got a lot to learn, kid."

"Like how to siphon gas from a car or snap a bra?"

Stung, Spark's head jerked back, a barely perceptible movement, as if Hally had pinged him with an elastic band. "Forget it," Hally said, opening a drawer, reaching for a spoon.

"It doesn't figure. For a guy who got a peek into infinity, you sure don't seem very happy."

"How would you feel, do you think, if you saw what I saw? Tell

me, so then I'll know. I mean, I think I know how I'd feel if I ran out
on my own kid but it doesn't seem to bother you."

Spark bit his bottom lip, red color fading to bloodless white. "Hal,
what do you want me to say?"

"Gram said my mom was crazy. Why did she say that? I can tell
by the way Hugh is looking at me, the way he acts, that he wonders if
I'm crazy too. I'm not crazy . . ." Hally's voice cracked. He lowered his
head. The cereal bowl overflowed, milk dripping onto the counter,
down the side of the cupboard, pooling on the floor. "At least . . .
Maybe I am going crazy . . ."

Spark stood up. "You are not crazy."

"What if I am? What if it's something inside me nobody can see?
Including me."

Spark came closer. "Hal, mental illness isn't a secret you keep. It's
not something you entertain in your head or wonder about. There's
nothing sensitive or subtle about it, believe me."

"But Gram said—"

"Jesus, if I ever hear that phrase again . . ." Spark threw up his
hands, accidentally sweeping the cereal bowl and its contents onto
the floor. "Forget what Gram said. This is a woman who believed in
leprechauns and fairy bushes. This is the woman you're quoting on a
regular basis as if she were Pliny the Elder. Are you sure it wasn't Gram
you saw at Black Head?"

Spark, as usual, said too much, he went too far.

"Gram told me nothing was sacred to you." Hally walked over to
the sofa where I lay taking it all in and squatting, he pressed his face
against mine. Both his hands gripping my shoulders, he pulled me into
his arms and up alongside him as he sat down.

"You plan to clean up this mess?" Spark said indicating the over-
flow of milk and cereal, the broken bowl sitting in sharp pieces on the
floor.

"You can do it," Hally said, watching as Spark obligingly reached for an excess of paper towels—he could have mopped up an oil spill from a supertanker—frugality wasn't in his nature.

"Forget all your jokes and smart-ass remarks. What do you really think about what's happened?" Hally asked him finally. "Do you believe me?"

Bending to his task, Spark considered for a moment before straightening up.

"Believe is a big word. I don't think you're crazy. I am, however, willing to entertain the idea that you're a little bit nuts."

Eleven

It was still dark the next morning, when I heard someone downstairs in the kitchen.

"Hi, Ned, did I wake you or did you come to mock?" Spark said, gulping orange juice as he reached for his jacket and headed to the door. "See you later," he said, abandoning the half-full carton on the counter as I followed behind him. He paused, then turned back around.

"You want to come with me?"

"Never say never," Spark murmured as we arrived at the harbor where Beans docked *The Winnie Cat*, the thirty-foot wooden boat that his father before him had used to catch lobster in the same cold clear waters off Monhegan. Spark stood for a moment, hesitating. "I swore I'd never get in another lousy fishing boat as long as I lived." He bent down and ruffled my ears. "If I ever give you my word about anything, Ned, feel free to piss on it."

"Well, Spark Monahan, look at you, shining away like a bad penny. So you decided to show up, did you?" Beans said as Spark stood up with me in his arms. "I see you brought along shark bait." He gestured lasciviously toward me. I barked and growled in response.

"Don't worry, Ned. I won't let him feed you to the sharks. I promise. You have my word," Spark said as he held me tight to his chest and climbed aboard.

We were about twelve miles out from shore, Beans' signature purple-and-green buoys bobbing in the churning navy water. Lobster season on Monhegan ran from the beginning of January to the end of June, May being the busiest month, though Beans wasn't always scrupulous about observing the rules and tended to mix a little "accidental" lobster fishing into off-season net fishing, too. "No two-bit bureaucrat's going to shut me out of the fall catch," I heard him sputter on more than one occasion.

I was sitting on an upturned yellow plastic container on the rolling deck amid the ancient wooden traps and the blue milk crates, watching Spark prep the bait, redfish, herring, and porgies, and listening to Beans curse out the seals for their lobster habit.

"They've got to eat, too," Spark said. "There's enough for everybody. Anyway, didn't we have this conversation fifteen years ago?"

"If we did you obviously didn't learn nothing from it," Beans said.

Spark kept on slicing and chopping. "Beans, if my kid's the Second Coming, as you and others seem to believe, ever think about who that makes me?"

"Well, from where I sit, I figure it makes you the patsy," Beans said, opening wide the throttle.

"Sorry, pal," Spark said, measuring a four-inch lobster, using a pair of pliers to fit a rubber band around his claws before consigning him to a plastic blue bin along with all the others.

"I hate this fucking job." He looked over at me: "I am the lobster."

Sighing, he picked up the last straggler from the pot.

"What do you say, Ned?" He smiled and glanced at Beans, who was leaning over portside baiting a trap. Unconcealed, he tossed the lucky crustacean overboard and into the ocean—almost as if he wanted Beans to take notice.

"Why'd you throw him back in?" Beans demanded.

"Female. Eggs," Spark said, lying with the greatest of ease. A good lie, I thought to myself.

Beans grunted skeptically. "You better not be throwing away my money!" he said as he lowered the trap back down into the water. "Jesus, oh!" he shouted as the loose trapline looped and tightened around his rubber boot, lifting him up off his feet and leaving him clinging to the side.

Spark, rushing to help, reflexively grabbed a knife and managed to cut the line just in time to prevent the 125-pound trap from dragging Beans overboard and into the icy water, and pinning him below the surface.

Beans, gasping, slid down onto the slippery wet floor. "Thought I was for it, for sure. Last time I got in trouble like that was forty years ago. Thanks, Spark." He patted Spark's arm in gratitude. "Don't know what I would have done . . ."

"I cut the line, that's all."

"That's nasty-looking," Beans said, pulling himself up, examining Spark's left hand, the palm sliced open, a deep diagonal cut that spurted blood. "How'd that happen?"

"Stigmata," Spark deadpanned. He shrugged. "Grabbed the blade. It looks worse than it is."

"I don't know about that. Let's get you patched up and call it a day," Beans said.

∽∽∾∾∾∾

"You're home early . . . Oh no, what happened to you?" Hugh said, tripping down the loft stairs, catching sight of Spark, while I bounded ahead into the living room and jumped onto the sofa.

"Dumb accident," Spark said, holding up his heavily bandaged hand. "Beans got lassoed by a trapline and I cut the rope . . . and my hand in the process."

"Jesus, it looks bad. Honest to God, you have the worst luck . . ." Hugh, catching Spark's expression, stopped mid-exclamation and turned to more practical matters. "How many stitches?"

Spark wandered into the kitchen. "A few. A small price to pay to ensure that Beans Tansy lives to breathe another day."

"First Pop. Now you. What's going on?"

"You mean in a cosmic sense? Obviously we've angered the gods . . . or maybe shit just happens."

"I wish you'd think about doing something else, Spark. These bloody lobster-fishing boats. Two guys drowned last season after getting tangled in trap lines. Beans isn't exactly meticulous when it comes to safety."

"I'm just putting in time until that department-head position opens up at Harvard," Spark said, opening a cupboard drawer and retrieving a bottle of Pastor Ragnar's favorite Calvados. He popped the cork and took a slug straight from the bottle.

"It's medicinal," Spark said, waving his wounded hand, taking another drink.

"I know you don't want to hear this, but you're a good guy, Spark."

"Shove it, Hughie," Spark said, dismayed.

"Does it hurt?" It didn't take much to engender a show of empathy from Hugh, who deftly changed the subject.

"Yeah, it does, actually." Straightening up, he handed the bottle off to Hugh, and headed toward the staircase. "I'm going to take a bath."

"Don't fill the tub, please. We're on an island. Water conservation."

"How could I forget when you constantly remind me? What are you laughing at, Ned?"

I was trying to decide who I admired more—Hugh for never giving up or Spark for never giving in.

"Hey, wait, there's something you should know about first," Hugh said. His tone. Spark stopped and stared at him, eyebrows raised.

"Should I sit down? Do I need another drink?"

"Look, you're not the only one, I have reservations about it, too," Hugh said, back pressed against the mission chair across from Spark, who was stretched out on the sofa, looking up at the ceiling and listening, with me lying across his legs just above the knee. "I worry that by accepting the money, we're on a slippery slope. I don't feel comfortable about it. Not entirely, anyway." Hugh kept on talking. Hugh tended to talk too much when he was upset or troubled.

"When you do something that you don't feel comfortable doing but you put those feelings aside for the money, I ask myself, isn't that the first sign of corruption?"

"The answer to your question is yes," Spark said.

"On the other hand . . . What are we doing that's so bad?"

"What do you mean, *we*? I wasn't consulted. This is on you and Pop, but since you ask, I'll tell you exactly what *we're* doing. We're accepting money from a tabloid so they can interview *a child* and then they can put the most sensational spin on whatever it is he tells them. We're exploiting a kid for money, and exposing him to every nut on the planet while we're at it.

"What part has you confused, Hughie? It's pretty straightforward."

"It's not like we're merchandising stuff."

"What about the apparition prints you're doing for Pop?"

Hugh looked offended. "That's art!"

"Oh yeah, sorry, I forgot," Spark said as I stretched and moved to the bottom of the sofa.

"Look, Spark, try to understand, I'm going broke. All this is affecting my productivity. I've got these commissions due. I've got the big show in New York coming up with a prestigious gallery. I know it's somehow beneath your dignity to acknowledge such a thing but Pop's at real risk of losing the church."

"No! Not the church! Take me instead."

"That's unbecoming . . . even for you." Hugh paused to let his rebuke settle in. "Every cent coming into this house until the end of time will go straight to feeding the debt, unless we get some kind of miracle. This is Hally's future, too, that we're talking about. You want him to go to college, right?

"And, honestly, at the risk of seeming selfish, I wouldn't mind being able to make a few plans of my own. As it is, I'm contributing every cent I make to keeping the ship afloat . . . To me, there are plenty of good reasons to do this"—Hugh's expression brightened—"including for the public good."

Spark looked baffled.

"Who are we to say it isn't true?" Hugh said. "Hally insists it happened. He's never wavered. It certainly seems to have had an impact on him that's consistent with something true. It's not entirely without precedent. The Catholic Church has investigated and endorsed some of these sightings."

"Oh, why didn't you say so earlier? That settles it."

"We're not selling vials of holy water or packaging up dirt and claiming that it has healing properties. No one's getting hurt."

"Oh yeah?" Spark said, his bare toes rubbing my belly. "Wait five minutes . . . Remember, Hally's still got this criminal allegation hanging over his head that he is a thief, a vandal and a budding sex fiend. What if the Wrendle family gets inspired and decides they owe it to the world to go public with their accusations? Kind of hard for them to resist, don't you think? Once the press gets ahold of it, it's over, he's as good as convicted."

Hugh looked troubled.

"Look. I get where you're coming from, Hugh. I understand the urge to take the money and run." Spark leaned his head back and for a moment, effects of the booze and painkillers taking hold, I thought he might even fall asleep.

Hugh studied him for a moment. "Maybe you're right." He leaned forward in his chair.

"Wake up. You're his father. If you don't like it, put a stop to it."

She asked to talk to Hally alone in the study, a proviso I decided didn't apply to me. I hopped up onto Hally's lap, making evident my intention to stay, at which point the door opened and Pastor Ragnar slipped inside. Smiling and enthusiastic, he complimented her on her long, glossy black hair, kidded her about her accent—she was a Brit—cited previous articles of hers that he had read and admired, all of it designed to make her forget that she had ever asked to speak to Hally alone. She didn't forget, but she rightly decided this was a battle she wasn't going to win.

"Aren't you just the cutest thing ever?" the journalist said, scratching the sweet spot under my chin.

"I thought you were referring to me," Pastor Ragnar joked as she smiled anemically and Hally looked mortified.

Her name was Gina and over the next couple of hours I watched her try to extract information from Hally, who was polite, fitfully adolescent, occasionally borderline charming in that fresh unadorned way of his, but he held fast, stubbornly declining to deviate from the script, repeating in terse and truncated form essentially the same description of events as he had first related them. Pastor Ragnar, taking Gina's measure, kept his distance—like me, he was listening, soaking it all in.

"Hally, if you will pardon me for saying so, you seem sad, almost depressed by what's happened. Is that right?" Gina said, appearing sympathetic.

"I don't know," Hally said. "Maybe. I don't really want to talk about it. You don't believe me. I can tell. So what difference does it make?"

"I believe you," Pastor Ragnar said. He just couldn't say it enough, apparently.

"I want to believe you," Gina insisted. "I really do. Help me out here, won't you?"

Hally shrugged his shoulders and his lips lifted at the corners in wan impersonation of a smile. I could hear his heart thumping in his chest, could feel his breathing accelerate, though I'm sure Gina had no idea about all that was churning around inside of him.

"Were you always religious?" Gina decided to try another tack. "I understand your grandfather," she looked unsmiling over at Pastor Ragnar, who acknowledged her with a flirtatious nod, "is a well-known religious figure in this state."

"No," Hally said. "No. I don't really want to be religious. I'm trying but . . ." He glanced nervously at Pastor Ragnar, who showed no reaction.

Gina looked surprised. "I would think that the least that would happen to someone after meeting with the Virgin Mary is that you would become a believer."

"I never said I wasn't a believer," Hally said. "I'm just not . . ."

"What? Finish what you were going to say . . . Hally?"

". . . interested. I'm just not that interested," Hally said. "Maybe when I get old and I'm going to die . . ."

Gina sat back in her chair as if she couldn't believe what she was hearing.

"Even God can't crack a teenager's hard shell of ennui," Pastor Ragnar said as Hally rolled his eyes.

"I just don't care that much about praying all the time and thinking about spiritual things. I tried. I gave it a shot. I'm tired of it." Hally reached for a cookie from a plate full of goodies on the coffee table.

"It's only been a few weeks . . ." Gina reminded him.

"It's embarrassing . . . Everyone thinks I'm crazy. Well, everyone, that is, except for people who are crazy themselves."

"Why, thank you, Hally!" Pastor Ragnar said in stagy approximation of conviviality. I cocked my head and wagged my tail, trying to get Hally's attention. He reached out and scratched my ears, tips of his fingers emanating concealed desperation. Pastor Ragnar wasn't the only one putting on a performance. Hally's showy turn at hyperadolescence, the way he was spinning out the mythic narcissism of teenage boyhood with all its boneheaded solipsism, bore no resemblance to the bereft child who lay facedown in his pillow, that I slept next to at night.

"I don't mean you," Hally said. "It happened the way I said it did. I wish I never told anyone." Hally, biting into his cookie, sat forward on his seat. He was looking around as if he were searching for a method of escape.

"Hally, I don't know what to say but I think you must possess more personal confidence than anyone I have ever met in my life."

"An interesting way to put it," Pastor Ragnar said, considering Gina's remark. "People say knowledge is power, but really confidence is the ticket, isn't it?"

Doing her best to ignore Pastor Ragnar, Gina stared at Hally as if he were a code she was trying to decipher. *"Who are you?"* she said.

Hally looked back at her, eyebrows raised, slightly amused expression on his face. Like his father. I barked up at him, wanting to hold onto that phantom Spark before he disappeared. He laughed. I kept barking and Gina laughed, too.

"I think he's trying to tell me something. Oh," she said, snapping her fingers in sudden recognition. "Is this the little dog that everyone says turned blue? Are you the dog with magenta eyes?"

"That's right, he is . . . As you can see for yourself," Pastor Ragnar said, wanting to shift the conversation back where he thought it belonged. "Hally is a boy of rare humility. Not an ounce of manipulation in him."

"As a pastor does it bother you to hear your grandson say he's not religious, that he's uninterested in God's will?"

"Not at all. Why should it? The truth is a wonderful thing. It can also reflect a passage rather than a state of permanency. His lack of guile is emblematic of God's presence in his life, even if he isn't aware of it. I believe that when Hally makes peace with what's happened here, when he embraces his destiny, he will light up the world." Pastor Ragnar spoke with such restrained passion and conviction that I found myself temporarily in his thrall.

He even made me want to believe and it was with a tiny bit of disappointment that I shook it off. It didn't hurt that he had that transfixing mellifluous voice, animated with intelligence and a vaguely arch tone, which compels even as it repels—never underestimate the exotic power of an attractive and unique speaking voice in combination with a superiority complex. Singers aren't the only ones making music.

I looked over at Gina, who did indeed seem both compelled and repelled, emphasis on the latter. Hally was listening to his grandfather and as he listened something was happening, something inside of him had shifted, filled him up, I could feel it. He got up and walked over to where Pastor Ragnar was sitting and sat down next to him. Pastor Ragnar put his arm around Hally's shoulders and pulled him close. He kissed the top of his head.

Gina, I sensed, wasn't buying it. "If I didn't know better, if I weren't persuaded about what an honest boy Hally is, I'd think this was a staged moment," she said, meeting Pastor Ragnar's dark glance.

The day had been overcast and gray but now the sun was out and the living room, which had been gloomy and damp, felt warm and bright, the sun's rays pouring in unfiltered through the open windows, the yellow light billowing, blowing in on the offshore breeze. A sweet scent of beach roses filled the room and all those beaming streams of sunlight wrapped themselves loosely around Hally, shimmering in place, his golden hair set aglow.

Gina's subsequent interview with Pastor Ragnar, which she conducted with him alone, was a minor explosion of ideas, opinions, comments, and challenges. They were in the study with the door shut, Pastor Ragnar sweeping me out into the hallway with the polished toe of his shoe. Undeterred, I lay down with my ear at the door and listened as he attempted unsuccessfully to manipulate Gina with his standard seductive techniques, their tense back-and-forth punctuated with false laughter and feigned interest from him and terse questions and incisive analysis from her.

"Pastor Ragnar's launching his charm offensive," I heard Hugh say as Spark, back from a day aboard *The Winnie Cat*, wandered into the kitchen.

"You mean his offensive charm," Spark replied. "Yeah, he's a regular Southern belle, all right."

"She wants to talk to you, too," Hugh said as he reached for the boiling kettle on the stove.

"No she doesn't," Spark said.

"You must be Spark," Gina said, emerging from the study with a smile, extending her hand as Spark stood up to greet her. Her sudden appearance in the living room thwarted his intention to escape upstairs. Slim, of average height, wearing a short summer dress with a delicate floral pattern, her skin was alabaster-white and she wore rose-red lipstick. She had strong features, prominent brown eyes, prominent nose, prominent lips, prominent teeth.

Spark took her hand in his. "I'm embarrassed," he said, indicating his outfit, smeared in blood and fish guts, reeking of brine, fresh off the boat. "You've caught me working hard, which is a rare occurrence for me. Normally I don't do much of anything."

She laughed. "I doubt that."

"Oh, all right . . . you got me. Typically, when I'm not rustling horses, I ride the rails, engage in a little petty theft here and there, steal fresh pies baked by widows and left to cool on open windowsills, that sort of thing."

"What happened to your hand?" she asked.

"Gunfight. It's nothing."

"I didn't expect you to be so pleasant and friendly . . ." Gina said. "Nobody told me . . . "

"That's because we didn't know," Hugh said, Hally standing next to him, groaning. "You sound like an idiot," he moaned to Spark. Pastor Ragnar looked on, reserving comment, though not for lack of an opinion.

"You clean up rather nicely," Gina said that evening, as Spark reappeared after a shower and change of clothes.

"I do, don't I?" Spark said as he pulled out a chair and sat down across from her, everyone at the table in the kitchen, open windows revealing a sun receded, black clouds low in the sky, winds howling, the dangerous change in weather persuading Gina to stay for supper and spend the night.

"I insist," Pastor Ragnar said. "It's for your personal safety—and for the pleasure of your company."

"I was hoping after dinner we might get a chance to sit and talk," Gina said, deliberately shutting down Pastor Ragnar with her wintry disdain, sipping her wine, addressing Spark.

"About what?"

"Hally. The apparitions. Faith. Belief. Truth. Lies. Consequences. Fathers. Sons. What else?" Gina said.

"Oh right, that—no," Spark said, leaning back in his chair.

"I don't understand."

"That's not my problem, sister," Spark said.

"My son is appalled we've agreed to take money in exchange for giving your newspaper access to Hally and his story," Pastor Ragnar said.

"Oh, we have an idealist in our midst. I thought I recognized the symptoms," Gina said playfully.

"It's the hair, isn't it?" Spark said. "The hair gave me away."

"That must be it," Gina agreed. "Come on, surely there's a way to persuade you? You seem like someone only too happy to share his thoughts and ideas."

"What does that have to do with me talking to you in your capacity as a journalist?" Spark said.

Gina leaned across the table. "It's possible this is a truly momentous historical event. Your son claims to have seen and spoken to the Virgin Mary on two occasions and others have come forward to corroborate that claim. At the very least, something of interest, something inexplicable, took place at Black Head in front of a large group of people, many of whom state, and with great emotion and conviction, with intelligence, that they were witnesses to a spiritually shattering occurrence."

"Are you having a stroke?" Spark asked her.

She straightened back up before continuing. "Do you know what I think? I think you're in denial about what's happened here. Frankly, I think you're afraid of the implications, both personal and universal. I think you're terrified to take this seriously. I think"—she leaned back in—"you're afraid to lead a meaningful life. You're scared shitless to go on record about anything."

Seemed like a lot to conclude about a person after a single fragmentary dinner conversation, but as I reminded myself, dogs make similarly instantaneous judgments based on nothing more than a few indiscreet sniffs.

"Couldn't agree with you more," Spark said when she'd finished.

Gina looked surprised. "So," she said tentatively, "does this mean . . . ?"

"No," he said brightly. "Not a chance in hell."

"Seems hypocritical to me," Gina said, knowing she'd been had. "You agree to the article but then convince yourself you haven't really done anything wrong by declining to participate. You, above all, should agree to speak."

"Why? You might as well interview Ned about it for all anyone cares. We did it for the money. That's it. I agreed because my father and brother asked me to, because Hally wanted to do it for their sake. Unfortunately, we're in a bit of a financial jam around here in case you hadn't guessed. Anyway religion's run its course except among some over-the-top nationalities . . . No one will even read it."

Gina laughed. "Ah yes, the Canadians," she said, gently mocking. "Religion hasn't run its course with your father," she reminded him.

"My father's Irish and if that wasn't enough, he's also Canadian. I rest my case . . ."

Pastor Ragnar laughed, not the most reassuring sound.

Spark ignored him. "This is really no different from those nutty reports of weeping religious statues. It's a novelty act."

"A novelty act? This is your son you're talking about," Gina said.

"Don't listen to a word of it, Gina," Hugh said.

"I won't," Gina said.

I must admit I was enjoying every aspect of the whole fractious situation. I've always relished having guests come visit, especially the purposeful type. (You want to know from bored? There are only so many ways to extract a squeaker from a stuffed toy.)

"Just tell me this: Do you believe Hally saw the Virgin Mary?" Gina continued to press Spark, which is when I decided to take matters into my own hands, do the right thing and rescue him.

You'd be amazed at how disruptive it is when a dog lifts his leg on a visitor's cashmere cardigan.

"Can I come in?" Hally knocked on Spark's bedroom door after everyone had retired.

"Yeah, sure," Spark said, setting aside the novel he was reading.

Hally grinned. "I can't believe you wear glasses. You're a secret dork."

"Even Achilles had his heel," Spark said, parking his horn rims on the top of his head. He was stretched out on his bed, on top of the covers, two pillows scrunched at his back, the room illuminated by the dim glow of an old lamp on a wobbly bedside table.

"There you are," Hally said, spotting me at the foot of the bed. "I was looking for you. Should have known you'd be in here." He looked up at Spark, a little wistful. "He likes you better than he likes me."

"You've been a little preoccupied lately . . . that's all. I'm a port in a storm."

"Nah, but that's okay. I never knew before that sometimes a dog chooses you. I know he loves me, but he chose you and that's up to him. You can't make somebody love you the best."

"No, I guess you can't."

It wasn't a particularly gloomy exchange but it made me feel a little forlorn to hear it.

Hally sat down on the bed, ill at ease, nervously fidgeting with the fringes on the bedspread.

"I just wanted to say thanks for not talking to Gina about me."

"Don't thank me . . ."

"Don't get me wrong. I'm not mad at Hugh and Gramp for talking to her. I know why they did it. I mean, I talked to her myself. Nobody made me."

"I know."

"I was happy that you said no and that you wouldn't change your mind . . ." Hally smiled. "Do you ever change your mind when you make it up?"

"I guess I'd have to think about that . . . wait, one time at the last minute I switched my ice cream order from chocolate to pistachio."

"Gram said—"

"Jesus, no more . . ."

"She told me you were the most stubborn person ever born."

"God, how I miss that woman."

"I keep forgetting what a big mouth you've got . . . Don't say anything to Gramp and Hughie about Gina, okay? I don't want to make them feel bad."

"I won't say anything . . . The thing is, it's only money . . . right? . . . What's so funny?"

"That's exactly what Gramp said . . . You both give the same reason for doing the exact opposite thing."

"It's the one thing we Monahans are good at, making a case."

Hally leaned across the bed to pet me, running his hand from the top of my head down my back in a series of strokes. He had something else on his mind.

Spark eyed him. "Just say it."

"Did you love my mother?" Hally asked, his eyes trained on me.

The question caught Spark unprepared. He surprised all of us, including himself, by answering sincerely. "I did."

If you were a dog you might have heard what I heard, his voice softly ripping along the seams, as if it were an ancient fabric conceding its frailty.

Hally pulled himself back up into a seated position, looked down at his lap and linked his fingers before pulling them apart and rising to his feet.

"Guess I'll hit the hay," he said. "Are you coming, Ned?'

I looked at him and wagged the tip of my tail, a bid for understanding. I did love Hally but I had found my place with Spark.

"Go on, Neddy," Spark said. "Go with Hally."

"It's all right," Hally said, opening the door. "Don't make him. You're the chosen one, remember?"

Spark stared after him and then he reached for his book. He tried to read but it was no good. He closed the book and for a moment he held on to it, leaned it up against his chest, rested his chin on it. Opening his fingers, finally, he let it slide from his hands.

He leaned down and reached under his bed where he kept his cigarettes. Inhaling deeply, he shut his eyes, the carbonated rumble of the waves expanding and contracting, the long, low, moan of the foghorn giving lonely voice to the night.

Not long afterward, the house in darkness, I heard Spark's bare feet touch the floorboards. Within moments he was in a clean white T-shirt and blue jeans with his running shoes in his unbandaged hand. My tail thumped against the bedcovers. He put his finger to his lips. "Quiet, Ned. Stay here," he whispered as he left the room and tiptoed down the stairs. Ignoring orders, I jumped off the bed and followed him to the kitchen. Groping around for his jacket and a flashlight, he never noticed when I slid past him through the open kitchen door and remained unseen at the bottom of the deck stairs.

He waited until he reached the concealing grasses and the stout clumps of wild shrub roses in the field before turning on the flashlight. I stayed clear of its narrow glow and pitter-patted along behind him. Cloud cover flattened the horizon, monochromatically sealing the sky to the earth and the earth to the ocean so there were no longer any clear lines of demarcation. The wind was picking up again and I felt the distant roll of thunder as we walked the short familiar route.

Gina was waiting at the guest cottage. She tripped down the stairs of the small porch and ran to meet Spark beneath the giant tulip tree on that wild night with lightning streaking over the ocean and thunder reverberating in the skies above. Boom. Bang. Boom.

"You've done this before," Gina said, lying back in the grass and the sand, exhaling loudly.

"One-handed, too. Generously giving of myself to the female population of the earth one woman at a time," Spark said.

I finally crawled out from the underbrush, during what I judged to be a ceasefire, and revealed my presence.

"Neddy!" Spark said as I pounced on his head, playfully pawing his hair. "Have you been here the whole time?" He sat up, startled, just as I caught the trace scent of someone familiar.

"What is it?" Gina said, alarmed, instinctively reaching for her dress.

"Hally? Jesus." Spark grabbed for his pants, squinting into the night.

"Oh my God!" Gina said, pulling the dress over her head.

"Hally . . . Come back!" Spark shouted, but Hally had vanished, dissolved into the darkness, the scramble of his footsteps echoing.

Spark buried his head in his hands. "Oh." It came out more raw sound than spoken word, as if he'd been kicked in the stomach.

"I'm so sorry, Spark. This is awful," Gina said. "I want to die."

"My fault. He's my kid. It's up to me to protect him from . . . me, obviously . . ."

Gina put a consoling hand on his shoulder. "It'll be all right. You'll see."

"Before he only suspected me of being a louse, now he's got proof." Spark stood up and pulled on his pants. "I'm sorry, it's got nothing to do with you."

Something. A flicker. I looked up in time to catch brief sight of Pastor Ragnar watching from his bedroom window, the curtain arranged so he could see without being seen, only his black outline visible, a man in secret partial silhouette, and in the instant that I saw him, he let go the curtain and vanished behind its veil.

Twelve

"How's the other guy?" Hugh said, at first sight of Spark the next morning. "You look like shit. Are you sick? Your hand isn't infected, is it?"

"No. I'm fine," Spark said. "Is Hally around?"

The front door opened. Pastor Ragnar stepped inside. "You're up. How good of you to put in an appearance. Is there some special reason you couldn't drag yourself out of bed and give our guest a proper send-off?"

Spark was pouring himself a cup of coffee. He kept his head down. "Don't you worry about it. She was properly sent off by me last night."

Hugh seemed suddenly compelled to organize a drawer that was well beyond straightening out.

"You're a dirty business, James Monahan," Pastor Ragnar said, the room so quiet I heard the sugar dissolving in Spark's coffee.

It was midafternoon when Spark spotted Hally down at the shore, sitting on Skunk Rock, a large igneous outcropping, almost entirely black but for its conspicuous vein of white quartz. Spark didn't hesitate but headed out to him, as I ran on ahead. The sun shone lightly, casting a thin buttercup-yellow glow, more decorative than functional, as if the scene were being artificially lit to achieve a specific result. Gulls called out, primitive shrieks slicing through the rolling crash of the waves.

Even at the shoreline the setting was implicitly dangerous, unpredictable, rogue combers occurring without warning, especially after a storm.

Spark lifted me up onto the rock. I surprised Hally by jumping into his lap.

"Oh, it's you," he said, glancing sideways as Spark sat down beside him.

"About last night . . ." Spark had decided to forgo the small talk.

"I don't want to talk about it."

"You're a kid. I exposed you to something I shouldn't have . . ."

"You don't even know her. You just met her."

"Look, you didn't need to see that and I'm sorry. Shoddy stuff on my part. I should have been more discreet, but—"

" But . . . what? You love her? You 'care' about her . . . And you've got the nerve to call me a liar?"

"Okay," Spark said, committed to equanimity. "Maybe I deserve that . . ."

"Stop it. I like you better when you're at least honest about being a jerk."

"Hey, no problem, happy to oblige." Spark's natural instinct to defend himself was winning out over his attempt at contrition. "Grow up, Hally. This isn't Sunday school."

"Oh, so now I'm a square church kid, is that it?"

"It's only sex. I know you're embarrassed. Hell, so am I. But I never took a vow of celibacy. Too bad if my being a human being disappoints you."

"Why are we even talking about this? You're never going to change. Gram said you were addicted to squalor . . . she said you're a grifter . . . and a dirty legs . . . and she was right. She said you cheated on my mom."

Spark reacted as if someone had emerged from hiding, put the palms of both hands on either of his shoulders and violently shoved him backward. It took him a moment to regain his equilibrium and even longer to speak.

"Addicted to squalor? My mother said that to you . . ." Spark's astonishment was piercing. "I did not screw around on Flory. Whatever you think you know—"

"Liar. You make me sick."

"Who do you think you are, you little twerp? You weren't there. You don't know what you're talking about. For that matter, you don't know me."

"You're right about one thing. I don't know you."

Hally closed his eyes and rested the back of his head against the dark rock face, cool spray from the colliding currents forming tiny droplets on his cheeks. "Don't blame Gram," he said finally. "She told me because she didn't want me turning out like you. Or Mom." He paused. "She said . . . she told me . . . My mom went crazy, for-real crazy."

"Hally."

"For once, answer me. Don't just put me off or make up stuff. It's true, isn't it?"

"She wasn't crazy. She just . . ." Spark was having trouble talking.

"She just wasn't sane."

"It's complicated." Spark seemed to be in physical pain.

"It's complicated because you don't want me to know that my mom was mental and maybe I'm just like her. Maybe I'm crazy, too."

"That's not true."

"You're such a liar."

"I'm not lying to you."

"Did you steal Ned?"

"What? What's that got to do with it?"

"Just answer me. It's an easy question: Yes or no? Did you steal Ned?"

"No."

Hally looked disgusted. "You don't know how to tell the truth. Oh, wait, maybe it's a good lie. Is it a good lie, Spark?" Hally turned around, and started down the rock face. He stopped abruptly and spun around to face Spark directly. "You really don't get it, do you? Want to know how I feel? I feel like an idiot."

"Hally—"

"Last night, when you told me you loved my mom, you made me feel like it was real, that it was something good. For a moment I even thought that *you* might be good, down deep . . . all-the-way-to-China-deep, maybe, but good in your own weird way. I felt happy, like we were a real family, even if it was only in my head."

"Hal—"

"Don't tell me that what happened with Gina has nothing to do with my mother and me. It's what you are. It's what you do. You don't love anyone. You can't tell me you care about Gina, and at the same time tell me it didn't mean anything.

"Don't tell me how leaving me was for the best and all anyone was thinking about was me. I know all that. Don't tell me I'm crazy for imagining us as a happy family—don't tell me it's just one more thing I saw that wasn't real."

"Hally, I'm sorry."

"I'll get over it, okay? Just . . . everyone says you're trouble . . . What I want to know is are you worth the trouble?"

Hally began to climb down the rock and, pushing himself off, landed in a foot of foaming water. "One more thing," he said. "Quit acting superior because of the things you say you don't believe in."

Seeing him step onto the uneven shoreline and walk slowly

toward the house, I thought about following him. I continued to watch him walk away even as I elected to remain behind. It was the right choice. Hally didn't need me but I knew who did.

"That went well," Spark said, gathering me into his arms, trying to understand all that had just happened. "I didn't steal you, did I, Neddy? I rescued you. There's a big difference."

I wagged my tail, and licked his hand.

Gina's piece appeared in print about a week later, accompanied by a photo of Hally, his image taking up half-a-page, his tropical blue-green eyes staring out at the world daring everyone to disbelieve him. Her story was a bit of a departure, more thoughtful, almost medita-tive, relatively speaking, ultimately more Jonathan Livingston Seagull than René Descartes, but still, a bit of an anomaly for the tabloid, though not without the customary sensational elements, including the suggestion in vivid hyperbolic terms that Hally was special, that he was somehow important to the world.

As a stylist, Gina was big on catchy sobriquet. She referred to Hally as the Reluctant Messiah. She described him as the Accidental Savior. She even gave me a title: the Purveyor of Wonderment.

"You want to read this?" Hugh said to Spark when he got home from his day on the boat.

"Nope," Spark said, walking straight through the kitchen, then the living room, bounding up the stairs two steps at a time.

"Ad copy," Pastor Ragnar sniffed, archly enacting his revenge against Gina, as Hugh read aloud. "Though marketing, like propa-ganda, does have its place."

"Anyway, who cares?" Hally said, biting into a green apple, juices spurting. "I don't care what she writes about me. I only did it to help with the money."

"That *confidence*, remarkable," Pastor Ragnar said admiringly, seeming to chew on something less tangible than an apple. "Always remember, Hally, sometimes in life you do it for love. Other times you do it for money. You must settle up with your choices. Never make the mistake of confusing the two. You'll be a lot happier that way . . . " Pastor Ragnar counseled, picking up his teacup and blowing on the rising steam, watching it disperse into the air around him. ". . . or not."

That evening, after Hally had gone to bed and the others were retired to their separate corners, Spark pulled up a chair and sat at the kitchen table and read Gina's story. He looked up briefly when Hugh came into the room.

"So," Hugh said, "what do you think?"

"I got paid today. Money's on top of the fridge. Help yourself," Spark said, ignoring his inquiry.

"Thanks," Hugh said. "It makes a difference. I really appreciate it, Spark . . . Now, are you going to answer me?"

"I think we've made a golem and we've sent it out into the world to wreak havoc."

"Maybe a little dramatic," Hugh said, pouring himself a glass of ginger ale. He leaned with his back against the counter and took a sip.

"We've been reckless with something we should have kept to ourselves. Instead, we sold it."

Hugh sighed and his fatigue sounded bone-deep. "We sold an interview to a dopey tabloid that no one takes seriously. Unless you really can die from embarrassment the worst is over. What the hell, Spark? It's not like you to be so bleak."

From the inner sanctum of his study, I could hear Pastor Ragnar chuckling away. He was speaking to someone on the phone. He'd been on the phone most of the day, talking to this one and that one. He was as deadly with a phone as a gunslinger was with a .45.

Hugh and Spark were taken up with their own discussion, not paying attention. They were accustomed to the ambient noise of their father's relentless conversation, just as they were used to the constancy of the wind and the waves and the seabirds calling out.

"We should have locked it up in the attic when we had the chance," Spark was saying. "How do we stop it from falling into the wrong hands? How do we stop it from getting into the wrong head?"

I sat up and stared at them. Spark and Hugh were smart guys.

How could they not know it had already gotten into the wrong head?

It was just past midnight, the house still and dark as Spark and I climbed the stairs. He flopped down onto the bed. "Oh, Neddy," he said, "tell me what to do." Spark was so self-aware, he was like the annotated version of a human being. I would have told him what to do had I only known. I just kept thinking the same thought. If it looks like a duck and quacks like a duck, you should consider the strong possibility that it isn't a duck at all.

Not long after, just long enough for both of us to fall into the first twilight stage of sleep, I felt him tighten up beneath the covers, my ears twitching as Pastor Ragnar's disembodied voice wound its way up the staircase, entering the bedroom at the base of the door, volume slowly climbing in serpentine fashion, rising in widening, then narrowing circles of menace.

He was alone and talking to himself, in that habitual way he had, arguing, fighting with someone unseen and unknown, someone I suspected was himself, his voice growing increasingly violent, language becoming more profane.

"Goddammit," he said, almost shouting, raw physicality careening all around the house. It felt like a street brawl, each gritty word staining the air, clots of blood on a torn shirt.

"Jesus Christ!" he said from the living room below. "Goddammit."

The others must have heard him, Hugh and Hally, how couldn't they? They remained in their beds, faces forced to their pillows. He talked to himself, yes, argued even, but this was different. This was rage that he was struggling to force back into its locked cage.

I yawned anxiously, noisily licking my lips, whimper escaping, shaking with fear. Spark pulled me beneath the covers. "Don't worry, Neddy," he said. "He's talking to my mother. They fight. They make up. It's fine." Spark held me tight and I realized this was something he'd been telling himself since he was a little boy even though he knew the fantasy no longer applied.

After he had exhausted himself, Pastor Ragnar walked up the stairs. The door to his bedroom clicked shut. Spark drifted off. It was four o'clock in the morning.

I lay my head between my paws and thought about Old English mastiffs. Seemingly the sanest of dog breeds, or so humans think, anyway. With their steady gaze and noble demeanor, their quiet stoicism and levelheadness, their stability and their fearlessness, they make you feel as if you could bounce a dime off their taut intelligence, but really, as every dog will tell you, they are mad as apples.

Thirteen

The church was full of people, eyes gleaming like Easter Sunday, many of them waving palms, waiting to get their first sight of Hally.

Pastor Ragnar met us on the porch.

"You came," he said to Spark, mildly surprised, the edges of his mouth turned down. "Why must you bring Ned everywhere with you? You're like a baby with a favorite blanket." He frowned, my presence temporarily spoiling his fun. "No dogs," he said. "He can wait in the car."

"It's too hot. He's just a little dog. He begged to come," Hugh said. "No one will even notice."

"Count me out of this whole thing," Spark said. "I don't want to be here, anyway."

"No problem," Pastor Ragnar said.

"This is ridiculous," Hugh said. "You wanted Spark to come. He came. Enough already."

Exasperated, Pastor Ragnar, briefly considered his dilemma.

"All right," he said. "He is the blue dog, after all, the purveyor of wonderment, isn't that right, Ned?" The more he thought about it, the more appeal the idea held for him.

"Yes, he should be here. Bring him along. People will want to see him."

"Where's Hally?" Hugh asked.

From the back of the church I looked down the narrow aisle, creaky and sunken in spots. A yellow vase of wild purple lupines sat on the table that doubled as an altar. A soft umber light crept in through the windows where it faded to a golden glow. I glanced around and saw so many thick ankles crammed into so many cheap pairs of shoes for a moment I imagined a herd of cows had wandered into a Payless.

Spark bent down and picked me up.

"The dog!" A woman called out as a collective murmur arose. All heads turned. The place was sweating, overwrought, and humid, crammed with people red as tomatoes, flush and expectant, men, women, teenage boys and girls, alongside indifferent children and toddlers who raced their dinky cars in the pews.

They had read Gina's article, which conferred a certain legitimacy on recent events as the printed word tends to do. Many of them were present on the island for the second apparition, some of them loudly convinced they had borne historic witness. Most were persuaded that at the very least, something had occurred that resisted ordinary explanation. The Church in the Clearing, and its congregants, they surmised, had been selected for a special purpose by God.

It was all enough to make you rethink the meaning of "special."

Looking around, I recognized many of them from the island and from the odd church function I'd attended. Beans, of course, sitting front and center as always, Mrs. Houton and Tommy in the pew behind him, something new there—and something old, too— Mrs. Houton glowering over at Spark. Chip and Arche Wallace were there, "Hey, chief, how's it going?" ringing out with painful regularity as the younger man greeted everyone in sight; even the deputy, Bert Connor, was there. Not everyone was sympathetic or convinced, a trace scent of skepticism hovered in the air like a bad batch of incense.

I glanced behind me and saw the Sex Family file in and stand at the back of the church, for once fully dressed, clothes worn like battle-ready armor, accusatory stares sharp as swords.

"What the hell are they doing here?" Hugh said.

"Reminding us that Sunday is no different from every other day of the week," Spark said.

"Pastor Ragnar waited until we were seated at the front of the church before he began to speak: "We wake up. We take our show-ers. We eat our porridge. We brush our teeth. We begin our days as we begin every day, like a familiar song whose choruses we know by heart. Our days go along, they *sing along* to the same old tune. It's all right. It's good in its way."

He did love those musical references and he had this distinctive way of speaking—an elegant style combined with a resonant actorly voice. His sermons, which tended to rely heavily on metaphor, started out quietly and built momentum as they went along, acquiring a cumu-lative force that ended in a crescendo. A traditional enough approach, even a little corny, but I've learned never to underestimate the power of hokiness as a persuasive device.

"As much as we crave and extol the beauty of the familiar, that's how much we're drawn to the mystery. The mystery of *it all*, the feel-ing that the ordinary conceals the extraordinary, that prose is only preparation for poetry, that the grounding experience of earth is noth-ing more than basic training for the soaring experience of the heavens.

"Months pass, years go by, and then one day, it happens. We wake up to a day like no other, a day that changes everything, that writes its own lyrics, a day that makes its own music. A day comes along that reimagines the worn pattern of our lives, and invites our souls to become both song and singer. We find ourselves in the vital grip of a day that puts the ordinary in direct contact with the extraordinary, a day like that rings out like a bell across time."

Quiet descended over the room. Something was about to be born but something was dying, too.

"That day," Pastor Ragnar said, pausing for maximum dramatic effect, "has come."

"Holy shit, this is insane," Spark said beneath his breath. "Is he talking about *Hally*?"

"Shh." Hugh put his finger to his lips.

When Hally finally appeared he was wearing a white shirt and bran-colored khakis. He was pale, almost ethereal, the same way he'd appeared at Black Head the day of the second apparition. I gave my head a shake and took a closer look. In the wan light, he looked, in that moment, as if he were sustained by prayer, meditation, and solitude as opposed to his preferred diet of Pop-Tarts and practical jokes. His eyes were focused on his feet. Habitually bare, they were tucked into a pair of scuffed sandals. I heard him softly whistle beneath his breath, though I'm certain that only a dog could have picked up on it.

He briefly raised his eyes, scanning the crowd. Once he located us, he looked back down, his gaze sweeping the floor. Pastor Ragnar walked over to him and, taking his elbow, led him to the front of the altar. Moments passed in a vacuum—no sound, no oxygen, suspension of movement, heart fluttering, light dimming. The entire congregation seemed to be in a state of suspended animation, as if they were being immobilized by the sheer intensity of their collectively held emotions.

Hugh bowed his head. Hugh had simple faith, which isn't the same as having simple-minded faith. His belief possessed a certain gracefulness, arising as it did from humility and critical thinking tenderly applied. He believed in God, but gently, prayed in happy times and sad, treated others well, and tried to make good moral choices in his daily life, which, in my experience of human beings, made him no less intelligent than the average nonbeliever.

A man cleared his throat. There was a shuffling noise in the pew across from us. I heard shoes on floorboard and along with Spark I turned to see the Tick-Tock Girls, the same mother-daughter singing act that performed hymns at Black Head, rise up in a single motion from where they were seated and take up their standard formation, oldest to youngest, on the left-hand side of the altar.

The girls were wearing matching dark green and red dirndls and all of them, including the mother, sported pigtails tied off with white ribbons. A few clumsy strums on the guitar, one false start and regroup and they began to sing "Have Thine Own Way, Lord!"

Spark gave a sharp intake of breath and buried his face in my hair.

"Have thine own way, Lord!" the girls, desperate mouths agape like baby robins competing for the next worm, sang more in defense of tone-deaf passion than harmony.

I could feel Spark shake, struggling to maintain some tenuous claim on adulthood. He was beginning to tear down the middle, from toes to head, cracking from the inside out. Hugh glared at him, issuing a silent fraternal warning.

"Please, God," he whispered into my ear, practically panting. "Make them stop."

They didn't even pause to breathe, mania sustaining them, they just kept singing, they were relentless, growing ever more earnest and loud and implacable and glassy-eyed—their rabid conviction wouldn't have been out of place at a Nazi youth rally—imploring the Lord to have his own way. A homely and enormous woman, moved by their escalating zeal, dropped to her knees, the thud resonating throughout the room.

"Praise be! It's the baby Jesus!" She wailed suddenly, looking at Hally, raising her arms to the heavens, wringing her meaty hands while I briefly wondered what part of New England she was from, her wringing-wet frenzy not exactly emblematic of traditional dry Yankee stoicism.

The girls sang on, fervor intensifying.

Spark looked around in disbelief. He struggled to suppress a strangled half-sob, half-laugh. He broke, an involuntary spurt of projectile laughter escaping. What the hell? Blame it on my youth. I began to bark, a high-pitched stream of yips and yelps, which only caused the German Girls' League to sing even louder and more frantically.

"Have thine own way, Lord!"

Hally lowered his head. It hit me. He thought Spark was laughing at him. Spark was too caught up in his own feelings to notice the effect he was having on Hally.

If Hugh's pallor were a paint color it would have been called Embalming Fluid Gray.

Pastor Ragnar's fury was practically audible, a deathly rattle emanating from somewhere deep inside of him. "Will you ever grow up?" he hissed at Spark. I expected to see blood stream from his eyes when something strange and entirely unexpected happened. The homely woman, bless her enlarged time-bomb of a heart, started to laugh—at first it was a surprised chuckle but then it grew and it deepened and it took ahold of her and soon she was gasping for breath and wiping her eyes, and then she was joined by other members of the congregation who looked on in wonderment, a few people grinning in embarrassment and confusion, others nervously giggling, but then they, too, started laughing.

It was strange to see these neighbors, fellow congregants and strangers, some of them unabashed believers, others professed skeptics, but in sum, people for whom common sense was a governing principle, people who generally observed the normal agreed-upon demarcation points and civilizing influences, from hedges to fences to the familiar bouquet of small talk and the panacea of little courtesies, watch them come together in what was essentially a moment of madness or at the very least an episode of incautious abandon, as if they'd all decided to hell with beige, let's paint the living room chartreuse.

Within minutes the church itself seemed to loosen its tie and roll up its dress-shirt sleeves, the walls streaming with tears of laughter. People were holding their stomachs, covering their open mouths, they were overcome, weeping with joy. They began to lean against one another, their eyes shining with mirth. Not before nor since have I ever seen Arche Wallace laugh, but he was howling to the rafters that day. Pastor Ragnar, detecting a sea change, retracted his fangs and he, too, began to laugh, or do his best impersonation, anyway.

Now it was my turn to wonder what was going on.

"Glory be to God!" someone shouted in a fever pitch of merriment.

"Alleluia, praise the Lord!" A cackling chorus went up.

It seemed Spark was the only one who wasn't laughing. Spark and the Sex Family, that is, a bizarre if brief alliance. Oh, and Hally. Hally wasn't laughing. Hugh seemed to be praying for a quick death. Never one to miss an opportunity, Pastor Ragnar, a man for whom inspiration and opportunism were the same thing, raised his arms over his head in triumph.

"I declare this to be, now and forevermore, the Church of Holy Laughter!"

Hally, his eyes closed, managed to somehow make a safe space for himself, creating a psychic and physical barrier between himself and the crowd that no one dared breach. Spark, looking deprived of air, stumbling among all those human crosses, headed toward the open double doors and back outside, Hugh and I following, Pastor Ragnar and Hally dissolving into the laughter and the song. At the last moment, before I left the church I turned around for one final look. In the far darkened corner, near the kitchen, I could see Mr. Herman staring blankly, reaching into his pocket for a worm.

I stepped outside. The breeze was light though it carried the heavy odor of flowers. I looked to the field behind the church where the wild lupines grew, blue and purple, the little church at the edge of a vast ocean, powerful waves of fragrance making their invisible incursion.

Spark would go on to wonder how it was that Pastor Ragnar, of all men, could preside over a church and a community that never stopped laughing. From that time on, uncontrollable laughter, touted as a joyful manifestation of God's presence, dominated every Sunday service. Only the little children in attendance seemed immune, staring at the adults around them in confusion. Mr. Herman, too, seemed oddly resistant and took to loudly mimicking a train whistle when things got out of hand.

"Poor man," I overheard someone say at the end of one especially emotional service. "He's gone off the deep end."

As a dog, I, too, was insusceptible, though there was no confusion in my mind about why.

"Meanwhile, I may never laugh again," Spark said. He watched in growing dismay as Hally's special spark faded to candlelight, Pastor Ragnar shrewdly withdrawing him from public view, the church breaking through the roof with new members, becoming a fringe phenomenon, part religion, part performance art.

To be fair, Hally never claimed to be anything other than a regular boy who found himself in extraordinary circumstances. He never ascribed to himself any special powers, let alone suggested he had some sort of divine status. He didn't say he was the Second Coming, or call himself the Messiah, accidental or otherwise. He never referred to himself as a prophet.

Not only did he not have the slightest interest in becoming anyone's savior, the truth is if you were to scour the entire world, known and unknown, and quiz every living human being, you couldn't find a less likely candidate for godliness than Hally Monahan.

In the early days and weeks following the apparitions—besides an uptick in the numbers and freneticism at Pastor Ragnar's church, things had seemed calm on the surface, though not serene in the common sense, more like an untrustworthy prelude, an unkind remission. A pause, slightly surreal, as if the world's colors seemed off, a little ominously pale or disturbingly garish.

In the slow beginning, excuses were made for what happened to Hally at Black Head—the failed concert, the grinding money problems, Spark's unannounced arrival, the crazy girl's allegations, the incident with the mason jars at Cathedral Woods—the combined trauma, especially for an impressionable kid with an unsteady history, was enough to drive anyone into the arms of a hallucination.

Humans love pursuing an idea to its logical conclusion. So what's my excuse? I'm a dog, I should have known better. In retrospect, it's obvious everything that happened at the beginning of the summer was a sign.

Before any monumental event, always, there are signs; that is, if you're paying attention. Any dog worth his salt can tell you when an earthquake is imminent, though a Dalmatian would sleep through a direct hit from an atomic bomb—there's a reason those guys see spots.

In the days and hours beforehand, it's not unusual for well water to darken and bubble and turn to sludge, or maybe a fountain will appear inside a well or burst forth from the earth. Birds abandon trees and fly low to the ground, their traditional songs subverted by terror into an avian siren, rats panic, horses rear up, the earth moans, and babies rush to be born.

Later on, as things got bigger and more uncontrollable, and messier and dirtier, a tidal wave gathering junk along the way, Spark would say that it was a conspiracy of craziness, a "convergence of crackpots" that was responsible for all that happened. There were so many signs, injuries, near disasters.

I think my inauspicious arrival—something stolen—was a sign.

My father always was way ahead of me in his thinking—there were no bottoms to the holes he dug. I got exhausted and threw in the trowel at the first sign of soil turning to stone. I suppose I prefer the shallow territory of familiar ground, the retread to the fresh footprint. I like to return to the same old places; for me, the old places are the source of true discovery.

Even after all that's happened, I go back. All the time, in my head I go back, trying to make sense of it, wanting to reclaim it, back to the rising mists at Black Head, to the mossy silence of a cathedral forest, lichen hanging in nooses from arched tree branches, turning toward the same destination at the end of that lonely gravel road, traveling again as so many times before, to an isolated path on a bright sunny day, to an old country church in a clearing, field of wild lupines flooding its banks, turning the whole world into a perfumed ocean of purple.

Fourteen

~~~~~~

Between Gina's article about Hally and the outbreak of spiritual delir-
ium at Pastor Ragnar's church it seemed our little universe had caught
on fire. Local newspapers picked up the story, which had spread to
some New England news stations, gathering its own peculiar momentum along the way until it had become something of a regional sensation, even seducing tourists from the more traditional destinations of
Cape Cod and the Vineyard.

"You'll laugh, you'll cry. You'll wish you'd never been born,"
Spark said as Pastor Ragnar installed speakers outside the church to
accommodate greater numbers of people, so even the leaves in the
trees were forced to listen to what he had to say each week.

"Is there a church where you can pray to *lose* the powers of sight
and hearing?" Spark moaned, as the family gathered at home in the
evening to watch an area news broadcast, the reporter in brown suit
jacket and mauve striped tie, posed solemnly outside the Church of
Holy Laughter earlier that Sunday morning, the cotton-candy gushes
of joy emanating from within overpowering the sweeter choir of
songbirds and the natural quiet.

"You can see and hear for yourself, Ida Mae," he said addressing a studio-bound colleague as his report groped for its conclusion. "These people are clearly in the throes of something. I've never seen anything like it. Some say it's the power of the Holy Ghost manifesting in this humble little church on a remote rural road in coastal Maine. Some say that it's irrefutable proof this young boy, Hally Monahan, has been hand-picked by the Virgin Mary—so God, too, presumably, by extension—to a special holy purpose. Others, of course, less poetic, if that's the right term, insist it's a simple case of mass hysteria, ascribing a more clinical explanation. Faith versus science, as it were, a battle as old as time."

"My gosh. Interesting. Makes you think, doesn't it? We don't know everything, do we? A bit like haunted houses and such. Incredible. Hard, then, to dismiss out of hand . . ." Ida Mae said, her face shellacked in a layer of industrial-strength foundation, cheeks flush with an application of rosy authenticity as she traded comments with the station's meteorologist who grimaced and shuddered as if he were a street mime. He signed off with a joke about an impending rainfall "accompanied by intermittent bouts of hail, boils, gnats and locusts."

The incident at the church, while it may have been galvanizing to increasing numbers of Pastor Ragnar's exuberant followers (who now seemed to exist in a permanent state of paroxysm), had the opposite effect on Hally, who gradually withdrew within himself. He was alarming everyone with the extent of his solitude and his solemnity, Spark visibly recoiling every time Hally pulled out his rosary and headed for his room, his shoulders drooping whenever he caught him reading scripture.

"I never thought I'd hope to find my kid poring over *Penthouse*," Spark said to Hugh.

"Cheer up," Hugh said, raising an eyebrow. "Maybe when he says he's praying he's in his room smoking pot."

Then again, maybe he wasn't praying *or* smoking pot. Maybe he wasn't doing much of anything at all. After spending plenty of time alone with Hally in his room where he would lie for hours on his bed just staring up at the ceiling, or clinging to his mysterious miraculous medal, the necklace of dubious origins as I had come to think of it, I suspected he was depressed.

The Monahans were not a practical family. They read and painted and talked and felt, but the three men combined could barely figure out how to operate a can opener. Left alone, their women gone too soon, they were a bit lost, lacking tether to the everyday. For them, it was less concerning and ultimately more satisfying to decide Hally was a minor god in the throes of an epic spiritual crisis than that he was an unexpectedly sensitive kid struggling with puberty, a series of fraught episodes and (big maybe) an encounter with the divine.

Now, as word spread about the catharsis of the church, he had a whole new burden with which to contend—followers, disciples, groupies, fans—a swarm of human deer flies capable of biting through clothing. People—in small numbers at first, though those numbers had begun to multiply at accelerating rates of speed—had begun to make the pilgrimage to the island to see Black Head and the spot where the Blessed Virgin appeared to Hally, but mostly they wanted something else from their purposeful wanderings, a little flesh and bone, blood, some human content.

They wanted Hally.

His distinctive looks made him easy to spot among a skeleton island population, even during tourist season. His everyday appearances, the attempted regular conduct of his life was accompanied by stares and whispers, pointing, sneaked glances, even the occasional confrontation. "This too shall pass," Hugh said as Hally grew more reluctant to leave the house, his world growing even more circumscribed and isolated.

"It's all right," Hugh said, putting his arm around Hally as he sat beside him on the stairs of the deck. "Don't worry. I know you don't believe me but this is just a temporary setback in your life."

"Fuck 'em all," Spark said from where he stood on the other side of the deck.

"Doesn't matter," Hally said. "This is the way it's going to be from now on."

"You don't know. How do you know?" Hugh said.

"I just do, that's all. I haven't chosen this life. It's chosen me."

"That's Pastor Ragnar talking," Spark said.

"Spark," Hugh said, exasperated, "you want to dial it down a little?"

"When will you get it in your head that it's me talking for myself?" Hally confronted Spark. "My old life is gone. This is my new life. The rest is just pretending."

A part of me—the part that saw the creative potential in failure—agreed with Hally's doleful estimation of things to come. It was hard to ignore the accumulating evidence. Something had changed and was changing, still. Something was circling overhead, lightly touching ground.

Hally turned thirteen the end of July and though seldom seen in public anymore, he had come to constitute the invisible cornerstone of Pastor Ragnar's exploding ministry. Like those venerated bone fragments and tufts of hair, the remaindered biology of saints, he was now embedded in the spiritual reliquary of a growing movement sanctified by his encounter with the divine. The odd understated appearance among the converted wasn't going to be enough—Pastor Ragnar knew that if he were to establish Hally (and himself) in the style and at the level he hoped, he would need to seduce a tougher, more discerning audience and not merely as a novelty act.

He unilaterally ramped up the campaign before the others even realized there was a campaign. I made it my business to listen in on his conversations, surprising him by joining him in the study where I curled up in the armchair in the corner while he talked away the mornings, haranguing his worshipful accomplices.

"Serve up a little of that old-time religion along with a big helping of potato salad, let's reach out to some southern churches. The goal now is to conquer the Eastern Seaboard. Blue-collars may be susceptible to a carefully selected proverb, but white-collars are a sucker for a pretty face."

He sounded like a cynical Washington political operative, one of several interchangeable identities he assumed on a daily basis, depending on his audience. When it came to money, however, he stayed consistent: "Pass the hat," he used to say. "Do not go hat in hand."

Pastor Ragnar was firm, unapologetic, and unwavering about the importance of asking for money as opposed to begging or scheming for money. His straightforward approach to raising funds was working, too, as donations began to come in from around the country and even places beyond.

By August, word had spread that Hally had cured a preteen girl brought to Pastor Ragnar's church because she was in the final stages of cancer, simply by touching his hand to hers. Even her doctor, a specialist from Sloan Kettering publicly professed astonishment at the instantaneous turnaround.

Hally's seeming ability to cure the sick had bumped up what was still essentially a regional story to a few national outlets, who used it to solemnly debate the merits of faith healing. The tone was generally if implausibly respectful—it was Hally who was breaking rank, not those charged with writing about him. That he wasn't comfortable with his new role made his story all the more compelling. Hally wasn't interested in convincing anyone of anything, which, ironically, proved to be the most persuasive thing about him. Also, it appeared he couldn't cure everyone, which made him seem like his own game show.

"Never underestimate the power of a cute nonthreatening boy on a dying girl on the brink of puberty," Spark joked about the young cancer patient.

"Nice," Hugh said.

Interest in Hally soared after that, there was no controlling it. It felt as if our world had become something sentenced to run wild in the streets. I dug a deep hole in the dirt beneath the deck and sought refuge there. People showed up at the church throughout the week. Some even came to the house, including one feverish soul who simply appeared at the kitchen table as if he were an extra place setting. We started locking the door after that. They all wanted something, begged for Hally's intercession in their troubled lives, insisted that he cure them of illnesses, find lost family members, restore cracked dreams, revive curtailed romances.

Through everything, Pastor Ragnar was soaring. Pastor Ragnar had emerged from all that cocooning madness with wings. Spark had begun calling him Colonel Parker, his fame continuing to grow along with Hally's—and through everything he never broke a sweat. Imagine Cary Grant presiding over a tent revival meeting. He held a broad, more eclectic range of appeal, attracting the attention of an elitist audience who normally would rather ingest Kraft dinners than be caught up with a preacher man, which brings us to the next point—his fundamentalism wasn't all that fundamental.

His religious views were a self-generated pastiche that evolved and changed as he did. The lower-case god of his own cultivated doctrine, Pastor Ragnar was an arborist, taking from this tree and grafting onto that tree, growing a conscious collection of traditional foundation trees and mixing them with showy ornamentals, the odd overarching giant, some sculptural exotics, and an abundance of fruit-bearers. He believed in function but he knew well the power of esthetics.

Maybe it was because he had more than a passing acquaintance with dirt beneath his fingernails. Although he came from a long line of godly men, he grew up in his mother's family business, a tobacco farm in southwestern Ontario. Every summer he was expected to work in the fields and the kilns, where he developed a lifelong aversion to cigarettes and manual labor. His father, who left Maine for Canada when he got married, presided over an Anglican church in a small Ontario town called Port Dover on the shores of Lake Erie.

Pastor Ragnar had no interest in becoming a minister, despite his father's insistence. He wanted to go into politics, was president of the Young Liberals as a high school student, but when he was seventeen he had that powerful dream that propelled him into the religious life. His dream was the source of great mystery, although I was somewhat underwhelmed when I overheard him tell Hally about it (perhaps as with most personally transformative events, you had to be there).

"Maybe it's the secret recipe for Kentucky Fried Chicken," Spark speculated.

I was convinced, based on something my father once told me, it was his Canadian background that contributed to setting Pastor Ragnar apart from the usual vibrating id.

"Canadians distrust people who breathe fire," he said. "They prefer to tamp down the visible flames, though it doesn't mean they don't burn away in secret. The rest of the world hasn't a clue as to their real character. Canadians are quite mad, Lupine."

Grind down most religious zealots into something you could stuff into a capsule and they would be the ultimate cure for insomnia. Pastor Ragnar knew how to be interesting and he had an edge—for simple allure, you can't beat the combination of a man with wicked margins who plays at being good. It's hard to dismiss someone who *looked as good* as Pastor Ragnar looked, or more significantly, it's hard for the press to ignore anyone that photogenic.

I wish I could say such superficiality was a distinctly human trait but dogs are no better—we may even be worse—when it comes to one another. Why do you think that Nova Scotia Duck Tolling Retrievers are held in such contempt by other breeds at the benches of Westminster? Because they look as common as some feral you'd find rooting around a dumpster. Don't get me started on Australian cattle dogs. I once watched a Chinese crested trying to chat up a Maltese terrier with a ribbon in her hair and found myself blinking back tears of embarrassment for him.

Taking full advantage of his assets, Pastor Ragnar held his nose and started appearing regularly on various religious networks—only a reluctant first step, his ultimate goal was to win over the secular media—and managing his ascendancy as if he were a wartime general strategizing a battle plan. Hally was a critical aspect of the campaign, albeit an elusive one, which was part of the design.

"Overexposure is the enemy of mystique," Pastor Ragnar said, knowing enough to dole Hally out judiciously and in tiny precious portions.

How he loathed "my so-called peers," as he called them, men such as Oral Roberts, Jim Bakker, Jimmy Swaggart, Marvin Gorman, Jerry Falwell.

"Hillbillies," he sniffed, though he took full advantage of the popularity their ministries enjoyed while comparing it privately to the massive following reserved for professional wrestlers.

Often tactically outrageous and provocative in his role as religious leader and craving the freedom to do as he wished with Hally, he had to be both creative and subtle when it came to handling Spark, who was, in principle at least, growing more resistant to Hally having a public profile. Still, there were ways to get around his disapproval and Pastor Ragnar was a master at devising new strategies and methods of attack.

Spark had critical areas of weakness—for one, he had a bad habit of letting the world entertain him—and Pastor Ragnar, like a mad scientist locked away in the secret laboratory of his darker imagination, was always experimenting with new mixes and potions designed to make Spark more malleable. The central problem, pathetically obvious to my canine self, was that Spark, despite outward appearances, wanted to please his father. He couldn't help himself.

In our relationship to humans, dogs are hard-wired pleasers, so we've had ample opportunity both to recognize the pitfalls and to codify insurgence as a means of counterbalance. That's why civil disobedience is so important to the meaningful prosecution of our lives, why we shred pillows, tear open garbage bags, and stretch out on the off-limits sofa in your absence.

It's self-declaration. Woe to the dog who doesn't impose his reckless free will on an empty house; he has no soul. Humans should think about that the next time they applaud their dog's spiritless come-to-heel or willingness to curl into a crate. See his head hang, the droop of his tail. A submissive dog is a wingless bird. A dog with no secret life is like a human being who hands off his moral compass to another navigator.

Pastor Ragnar's profile as a religious leader and authority continued to expand, especially after he was interviewed by Charlie Rose, which attracted all sorts of comment from sources both likely and unlikely—the world, let's face it, loves a star. Not like my father, who was a hard guy to impress. "Charlie Rose is all right," he used to say. "He's no Bill Moyers."

Fifteen

Without consulting anyone, Pastor Ragnar had the church's public relations woman—one of his first hires when the money started flowing—approach *Life* magazine about the possibility of a story. Then he set about influencing the choice of photographer, and succeeded in persuading Rusty Cipolla to undertake the assignment.

Cipolla's career as a photographer of celebrities had made him a celebrity photographer, the sequined social equal of his subjects. His photos were like opulently staged musical production numbers. No portrait was complete without a topless woman, an exotic animal, and a man in drag. Everything he did was to advance the setup, the fantastical disguise. His high-concept imagery sold magazines and generated regular debate about style and wit among people with neither.

"This is turning into 'Hallywood,'" Spark said when he heard. He was in the kitchen sitting at the table trying to resuscitate a pair of old work boots. "Soon you'll be using the kid's image to sell Count Chocula."

"Jealousy doesn't become you," Pastor Ragnar commented.

"You think this is about jealousy?" Spark asked him.

"No need to be defensive. Given Hugh's artistic success and now with what's happened to Hally . . . it must be difficult to find yourself always being relegated to the role of the anonymous brother."

"I'm Hally's *father*," Spark said, looking at Pastor Ragnar in disbelief.

"I misspoke. It's easy to forget," Pastor Ragnar said.

"Especially when you want to."

"Jamie, I've rarely felt misunderstood, but you truly misunderstand me," Pastor Ragnar said, reaching out and putting his hand on Spark's forearm.

"If I understood you, I would be you. I don't want to be you," Spark said, shaking off his father, picking up his boots, and heading toward the stairs.

"Those boots have given up the ghost. Let me buy you a new pair," Pastor Ragnar said.

"Thanks but these are fine," Spark said.

I brushed against Pastor Ragnar's leg. He gave me his look. Frost formed on the tips of my eyelashes.

It was decided that Cipolla would shoot Hally at home on Monhegan Island. The trick was to get Hally to agree to be photographed. While Pastor Ragnar treated religion as if it were a cat he was attempting to strangle with his bare hands with all the incumbent claws and screeching, Hally, the boy who once professed indifference to God, was growing more quiet and introspective, less religious in the dogmatic sense and more spiritual, well, his version of spirituality, anyway.

His reluctance to seek out a public profile was occurring in direct opposite trajectory with Pastor Ragnar's escalating pursuit of greater fame. So it was with extreme care that Pastor Ragnar pitched Hally on the merits of the *Life* magazine shoot. Told him it was part of an essay on the power of prayer and faith healing. "Think of all the souls you can potentially influence to pick up a rosary," he said. Hally took it in, never commented.

The night before Rusty Cipolla was to arrive, Hally marched into the living room and announced he wouldn't be photographed.

"I don't want to pursue personal glory or attention. I'm not supposed to," he told Hugh who had been minding his own business throughout the whole matter, and was watching TV.

"First, you're not seeking fame . . . second, what do you mean? You're 'not *supposed* to'?" Hugh said, turning down the volume. "I said it was okay. Your father said it was okay, well, he didn't say it wasn't okay. Pastor Ragnar instigated the whole thing. This guy is an amazing photographer, Hal. He doesn't agree to shoot just anyone. Who told you that you weren't supposed to do it?"

Hally didn't speak. Neither did Hugh. His expression said it all.

"You leave Hally to me," Pastor Ragnar said in a phone call from the church, confirming the arrival early the next morning of Cipolla and his entourage, including a writer from *Life*, though there was to be no formal interview with Hally. This was a story in photos to be accompanied by sparse "lyrical" copy.

"He'll be relying on atmospherics and impressions," Cipolla had explained.

"I hope he's seen *I Was a Teenage Werewolf*," Spark cracked as Hally continued to resist.

The next day, Pastor Ragnar and the crew arrived in a rented boat. They came on foot, carrying tons of lighting and camera equipment, Cipolla in a frenzied state of artistic ecstasy, having been driven slightly mad by all the photographic possibilities on the island. Hugh had prepared an elaborate brunch for everyone and he and Cipolla

instantly hit it off, talking animatedly about art and painting and pho-
tography and galleries and people they knew in common, Hugh chatting excitedly about his current collection.

Listening to him talk away so happily about his painting to someone who reciprocated with equal passion, I felt a bit of a pang as it
occurred to me that Hugh, a man of true devotions, was often con-
signed to the sidelines of all that swirling family drama. He had a
serious career but sometimes the rest of the Monahans behaved as if
he were selling caricature portraits for $15 a pop at the church bazaar.
Even the locals seemed more interested in Spark's various scrapes and
skirmishes than in Hugh's growing stature as an artist, though Hugh
never seemed to mind.

"I just want to paint. I don't care about the rest of it. Why should
I expect the world to be as interested in my work as I am?" he was
saying to Cipolla as they compared notes, the photographer promising
to attend his show.

"I think it's my best work to date," Hugh said after much prodding
by Cipolla, instantly qualifying. "I hope so, anyway."

"Where is Hally?' Cipolla asked finally.

"Oh, he'll be here soon. He's just a little shy—that self-conscious
age, you remember," Hugh said, avoiding any reference to the soap
opera occurring behind closed doors. Hugh was now participating
in the freewheeling marketing of Hally, though he would have been
appalled to hear it described that way.

"Tell you what, why don't you take the crew to Black Head, let
them get an idea about the location for the shoot? What's involved,
and so forth. I think you'll be amazed. Spectacular life-affirming—
even God-affirming site, if I may say so. I assume you New Yorkers
can survive the occasional reference to God without turning into pil-
lars of salt," Pastor Ragnar said as he led the photographer outside.

"Sounds like a plan," Cipolla said. He surveyed with open arms the ocean's vastness, its rough waters. "Where has Monhegan Island been all my life?"

"I'll be along shortly with Hally," Pastor Ragnar said as Hugh picked up some of the lighting equipment.

"I'll stay here with you," Spark said, appearing on the deck as the others prepared to head out.

"Oh no," Cipolla said. "Come. I'd like to photograph you, too. The Monahans have been blessed with good looks. You and Hally are just begging to be shot in black and white, light and dark."

"Nah, not my bag," Spark said.

"Go with them, Spark. They might need you for something," Pastor Ragnar said.

"Like what?"

"Oh, I'm sure they'll want someone to point out to them what makes one rock different from another rock. Failing that, you can always pick up sticks."

I stayed behind. Intuition, maybe. All right. Truth was I never could resist a fireworks display. I was in the kitchen with Hally and Pastor Ragnar. Hally, eyes cast downward, was sitting at the table, drumming his fingers softly on its wooden surface, his familiar adolescent precursor to battle. Tail keeping up a steady muted thumping, I sat expectantly in the middle of the kitchen floor, so I would have a clear view of both of them. I'm ashamed to say this was one collision I was looking forward to.

Pastor Ragnar was standing near the sink, temporarily distracted, looking for the source of a small scratching sound. Finally, he opened the bottom cupboard door and discovered a live mouse trap.

"Bloody mice," he said as he retrieved the trap.

"Hugh releases them into the woods. He doesn't have the heart to kill them," Hally said.

"So they come back. It's inevitable. No place like home, even if you're vermin," Pastor Ragnar said agreeably, looking down at me in unsubtle fashion. Pointing, he said, "He's established himself as a fierce little creature. Maybe he should start to earn his keep by helping to control the mouse population around here."

Who did he think I was, some scruffy, single-track, pest-obsessed Border terrier?

"So." Pastor Ragnar hung the word in the air, implication keeping it afloat.

Hally stopped drumming his fingers. "I'm not doing it, Gramp, I'm sorry. You do it. I don't think it's right for me to do it. I don't want publicity. It's wrong for me to exploit this. You understand, right?"

"I understand that you need to step up and assume a leadership role if our ministry is to succeed and you need to accept that becoming a public person is part of your duty. Do you have any idea what's happened here? In a matter of a few months, you, we, the church, have become a mighty force for good. This may come as a shock to you but this isn't about your personal preferences. There is something greater at work than your paltry opposition."

"What?" Hally said, clearly taken aback.

"We survive on the support of the public. No donations—no ministry. You need to play your part."

"I'm not asking people for money. This isn't about money . . ."

"Oh, I see, you leave the uncomfortable parts to me, is that right? Let me put it to you this way, Hally, it's gotta be fed and it don't eat hay," Pastor Ragnar said, uncharacteristically crude. He was growing impatient and it showed.

"I've never heard you talk like this before," Hally said. "I don't like it."

"Here's what I don't like. You putting vanity and personal considerations ahead of your obligation to spread the word of God and help the spiritually impoverished."

"Not this way," Hally said. "Anyway, I'm not that important. Not the way you make it sound. I'm just me."

"What you are is a selfish little fraud," Pastor Ragnar said. "You're obviously not up to what God has asked of you."

"Gramp, why are you saying this stuff?" Hally looked stricken.

"Have I not supported you when no one else would?" Pastor Ragnar asked him, hand to heart. "I'm asking you to do this thing. Who are you to challenge the will of God? Get it in your head, kid, you're not the driver, you're the car."

"I don't want you to be mad at me but I can't do it and you shouldn't ask me to do it when you know how I feel about it." Hally stood up. He turned to leave when Pastor Ragnar sprang forward in a singular violent thrust of anger, and knocked him down onto the floor.

Stunned, Hally landed on his side, his grandfather towering over him. I ran over to Hally, barking and growling, poised to fight. Hally grabbed me, held me close, and propelled himself backward using the heels of his running shoes, trying to get away as Pastor Ragnar leaned over, his face inches from Hally's.

"Get up! Get out there," he ordered, "and . . . smile!"

The smiling word "smile" in combination with the unsmiling tone in which it was spoken, was an unnerving juxtaposition that lingers in my memory to this day.

Pastor Ragnar's anger was sudden and shocking. Almost as unnerving was the disturbing way in which it instantaneously dissipated, giving it the feel of something almost supernatural.

Terrified, Hally nodded.

Straightening himself up, Pastor Ragnar held out his hand to Hally and helped him to his feet. Solicitously, almost lovingly, he brushed him off and patted his hair and dusted his shoulders as Hally, numb and shaky, warily submitted, too fearful to object.

"You look perfect. See how easy that was? Come along, sweetheart," he said, giving Hally a quick overall appraising glance. "Shall we go join the others?"

Pastor Ragnar paused at the door. "On second thought, you go ahead. I'll catch up in a minute." He shut the door behind Hally before I could follow, trapping me with him. He walked to the middle of the kitchen and ran both his hands through his hair. He was breathing heavily.

"Goddammit," he said, looking around. He spotted the live trap on the counter, walked over, opened it up and lifted the mouse out by its tail. In one indelible and swift motion he flung it against the crumbling plaster wall. Stunned, the little mouse slid slowly down the wall and onto the floor where it remained motionless.

"Watch out, you little bastard, or next time it'll be you," Pastor Ragnar said.

My ears shot forward. He was talking about me and for that moment, at least, he had my full attention. He opened the door and I dashed past him and outside and I ran ahead to find the others.

Hally's distress levels the day of the shoot were so acute that in combination with the blackness of the bluffs, the gray burden of the clouds, the circling ebony birds overhead, and always, the surpassing waves, his unhappiness seemed to light him from within, causing him to appear on the page like some rain-and-wind-lashed lantern struggling to stay lit.

(There was a portrait of me that turned out rather well, too, my red coat stealing the scene from the gray-and-black surrounding landscape.)

As for Pastor Ragnar, well, everyone said didn't he look just like a movie star? People were smitten with him and with Hally, whose discomposure was translated by the camera as languor, his pain as intensity—in other words, Hally found himself abruptly cast into the moody role of the sexy Second Coming.

"Jesus, Hal, you look like Brigitte Bardot," Spark said as he looked at the photos in print for the first time. "Next they'll be calling you the Baby-Dolly Lama. Look for yourself."

"Thanks. I don't want to see them. I mean it," Hally said as he walked from the room and toward the stairs.

"Come on, I was just kidding," Spark said. "You can't help it if the camera loves you." Looking amused as he came around the corner, Spark found Hally standing at the foot of the stairs, his hand on the banister, as Hugh bumped down from the second floor.

"What's wrong? Look. I was just joking around . . . Holy shit, now you can't even laugh? Hey, Hal, where are you going? Come on, I was kidding," Spark said, growing progressively more contrite as Hally brushed passed him in the hallway. In the background, Pastor Ragnar was talking loudly on the phone to someone, gleefully telling him about the *Life* magazine photos, about what this kind of exposure could mean for the church.

"It's not what it sounds like," Hugh said to Hally. "You know how he can be."

"Yeah. Sure. It's okay," Hally said to Hugh. "Don't worry about it." He kept on walking into the kitchen, Spark staring after him.

"Hally," he called out. "I really am sorry. All this . . . what's happened, it's not a joke. I know that."

Hally paused. "Except that it is a joke." He turned in one direction, then in another, almost as if he didn't know where to go, bumping into himself on all sides. He fled to the kitchen. The door opened, then shut behind him. I jumped up and looked out the window. He set out at a run, heading for the meadow.

"He'll be all right," Hugh said.

"Should I go after him?" Spark asked.

"I'd let him be."

"I'm never going to get this father thing right."

"It's not wrong for a kid to see his parent as a human being. You make a mistake. You say you're sorry. You try to do better. You're doing okay," Hugh said.

"Something seems off between Hally and Pop. Ever since the Cipolla thing. Have you noticed?" Spark said, fingering through a copy of the magazine, one of several spread out on the table.

"Maybe." Hugh seemed evasive.

"Something's happened," Spark said. "I recognize the symptoms."

"Spark. The rough stuff with Pop is behind us. I know, believe me. Why do you think I stuck around? I wanted to make sure Hally wasn't manhandled."

"I know that," Spark said, eyes lowering. "I owe you, Hugh."

"You don't owe me anything. All those years ago, when Hally was a baby . . . Spark . . . I should have intervened when Pop came after you that last day."

"Forget it."

"No, I can't forget it. He had no right to attack you like that. I watched him beat you up and I never spoke up or tried to defend you. You hadn't even been out of the hospital that long. I'm ashamed when I think about it all . . ."

"What were you supposed to do? You were just a kid. We were both terrified of him. Let's forget all that stuff. Crazy part of it is . . . I think he even feels bad about it."

"I know he does. He never laid a hand on me again after that day. He's never touched Hally except in affection. I swear to you, Spark, I wouldn't have allowed it."

"I know."

"If Pop got rough with him, Hally would say something."

"Would he?" Spark said. "I didn't."

"Pop's mellowed," Hugh said. "He's not proud of what he was like. He's changed. He's crazy about Hally . . . and . . . we'd know."

"Would we? Not all scars are visible," Spark said.

⧫⧫⧫⧫⧫

Thirty minutes and one slammed door later and Hally was back, pacing frantically, running his hands through his hair. "What do I do?" he said. "Where do I go?" I felt a ripple of dread.

"What's going on?" Hugh galloped down the stairs from the studio, paintbrush in hand.

"Bunch of people, they were waiting for me on the trail. I took off and some weird guy sprang out of the bushes and tried to grab me by the arm. I shook him off . . . Jesus, where do I go? What do I do?" He kept repeating himself. "I tried, Hugh, I don't want to do it anymore. I quit."

"Bloody lunatics," Hugh said. "Try to calm down. What did they want?"

"They want me to fix them. Some big fat guy with osteoarthritis in his knee is begging me to make him better. Quit stuffing your face! They want me to cure them. Cure them? I want to kill them!"

Hugh laughed. "I wouldn't want to be the guy who recommended you to God for the Miracle on Monhegan assignment right now."

"Oh man," Hally said, sliding into the chair next to Hugh at the kitchen table, "I hate to admit it but Spark's right. I'm not cut out for this. You probably have more faith than I do." He sounded miserable.

"What's that supposed to mean?" Spark caught the last bit as he walked in the front door. I rushed over to greet him after his trip to the village. "Are you saying you didn't see what you said you saw?"

"Don't get so excited . . . I saw what I saw, that's the point. It's not faith when you *know*, right?

"Ever think you've just moved on to a whole different set of faith questions? Maybe God's challenging you to have faith in what He's got planned," Spark said.

"Yeah, well, maybe I don't like what I'm seeing all that much. You want to think about what that feels like?"

"No, I don't. I'm way behind you on all this stuff, Hal. I'm still work-ing on having faith in you."

"You guys just don't get it."

"Hally, did Pastor Ragnar do something to upset you?" Spark said.

"No."

"He didn't hurt you?"

"No! Why would you guys think something like that? He's not like that."

"Because you don't seem like yourself," Hugh said.

"What's happening to you, Hally?" Spark said unhappily. "It used to be that all it took was a whoopee cushion and a Mars bar to make you jump for joy. Now, supposedly anyway, you know, I mean, you *really know*, the answer to the big question—there is a God, there is life everlast-ing—everybody thinks you're the Second Coming, and you're a big sack of misery. What's it going to take to make you happy?"

"What makes you think that I'm supposed to be happy?" Hally said.

There was so much noise on the shoreline most of the time—the colli-sion of wind and wave, the consonant shrieking of birds rippling in black waves across the sky as they were practically deboned by intermittent gusts. It was unaccountably quiet that clear night, the ever-circling birds, like sleek capsules, silently gliding, the only sounds the spooky swish of water against mossy rock and the low whistle of a solitary slender strand of wind.

Hugh held the door open for me as I stepped out onto the deck and lay down by the top of the steps. I liked to relax outside for an hour or so at night by myself. I had always needed time alone, time to think. My nose held high, the breeze blew back my ears, ruffling the hair on my head.

What was that? My ears rose up and forward even as my tail stiffened, the hair along my spine rising in a single spiked gesture, an ancient sequence of behaviors outside my control. I felt a deep rumble collect in the back of my throat.

Springing up, I barked with so much urgency that Hugh and Spark both came to the door while I rushed down the steps and howled into the darkness.

"What's going on, Neddy?" Spark asked, knowing I wasn't a frivolous barker.

"Who's there?" Hugh hollered, then waited as Spark went back into the house for a flashlight. He shone its beam out over the rocky beachfront to the part of the property where the long grasses grew. I barked louder as the beam of light picked them out where they squatted, here and there among the grasses, illuminating them in outline, singly and in couples and clusters. An infestation of people, men, women, young, old, and in between. One, there. Two, over there. Five, there. Three, over there. Another one, and another.

I kept barking but nobody moved.

The screen door opened and banged shut. Pastor Ragnar stopped to revel, marveled aloud, and began to take captivated inventory, as if he were charting stars in the evening sky.

"We'd like all of you to leave," Hugh said in a loud voice. "This isn't helpful to anyone."

"'It is good that he waits silently for the salvation of the Lord,'" said Pastor Ragnar.

"Go away. Get lost," Spark shouted into the blackness, the tall grasses swishing in hushed response. It sounded like whispering but it was only the lonely wind moving through the grass. No one moved. No one spoke. It wasn't human. How do people do it? Cease to be human while the ocean rocks inauspiciously this way and that and tall grasses rustle according to their nature and a dog barks.

Silent and full of purpose, they just continued to stare at the house in the belief that Hally would appear.

Sixteen

〰〰〰〰〰〰〰〰〰〰〰〰〰〰〰〰〰〰〰〰〰〰〰〰〰〰〰〰〰〰〰

Hally's mute acolytes were gone when we woke up early the next morning, leaving behind warm cradles of flattened grass, randomly arranged in the field like abandoned ground nests.

"Come on, Spark, let's get going," Hally said from the hallway, calling up the stairs. They were heading to the harbor to meet Beans. Hally was going out on the boat with Spark for a day of mackerel fishing. All part of Spark's latest plan to conventionalize Hally's life. Nothing more normal than the daily grind of a despised occupation, he said, outlining his strategy to Hugh.

"Hang on," Spark yelled from behind a closed door. "I'll be down in a minute. I just got out of the shower."

Hally's arm rose impatiently with his voice. He sighed and his fist dropped with a thud onto the balustrade, as if an invisible string overhead snapped.

"Tell Spark he can catch up with me," he said, dashing through the kitchen, reaching for a jacket and grabbing a pear from the fruit bowl on the counter.

"Can't you wait?" Hugh said. "I don't like the idea of you heading out alone . . . especially after the night of the living dead . . ."

"I don't need a bodyguard," Hally said, taking a bite of the pear.

"I'm not so sure about that," Hugh said.

"Have you seen these people? They're not exactly special forces."

"Hally—"

"I'm fine, Hugh. See you later." He popped open the screen door and was gone before I had a chance to follow. I watched from the window as he ran toward the trail in the half-light, tossing the partially eaten pear high overhead and into the wildflower field. Jumping down, legs throbbing to get going, I leapt up at the door.

"No, no, Neddy," Hugh said, latching the door. "You can't go. They're going out on the boat. You stay here."

I flopped down in place and curled up in the corner by the door, making plans of my own. I didn't need to wait long. A few minutes passed and I heard Spark coming down the stairs. Hugh went into the study. I jumped to my feet and scratched on the screen door when Spark walked into the room.

"You want out, Ned?" Spark asked absently as he unlatched the door. I pushed it open with my nose and bolted. Leaping out onto the deck, I sprinted toward the meadow, free as dogs were meant to be, scrambling over rock and bounding along the winding trails, running to find Hally. The moment I spotted him I headed off at full tilt to join him, was in mid-dash when I saw a man appear from the trees along the trail. I paused, momentarily surprised.

The man was speaking to Hally. I could see him smiling, a big friendly grin. By the way he was moving, pleasant, scratching his head, gesturing with arms out wide, I guessed he was asking for directions. Something about Hally's demeanor was a little off, but then I got close enough that I heard Hally say goodbye, saw him as he resumed walking, the man moving away, in the opposite direction.

I put my nose to the ground, distracted by a fresh scent—rabbit, maybe, or a groundhog. I snuffled around for a minute or two. When I looked back up Hally was gone. I ran to the spot where I'd last seen him.

"Neddy!" Spark said, arriving seconds later, panting, catching up with me. "Now I've got to take you back home. Oh, what the hell? Do you want to come fishing?"

I wagged my tail in halfhearted greeting. He looked at me, confused by my lack of enthusiasm. Then he noticed Hally's backpack in the tall grass beside the dirt trail. My tail drooped.

"What's going on? Where's Hally?" He looked around and called Hally's name. From the woods came a muffled sound, like a thwarted cry. I dashed into the brush, followed by Spark.

"Hally!" he shouted.

In a small clearing ahead, we saw him. Hally was down on all fours, crawling, scrambling, and trying to get to his feet, blood on his face, dirt on his pants, his shirt. Shock—I felt its platinum surge, as if I had touched a live wire. I can still see his white skin, his red blood, the terracotta dirt stains on the knees of his pants. For the briefest of seconds, I felt as if I had been turned inside out, all that was inside me raked by claws.

As we neared, the man I'd seen earlier rushed up behind Spark and spun him around by the shoulders. He was middle-aged, long hair hanging to his shoulders in oily coils, a big man, wearing cutoff jeans and a dirty white T-shirt embossed with the image of the Shroud of Turin. He wound up and threw a punch at Spark, hitting him in the eye.

Spark reeled backward as Hally staggered to his feet, Spark yelling at him to run, run, run. The man grabbed Hally by his forearms and was pulling him down the path and deeper into the woods. I charged, leapt up and chomped down on his exposed calf. Still he held on to Hally, who was struggling violently to get free as Spark, recovering, threw himself at the man, climbing onto his back, pulling his hair, punching him in the head, causing him to twist and swing his arms, forcing him to let go of Hally's right arm.

Spark was a scrapper, not a slugger like this brute he was up against. He tried to strike out at Spark, finally scraped him off against a tree, all the while kicking out with his feet trying to get free of me. Hally fell down to the ground and before he could recover his balance the man was dragging him by his arm along the rocky path again.

He half hollered, half growled at us as we kept on him, he was breathing hard, kept lashing out at us, a bear among bees, all the while trying to maintain a grip on Hally who was twisting and fighting. Hally wasn't a big kid, nor especially powerful, but in his own way, he had a ferocious spirit and he wasn't going down easy.

It was awful but it was wonderful, too, all of us in there swinging. You think you couldn't kill anyone and then something happens, something like nothing you've ever experienced in your whole life and all you taste is their blood. What I wouldn't have given in that moment to be a Tibetan mastiff. I would have torn out his throat, painted my face with his shredded remains, and bayed at the moon until sunrise.

Spark broke off, frantically looked around and grabbed a thick tree branch lying on the ground. Using both hands he brought it down across the back of the man's skull. The man tumbled forward. There was a moment, an opening. Spark grabbed Hally's hand and yanked hard, the two of them took off, Hally stumbling, Spark pulling him along, keeping him upright, heading for the trail that led back home. My teeth were still buried in that bastard's fleshy ankle—he tasted like spiced sausage and rust.

"Neddy!" Spark shouted. "Neddy! Come on!"

I bit down hard. The man yelled and swore and tried to kick me with his other foot, dealing me a glancing blow in the shoulder. I flew forward and spun out onto the ground but quickly jumped to my feet and dashed ahead just out of his reach as he followed, running after us, oh, but there wasn't a chance in hell that big fat son-of-a-bitch could catch us.

I was sailing in the air and singing, that's how exhilarated I was as we made our dash to freedom. I couldn't have been any more excited than if we'd left him for dead.

The bastard had hit Hally in the head with a rock, leaving a big oval bump at his hairline that oozed blood onto the sofa cushions and stained his face. His shirt collar was red.

Pastor Ragnar stayed with him in the living room, covered him with a blanket, held a compress to his forehead, and spoke softly to him. Hugh was there. Spark was there, too, his eye black and swollen and nearly shut. He dropped off Hally and immediately left again, though Hugh insisted he stay put, but he wouldn't listen, took off sprinting in search of the man who'd done this. Hugh reached for the phone. He called the sheriff's office, he called for a doctor, he called island people he knew and they immediately started searching the area.

"Who else do I call?" Hugh said, helplessly looking to me for an answer.

The sheriff wanted to speak to Hally. He came to the house but by the time he got there, Hally was sedated and upstairs in bed where he was ordered to remain by the doctor. Pastor Ragnar said tomorrow was soon enough. Anyway, Spark could provide him with all the details he needed when he got back.

Have Spark call me, the sheriff said—just as Spark appeared in the wildflower meadow, walking slowly toward the house.

"Ow, that's quite a shiner," the sheriff said, wincing when he saw Spark's eye, which by now was fused shut, the right side of his face black and blue. Everyone turned around and went back into the house. Hugh wrapped a bag of frozen peas in a tea towel and gave it to Spark, who pressed it against his eye, his cheek, his forehead.

He took some aspirin and sipped tea from a mug. Hugh gave his shoulder a squeeze. Spark reached up and put his hand on his brother's in a gesture I felt in my heart more than I saw with my eyes.

"The doctor wants us to wake Hally up every couple of hours, make sure he's okay," Hugh was explaining.

"He's all right, though?" Spark asked.

"It seems like it," Hugh said.

"He's going to be fine," Pastor Ragnar said.

Spark answered the sheriff's questions. This is a very serious incident, the sheriff said, obviously instigated by a man with bad intentions. He welcomed speculation as to his identity. Spark said he didn't recognize him specifically. "I do recognize the type," he said. "I recognize the fanaticism."

"Go on," the sheriff said.

"These night-crawling crackpot followers of Hally's. They show up at dusk and stay until dawn."

"How do they get here?"

"Spaceship," Spark said. "I don't know. The guy I work for says he's seen them arrive by the boatload."

"I see where they must be a nuisance . . . but this guy seems to be a horse of a different color . . . Kind of a rogue elephant . . . Any idea what he might have been after?"

Spark shook his head. "Nothing good. Who knows with these kooks?"

The sheriff, seldom looking up, finished writing in his notepad, thanked him and stood up to leave.

"Say," he said, slightly hesitant, "since I'm here . . . it's maybe not the best time to bring it up but about the other matter that's still pending . . . Where does Hally's mother fit into all this? Who is she, by the way?" he asked awkwardly.

"Sounds to me as if you already know the answers to those questions," Spark said.

"Look, Spark . . . people will talk. One of the old-timers says Hally is Frederick MacNamara's grandson."

"Let me guess: Arche Wallace . . . no, not Arche. Mrs. Houton," Spark said.

"The source doesn't matter. It makes no difference to me except that the MacNamaras are a very prominent family with money and influence and powerful connections. The Wrendles have got wind of it somehow and they're all over me about it, accusing me of not charging the boy out of fear of the family, even suggesting the sheriff's office has been pressured. They're threatening to file a complaint. I guess I would have appreciated hearing about it from you in the beginning."

"Not so great being on the receiving end of a false accusation, is it?" Spark said.

Pastor Ragnar, who had been silent, tried a more conciliatory approach. "Think about our side of it. What would you have concluded about our intentions if we had brought up the connection?"

"Fair enough," the sheriff conceded. "I'm surprised, though, with all the . . . recent . . . um . . . attention in the press that the relationship hasn't come out."

"It's not common knowledge or is mostly forgotten and the people who do know or suspect they know aren't the type who are going to gossip to the press," Pastor Ragnar said. "I've always assumed it would become public at some point. Why volunteer?"

"Just consider this a friendly heads-up—the Wrendles are also threatening to tell the press about everything. They figure this stuff with the um . . . Virgin Mary sighting . . . is, in Bill Wrendle's words, 'a snare and a delusion,' whatever the hell that means . . . either that, he said, or the boy needs a good psychiatrist."

"Another great mind at work," Pastor Ragnar said.

"Well, so you say, but, plenty of folks might see his point," the sheriff said. "He could do your boy some harm. You and your church, too, I'm sorry to say, Pastor Ragnar—he's bringing up the controversies about the failed concert, the rumors you stole money, says you're a bad family and someone needs to put a stop to you and he says he will, if we don't bring charges soon."

"You're still thinking about charges?" Spark said. "I thought this thing had crawled away and died a natural death."

"Nothing's final yet," the sheriff said. "I've got the Wrendles hounding me about when I intend to lay charges and the Monahans insisting I drop the whole thing. I'm just waiting for the MacNamaras to descend."

"You have no evidence," Hugh said.

"What I do have is a serious allegation of break and enter, of theft, of serious vandalism, to say nothing of impropriety. I have a girl's testimony. You wouldn't be the first family to believe their perfect son could commit no wrong."

Spark rolled forward onto his feet. "I really resent that remark. Hally's the one under attack. The girl is lying. These goddamn Wrendles are like circling vultures."

Pastor Ragnar put his hand on Spark's shoulder, holding him in place, symbolically at least.

"You'll have to forgive my son," he said. "He's had a tough day." He let go of Spark and moved toward the door alongside the sheriff. "Thank you, sheriff, for all you've done. We appreciate your fairness and continue to count on your balanced approach. I have every confidence you'll do the right thing. As for the Wrendles, they had better look out."

"Don't know whether I like the sound of that," the sheriff said.

"I mean only that there are laws protecting people from libel and slander and defamation. For that matter, Fred MacNamara isn't a man to be trifled with. They might want to think twice about invoking his name unfavorably in the press."

There was a hint of intimacy, of immediacy, circulating in the tone of his voice. I wondered if Spark and Hugh had caught it.

"Yes, well, none of that's my concern," the sheriff said, putting away his notepad and offering assurances that he would do his best to track down Hally's assailant.

Spark, who had obviously picked up the same thing as me, waited until the sheriff left before confronting his father. "Have you been in touch with Old Man MacNamara?"

"We've spoken over the years. I thought it was prudent."

"Recently?" Spark couldn't conceal his surprise.

"A few days ago."

"Why didn't you say something?"

"I didn't want the headache, frankly. You and Fred MacNamara aren't exactly a mutual admiration society . . . Hugh knows all about it."

Hugh responded to Spark's inquiring look. "It's no big deal, Spark. MacNamara calls maybe once or twice a year to find out how Hally's doing. Flory was their only child. Hally is all they have of her. It's no big secret. I didn't mention it because I figured, why get you all worked up unnecessarily? He's never asked to see Hally. It's not like he helps support him."

"Oh, he's tried. I won't have it," Pastor Ragnar said.

"What?" Hugh looked stunned. "That's news to me. He's tried what?"

"To see him—on the down-low, of course. To send money. The moment we accept money and attention from that family they will feel entitled to interfere with how we raise Hally," Pastor Ragnar said. "This way they're relegated to the role of interested bystanders."

"I can't believe I'm saying this, but I agree with you," Spark said, though Hugh looked a little long suffering. "Does Hally know Mac-Namara calls about him?"

Hugh shook his head. "No. Why start something percolating inside him for no good reason?"

"Fortunately, they're not inclined to press matters because they don't want people to know Flory had a baby outside of marriage. A baby she subsequently deserted after . . . well, they don't want to start talking about all of that. They managed to keep everything under wraps, thanks to our cooperation all those years ago. Thank God for the gift of their small medieval minds," Pastor Ragnar said.

"Except that I did marry her," Spark said casually. My turn to be surprised. "What? Did you think I'd forgotten?'

"You *did not marry* Flory," Pastor Ragnar said, "because if you had married her the MacNamaras would be all over Hally. Even if we threatened to reveal everything—"

"Which we wouldn't do in any case," Spark interrupted, making his feelings clear.

"We wouldn't be able to compete with their resources. He would be lost to us."

"You really think so? Even now?" Spark said. "I never really got the secret marriage thing. I only went along because Flory was terrified her father would have her kidnapped and the marriage annulled if he ever found out about it. Then you got involved . . ."

Hugh got up and adjusted a painting that was hanging crookedly on the wall.

"Flory was right. The only thing worse in Fred MacNamara's mind than having an illegitimate grandchild was having you for a son-in-law. If he knew your union was legal, he would have cut his losses, pounced on his grandson, and may have had you murdered to boot. Anyway, what does it matter because a marriage never took place?" Pastor Ragnar said.

"I guess you figure if you say it enough it won't be true," Spark said. He held his hand to his forehead, wincing in pain. "Hally should know. He already has me pegged as a guy who knocked up his mother, didn't give a damn, then ran out on her after running around on her. Maybe if he knew we got married . . ."

"Are you quite sure it's Hally's romanticism that you're thinking of?" Pastor Ragnar said.

"How's your eye, Spark? Can I get you something?" Hugh said.

Spark shook his head and looked appreciatively over at his brother before turning his attention back to Pastor Ragnar. "Does MacNamara know I'm back home?"

"No. He's quite happy to think you're not involved with Hally's life. Let's keep it that way. He still blames you for what happened, swears you drove Flory to madness."

"How? By leaving dirty dishes in the sink? She had a disease. I can only imagine what the old man had to say about the apparition stuff," Spark said, changing the subject, lying back down on the sofa, compress to his face.

"Predictably conflicted," Pastor Ragnar said, picking up on his cue. "Worried that history may be repeating itself. I assured him that's not the case. Hally's mind is sound."

"The MacNamaras are Irish Catholics. They're not that far removed from believing in the little people. Of course, they already see themselves as special in the eyes of God. The Virgin Mary appearing to their grandson only makes it official, though Fred's still having trouble understanding why Hally's status as a bastard entitles him to a visit from the Holy Mother.

"He appears to think he has higher moral standards than God."

"If I didn't know better, I'd say that you're sounding a little skeptical about the apparitions," Spark said slyly, pulling himself up into a sitting position.

"Ah, but as you say, you know better," Pastor Ragnar said, patting him on the knee.

Late that night, Spark sat in a chair next to the bed where I lay beside Hally as he slept. The door opened and Hugh slipped inside.

"You should go to bed," he said. "You look wiped out. I'll check on Hally through the night."

"Thanks," Spark said. "Think I'll just sit for a little while longer."

"Sure," Hugh said, pausing. "He looks so much like Flory, lying there. Amazing, the resemblance . . . You don't see it?" Hugh said, reacting to Spark's noncommittal expression.

Spark shrugged. "I guess. A bit."

"That conversation with Pop earlier . . ."

"I know. Makes me want to blow my brains out."

"Go to bed. Sleep it off."

"Soon," Spark said as Hugh left. He looked sideways at Hally, his glance furtive. Legs extended, he leaned back in the chair, back of his head touching the wall, head bent forward now, tears flowing unchecked down his cheeks.

"Spark, are you okay?" Hally asked, waking up.

Spark rubbed his eyes and, reaching out, flipped off the switch on the table lamp, so the room's only illumination was the light from the moon.

"Yeah, I'm fine," he replied, hastily pulling himself together. "What about you? How are you doing?"

"My head is killing me."

"Go back to sleep. You'll feel better in the morning."

"Did they catch him?"

"They will. Forget about him. You're safe. That's all that matters."

"It was the same guy . . . as the other day. The guy who jumped out and tried to grab me by the arm . . . It took me a minute to recognize him. There was something different but . . . Remember, I told you about him."

"Yeah, I remember. Don't worry. He's not going to bother you anymore."

"You don't need to stay with me."

"Sure I do," Spark said, hands on the bedcovers. He reached out and stroked the top of my head.

"Spark?"

"I'm here."

"I wish none of this had ever happened. I wish she'd appeared to somebody else. Somebody who cared about religion and being holy and doing good works. Spark, I don't even like it when the school makes us volunteer at the old folks' home."

"I used to hate it, too."

"I even quit the Red Cross Club."

"Me, too."

"So why'd she pick me? Why didn't she pick somebody like Ansel Roberts?"

"Who's Ansel Roberts?"

"This kid at my school who's always thinking of ways to help his community and he's always lecturing everybody about doing more. It's like, no matter what you do, it's never enough."

"Every school's got a kid like that. Mine was Brad Landymore. He was always holding car washes for charity and organizing rallies, trying to get everyone to donate their Christmas gifts to the poor. Shaving his head in solidarity with some cause or another. Acting disappointed when you didn't volunteer to spend your Saturday afternoon at a soup kitchen. I told him I'd start going when he stopped so I wouldn't have to run headfirst into his wall of goodness."

"Ow . . . don't make me laugh," Hally said.

"Landymore was the type who makes a career out of whining that girls never go for nice guys. Meanwhile, I once caught him pouring lighter fluid on ants and setting them on fire. Obviously, even God can't stand these guys," Spark said. "I mean, if you've got all the kids in the world to choose from, are you really going to single out some secret sadist and budding junior Rotarian? Hey, Hal, think about it. Looks like the Virgin Mary is just another example of a woman who's bored by nice guys . . ." Spark was just getting warmed up.

"Stop, I mean it," Hally begged, holding his hands at his temples. He took a deep breath. "What about my mom? Was she bored by nice guys?"

"What do you think?" Spark said.

In the small silence I heard them. I leapt to my feet and rushed to the window barking. Spark told Hally to stay in bed as he came up alongside me.

"What the hell?" he said as we watched the singing sisters, their mother, and others from the church gather, assembling soberly below Hally's bedroom window.

"Bring flowers of the rarest, bring flowers of the fairest . . ." It was the Tick-Tock Girls.

"Oh no," Hally whispered weakly from his bed, recognizing the singers and the song.

"Your virgin brides await, O Lord," Spark said.

"Everywhere I go, they're there," Hally said. "Spark . . ."

"Yeah?"

"What you did . . . coming after that guy . . ."

"I know. I even impressed myself," Spark said.

"Would you cut it out for once? I'm trying to thank you."

"Forget it. You're my kid."

Maybe Spark didn't want thanks, but I barked sharply, looking for a little recognition for my own part in the rescue. They laughed.

"I swear Ned understands every word we say," Spark said.

I barked again in acknowledgment. Amused, Spark opened wide the window, leaned outside, and shouted for everyone to get lost, but it didn't matter, they acted as if they hadn't heard him, just kept on singing.

It didn't matter to them if they were wanted or not, their group growing in numbers through the night, something aberrantly Zen about their unblinking zeal, the same song, like a chant, repeating again beneath the blue-gray light of the moon.

"O Mary, we crown thee with blossoms today / Queen of the angels and Queen of the May."

Seventeen

"Classes start next week. We need to make a decision. We need to pull Hally from school," Pastor Ragnar announced from the kitchen table, the matter already concluded. "It's not safe for him. There's no point pretending any longer he's ordinary. Sometimes special people require special handling."

Hugh's unhappiness tended to express itself as a household chore or a sudden intense preoccupation with a spot or a stain. He got up from the kitchen table and mindlessly began to wipe down the counter.

"It's the only experience of normalcy he has," he said, without much conviction.

"Do you want to risk another episode like what happened here a week ago?"

"How can you ask me such a thing?" Hugh stopped cleaning and looked at his father.

"You want to continue to pretend . . . well, keep it up. Especially with that lunatic still on the loose. You're playing Russian roulette with his safety. No one is suggesting that he can't have friends." Pastor Ragnar paused to reach for a slice of banana bread. "Friends are overrated."

"It won't be the same for him."

"Well, that's the point, isn't it? Nothing is the same anymore."

"You need to talk to Spark about this. He should have a say in what happens to his own son."

"He forfeited his right to a vote all those years ago when he walked out on him."

"It's not quite that simple. He was only a kid himself. Everything was a mess with Flory. He was a disaster. The two of you were at odds. Same with Mom. He did the best he could."

"You're your brother's champion now? What's brought this on?"

"I'm older. I see things a little differently. That last day, all he wanted to do was say goodbye to the baby. You . . . forced him from the house. Wouldn't take his calls. After everything he'd been through . . . It wasn't right, Pop."

"It didn't give me any pleasure. He was drinking. He was behaving irresponsibly. He was upsetting your mother and making life at home miserable for everyone. He wasn't safe around the baby. It was going to end in disaster for all of us. I gave him several chances to straighten up. He gave me no choice."

"I used to believe that, too, but I was wrong."

"I had a ship to keep afloat and it was sinking fast. I did what needed to be done. I make no apologies."

"Pop, it was hard for everyone. I'm not trying to cast blame. I think we should cut one another some slack . . . Anyway, I'm glad Spark's home now. It's been good."

"Bully for that, but right now Hally is what's important. Hally and his visions should be our uppermost concern."

Back to scrubbing. "I don't want to talk about the stuff with Hally, what he claims he saw . . ."

"You mean the Virgin Mary? You can say it. Nobody's going

to cancel your subscription to *The New Yorker* just for saying her name."

"Come on, Pop. Give it a rest, please. I've got commitments. I've got a show to mount, for crying out loud. I've already postponed trips to New York. My gallery is starting to think there's some kind of issue with me. I can't think straight . . ."

"I see. I'm sorry the monumental events of the summer are interfering with your little art show."

"Do you have to act like this? I've tried to be supportive. I don't know what more I can do. We have different beliefs, that's all."

Pastor Ragnar eased backward in his chair, breaking off a piece of banana bread and putting it in his mouth. "This is delicious, by the way . . . Right now, Hugh, what I believe is that it's in the best interest of my grandson to leave school."

"What happens now?" Spark said, home after his first day back on *The Winnie Cat* since the attack. "Hally starts collecting cans by the side of the road?"

"We can arrange for a tutor and he can finish his year doing independent study," Hugh said. He was cleaning out the kitchen cupboards and avoiding Spark's eyes. "It's not so bad, Spark."

"We promised we'd keep him in school. He's so alone. He needs to make some friends . . ."

"There are too many nuts around. For all we know that creep is still lurking on the island somewhere."

"That's the point of a promise. It's something you keep no matter what, or you don't make it."

Hugh looked frazzled. He ran his hands through his hair.

"Talk to Pop, . . . not me."

Spark was standing in the middle of the living room.

"Don't look at me that way, Spark. I mean it," Hugh said without turning around to see exactly how Spark was looking at him. He didn't need to. He knew. It was the same way he was looking at himself.

Once he accepted he wouldn't be going to school, Hally used to spend most of his time in his bedroom, sitting by himself staring out to sea, late summer air rushing in through the window screen. Sometimes he whistled for me to join him.

"You're alone way too much, Hally," Hugh said one day in the studio as Hally watched him paint. "You should be out having fun, making friends, playing spin the bottle . . ."

He looked disappointed when Hally let his deliberately dated reference go unchallenged, but carried on, trying to goad him into rallying. ". . . Lying to all of us and sneaking around. There's something to be said for sneaking around." He gave him a hopeful glance, but Hally wasn't listening.

"Hugh, do you think I can ever be normal again?"

Hugh stared at the canvas in front of him, focusing intently, acting as if he hadn't heard him.

"Hey, Hal, would you mind grabbing me something to drink?" he said.

Hally stared at him for a moment, a futile attempt to get Hugh to put down his paintbrush and look at him.

"Sure," Hally said finally as he got up and went downstairs and opened the fridge and poured a drink. Apple juice. No ice. He came back up the stairs and handed the tall glass to Hugh and then he left the room, tripping down the stairs, with their scuffed and peeling hand-painted flower and bird and animal motifs, and Hugh looked after him for the longest time, and even after he had disappeared he kept looking after him.

〜〜〜〜〜

Pastor Ragnar hired DeeDee White, a schoolteacher and dance instructor (the same woman Hugh tried to convince Hally he'd seen on Black Head), to tutor Hally four hours a day. She had become a member of his congregation after the apparitions and was visibly thrilled to be playing a role in Hally's education. Despite her eccentricities, she was highly qualified academically, which made her "proclivities" all the more glaring—imagine a fairy armed with a master's from Radcliffe.

A certifiable adult—she was in her mid-forties—she tended to favor flowing dresses and wore her long brown hair in a kind of frizzy Renaissance canopy that hung below her shoulders to mid-back, suggesting she had arrested stylistically in the sixties, a forever ingenue with a doughy jawline and a skewering earnestness that made every conversation with her feel as if you were a hapless butterfly pinned to a spreading board.

Her daily presence around the house was keenly felt and made its own patchouli-scented contribution to the summer's madness. Hugh had perfected the art of being friendly while maintaining a comfortable distance, giving the polite impression he'd love to talk if only he weren't on such a tight deadline with his show. Pastor Ragnar was always on the verge of departure, with—so sorry!—barely time to say hello. Hally sat attentively enough during her lessons—she was an inexplicably good teacher—exiting the room at the first opportunity, before things turned personal. Spark, on the other hand, not so much. Everything he was, everything he thought and felt, was on open gaping display for everyone to see and his engagement levels were epic, which tended to make him the target of anyone with something to say.

Hugh, Hally, and I listened from the top of the stairs in the studio one morning as Spark, waylaid by DeeDee, tried to eat his breakfast before heading out to help Beans do repairs on the boat.

"I'm quite comfortable in other dimensions," DeeDee was telling him.

"Oh yeah? I can see where that might come in handy," Spark said agreeably.

"Yes, I've spent a great deal of time with a medium, regressing . . . I was a man in another life. I was decapitated fighting the powers that be . . . It's made me realize how unimportant gender is."

"Heads, too, I guess . . . Regression is kind of a specialty of mine . . ." Spark said, obviously enjoying himself. Spark loved fools almost as much as they loved him.

"Oh, I'm not surprised," DeeDee said. "The moment I met you I sensed we were kindred spirits. You felt it, too, didn't you? Something special between us?"

Hugh and Hally looked at each other in silent delight at this new turn of events.

"I didn't *not* sense it," Spark said.

"I'd love to make you dinner some night. The thing is . . . I don't play games, Spark, I find you very sexually attractive," she said as Hally clapped his hand over his mouth, Hugh shushing him, eager to hear more.

There was a moment of silence before Spark finally spoke. "Um, thank you. You're . . . a handsome woman, and as much as I'd love to explore your suggestion . . . I feel a little uncomfortable because you're Hally's teacher. It might not be appropriate under the circumstances, if you see what I'm saying . . ."

"I never imagined you were such a traditionalist. You don't give that impression. Oh well, that has it's own appeal, doesn't it? I think I admire you, Spark Monahan," she said perkily. "Just remember, my door is never locked. In your case, it will never even be closed."

"Good to know," Spark said, the chair scraping against the floor as he pushed himself away from the table.

"Hally tells me you like to read, another thing we have in common," DeeDee said. "I'm reading the Tibetan Book of the Dead. I'll lend it to you when I'm finished."

"I can't wait," Spark said, the sound of the kitchen door opening and closing behind him.

"Oh man," Hally whispered to Hugh, "this was worth being pulled from school."

Later that evening, at dinner, Hally asked Spark to please pass the salad. "This is really good, Hugh," he said as Hugh looked pleased. "Have all you want, there's lots," he said.

Everyone looked up as Pastor Ragnar emerged from the hall and sat down at the table. He closed his eyes as if he was saying a silent prayer, then reopened them. "That was the sheriff. The Wrendles have withdrawn their complaint against Hally. The girl has admitted she was lying after her parents found some of the money hidden in her room. The whole thing came out. She said she destroyed her father's research as part of a plan to discredit Hally and protect herself."

"Oh, thank heaven," Hugh said, putting his arm around Hally, who was sitting next to him. "Such a relief."

Hally's head lowered. When he looked up, he was smiling, eyes moist. "Wow," he said, biting his bottom lip.

"That's really great news, kid," Spark said, leaning across the table, taking both of Hally's hands in his. Straightening back up, he looked down at the food on his plate, poked around with his fork, and then glanced up at Pastor Ragnar.

"Do you know anything about this?" Spark asked him.

"What do you mean?'

"The timing just seems weird. The girl has had ample opportunity to tell the truth. Why now? One minute this Wrendle guy is threatening to blow up the world if Hally's not arrested and the next he's calling to say, 'Oh, never mind.' Seems strange, that's all."

"'Every good gift and every perfect gift is from above, coming down from the Father of Lights, with whom can be no variation, neither shadow that is cast by turning,'" Pastor Ragnar said.

"A simple 'Yes, I know' or 'No, I don't' would work," Spark said.

"Anyone like some tea?" Hugh asked getting up from his seat. Poor Hugh. I wagged my tail empathetically.

"I only know what the sheriff told me and that, my dear Jamie, is cause for celebration," Pastor Ragnar said, leaning back in his chair. "Did I hear a rumor about a peach pie?"

"You did. Anybody else want some?" Hugh asked. "Spark?"

"Sure."

"Hally?"

"Yes, please," Hally said, glancing down at me. "Want to share with me, Neddy?" I jumped into his lap. I had a terrible weakness for pastry and Hally could always be relied on to be generous.

"Crack open the vanilla ice cream while you're at it. Let's do it up right," Pastor Ragnar said, reaching out and fondly rubbing the top of Hally's head.

I looked on happily though I couldn't help but wonder about the necklace Hally kept hidden away in his room. If it wasn't the Sex Family girl's miraculous medal, whose was it?

Later that night around midnight, after Hugh and Hally had retired for the evening, Spark sought out Pastor Ragnar in his study. His father glanced up briefly from his desk when he saw Spark enter, then continued working on whatever it was he was writing.

"Make your point, Jamie," he said, without looking up.

"So what was it? Threats or money or a combination of both?"

"Fred offered Bill Wrendle a sizable amount of money to drop the allegations against Hally and he was also prepared to threaten him with all sorts of unsavory consequences if he didn't agree. It never got that far."

"You two guys do know you're breaking the law . . ."

"Since when is that any sort of concern to you?"

Spark ignored the familiar paternal rebuke. "Why take the risk? Wrendle could have flipped his lid and gone to the sheriff and the press with the whole story. This thing was dead in the water. They were never going to charge Hally. They would have been forced to, though, if Wrendle had proven to be a man of integrity."

"Highly unlikely." Pastor Ragnar laughed. "You're not old enough to realize how few such men there are in the world. Everyone has a price."

Spark didn't look impressed. "That's not true."

"Dream on, laddie . . . We didn't even factor it into the equation. It was precisely because there weren't likely to be charges that we had to act. Wrendle was getting ready to go to the press about everything. He *longed* to do it. It would have been a disaster for the church, for the family, for Hally, and might also have resulted in face-saving charges being laid by an embarrassed sheriff's office, to say nothing of a civil suit, which was surely in the offing, regardless."

"So Wrendle takes the money and what's to stop him at some point from growing a conscience and coming forward with the whole tawdry mess?"

"It's a great deal of money, Spark. Besides the fact that he'd have no credibility if he were to reverse himself at some later date, the man isn't a fool. MacNamara would destroy, not just him, but his entire family. Even his lawn wouldn't be safe."

"The emperor of all things strikes again."

"Don't kid yourself. He could make it happen by snapping his fingers and Fred likes to snap his fingers."

Spark walked over to the bookcase and randomly pulled a volume from a crowded shelf. He leafed through the pages.

"I don't know why you want to be involved with that ruthless SOB."

Pastor Ragnar set down his pen and closed his notebook. "We understand each other and we have a mutual interest in our grandson."

Spark replaced the book. "Maybe. What if the dam breaks?"

"The dam will hold."

"Hubris, Pop." Spark said. "Nobody's ever got all the angles figured. Not even God, according to you—isn't that what Cludo's all about?"

"Why, Jamie, I had no idea you were paying attention." Pastor Ragnar rose to his feet, ending the conversation.

"Oh, you might be surprised how attentive I am," Spark said as the two of them headed toward the stairs, Spark, pausing to let his father go on ahead even as he reached out and touched his sleeve, both of them stopping in the middle of the stairs. "You're wrong, you know, when you say that everyone has a price."

"Jamie, I've fought in a war, traveled the world and lived in three different countries. I've seen things . . . How would you know anything about it?"

"Frederick MacNamara once told me to name my price to stay away from Flory."

Pastor Ragnar looked momentarily surprised but quickly checked himself. "What did you say?"

"There was nothing to say. I don't have one."

"Oh my God, Jamie, how deluded you are," Pastor Ragnar said. "You're like your little red shadow here." He nodded in my direction. "You can be owned outright for the cost of a tender glance, a kind word, and a warm bed."

Don't forget the peach pie, I thought to myself, even as I found myself hating him for his cruelty in that moment. For all Pastor Ragnar thought he knew about the price of others, he seriously discounted, as men of his type inevitably do, the capacity of others to surprise.

※※※※※

Pastor Ragnar's mission was to make Cludo and himself a mainstream cultural presence and with Hally's help, and now Frederick Mac-Namara's, he was succeeding. Cludo, his demeanor suggested, was neither a cult nor a religion, it was a caste.

His refusal to recruit followers by means of the classic come-ons—prayer for hire, histrionics, scriptural acrobatics, the erection of monuments to God, dubious retreats and expensive seminars—even helped persuade the public that there was legitimacy to his claims about Hally and his visions at Black Head.

Observing it all from my privileged seat—the lies, the deceptions, the stumbles, the pratfalls, the doubts, the certainties, the delusions—one thing stayed true: Hally Monahan was being groomed by his grandfather to be an imperfect god, the ideal modern messiah, a baby Jesus with relatable flaws, an aversion to preaching, and great hair. Good but not so good as to be off-putting. Wicked enough to be interesting but not so wicked as to be unkind.

A savior in need of saving.

Pastor Ragnar had his redeemer.

Eighteen

"What do you think?" Hugh said, barely able to conceal his excitement, summoning us upstairs to his studio. It was the second week of September. He wanted us to see his work before it was shipped to New York for his upcoming show the beginning of November.

"Wow," Spark said, looking at the series of oil paintings crammed on every inch of the whitewashed walls of the loft studio. They ranged in size, some smaller than a cereal box, others were as high as the ceiling and ran the length of the wall. When he ran out of places to hang them, Hugh leaned paintings against one another and piled them on the floor. One was propped against a steel cart he used to hold his paints and brushes.

"This is fantastic. What do you think? You must be happy."

Hugh looked pleased but he was a modest guy at heart. "I don't know. I hope they're okay. Not for me to say. I'm just glad to be done."

"Hugh, these are all awesome," Hally said. I followed his gaze. Tucked away around the corner in a separate nook was a large painting displayed on an oversize homemade easel. I was stunned to see my portrait in oil, painted in various striking shades of blue on a huge canvas, my eyes glowing magenta.

"That's wild," Spark said, delighted. "Ned, what do you think about being a muse?"

"That is so neat. What's it called?" Hally asked.

"Purveyor of Wonderment," Hugh said. "What else?"

"This is one time when I have no objection to a member of this family being elevated to the status of a god," Spark said. "You've earned it, right, Neddy?"

Hugh and Hally continued to talk and I was vain enough to enjoy being the focus of their attention, though I kept an eye out for Spark, who wandered off among the paintings. One in particular compelled his interest. He examined it for a long time until finally Hugh came over and stood alongside him. Spark glanced up at him: "Why don't you tell us what you really think?" he said.

The painting, a nocturne, a good size, more long than wide, was executed, like my portrait, in shades of blue, though the effect was not the same. A blue-black night sky, with pinpricks of starlight, wrapped a little girl in its vastness, making her seem as if she were both fixed and floating somewhere in space. She had bare arms and wore a simple white-blue dress, Mary Janes on her small feet. On her head was a tall pointed hood, and in her hands she clutched to her chest a large crucifix with mournful Christ figure, while seeming to extend it outward and away from herself. Her mouth was open as if she was crudely hollering—a lovely child made ugly, harsh, stupid even, by the hardness of her eyes and the cruelty of her shouting mouth.

"What have you been hiding all these years? I had no idea you had it in you, brother," Spark said as Hugh's face flushed pink. "Has Pop seen this?"

"No. Pop's not interested in my work. I'd have to get picked up by a museum before he'd take notice and I don't see much chance of that happening in my future." There was no self-pity or recrimination in his words. Hugh may have been the younger brother but Spark had a tendency to lean on him and I was starting to understand why.

"Don't sell yourself short, Hugh," Spark said.

Hally approached the painting of the girl and taking up a spot next to Spark, looked at it for the longest time before commenting.

"It's the littlest Tick-Tock Girl," he said.

"How'd you like to come to New York with me tomorrow, Hal?" Hugh asked a little later as he packed his bag. The invitation may have seemed spontaneous but the plan to take Hally had been in the works for a while. His attacker was still on the loose and though we had begun to relax, we were still wary especially since, in the last couple of weeks, Hally's groupies had resumed their nightly vigil at the house. Even as the weather cooled and the ground grew hard, some of them had taken to hanging around in the daytime, occupying the sparse meadow, huddling among the leftover bran grasses, as they crouched on the ground for hours at a time, unmoving, as if they had plans to hatch something.

"Are you serious?" Hally asked.

"It's just for a couple of days . . ."

"I don't care how long it's for," Hally said. "Get me out of here."

After taking the ferry to the mainland, Spark and I drove Hugh and Hally to the airport and Pastor Ragnar was in Portland on church business so the place was empty when we got back home. We came in through the front door. I knew immediately someone had been in the house. The hair on my back stood up and before Spark could set me safely down I leapt from his arms, crash-landing on the floor, barking and circling, going room to room, nose to the floor.

The back door leading from the deck to the kitchen had been kicked in, wood frame smashed and broken, glass shattered. Spark took quick inventory of the house. I was in Pastor Ragnar's study following the trail when I heard him.

"Oh no," he said.

Hugh sat on the floor in the middle of his studio, not speaking, his head in his hands.

"Hugh," Spark said.

Hugh opened up his hands, spreading wide his fingers. "Give me a minute."

"Oh my God," Hally said.

"It was like this when I got home," Spark said, surveying what was left of Hugh's work.

Slashed and shredded paintings hung in strips of vivid canvas, reduced to fringed remnants on snapped and broken frames, every painting destroyed and beyond salvage, victims of frenzied overkill, as if a pack of starving wolves had set upon a herd of sheep—the studio still stank of violence.

"Hugh, I'm so sorry," Spark said. "I don't know what to say."

Hugh nodded. He looked around. "I don't know what to do."

Hally walked over to the corner where a frame stood propped against a stool, still intact, though a razor or a box cutter had been used to cut away the painting, so only a large rectangular hole, bordered by irregular tufts of canvas, remained attached.

"The painting of Neddy is gone," he said even as something else caught his eye. "Look over here."

"I can't," Hugh said. "I've seen enough."

The nocturne, the painting of the little girl holding the crucifix, was partially concealed behind a larger canvas. It was untouched. An arrow tattooed the wall in thick smears of black oil paint, and pointed from the painting to a single scrawled word: ThiS.

"What does 'this' mean?" Hally asked.

"This is all there is," Hugh said.

"This is who I am," Spark said.

"This is it," Hally said.

"Who cares what he means? Fuck this," Spark said.

Later on, gathered in the living room, when they were sufficiently put together to think about what had happened, everyone first briefly entertained the idea that Bill Wrendle might have decided to extract his own anonymous revenge against the family by destroying Hugh's paintings. Hugh was the one he'd dealt with after all.

"Why would he take the painting of Ned? Why leave the one of the little girl and the weird message?" Hugh asked, leaning forward in one of the Morris chairs. "Unless he was deliberately trying to throw us off the scent, it makes no sense."

Besides, the attack was so savage it seemed less like calculated revenge and more like a snuff film. "Wrendle's a botanist, not a werewolf. It feels like something unleashed, some strung-out id on the loose," Spark said. "Like the ambush on Hally, that guy, the Shroud of Turin guy."

"It was him," Hally said.

It *was* him. I could smell him on the house.

Nineteen

In subsequent days even the house suffered without Hugh's warm active presence. It felt as if there'd been a power failure and nothing was working. Hugh alternated between staring up at the ceiling in his bedroom and staring up at the ceiling in the living room, not talking, uninterested in food or any aspect of personal hygiene or daily life. The destruction of his work was such a devastating loss that no one, including Pastor Ragnar, even considered mounting the usual platitudinous campaign to rouse him from his despairing state.

Spark tried to take over caretaking duties but the overall effect of his efforts was to plunge everyone into the kind of misery that only four nights of hot dogs and store-bought macaroni salad can produce in a family. On the fifth day, the squeaky desperation of Hally's plaintive wondering about what we were going to have for supper reached somewhere deep inside of Hugh, pierced the part of him driven to take care of others, to be useful, and he got up from the sofa, walked into the kitchen, and opened up a cupboard door.

"Anyone for homemade lasagna?" he said.

⊗⊗⊗⊗⊗⊗

The sheriff met with Pastor Ragnar and Hugh over coffee at a little restaurant in the village. Grinning broadly, he reached out with both hands, clasping Pastor Ragnar's hand in greeting.

"Saw you on CNN. I feel as if I'm in the presence of the pope," he said.

"Why does that seem like a demotion?" Pastor Ragnar replied.

It was a sunny day, still warm enough to sit on the patio overlooking the harbor. I was squeezed alongside Hugh, hind leg dangling between the chair's spindles, my head in his lap. Hugh, like Spark and Hally, was always willing to endure a little discomfort to make room for me.

Spark was out on *The Winnie Cat* with Hally and Beans.

The sheriff—unofficially at least—conceded it was not unreasonable to surmise that the person who broke into the house was the same man who had attacked Hally and Spark.

"That doesn't mean it's him. We have no evidence," he said.

"A high degree of probability, though," Pastor Ragnar said.

"A degree of probability," the sheriff corrected. "Look, to be frank, there are so many oddballs hanging around the island and at your place in particular because of Hally and the . . . uh . . . apparitions . . ." The sheriff coughed, his face reddening.

"Honestly, this grows wearying," Pastor Ragnar said. "Perhaps if Hally had seen the spirit of Sally Rand it would be more palatable."

Hugh handed the sheriff a glass of water. "Who the hell is Sally Rand?" he asked, getting no reply.

"Thanks." The sheriff, sputtering, took a sip. He cleared his throat. "It could be any one of Hally's followers or none of them. My suggestion: Tamp down the flames."

"You make it sound as if we've been setting off fireworks. A grass fire would be a more accurate analogy. So we hose everything down. What difference will that make?" Pastor Ragnar said. "All we'll do is curtail legitimate interest in Hally and what's a growing and import- ant ministry, while not doing a thing toward catching this lunatic."

"I wouldn't say that," the sheriff said, tossing pieces of his choco- late chip muffin to the seagulls. "We have no idea what's driving him. So many of these types are attracted to famous people. Look what happened to John Lennon."

"I don't see the connection to Hally or Cludo," Pastor Ragnar said.

"Moth to the fame."

Hugh grinned at him appreciatively. "Not bad."

"You like that, do you?" The sheriff smiled as Pastor Ragnar sighed and gestured impatiently for him to get on with it. The sheriff obliged. "These predatory types see themselves at the center of the universe and they want everyone else to see them in the same way. Carry on your daily business. Just cool things down a little, avoid the press and our guy may no longer be in such a lather."

"Possibly, but in my opinion, it's a waste of time to devise a strat- egy based on speculation about what the other guy is thinking. If you'll indulge an old cleric: 'For who among men knows the thoughts of a man except the spirit of the man, which is in him? Even so the thoughts of God no one knows except the Spirit of God.' "

The sheriff nodded amicably. "I freely admit I can't figure out what most people are thinking. God either, plenty of the time. Hell, I don't even know what I think at any given moment. What I'm sug- gesting is based on experience and common sense. You want to avoid more trouble while we look for this guy, that's my advice."

Pastor Ragnar continued to press his point but in the end, with prodding from Hugh, he reluctantly agreed to keep the details of the recent incident confidential. Hugh had already explained everything to his gallery dealer, but he was confident he could count on her to keep things to herself.

"Good, let's throw this guy off balance. He'll be scouring the papers expecting to read about what he did and what he might do next. We don't need to be reinforcing his sense of destiny." The sheriff stood up to leave. He bent down and scratched my ear. "Good to see you again, Ned."

"I don't want to leave him alone at the house," Hugh said.

"I think that's smart," the sheriff agreed, both of them underestimating my ability to take care of myself.

"You really think adopting a lower profile will discourage this guy?" Hugh asked him as the sheriff prepared to head out.

The sheriff looked doubtful. "At this stage, going to ground is all we've got."

"Then we've got nothing," Pastor Ragnar said.

"Oh, sorry, didn't mean to disturb you," Spark said later that night as he stepped out onto the deck where Pastor Ragnar was sitting in his rocking chair, looking out over the ocean, clouds rolling in, wind picking up. He turned around to leave.

"You're not disturbing me. Stay, if you'd like. I could use the company. Where are the others?"

"Gone to bed," Spark said, responding to the unusual invitation, pulling up one of the weather-beaten Adirondack chairs and sitting next to his father. I hopped up into Spark's lap, feeling suddenly energized at the prospect of a late night conversation between these two.

"We don't get a chance to spend much time alone together . . . Looks like we're in for quite a storm," Pastor Ragnar said.

"Yep, gotta love a good storm."

"You're right. What good are you if you can't enjoy the eventfulness of a great storm?"

Spark laughed. He sat forward, glancing around. "Kook-free zone tonight. Seems like Hally's friends are fair-weather disciples."

"Don't be unkind, Jamie . . . I suppose we're all fair-weather disciples in some capacity or another."

Spark ran his fingers forward and through my topknot of hair pushing it over my eyes, then back again in playful sequence. "Pop, I know you're not happy about putting 'The Hally Show' on hiatus . . ."

"Is that what you think this is?"

"In some ways, yeah."

"That's just crude thinking."

"Maybe so, but this is what I know: You're not exactly content to be a country preacher with a cozy little flock dozing off during your weekly sermons. You've been exploiting the hell out of Hally and Black Head from the beginning and you've done it to push your own personal agenda. You want to make Cludo a part of the discussion. You want to be seen as an important religious figure . . . whatever that is . . . It's been your goal for as long as I can remember."

"Go on."

Pastor Ragnar was in an unusually tolerant and conciliatory mood. I cocked my head. Could it be that success was mellowing him? Spark decided to take full advantage and pressed on.

"You don't want anything shutting down the momentum. That would be your business except that Hally's a big part of all this. I don't want anything bad to happen to him or anybody else in the family."

"Neither do I."

"I know you don't, but your ambition might be clouding your judgment."

"There's nothing wrong with ambition especially when it's in the service of an idea. Why not seize this rare opportunity? Especially since God appears to have taken a personal interest in this family. With Him in favor, who dare stands opposed? Not me, certainly. Have you ever thought it's a sin to ignore your calling?"

"I know you're not after money, but money's not the only corrupting influence," Spark said, pushing on. "Face it, Pop, you want to be one of the immortals. You and I both know you're pursuing the cult of personality to that end."

"It's nothing I can chase and catch. Such a thing is conferred, not earned. In any event, it isn't me. Hally. He's the one."

Pastor Ragnar's burst of intensity seemed to light up the darkness. He leaned forward in his chair and turned sideways to face Spark.

"Think of it, Jamie. Really. Think of it. What's happened here: The clouds parted and the skies opened for your son, for Hally. He has a grand purpose to fulfill. What could be clearer?"

"It's a story, Pop," Spark said. "What if the Bible's just an inflated collection of stories told by the Jim Bakkers and the Oral Roberts of their era?"

"If that were true, then the Dead Sea Scrolls would be written in crayon," Pastor Ragnar said drily, sitting back in his chair. "Anyway, I've put aside some of my own personal and intellectual reservations, because in the end, they are fluid and ever-changing and unreliable. What's important is the central idea, do you see?"

"I see plenty of 'flexibility' happening. I don't see how that is such a shit-hot idea."

Pastor Ragnar laughed. "When I was your age I felt exactly the same way. I thought the truth was engraved on stone tablets."

"Don't patronize me, Pop, please."

"I'm not. How can I explain? When I was younger than you, I worked with a man who was middle-aged. He used to call his wife every morning, midmorning, and one of the first things he would say to her is, 'What do you want to do for supper?' Then they would go on and on about the menu, what to have, how to cook it.

"I was so disgusted that life should come down to this. 'What's to eat?' Is this all you have to say to each other? Pork chops, mashed potatoes, this is what you wake up thinking about? My God, why talk about food? Who cares about food, when there is so much to do? So much that truly matters? Who cares about planning dinner, when you can fight, when you can undertake the world's challenges, when you can make your voice heard? Who gives a damn about the ordinary things of life?"

"That's when you married Mom?"

Pastor Ragnar ignored the dig.

"I vowed never to become such a passionless man. Well, I'm now that man's age and what do I find myself thinking about over the course of the day? What's for supper? I've slipped, Spark. I'll slip even more before I'm through."

"That's *never* going to happen to me," Spark said.

Pastor Ragnar got up, his silhouette practically invisible in the darkness. He laughed and put his hands on Spark's shoulders. "Jamie, in your case, I'm tempted to think it might even be true. Just as I continue to hope ultimately it will prove true of me," he said, and then he released his grip, gave Spark an affectionate pat on the back, opened the door and went inside. The kitchen light flickered on, then just as quickly died.

Spark and I stayed where we were, thunder in the distance, flashes of lightning illuminating the horizon. He stroked my neck, then he rested his hand on my back and watched as the waves rose higher and grew louder.

Spark took a shower before bed. While I waited, I went downstairs, summoned by the murmur of Pastor Ragnar's voice in the den. On impulse I scratched on the door and he let me inside. He was on the phone. He sat down behind his desk as I jumped up on the chair opposite him. He was apologizing for the lateness of the call, his voice low and uncharacteristically subdued.

I've given it considerable thought, he was saying, I've decided to go ahead.

Go ahead with what? I wondered, though not for long. Pastor Ragnar had plans to make public what had happened to Hugh's paintings. He wanted the whole story out in the open, he said. It was for Hally's sake. It was for the good of the family. More than that, it was a moral imperative.

"Secrecy protects the perpetrator, not the victim," he said to apparent agreement on the other end.

"Use your contacts in the press but make sure to keep my name out of it. My family has been frightened into silence. Never act out of fear," he said, digressing. "The sheriff here is a decent enough guy but he's hopelessly reflexive in his thinking and my boys are inexperienced. They'd have my head if they were to find out. I'm acting on my own."

He was willing to risk their wrath, he said, because he knew it was the right course to take, telling the world about the threat against Hally. About the destruction of Hugh's paintings.

"This guy thinks he can threaten my family, come into my home with impunity, and I'm supposed to sit in a corner with a set of worry beads and wait for him to make his next move? I hope the publicity does flush him out because, believe me, I'll be waiting for him and he's not going to know what hit him."

In the early hours of the morning, I wandered downstairs, unable to sleep. The wind bore down on the house, shaking the life out of the windows as they rattled. When I was young, violent storms terrified me. "O ye of little faith," my father said as he watched me shake.

"What's that supposed to mean?" I said, annoyed at the implicit suggestion of cowardice and upset at being called out for inconstancy—

no dog, ever, wants to be castigated for faithlessness—there can be no greater personal failing in the canine world. My father had his own ideas about faith and faithfulness. "Put your faith in science, you get the atomic bomb and thalidomide. Put your faith in God and you get the Inquisition and injunctions against dancing."

"Where do you put your faith, then?" I asked him.

"You put your faith in yourself and even then you need to be skeptical. Believe me, Lupine, there is plenty of God, scientist, and the devil living inside us all. You don't need to go looking for any of it."

I finally fell asleep in front of the waning fire, a deep sleep. Something woke me up though I couldn't say what it was. The house was in darkness but for the diminished red-gold light of a single flame among the dying embers. I felt a pang, the hollow ache that comes when sound sleep gives way to sharp awakening. Standing up and stretching, I tried to shake off that melancholy feeling as the world outside our door continued its mad spin. I took a small detour on my way up the stairs to Spark's room—and from the second floor of the landing I looked out over rock and sea and bending trees, their images occurring in nonstop, seizure-inducing flashes of lightning.

The waves rose ever higher, spilling onto the rock, the water advancing on the house. The whole island seemed to have come unmoored, as if we'd been heaved out into the ocean, a message in a bottle, trying to staying afloat in the deluge.

The black and midnight-blue sky ignited, orange and gold light illuminating the darkness. It was then that I saw him. Standing on the edge of the low-lying bluff, in the concentrated crucible of all that craziness, looking out over the ocean.

It was madness. Who would be crazy enough to go out into a storm on a night such as this and risk being swept away, lost forever to the certainty of the Atlantic? I took a closer look, the lightning telling the story, and there it was, the reckless stance giving it away, all those exposed vulnerabilities illuminated in the darkness, puny humanity facing down all that wildness.

It was Hally.

Disquietude took hold of me, suppressing the ancient instinct to bark, to rouse the household. Hally was in need of saving, but seeing him out there alone at the mercy of all those unleashed forces, I knew in the deepest part of me he was beyond whatever a round of barking could accomplish, and in my humility I kept silent and maintained a secret watch.

Twenty

We were nearing the old lighthouse when Spark bent down and set me free of his backpack. He had slipped away from the family to enjoy a few hours hiking the island where he grew up. The lighthouse loomed up ahead, the sun's rays reflecting off the surrounding stark white buildings with their red roofs—the keeper's house, the oil house, the chicken coop where I could still discern the phantom scent of an ancient flock.

We climbed into an old wooden rowboat. Spark lay back and closed his eyes, sun on his face. I curled into him, my head at his shoulder, soft breeze rippling through my hair, crunchy scent of autumn in the air as I hovered in the twilight state between awake and asleep, imagining us gently adrift, the rowboat rocking serenely on amber water, aimless and floating, devoid of industry.

"Spark, wake up." Hugh was on one knee next to the rowboat, his hand on Spark's shoulder.

Pulling himself up onto his elbows, Spark, surprised and momentarily disoriented, rubbed his eyes and shook his head, trying to get his bearings. He squinted in the brilliant white light as I cracked open first one eyelid, then the other. Tender dream of life interrupted, my dry-docked consciousness landed with a thud.

"I must have fallen asleep," Spark said, face burnt red by the wind and the sun. Leaving himself exposed was a way of life for Spark. He yawned, then stretched. "What's up?'

"Somehow the press found out about my paintings being destroyed. A reporter from the Associated Press called wanting us to comment on the break-in and the rumor that Hally has a violent stalker and what are we doing about it?"

"What?" Spark, fully awakened now, climbed out of the boat. "How the hell did they find out?"

"I don't know. Maybe somebody from my gallery. Could have been someone in the sheriff's office who leaked it. That stupid deputy is a likely candidate."

"Pop."

"No way. He agreed to keep it under wraps."

"To placate us. To shut us up. To keep us off his back so he could do exactly what he wanted to do."

Hugh just kept on insisting it wasn't the case. You weren't there, he told Spark, describing how Pastor Ragnar had given his word he would remain silent. Since when, Spark countered, had Pastor Ragnar ever deferred to the convictions of someone else when they clashed with his own?

"Come on, Hugh, think about it," Spark said on the trek back home, as side by side the two brothers climbed a rugged incline, Spark extending his hand to Hugh to pull him up after he lost his footing. "He's never going to agree to back down, even when he agrees to back down, because he doesn't know how to retreat and he's not interested in learning. He'd see himself and all of us blown sky-high before he'd ever take the path of least resistance. Pop's not a peacetime general. He's not even a wartime general. He's like a permanent cosmic disturbance."

Hugh walked alongside him listening. "You're exaggerating as usual . . . " He stopped in his tracks, looking sheepish. "Though I will admit, it didn't take him long to grab the phone from me to talk to the reporter."

"Ha, you never mentioned that. Jesus, Hugh . . ."

"Hey, you can't blame a guy for wanting to believe."

"You poor deluded sap."

"What the hell, Spark? Who are you trying to kid? Don't tell me you weren't clinging to some shred of hope he'd keep his word."

"Okay, maybe a little," Spark admitted. "Son-of-a-bitch. He worked me over good the other night. No wonder he was being so friendly and agreeable," Spark said as Hugh grinned over at him.

"Should we say something to him? What do you think?"

Spark thought about it for about thirty seconds. "What's the point? Besides, Hally's got enough to deal with. He'll catch on to Pop's methods soon enough. Not that it will make any difference. Then he'll just be like you and me—with fewer bruises."

The story once unleashed proved irresistible—it seemed less to run than to detonate in the pages of newspapers across the country, and from that point it was quickly picked up by TV, fallout raining down everywhere around us. Human interest and gossip was beginning to supplant news stories in legitimate media outlets and soon we found ourselves besieged by journalists wanting to interview the family, and expose every aspect of our lives.

Hally, his stalker, the apparitions, Cludo, Pastor Ragnar, the controversial concert, Hugh's rising star in the art world—it was only a matter of time before the inevitable question got asked: What about Hally's mother?

"A local girl," Pastor Ragnar said, unflappable and trying to appear matter-of-fact. "Sadly she died as a result of illness shortly after he was born."

～～～～～

"What was Pop thinking?" Hugh asked Spark, when Flory's name first appeared in print a few days later. "How could he think with all these reporters involved, all of this interest he's whipped up in Hally, that it wouldn't come out? All anyone ever had to do was look at birth records or ask around the village. God knows where it will all lead."

"What makes you think he didn't plan it this way?" Spark said bitterly, the two of them working together to clean up and reorganize Hugh's studio. "The MacNamara connection is pure gold. I mean, it's one thing for God to take a special interest in Hally but even God can't compete with the power and mystique of the MacNamaras here on earth."

"That's cynical stuff even by your standards," Hugh said, dismantling damaged canvases and piling the debris into the corner. "The last thing Pop wants is for the MacNamaras to exert any sort of claim on Hally."

"You know, I've been thinking about it, Pop's alleged paranoia about the MacNamaras. I know the family pretty well. For them, death is preferable to publicity. Even if they wanted him, which they don't, Hally's not a little kid. He's not powerless. His opinion would count. They'd have to carry him out of here kicking and screaming."

"Carry me where?" Hally was on his way up the stairs. "What are you guys talking about?" He stepped into the open loft area of the studio. "Are you planning to put me in the nuthouse or something?"

"No, of course not," Hugh said, indignation in his voice. "Why would you say something like that?"

"No reason," Hally said. "Just something to say."

"We were talking about the MacNamaras," Spark said. "We were speculating about how you might react if they ever decided to do something unpredictable, like pursue custody of you, which they won't," he hastened to add.

"I'm not a criminal. I don't need anybody having custody of me," Hally said.

"You're a kid. Somebody has to take care of you. It's just a legal term," Spark said.

"I can take care of myself. From what I can see, you guys need somebody taking care of you more than I do."

Hugh sighed noisily as he straightened up, the special anguish of dealing with an adolescent written on his face. "Well, anyway . . . how do *you* feel about all this stuff with the MacNamaras?"

Hally sat down on the top step. He shrugged and called me over to him. He rubbed my face and covered my eyes with the tips of my ears.

"Whatever. What do I care?"

"Do you have any interest in meeting them? They're your family, too," Hugh persisted, exchanging a quick commiserating glance with Spark.

"Kind of. I guess. Maybe they could tell me things about my mom, when she was little and stuff. What she was like. What she liked, you know, her favorite music and I don't know, just personal things about her. Nobody else around here will."

"Phil Ochs. She loved Phil Ochs," Spark said as he snapped a large wooden frame into two smaller pieces and tossed them onto the growing pile of garbage. "You do know who Phil Ochs is, right?" Spark could be a bit of an adolescent boy, too, when it suited him.

"I know who Phil Ochs is," Hally said.

"I can tell you whatever you want to know about your mom."

"Since when? Like what?" Hard as he tried to appear indifferent, Hally couldn't resist what Spark was offering.

"Like . . ." Spark scanned the mess and thought for a moment. His face brightened. "When she was little she used to steal dogs."

"Right," Hally said, disgusted.

"I'm serious. From her earliest memories, she'd wanted a dog and her mother said she needed to wait until she was a bit older. They were always traveling, they were too busy, they couldn't afford it."

Hugh and Hally exchanged the same confused expressions.

"Just wanted to make sure you guys were listening," Spark said. "There were a million excuses for why she couldn't have a dog. So your mom used to take a jump rope and head out into their neighborhood— this was at the Georgetown house in Washington in the days when dogs and kids still roamed free, and before they moved to their 'heritage seat' in Middleburg, Virginia—and steal dogs, loop the jump rope around their necks and take them, lead them away, sometimes steal them right from their yards.

"She once stole a cocker spaniel puppy from a front yard and she hid him in the attic of the house and fed him potato chips and jelly beans. She got caught, of course, but it didn't stop her. She terrorized the neighborhood. Kept taking dogs. Her parents found ways to return them without anyone knowing who took them. They finally got desperate and relented and got her a puppy of her own, a fox terrier she called Zing.

"Flory was a little single-minded. She tended to get what she wanted through attrition."

Hally looked suspiciously at Hugh. "Is that true?"

"It is," Hugh said. "She told me that story herself."

"Great," Hally said. "So I come from a line of dog thieves."

"And Jesus freaks," Spark said, opening wide the studio window and tossing the remains of Hugh's ruined paintings onto the rocks below. "Don't forget about them."

〜〜〜〜〜

The next morning, Spark out on the boat with Beans, and Pastor Ragnar at the church, Hally and Hugh set about to burn what was left of his work. Hugh, true to his character, made sure to set up proper perimeters for the fire before he lit the match. He and Hally quietly fed the flames and then stood and watched the fire as it burned. I lay at Hugh's feet, the heat in my face.

"Hugh," Hally said, "if I ask you something will you promise to tell me the truth, no matter what?"

Hugh glanced at him sideways and only briefly, before he resumed staring at the fire.

"I promise."

"Did Spark play around on my mom? You know, see other girls behind her back?"

"No."

"Gram told me—"

"I know what she said, but she was basing her conclusions on false information." Hugh threw some kindling onto the fire.

"What false information?"

"Well, Flory told her things . . . She became convinced that Spark was having affairs with every woman within a hundred-mile radius. She even went and confronted other girls, made scenes . . ."

"Why did Gram think it was true if it wasn't? You didn't. Why didn't you believe my mom?"

"Because she wasn't in her right mind and as for Mom, let's face it, Gram was a busybody. It appealed to that side of her nature to take up these things."

"She was his mom. Why did she want to believe bad things about him?"

"Because in a warped way it wasn't bad to her. It only confirmed her belief her son was irresistible to women and could have anyone he wanted. She took weird pride in it. I think she liked to imagine Spark was indifferent to Flory's money and pedigree, which he was, but not in the way she thought."

"She told me she was only telling me about it because she didn't want me to make the same mistakes."

Hugh covered his face with his hands. "Oh, Hally, I don't even know where to start . . ."

"Okay," Hally said, shoulders drooping. "If you don't want to talk about it."

"Come on, let's stand back a little," Hugh said as the fire grew hotter and the flames soared higher. "It's not that. It's just complicated." I followed them to where they sat down at the side of the old spruce tree just beyond the house.

"Forget all that other stuff. I think the important thing for you to know is Spark was crazy about your mom. I don't think he's ever gotten over her. I wonder if he ever will."

Hally was listening, not saying anything. He pulled me onto his lap. Hugh sat quietly for a moment, as if he were conducting an internal debate with himself.

"She loved him, too, which made what happened even sadder." He picked up a stray branch and focused his attention on peeling away the bark with his fingers.

"You mean because she died?"

"It was a terrible time. A dark time. Everyone was walking around like zombies. We were all worried about Spark, about what he might do. I remember one day, seeing him leave the house and head out by himself, and I honestly thought I would never see him again."

"What do you mean?"

"I mean I thought he was going to disappear and never come back. I'll never forget the relief I felt hours later seeing him come up over the ridge in the wildflower meadow."

"Did you ever ask him about it?"

"We weren't that kind of family. Some things you don't need to talk about. Some things you just know. I knew he was wrestling with something deep inside himself that wasn't accessible to anyone else and I hoped and prayed he would win the battle. He did. Then, of course, eventually he did go away. But not in the way I'd feared."

Hally took several deep breaths. "Some things I just know, too. I know you're not telling me the whole truth. You're not, are you, Hugh?"

Hugh shook his head.

"My mom went crazy, didn't she? I mean in the real sense."

Hugh put his hand on Hally's shoulder and rested it there. "Hally . . . "

"It's all right. What happened?"

"Flory was always a bit high-strung, I guess you'd say. Kind of temperamental but we just figured she was spoiled . . . I was a kid. What did I know about anything? She started having real problems during the pregnancy and then after you were born, things just got worse and she was hearing voices, she was despondent and paranoid, imagining things that weren't true. Doctors couldn't seem to help her. Nothing helped."

"She killed herself, didn't she?"

"She did." Hugh lowered his eyes.

"How?"

"She put a plastic bag over her head. The doctor told us it's actually not a bad way to go, if that helps."

"I wish I knew this stuff before," Hally said after a long moment.

"Maybe we should have been more open with you. I should have . . . I don't know what I should have done. We all just kind of shut down and nobody wanted to talk about it. Seems wrong in retrospect but it was the only way to get through it at the time. And you were so little. Nobody wanted to burden your young life. We

knew you'd have to find out someday. We waited too long. I can
see that now.

"I think I was a little bit ashamed, too. I guess I didn't really know
what to say and I was mad at Spark for leaving. I should have had more
compassion for the situation. He was in terrible physical and emotional
shape. He wasn't able to make proper decisions. Nobody knew what
to do and we had a baby to take care of. Spark couldn't stand living
here. All the reminders of Flory and what happened. He just wanted
to run away from everything."

"From me, too?"

"No. He honestly thought he was doing the better thing by leaving you here with Mom and Pop. The thing is: He was right, Hal. He
had started drinking and acting kind of wild and all the grandparents
were deathly opposed to him raising you alone."

"Pop took the tough love approach, which was probably the worst
thing to do. My parents had all these financial problems. We were
worried at first the MacNamaras might try to take you from us. We
were even worried about what Fred MacNamara might do to Spark.
He was out of his head with grief. He blamed Spark. It was a mess.
Oh, Hal, I don't know what to say about all of it, even now."

"I wish Spark would talk to me about it, the way you are."

"Your dad isn't the kind of guy to spill his guts. I think it's one of
those things in life . . . if he were to give in to all the sadness he feels
about Flory and leaving you, he would never be able to find his way
back from it. I know it's difficult for you and it's not fair, but can you
try to understand? Hally?"

I leapt from Hally's lap before he could answer, shot forward at
first sound of them, charging at them, barking, wanting them to go
away and never come back, the breeze enveloping me in their familiar
bubble-gum fragrance.

"Oh no," Hally said. "The Tick-Tock Girls."

Twenty-one

No one thought it was a good idea. No one except for Pastor Ragnar, who had been planning the concert since late May. Hugh and Spark argued—you might even say passionately—against it. In desperation, they recruited Sheriff Guerin to enumerate all of his various objections, which included the folly of potentially exposing Hally to a man who meant him obvious harm, a man who could disappear among the crowd, and get within striking distance undetected.

"It's kind of hard to pick out a single almond from a bushel of mixed nuts," the sheriff said with a wink in a much-appreciated aside to Hugh and Spark.

Nothing worked. Pastor Ragnar would not be dissuaded from his plan to host a musical concert on the grounds of the museum, a site overlooking the harbor, on Sunday, October 12, the Columbus Day holiday weekend. He held it in honor of the Holy Mother's birthday, December 8, the Feast of the Immaculate Conception, but scheduled it early to avoid the ice of winter.

"'Of whom shall I be afraid?'" he asked.

"Oh, I don't know," Spark said. "How about the guy who nearly brained Hally and me, for starters?"

"Good luck. Pop's on a journey of redemption after the last fiasco and now he's got some money behind him," Hugh said. "There'll be no stopping him now."

Without consulting anyone, Pastor Ragnar and Rusty Cipolla had entered into an agreement concerning the making of a documentary about Cludo, the laughing church, the apparitions and Hally, with the concert as its narrative centerpiece. The Portland Symphony Orchestra agreed to perform, compelled by the uniqueness of the location and heartened by Cipolla's involvement. Tara Hogarth, the acclaimed soprano would sing, along with Evelyn Katarsos, who shared billing with the Virgin Mary when she made her second appearance at Black Head.

"They singing Kurt Weill?" Spark quipped, parked on the counter, resigned to the inevitability of the celebration. "Hosanna Rockefeller!" he shouted.

"You never know," Pastor Ragnar said cheerfully, sitting at the head of the kitchen table, taking a last bite from his sandwich. He dabbed at his lips with a napkin. "If you'll permit me an observation: I don't think fishing agrees with you, Spark. You're beginning to put too much faith in bait."

"I hate the opera," Hally said, speaking up from where he sat in the living room assembling a model sailboat. He hadn't appeared to be listening.

"What are we talking about?" Hugh said, entering the kitchen through the screen door, sketch pad under his arm. He had started working again. I warmed to the sound of his voice. Hugh was as reliable as the tides.

"Pop's night at the opera," Spark said.

"Ugh, I hate the opera," Hugh said.

"You can't understand a word they're singing," Hally said.

"Be grateful. It only gets worse when you know what they're saying," Spark said.

"That's the power of it—music is its own transcendent language," Pastor Ragnar said. "It's all about greater meaning and emotionally subjective translation. Music sung in a foreign language engages our imagination at a primal level. Music unfiltered by familiar language reaches into our souls, flooding us with mystery. No word recognition to harden us against what we're hearing in our hearts."

I caught Spark sneaking amused glances with Hugh as Pastor Ragnar continued.

"The Bible says, 'It is the glory of God to conceal things.' Scripture asks of us: 'Can you find out the deep things of God?' Knowing the words, understanding their meaning, is of the prosaic earth and not the poetic spirit."

"And that, my friends, is why God put the bop in the bop she—" Spark said.

Before he could finish, Pastor Ragnar interrupted. "Even your usual nonsense isn't enough to spoil my good mood today."

"Sorry, Gramp, but I still think it's going to suck," Hally said.

"Unfortunately for the three of you, Black Flag was already booked. Maybe next year," Pastor Ragnar said as he took a final sip of tea and headed out to meet with Cipolla in town.

After he left, Spark, sliding down from his perch on top of the counter, turned to the others.

"What does the Bible say about what it means when somebody's speaking to you in plain English and you still don't know what the hell they're talking about?"

"When did you first meet my mom, anyway? Talk to her and stuff,' Hally said, standing next to Spark on *The Winnie Cat*, both of them in black knit caps and red-and-blue foul-weather bibs and brace pants. It was just the three of us—Beans' gout was acting up, so Spark recruited Hally's help, physically dragging him half-asleep and complaining from his bed at 4:30 a.m.

The boat rocked back and forth in the choppy chilly early morning hours, the sun's rays briefly piercing the gray clouds, warming me where I lay on top of an old blanket in a plastic milk carton, my designated fishing spot, watching Spark and Hally check the gill nets.

"It was the first summer the MacNamaras opened up the house on the island. It had been shuttered for years. Hugh and I used to think it was haunted when we were kids."

Spark, typically, took a temporary narrative detour telling Hally about how they had found a way inside the house by scaling the rose trellis to the second-floor balcony, gaining access through a door with an unreliable lock.

"You broke into the house?"

"No. We found an unlocked door, there's a big difference."

"Yeah, okay. Whatever you say."

"You want to hear the story or not?"

Hally nodded.

"I occasionally saw Flory around the island, always from a distance. She was friends with this girl, Becky Hardiman, a real pill so I made a point of avoiding them. The first time I ever really met her was high school. She announced to her parents that she was leaving Marymount, a hotshot Catholic prep school in New York, to go to high school in Boothbay Harbor with the bourgeoisie. Part of her personal rebellion. In those days, she had a picture of Danny the Red, this self-styled French anarchist, in her locker, next to her idol Phil Ochs. She had it all figured out. She was going to live with Becky and her parents."

"Her mom and dad let her?"

Spark laughed. "They didn't have anything to say about it, believe me."

"It was the first few weeks of the school year and this goofy singing group, Up With People, was scheduled to appear at an assembly. They were like hippie anti-venom, so hysterically optimistic you just wanted to punch them in the face, nationalistic, hyperpatriotic, the works, clean-cut and so cheerful they came across as deranged."

"Sound like the Tick-Tock Girls," Hally said.

"Yeah, exactly. So there they are, singing their little hearts out onstage in front of the whole school, and your mom gets up from her seat and charges the stage and starts challenging them to a debate about their dubious origins."

"What happened?"

"Everybody goes nuts. Chaos. The concert's over. The group flees. Staff converges. All of these kids start raging at Flory but she never backs down. A group of guys surround her in the hallway and some of them start threatening her, saying what they're going to do to her, she'd better watch her back, that kind of crap. This creep, Kevin, starts making sexual threats and that's when I tell him to fuck off and boom, we get into it, and then Flory steps in between us and tells both of us off."

"You were trying to help her, though."

"She didn't need my help, and she let me know about it. Then she stomps off. I can still see her, smoke coming out of her ears. Some guys try to block her way and she pushes right through them." He laughed. Even all those years later, Spark couldn't conceal the pleasure he took in her courage. "Anyway, I looked for her and I told her I wanted to learn more about Moral Rearmament, the group behind Up with People."

"Did you? Want to learn about it, I mean?"

"No. Are you kidding? I grew up with Cludo, remember? I could have given her a master class on the subject of cultish doctrines. Anyway, that's how I met your mom."

"Did she get kicked out of school?"

"Nope. People said it was because she was a MacNamara but that wasn't true. Sometimes that can turn you into a target of reverse snobbery, which you'll probably find out before you're through. Some of the teachers spoke up for her, that's what saved her. The vice-principal, a guy I always thought had a stick up his ass. Unlikely places, Hal. You just never know."

"Did you guys fall in love right away?"

"We fell so fast I think it happened someplace outside ourselves before we even met. It's like our feelings had already arrived and were drumming their fingers waiting for us to catch up. I was so punchy I didn't even know where I was."

"So . . ." Spark stopped talking, face darkening like the overhead sky. "Uh," he said, looking around, behaving as if he'd forgotten something, though it was obvious to Hally and me, remembering and not forgetting was the problem.

"She didn't have meningitis, did she?" Hally wrapped one arm around his chest and with the other hand pulled up his jacket collar, concealing most of his face.

"No, she didn't."

"Hugh told me."

Spark glanced skyward, squinting, said something about a possible storm, and then he folded his knit cap down over his eyes before rolling it back up again.

"Good day for us, bad day for the fish," he said, the nets surging with life and death.

Hally came over to have a look. "I feel sorry for them," he said.

"Yeah," Spark agreed. "It stinks. I'll never eat seafood again as long as I live."

"Spark, do you think you'll ever get married?"

"Nope."

"Why not?"

Spark focused intently on the day's haul. Among the mackerel was a bycatch of a few errant lobsters, which Beans wasn't inclined to part with, even though lobster season didn't start until the end of December. Unlike Beans, Spark handled the lobsters with care. Beans used to get after him for being slow but he was wasting his time. "You do know these guys are living creatures," Spark said. "They're not tennis balls."

He picked up a hermit crab and released him overboard.

"Spark? Why not?" Hally repeated.

"Because I've been married, that's why."

"What?"

"Flory and I got married just before you were born, the same weekend."

"You did? Why didn't you say anything?"

"Because I'm stupid and I allowed myself to get talked into something dumb."

"I don't get it."

"Your mother was afraid of how her dad would react. She thought he would make her get an annulment. She thought he would take you away from us. He's a powerful guy with endless resources. Pastor Ragnar shared the same concern, especially after Flory died. He was convinced your other grandparents would have swooped in and got custody of you if they knew you were uh, legal . . ."

"Why didn't they anyway?"

"Because they're jackasses." Spark took a deep breath and tried to self-correct. "Maybe a better way to put it is they're traditionalists about the way they view things. In their narrow interpretation of the world—and they're strict old-world Catholics, too, remember—it's socially and morally embarrassing to have an illegitimate child in the picture. Especially the child of a daughter. The era didn't help either.

Things were changing but it was still a stricter time when it came to this stuff. Maybe if Flory had been a son she could have gotten away with it better."

"Did you feel like you had to get married because she was pregnant?"

"Not exactly. I felt like it was the right thing to do, but that was secondary. I wanted to marry Flory. She was the one who stalled, not me. I wanted to marry her from the moment I met her."

"So, I guess you're old-fashioned, too," Hally said.

"Nah," Spark said.

"My mother's dead. She's been gone all these years, why are you so sure you'll never get married again?"

"Flory was it for me," Spark said.

Then he stood up, bent over, picked up the milk carton containing the day's illicit catch and dumped them overboard.

We were on the way home, Spark at the wheel, the boat clipping along, bumping against the waves, cold spray shooting onto the boat in wide spurts, Spark steering *The Winnie Cat* faster than Beans would have liked.

Hally, hair dripping, salt water streaking his face, zipped me into his waterproof jacket to keep me from getting soaked. Only the top of my head was visible.

"Do you hate me for not telling you sooner?" Spark asked him.

"No," Hally said, reaching out, his hand on Spark's hand. He had tiny drops of salt water like crystal prisms on the tips of his eyelashes.

"I don't hate you," he said. "You loved my mom and anyway, everybody's got their secrets."

That night, Spark in gray sweatpants and a dark turtleneck sweater, plopped down next to Hugh on the sofa. "Jesus," he said, teeth chattering, "it was cold and damp out there today. I can't get warm. Took a shower, didn't help."

Hugh shifted and pulled the woolen throw cover from beneath him and, rolling it into a ball, tossed it at Spark's head. "You want some Ovaltine?" he said. "I'll make you some."

"Ovaltine? What am I? A thousand years old?"

"I forgot I was dealing with Sinatra. How about a hot toddy then? Heavy on the booze." Spark agreed that sounded good and Hugh headed into the kitchen, put the kettle on and began pulling what he needed from the cupboards—lemon juice, honey, bourbon.

"Money's not such a big deal around here anymore. Why don't you quit that stupid lobster boat before you wind up drowned by a trapline? It's not as if you like it."

"Penance," Spark said, blowing into his cupped hands.

"You're not serious?"

"No . . . and yes. No. Maybe," Spark said as Hugh handed him a glass mug. He took a sip.

"That's great, thanks, Hugh." He took another drink. "Hey, brother, let's get drunk. Find us some fast women. Take in the pleasures of the harbor. What do you say?"

"Uh. No. This is Monhegan, not Shanghai. Settle down, sailor."

Hugh, kneeling, reached for another log to put on the fire. The wind drummed in the chimney as he swept away the loose ash, Spark studying him as he worked.

"We should do a little work on the house next spring, fix it up before it collapses. My foot went through the porch step earlier," Spark said.

"Are you being serious? I just assumed we were going to let the House of Monahan continue on the road to perdition," Hugh said.

"Sure. Why not? It's our inheritance," Spark said, amused at the notion.

"Yeah, okay. I've got a hell of a lot of work ahead of me but it might be a healthy diversion. Maybe Hally could help. Be good for him."

Spark, who was sitting in the corner of the sofa, wrapped the blanket tightly around his feet.

"Hal said you guys had a talk. What about?"

Hugh looked hesitant, but then decided to be frank. "You. Flory. You and Flory. He wanted to know if you ever played around on her. If you loved each other. What it was like back then . . ."

"What did you tell him?"

"I told him the truth." Hugh looked a little sheepish. "I just didn't tell him the whole truth." Hugh turned his back and swept ash from around the hearth. "Spark, I told him about Flory's illness. I guess it's more accurate to say I confirmed his suspicions. He guessed the outcome. I think in some ways he's always known." He turned back around to face his brother.

Spark took a sip of his drink. "Yeah, well, he had to find out at some point . . . Better he found out from you. You've been more of a father to him than I have." He waved away Hugh's protests. "Whatever you said . . . It helped. Thanks, Hugh."

"Good. I'm glad."

"I told him we were married. It was time. He had a right to know."

"Wonder how Pop will take it?"

"I'm sick of thinking about how Pop will react to things . . . Hally's not a baby. He's long past being snatched from the cradle by the MacNamaras."

Hugh got up from the hearth and sat down on the sofa, at the opposite end from Spark, poker still in hand. I was lying in between them. Spark seemed to have something more he wanted to say. Hugh waited expectantly.

"Hally asked me if I would ever get married again."

"What did you say?"

Unable to speak, Spark just shook his head.

Hugh put down the poker. "Spark, I get it . . . I do . . . but . . . you just turned thirty-two. If you're still this nuts about Flory after all that happened, think about how you might feel about a woman who won't stab you in the back with a kitchen knife."

Pastor Ragnar was trying to teach Hally the correct way to chop firewood for the fireplace, though he pointed out the word chopping was a misnomer. The aim wasn't to cut the wood but to split it, he explained. He demonstrated the correct stance and instructed Hally to rely on controlled speed and momentum to help the weight of the ax do its job.

"Look out, Ned," he said, ordering me up onto the deck. "We wouldn't want Spark to come home from fishing and find his best friend's been dispatched by a piece of wood in flight."

"Go on, Neddy," Hally said.

Pastor Ragnar turned his attention back to Hally. "There are certain things every man must know. They are, in no special order— how to change a flat tire, do a chin-up, make scrambled eggs, do laundry, throw a punch, get down on your knees and pray, fasten the clasp of a woman's necklace, handle a horse, change a diaper, and split wood."

He pointed over at me. "Earn the love of a dog."

"Do Spark and Hugh know how to do all those things?"

"I made certain of it."

"I can't imagine seeing Spark down on his knees praying."

"It's not a spectator sport," Pastor Ragnar said, positioning Hally's hands correctly on the ax.

Later on, as they stacked the newly split logs against the side of the house, Pastor Ragnar got around to talking to Hally about his day on *The Winnie Cat* with Spark.

"I hear your father told you—"

"Yup," Hally said, not waiting for Pastor Ragnar to finish, as he added to the neat pile, one log snugly positioned on top of another.

"How do you feel about it?"

"Fine. Kind of happy, I guess. I don't get why it's such a big secret, though. Nobody cares about people being married anymore."

"I can assure you, your other grandparents care a great deal about it. It may seem an archaic notion to you, Hally, but to Fred Mac-Namara it makes all the difference to how he perceives you—as his only grandson and legitimate heir or as Spark Monahan's bastard kid intent on picking his pockets."

"I don't care about their money."

"Of course not, but you'll never convince him of that. It's a disease among the wealthy, especially Old Money. They're raised to think people are only interested in them for their money and it becomes a self-fulfilling prophecy since, as a result of their neurotic preoccupations, there is little else about them that's interesting *except* their money."

"Hugh told me about the other stuff . . . about my mom."

"Yes, it was a great pity about your mother. She was a lovely girl. A real pistol, Flory."

"I still don't see why Gram hated her so much . . . She couldn't help it if she was mental."

"She loved your mother at first but then . . . Ellen tended to be overprotective when it came to your father. She wasn't entirely rational in her response, after seeing him so unhappy. The situation put a great deal of strain on everyone."

Hally stopped to remove his jacket. It was a cool fall day but the work was hard and the sun's rays were strong. "Are you going to tell my other grandfather? About them being married?"

"I'll do whatever you'd like me to do. At this stage of the game, at your age, it's lost some of its power to do harm."

Hally resumed his task. "Don't tell him then. If he didn't care about me before, why should I care about him now?"

Pastor Ragnar nodded. "We'll leave it at that . . . Did you and Spark have a good time together on the boat? You seem to be getting along better lately."

"Yeah. It was good. It's just . . ."

"Just what?"

"I hate catching fish . . . seeing them gasp for air . . . I hate catching lobsters the most. It's horrible, all of them in those crates piled on top of one another like wood, as if they weren't alive with feelings of their own, as if they didn't have lives they loved just as much as we love ours. Spark doesn't like it either. Sometimes he throws them back in."

"Keepers, you mean?"

"Yup," Hally nodded.

Pastor Ragnar shook his head, small smile escaping. "Not surprised. Beans has insinuated as much."

"You would have thrown them back in, too, Gramp, if you'd heard them."

"What are you talking about?"

"They make this sad sound, like they're crying."

"Hally, lobsters don't make noise. They don't have vocal cords. Anyway, it's good to be compassionate but you don't want to be like your dad, anthropomorphizing fruit flies."

"Try telling the lobsters that. I know what I heard. They scream when people throw them into boiling water to cook them. They scrape at the sides of the pot trying to escape. Haven't you heard it? I've heard them. It's terrible. It's real. I'm not making it up." Hally pulled off his gloves and threw them on the ground. "I'm so sick of everyone telling me what I should think or how I should feel."

Pastor Ragnar frowned. He put a comforting hand on Hally's shoulder.

"Never mind, Hally, I believe you. You can confidently tell me anything."

Late that night I was with Hally, Spark, and Hugh watching TV when I heard Pastor Ragnar slip quietly downstairs and into the den, the door clicking softly behind him. The guys, in high spirits and talking, noisily headed into the kitchen to make popcorn. I hopped down from the sofa and made my way down the hallway. I lay down next to the door with my ear at the threshold.

Pastor Ragnar spoke in a low voice but not so low that I couldn't hear him.

"Fred, yes, I'm quite well, thanks . . . I wonder if I might talk with you about something important. I think it will prove most interesting to you. There's something you should know. Do you have a moment?"

Twenty-two

It was the day of the concert. The morning started inauspiciously with cold rain and sleet, the branches of trees sagging, almost touching the ground, but by late afternoon the sun, the color of tarnished brass, pierced the gray clouds with sharp spears of light. The hardening ground, black and charcoal, softened slightly as the sun's rays intensified.

Some people insisted it was a miracle, the skies clearing at the last moment, but then some people think it's a miracle when a parking spot opens up.

Spark, Hugh, Hally, and I, with Rusty Cipolla filming, headed out around dusk for the concert site in the village. Everyone was feeling merry, laughing, teasing, kidding around, hamming it up in front of the camera though Hally was a little reserved. Spark, even more irreverent than usual, entertained all of them, including himself, by making endless fun of the day's events.

The performance was scheduled to begin at 8 p.m. Hally didn't get far from the house before people began to appear from the field of tall grasses and from the wildflower meadow and then they emerged in even greater numbers from the wilderness areas beyond the trail.

They whispered excitedly and pointed when they saw Hally, some clamoring for a closer look.

"This is fantastic," Cipolla said from behind the camera where he subsisted on a slender diet of observations. Hally looked at him as if he was out of his mind.

Spark wanted to turn back but Hally said no, he couldn't disappoint Pastor Ragnar, and then, barely having finished speaking, he took off running, shouting for everyone to catch him. I dashed out ahead of him and Spark quickly caught up, leaving Cipolla shouting for us to wait for him. Hugh, good old Hugh, stayed behind to help him, and Hally's followers were left to scramble, stumbling, uncertainly jogging, tripping over one another, trying clumsily to navigate the uneven ground, steep inclines, and sliding rocks.

As we neared the museum grounds, the area lit up by the lighthouse, Hally groaned at first sight of all those people and pulled his hooded sweatshirt over his forehead, partially covering his face, and Spark picked me up and popped me into his backpack so I wouldn't get trampled or recognized. A temporary stage had been erected not far from the harbor's edge, and we saw Pastor Ragnar, everywhere at once, dealing with last-minute problems, wading through the off-kilter swill of humanity, the waters neatly parting in deference to his natural authority.

He ignored us but no one took it personally. "Executive-brain trance," Spark called it.

Religious zealots, pilgrims with vacant eyes and curiosity-seekers, people with nothing better to do, and genuinely interested "seekers" mixed with secular fans of classic music performance, all of them just kept on coming, rolling in like the waves, jostling together in relentless giddy surges, setting up their lawn chairs and spreading out their billowing fur- and sheepskin-lined blankets.

They came in boats that rocked back and forth in the wharf's waters. They filled the adjacent deserted island of Manana, lining the shoreline and dotting the higher ground.

There was an identifiable raucous cadre of extremists—you will know them by their shouts of uncontrolled inappropriate laughter. Pockets of prayer and laughter and hymn-singing, contagions of grotesque happiness, burst forth from their ranks and bubbled over like symptoms of an ailment that resisted easy diagnosis but raised all kinds of concern.

"Any one of these nuts could bring down a plane just by looking up," Spark said uneasily, holding tight to Hally's forearm as we made our way toward the big white tents set up for the performers and staff.

No one at the site had officially recognized Hally but it was only a matter of time, a handful of people kept trailing us, sniffing the air, suspicions raised, the regulars from the house and the church prowling around. We were relieved to see the sheriff and several of his deputies, along with private security hired by Pastor Ragnar, who were assigned to protect Hally and help manage the crowd.

Hally was scheduled to appear briefly onstage with Pastor Ragnar, though the time was a secret—nobody wanted to make life easy for the Shroud of Turin guy by providing him with an itinerary.

There never were so many stars as there were that night. Sparkling pinpricks of white light softly illuminating the black sky, the night crisp but glowing like candlelight, lanterns in trees lit and shimmering. Poplar leaves rustled on the cold breeze in shadowy accompaniment to the music, as the waves tumbled and rolled and the symphony played and the singers sang, the air itself seeming to ring out clear as cathedral bells.

When Hally finally appeared onstage, the chant went up. Three times the crowd cried out in unison, even the secularists got caught up in beseeching God for salvation.

Hosanna. Hosanna. Hosanna. Pastor Ragnar led the chant.

"A new low," Spark said on the walk back to the house, flashlights showing us the way in the dark.

"Don't be so cynical," Cipolla said. "That was one of the most moving experiences of my life. Wonderful flow of energy and spirituality. All those people joined in perfect harmony. The ocean. The stars. The music. The sweep of light from the lighthouse. It was a miraculous convergence. It made me happy to be human, to celebrate glorious humanity."

"I understand people had the same reaction to the Nuremberg Rally," Spark said. He was being even more contrary than usual.

"Spark . . ." Hugh said, his voice urging restraint.

"I don't appreciate that comparison, or the implied suggestion," Cipolla said curtly.

"Anyway . . . we couldn't have asked for better weather, especially this time of year. What a beautiful night," Hugh said.

Spark and Hugh were already inside. Hally and I were lingering on the deck, taking advantage of a brief moment of solitude. He was clearly unnerved by the attention he'd received at the concert and was trying to pull himself together. He was trembling, his hands shaking as he pulled me close to him. We could hear voices carrying on the wind from the rocky shore where there was an informal gathering, Pastor Ragnar and Rusty Cipolla, other voices I didn't recognize, excited and animated, laughing, thrilled at how things had gone.

"It was magisterial," I heard DeeDee White say.

"Sublime," someone else agreed. "I felt the presence of God."

The familiar voices of the Tick-Tock Girls, in their matching dresses, and their mismatched harmonies, grew louder and more confident as they sang "The Old-Fashioned Way."

Hally swore quietly and then, summoning me, he opened the back door and as he stepped inside, beckoning me to follow, I had the most disconcerting feeling, the hair on my back standing straight up. I stopped at the threshold, turned my head and barked at the darkness.

In the cold, as I barked, I could see my breath take shape and then disappear.

I scratched at Hally's bedroom door and it took him a long time to let me inside. He didn't say a word but covered his ears with his hands, trying to drown out the sounds of the Tick-Tock Girls as they sang. Increasingly distressed, he crawled inside his closet door and curled up in the farthest corner, trying to make himself small. He stayed there for what seemed a long time and then he got up and, picking me up, he held me close, kissed me on the top of the head and, opening his door, put me outside on the floor in the hallway. Then he shut the door and wouldn't let me back in.

Spark had fallen asleep on the sofa in the living room where I eventually joined him. It was an uneasy night. Before sunrise, I followed Spark up the stairs to his bedroom, next to Hally's room. Spark sat on the edge of the bed and I lay on the pillow beside him, both of us listening to Hally throw up in the bathroom at the end of the hall. Spark waited for a little while after we heard Hally's footsteps coming down the corridor and then the door to his room clicked shut. Spark got up and knocked on Hally's door.

"Hally, where are you?" Spark asked, confused, looking around the small room.

The curtains blew, fanning out over the bed. Spark, hands on the windowsill, stuck his head out through the wide opening. "What are you doing out here?"

I jumped up onto the windowsill and saw Hally, his back to the chimney, knees pulled up to his face, sitting on the mossy roof, his outline smudged but visible in the silvery predawn grayness.

"Go away, Spark," Hally said, his voice hoarse. Spark climbed onto the roof beside him, me tentatively following, taking refuge in Spark's lap—not a huge fan of heights, but this was not the time to be thinking only of me.

That night on the living and breathing roof, something was averted beneath the cool spare light from a waning moon, the three of us alone in the sky, the early morning a shallow pool of silence.

No one spoke but sank into the quiet, listening to the beating of each secret heart.

The next morning, while taking a brief tour of the property, I came across a clumsily dug hole covered over with leaves and hidden behind a boulder in the long grasses of the wildflower meadow. There was a battered backpack shoved into the corner of the shallow dugout. Recognizing the scent, I ran back to the house, summoning the others with my barking. The sheriff, called to the scene, found masking tape in the bag and a shabby wallet containing worn clippings about the apparitions and a picture of Hally torn from *Life* magazine.

Hally's stalker was named Jonah Harkness. He was a religious fanatic, used to preach on the streets and parks in Portland—that is when he wasn't dodging jail for a series of sex offenses.

"A sex offender? Oh Jesus," Hugh said, sounding sick.

"This is insane," Spark said. "Hally's turning into some kind of pop star slash Jesus hybrid. Those goddamn apparitions . . . "

I had a hunch it was likely the first time the words "goddamn" and "apparitions" had ever appeared in apposition to each other in the same sentence but it was hard not to empathize with Spark's fury. We were in the living room. Hugh was sitting on the sofa, knees spread apart, elbows resting on his knees, his head in his hands. Spark was pacing. "That's it. This—all of it—is over."

"Spark, I don't know what Hally saw but he believes he saw something . . . He believes he heard someone speak to him. He's never wavered . . . Maybe we have to consider . . . the possibility . . ."

"No," Spark said, shaking his head. "No."

"Yes, like Flory. Yes, Spark. Yes," Hugh said gently.

"For Christ's sake, Hugh, do you hear yourself? Flory came up behind me and stuck an eight-inch carving knife into my back. She tried to kill me."

"I know," Hugh said. "How could I ever forget?"

"Hughie, think about what you're saying . . . She left me to bleed out on the floor . . . She put a plastic bag over her head and—"

Pastor Ragnar appeared in the doorway. "Be quiet, the two of you," he said wearily, seeming depleted. "He'll hear you."

Hally crept up behind him. "It's too late," he said as I wondered what he meant.

In an official first for the Monahan family, no one knew what to say.

Twenty-three

"We'll find the bastard, I promise you. Now we know who he is. We've got everybody in the state out looking for him. His face is in every paper and on every TV set in the country. I know it's tough. Just sit tight. We'll get him."

"I know you will, sheriff," Pastor Ragnar said, though Spark and Hugh, all of us together in the living room, didn't look quite as persuaded. "We should never have let down our guard. To think he was probably out there all night long lurking and plotting. Everyone was just so euphoric."

"I have to accept my own share of responsibility," the sheriff said. "Concert went off without a hitch. We were all feeling good. Too good, obviously. Hally was home safe. This guy is a true predator, watching and waiting for his moment. Thank heavens he never found one."

"You can thank Ned it wasn't worse. He sounded the alert," Spark said.

"You can't beat a dog. You did our job for us, didn't you, buddy?" the sheriff agreed. He bent down to give me a pat on the head. When he straightened up, he said. "This guy must be feeling desperate right at the moment. Nothing to lose. No telling what he might do, so I'm sure I don't need to remind you, utmost caution is warranted."

"Where's Hally?" Spark asked Hugh, his voice barely above a whisper. They were standing across from each other in the kitchen.

"Still in his room," Hugh answered. "You can't blame him. All these people tracking his every move. This creep after him. Then finding out about Flory in the worst possible way . . . I wish to God we had told him the truth before now."

"Is there a right way or time to tell a kid his mother tried to murder his father and then killed herself?"

"What if he heard me? What if he heard what I said about him inheriting Flory's problems? What must he be thinking?"

"I don't know. I've got no answers. I don't think there's a guidebook covering off what's happened here." Spark, whiter than usual, eyes red from sleeplessness, suppressed a yawn. "I've got to get some sleep. I can't think straight."

Hally was waiting in Spark's room, sitting in the old leather club chair, dressed in jeans and faded cotton pullover, wrapped in a worn Hudson's Bay blanket, cold wind whistling outside, making eerie incursion through the cracked and rotting window frame.

"Hally," Spark said, hand to heart, startled. "Holy shit, you scared me."

"What happened that day? Between you and my mother?"

"Hally." Spark sat down on the edge of the bed.

"Tell me."

"Jesus."

"Spark . . ."

"She came up behind me. That's it . . . No warning. She came at me from behind."

Neither Spark nor Hally said much after that. After a little while, Hally stood up and left.

My ears blew back in the wind. Spark's hair was in my face. "It's freezing," Spark said, wrapping his scarf tightly around his neck and shuddering, hunching his shoulders toward the blowing gusts coming off the ocean, the churning water a cold and ruthless blue.

Not far from the house we ran into Chip Wallace, who pounced merrily on Spark.

"Hey, chief, how's it—"

"Not now, Chip, for Christ's sake," Spark said as Chip looked crestfallen and apologized and kept on walking in the opposite direction, eyes cast downward. "Jesus," Spark muttered to himself. He spun around. "I'm sorry, Chip," Spark hollered after him. "There's trouble at home."

Chip raised his hand up over his head. "That's too bad," he shouted.

We resumed our walk along the Burnt Head trail, heading toward the island's rugged back side, noted for its fatal currents, slippery surfaces, and unforgiving comber waves.

"Pop," Spark said, looking down from the trail, spotting Pastor Ragnar up ahead in the distance, walking stick in hand, navigating the cobbled beach just shy of the tidal line. Spark and I maneuvered our way downward and off the trail, heading toward him, walking the rocky shoreline we had walked many times before.

The black rocks were stained white with gull droppings, the power of the blowing wind no match for the primitive stink of centuries of accumulated bird shit. I wobbled slightly from its overwhelming effects.

The wind and the waves were so loud we were on top of him before he knew we were there at all. "Hey, Pop, what are you doing out here?" Spark touched his father on the shoulder.

"Spark." Pastor Ragnar, startled, stopped and turned around, quickly recovering. "Same as you, I imagine. Seeking solace in nature. Where's Hally?"

"He's resting. Hugh is with him."

"Good."

"Yeah, good," Spark said as he walked, stopping occasionally to stamp his feet or blow into his cupped hands, refusing his father's offer of his gloves. "Pop, I've been thinking. You may not want to hear what I have to say but I think this thing with Hally needs to be put to bed for good. He's too vulnerable. Even when they're well-intentioned, or think they are, these followers of his, or whatever you want to call them, make his life hell.

"So we find this guy. One monster down. There'll always be another monster. The only way Hally can have a chance at a normal life is if he withdraws from the church, Cludo, the public eye, just disappears and no more conversation about him or the apparitions. It all just stops."

"Or it accelerates. Nothing fuels the human imagination like mystery and inaccessibility. Why do you think death is the best career move some celebrities will ever make?"

"Pop, please," Spark said, tone of desperation in his voice. "Who cares about this crap? Just cut it out. No more bullshit."

"Yes, Jamie, yes," Pastor Ragnar said, patience being tested, sounding the edgy way people do when assailed yet again by a familiar accusation.

"Look, I don't want to pin this whole mess on you. I played my part. Why don't we both agree enough is enough and make a few changes? Start by declaring a truce. We've been fighting with each other for so long I can't even remember what it's about anymore."

"What exactly would you like me to do?"

"Stop talking about Hally and the apparitions for a start. You're smart. I'm sure you can do it in such a way it works for you and for Cludo."

"It's not that simple. Some things can't be called back into the cage."

"Use your imagination. What the hell? Jesus has years of his life unaccounted for."

"The world's in trouble when Spark Monahan is relying on scripture to make a point in an argument."

Spark laughed a little in concession, which helped to soften the intensity of their exchange, and then Pastor Ragnar, a bit tentatively for him, questioned Spark about the Wrendle girl's accusations against Hally. He asked Spark if he'd ever considered the possibility Hally had done what she said he'd done.

Spark shook his head. "No."

"Why not?"

"For one thing, I saw them together that night. The dynamics weren't there, which is putting it mildly. Hally was so obviously scared. She was so obviously enjoying tormenting him. Hally isn't exactly a criminal mastermind. Even if I hadn't seen them, I just knew."

"You had faith in Hally."

"It was more than that."

"Yes, some things you just know," Pastor Ragnar said, seeming momentarily enamored with the realization. Pastor Ragnar pointed to me. I felt slightly irritated. What did I have to do with it?

"The moment I saw him, for example," Pastor Ragnar said, "I knew you'd stolen him."

"So you have the same reflex, in the inverse, when it comes to me. You *just know* not to have faith or believe in me."

"I'm not saying that at all. I'm pointing to one incident, which becomes significant only because you insist on denying it. Admit it, Spark, you took the dog."

"I can't," Spark said. "I can't admit it because it doesn't seem true."

I had been running alongside them, scurrying about, paying attention to their conversation, while tracking the fresh wild scents in the moist air and on the ground, at least the few strong enough to hold their own against the prevailing stench. What Spark said. It didn't feel true to me either. It felt like fate, not like a petty crime.

"All right," Pastor Ragnar said unexpectedly. "Fair enough."

"Have you got something else on your mind, Pop?" Spark said. "Something you're not saying?"

Pastor Ragnar shook his head but his demeanor belied his words. He seemed morose, worse, he seemed amenable. It was disconcerting.

I circled them barking—wanting to try anything, even embarrassing dog antics, to lift the mood—and even Pastor Ragnar looked amused. He and Spark, wearying of the battle, talked a little about the success of the concert. We veered around a large outcropping of rock, which took us nearer the shoreline.

"How did we wind up here?" Spark said, realizing we had wandered below the tide line. "We should head back up."

"Jamie," Pastor Ragnar said, slowing to a stop, circling back to the beginning of their talk.

"Believe it or not, it's occurred to me Hally could stand to step away for a time . . . You should know, I contacted Fred. He's expressed interest in getting to know Hally, for real."

"I'm guessing you told him Flory and I were married."

"I did."

"How'd he take it?"

"He was pleased in his own way."

"So now, Hally's acceptable to him and Joanna."

"He is."

"I'm just supposed to walk away—*again*—and turn over my kid to Fred MacNamara, a man who hates me . . . "

"No. Of course not, but we can't keep Hally safe. Fred MacNamara can. He can make Hally disappear and still give him the world. Our only option is to lock him up in his room and stand guard. Unfortunately, after a great deal of thought and prayer, I have come to believe, as you say, there will always be another Jonah Harkness. It's the nature of this thing. Something about Hally, too, attracts these unstable types.

"It would be a temporary informal arrangement. We still retain custody. Hally can come and go as he pleases. Fred's agreed you can see and talk to him whenever you like."

"How good of him . . . I don't get it," Spark said. "Why are you suddenly promoting this idea, the very thing you dreaded happening, now you're all in favor? Why?"

"Not sudden. Not really. I've been thinking about it for a while."

"Pop, there's more to this than you're saying. What's going on?"

They had begun to walk again. Almost instantly Pastor Ragnar wobbled, slipped, and fell against the black rocks. Spark lunged for him but too late, Pastor Ragnar had begun an uninterrupted slide to the icy edge of the shoreline and into the water, the currents grabbing him, gobbling him up, pushing him under and back up again. He tried to get out but there was nothing to grasp.

"I'm coming," Spark said as he headed toward the shoreline, moving perilously fast, me slipping and sliding behind him.

"Jamie, go back." Pastor Ragnar gasped when he saw us.

"Hang on," Spark said, trying to safely maneuver the treacherous black rock, slick as polished ice, knowing that when people go into the waters off Burnt Head, they don't generally come out again. He glanced quickly around and reached for Pastor Ragnar's walking stick, lying at a random angle on the rock near the water's edge.

Moving purposefully and methodically, Spark lay down near the shoreline and extended the stick. "Grab it. Hold on," he ordered Pastor Ragnar, who was struggling against the waves to keep his head above water. After several failed attempts, he was finally able to latch onto the stick.

"Don't let go," Spark shouted, pulling with both hands, arms shaking with the effort, shouting to be heard over the waves and the wind. Slowly, he dragged his father from the water—Pastor Ragnar was strong and fit and was able to participate in his own rescue. Once out of the water, with Spark's help, he crawled over the rock to where we were.

"Jamie," he said, reaching out, clasping his shoulder. "I've wronged you. Forgive me."

"Come on, Pop, that's just the hypothermia talking. Save your energy. We need to get back up and out of here. Why the hell did you come down here anyway?" Spark said as he stood up and then extended his hand, helping to get Pastor Ragnar to his feet. "Be careful." He pointed to higher ground and Pastor Ragnar nodded, his teeth chattering, clothes dripping, black hair gleaming in the stark sunlight, wet tips icing over, the wind almost blowing us off our feet.

They were walking side by side, Spark's arms around his father, moving at an even, careful clip. "Be confident," Spark said. "Walk like you mean it. This isn't the time to be tentative."

The rocks were wet, the spray from the wind making them even more perilous than usual. Spark knew those rocks so well, had navigated them a million times, knew the dangers of going past a certain point, the black rocks covered with an invisible treacherous moss. That day they were as sleek as I would ever know them to be. I trotted out and away so I was in front of them, the scent of Pastor Ragnar's cologne preceding him. There was that cold pipe smell I recognized. Equipage. Pastor Ragnar, directly behind me, pivoted, his feet sliding out from under him. He started to slide. Spark grabbed him, hoisting him back on his feet. "We're almost there," he said. "Hang on, Pop. I've got you."

"This has been the season of slippery slopes," Pastor Ragnar said. "You've got me. Who's got you?"

Twenty-four

"What if he doesn't come back? What if he decides to stay?" Spark said as he and Hugh worked away on the porch, ripping out the old rotting and mushy wood, the rusted nails. It was Hugh's idea to demolish the old veranda before it collapsed altogether and someone got hurt. It was the same weekend in November that Hally first went to visit his grandparents in Virginia.

"That's not going to happen," Hugh said, struggling with an especially resistant board.

"Sure it could. Hell, I don't think I'd come home."

"Yes, you would and he will, too. It's only a few days. Have some faith and just keep banging away."

"Just his state of mind is so lousy. He was so upset. I think he hates me. He's barely spoken to me since . . ."

"Spark, he doesn't hate you. He's struggling with all that's happened."

"What if they get him a pony?"

"He's a little big for a pony."

"Nobody's ever too big for a pony," Spark said unhappily.

〰〰〰〰

"Neddy!" Hally bent down and pulled me into his arms, crushing me against the buttercream softness of his Italian leather jacket. "Look what I've got for you."

He presented me with a hand-tooled leather collar and for a second I thought about the bony strays roaming the mean streets of Dorchester but the moment quickly passed and I ran down the hallway dragging Hally's silk scarf in my teeth.

"Nice hair," Spark said, after greeting Hally as he came in the house through the kitchen entrance. "Is that the Choate taper, by way of Brideshead Castle?"

"It's just a haircut, Spark. It's not a brain transplant," Hally said tolerantly, smiling broadly as Hugh stepped forward and gave him a big hug.

"I think it's great," Hugh said. "Wow, look at you. You look as if you just stepped out of the pages of GQ."

"And people thought you were a god before," Spark said, leaning up against the counter.

Hally dropped his luggage on the floor, where it landed with a thud. "Okay, I get it, Spark. You don't approve."

"Of course he does, don't you?" Hugh said, giving his brother the verbal equivalent of a pointed kick under the table.

"Yeah, sure, you look good, Hal. Don't pay any attention to me. I'm just being a jerk."

Hally began excitedly pulling gifts for everyone from his bag. "Oh well, if that's all it is, then don't worry about it. Just you being you."

Just then, Pastor Ragnar made his controlled entrance into the living room. He had been working in his office.

"Welcome home," he said. "Are you still speaking to your poor relations?"

"Yes! Come on, you guys . . . Can I tell you about it? Or are you going to act like freaks?"

Pastor Ragnar pulled him in for a kiss on the forehead. "Oh, I insist on hearing about everything, from the smallest detail. Leave nothing out."

His grandparents wept when they saw him. You're the image of your mother, his grandfather told him, holding him tightly to his chest. His grandmother was too overcome to speak at first. The house was so big he kept getting lost. They gave him his own bedroom and told him he could decorate however he wanted. His bedroom had a balcony overlooking the grounds and the stables.

"They said I can have my own horse!" Hally said as Hugh ignored Spark's I-told-you-so stare. "Whatever kind I want."

"What about a unicorn?" Spark said.

They took him shopping. His grandfather opened a bank account for him and said he would give him a weekly allowance. They talked about traveling together.

"To another dimension? Maybe DeeDee can be your guide," Spark asked.

"Jamie, your resentments are showing," Pastor Ragnar said. "Not a good look for you."

"They said I could have Tutela Heights. It's mine. They're going to fix it up for when I'm older."

"Oh, I don't know about that. Really? Maybe that's not such a great idea," Spark said, looking pained.

"They want you to come and visit sometime," Hally said. "All of you. I said you would."

"Of course we will," Pastor Ragnar said.

"You, too, Spark," Hally said.

"They're just being polite, Hal," Spark said. "I'm the last person they want to see."

"Maybe," Hally conceded. "But politeness is a start, right? Maybe you could be polite, too, and try."

Spark shrugged. "Maybe."

"Hughie, I talked to them about your work. My grandfather collects art and he said he'd seen some of your paintings and he really liked them and said how talented you were and that he wants to talk to you some time."

Hugh made no attempt to conceal his pleasure. Spark regarded Hugh with a combination of contempt and disbelief. "Old Man Mac-Namara is just trying to ingratiate himself with us and he's pulling out all the stops."

Hugh grinned over at him. "Yeah, well, whatever he's doing, it's working."

As Hugh and Spark bantered back and forth, Pastor Ragnar took Hally aside. The two walked into the study while I trailed behind them.

"They were good to you, then?" Pastor Ragnar asked Hally in a low voice.

"Yeah," Hally said, nodding. He paused, going over something in his head. "They think I should be in school, though. They want to send me to Georgetown Prep in Washington. That's where my grandfather went to school. He said he was going to call and talk to you about it."

"Fred wants you in the hands of the Jesuits. I'm not surprised. How do you feel about it?"

"I want to go to school. I feel okay about it. Maybe a little weird about moving away."

"So it begins," Spark said, appearing in the doorway. He had obviously been listening. "How long did it take him to mention prep school? Five minutes, ten?"

"Spark, he only wants the best for Hally," Hugh said, joining them.

"You mean he wants his idea of the best for Hally," Spark said.

"What was that?" Hally said as Spark darted from the room. There was a loud thump against the kitchen door. Footsteps on the deck. Faces peering in through the door, through the window, visible from the living room.

"Goddammit," Spark said, going for the door, opening it wide, shouting at them to leave. There was the sound of youthful laughter, teenage boys and girls, shoving and squealing as they scrambled from the deck. Someone had sprayed "Hail Murray" in white letters on the floor.

"Great, now we've got the toilet-papering brigade out in force," he said, slamming the door hard enough that it banged. Still we could hear them, their voices calling out to one another as they fled. Hally lowered his head, seeming suddenly drained of vitality.

"Is this your idea of what's best for Hally, Spark?" Hugh asked, but Spark's attention was on Pastor Ragnar.

"You did this," he said. "All of it. It's all on you. You orchestrated the whole damn thing from beginning to end."

"I've done only what I thought was best for Hally," Pastor Ragnar said.

"Everything you do is for you," Spark said.

Hally was fed up with listening. "Why don't I make it easy on everyone? From now on I'll make my own decisions. If I want your help, I'll ask for it, otherwise all of you, butt out."

Pastor Ragnar started to respond but then thought better of it, watching silently, along with the rest of us, as Hally left the room, his footsteps beating up the staircase, the door to his bedroom banging shut.

Spark turned to Hugh and Pastor Ragnar. "Oh, now I get it," he said. "Hally's the teenage antichrist, and lucky for us, he's got more money than God."

The next morning, early Sunday, before church services, Pastor Ragnar summoned everyone to the living room, saying he had something he wanted to discuss. Intrigued, I jumped up on the sofa between Hugh and Spark as Pastor Ragnar stood in front of the fireplace, assuming a slightly formal stance, as if he were about to give a major address. Hally sat poised on the edge of one of the Morris chairs. He was wearing a fleece jacket, hood pulled up around his head. I looked at him closely. Something seemed off.

"Don't tell me," Spark said. "You've decided to abandon the ministry and become an Irish step dancer."

Looking unamused, Pastor Ragnar explained he had been contacted by *Esquire* magazine about a portrait series they were shooting. It's called "Three Generations," he explained.

"Grandfather, son, and grandson," he said. "They're being very selective who they shoot and they want to photograph us. Part of the attraction, apart from the obvious, is the photographer. Yousuf Karsh."

"Karsh," Hugh repeated reverentially.

"I thought we weren't going to do this stuff anymore?" Spark said, agitated. "I should have known better . . ."

"This is different," Pastor Ragnar said. "This is an artistic project."

"Maybe so, but Hally isn't doing any photo shoot," Spark proclaimed. "I don't care if Michelangelo rises from the dead for the sole purpose of adding the Monahans to the ceiling of the Sistine Chapel. No more. Over. Done. Finished."

"Don't you think Hally has a right to make his own decision?" Pastor Ragnar asked.

"No. I'm his father and I'm saying no. After all that's happened. How can you even—"

"I'll do it," Hally said, interrupting, his mood dangerously black. He had been so buoyant on his return only hours earlier.

"Are you sure?" Pastor Ragnar said. "You have a day or so to think about it . . ."

"I have thought about it. Tell them okay," Hally said, glaring at Spark.

"Hugh?" Pastor Ragnar inquired.

Hugh looked over at Spark. "It's Karsh . . ." he said by way of appeal.

"You really figured this whole thing out, didn't you?" Spark said to Pastor Ragnar. "Trick Hally into thinking he's making his own decision when all he's doing is giving in to adolescent defiance and tempt Hugh with the opportunity by dangling Karsh in front of him . . . Well, you can count me out."

"Oh, I'm sorry, perhaps I didn't make things clear," Pastor Ragnar said. "The magazine was specific in its criteria: Three generations of three *high-achieving, high-profile* males from the same family. You weren't included."

"Jesus, Pop," Hugh said.

A few hours later, Spark and I were out walking the trail to White Head when we saw Hugh approach. He ran to catch up. "Found you," he said, panting. "Spark, I want you to know, I'm not going to do it. I told Pop to forget about me being photographed. It was lousy what he did. He set you up. I don't want to be any part of it."

We resumed walking. "Thanks, Hugh," Spark said. "I want you to do it. You should do it. You've earned it. It will be good for your career."

"What about Hally?"

"Uh, well, I'm feeling a little overpowered right at the moment. I'm not exactly a match for the assembled forces of Pop, Frederick MacNamara, and God."

"Sure you are," Hugh said. "Why do you think they've formed an alliance? Because they know who they're dealing with."

Spark laughed, a bit rueful. "The thing is, Hughie, I just have this uneasy feeling inside and I can't shake it. All these battles seem like skirmishes designed to distract us from the real war that's going on, the secret war we have no idea about."

I sat down at this feet and looked up at him but he didn't notice me. Reaching into the top drawer he pulled out a pair of sewing scissors and without benefit of a mirror or plan of attack, he began to methodically cut his hair, starting at the front, then the top, the sides, and the back, hacking away, lopping off big glossy chunks, until he'd accumulated a shiny pile of gold on the surface of the desktop.

He lay back down on his bed. I lay next to him while he stroked my head.

"Are you sleeping okay?" he asked himself.

"No," he answered.

"Are you eating what you should?" he asked himself.

"No," he answered.

"Are you feeling anxious all the time?" he asked himself.

"Yes," he answered.

Hally stopped mid-stroke and got up from the bed. He looked at himself in the mirror.

"So this is what it looks like," he said, reaching out, tracing the outlines of his face with his finger to the glass.

Twenty-five

Spark walked into the kitchen through the back door. He was home early from work, engine trouble on the boat. It was midmorning, around eleven o'clock. I ran to greet him. He picked me up, asked me about my day, and carried me over to the refrigerator. Reaching inside, he grabbed some orange juice, set me down on the floor, and drank from the carton. Hugh hollered greetings from the studio above. "Quit drinking from the carton!"

"How does he know?" Spark asked me.

"The same way I know you're eating peanut butter with a knife from the jar," Hugh shouted as Spark put the lid back on the jar.

"Well, you're wrong," Spark lied.

"You've gotta quit that boat. I can smell you from here. For a minute I thought you brought Salamander by for a visit," Hugh said as Spark, unfazed, grabbed a handful of cookies, kicked aside his backpack, and headed for the shower, me trailing him.

Sometimes I'd join him in the bathroom and I'd pester him until he'd put me up on the high shallow windowsill so I could see what was going on outside.

"Gee, are you sure that's a good idea? What if he fell?" Hugh said when he saw me perched up there at his eye level.

"Talk to Ned. It's his idea. He insists," Spark said.

"You sure do run a tight ship," Hugh said.

After showering, Spark pulled on a pair of blue jeans and a long-sleeved T-shirt. Rubbing his hair with a towel, he knocked on Hally's door, then poked his head inside.

"Hal?" he said.

Bumping down the stairs, he went into the kitchen. "Where's Hally?" he asked.

"In his room," Hugh said.

"No. I checked. He's not there."

Hugh frowned. "He told me a couple of hours ago he was tired. He hasn't been sleeping so I let him rest."

Hugh went into the hallway and called out Hally's name. We looked all through the house and around the property. We opened up the little guest cottage but we couldn't find him anywhere.

"Oh boy," Hugh said. "Where would he be? He knows not to go off with this creep on the loose."

Spark asked if Hally had seemed upset about something.

"No. No more than usual. I mean, I didn't see him. We exchanged a few words through the bedroom door but he seemed fine. Nothing alarming, anyway."

"Okay. Let's not panic. He's a kid and he's been kept on a short leash, especially since the concert. Then he's set loose in Virginia, which is its own fantasy world. Something was bound to give. Where would he go?"

"I should have kept a better eye on him. It never occurred to me he'd take off."

"It's not your fault. He shouldn't have sneaked off on his own." Spark stared out over the ocean, thinking. "He'd know better than to go anywhere obvious where he'd be visible. I wonder if he went to Tutela Heights?"

"Why would he go there?"

"Just thinking out loud—his grandfather gave it to him. It's his, wouldn't you want to see it? And we talked about it a while ago when we were on the boat. I told him how you and I used to get in through the upper balcony."

"Why would you tell him about that? Honest to God, Spark . . ."

"All this stuff about the MacNamaras, and the house being his one day, maybe that inspired him . . . I'll bet that's it. I'm going to run over and have a look."

"I'll come with you. Just let me close up the studio and . . ."

"Nah, don't worry about it," Spark said, already heading out. "Wait here and see if he turns up. I'll be back soon, with him or without him." He broke into a run. "Come on, Neddy, let's go find Hally."

The front door was left slightly ajar, creating an eerie effect. We stepped inside gingerly, Spark especially lacked enthusiasm for crossing the threshold, willing himself to walk through the doorway. There were giant copper urns on either side of the interior entranceway, posturing as house staff. I took a deep breath, inhaling dust, choking on the staleness.

I felt as if I had stepped inside a fairy tale, or maybe a ghost story, things I had only previously heard about and imagined, awakening, stretching, yawning to life, Spark and I at Flory's house, in the part of the kitchen where the windows opened wide to the ocean. A big kitchen, old-fashioned, white, traditional with dated appliances and plain straightforward cupboards from the twenties or thirties—only old money dares to be dowdy—it opened up at the side entrance to a large winterized porch.

Spark stopped and leaned against the counter with his eyes closed. I waited while he composed himself. After a few moments, he made his way—me matching his slow deliberate pace, adhering to his side like a crutch—to the dining room, whose walls were covered in decades-old hand-painted wallpaper with seashore motif. The antique table and chairs were dark mahogany, covered in dusty cream-colored bedsheets.

The MacNamara house, untouched and unpolished, qualified as a "grand old place," with its high ceilings, classic architectural elements, crown molding, and old hardwoods. I was in a different era when I was at Tutela Heights, a house that lent value to the theory of benign neglect as a working philosophy with many applications.

"Hally?" Spark said, voice echoing softly, human voice seeming somehow out of place, from the center hallway on the main floor. It wasn't long before Hally appeared at the top of the stairs. He was wearing blue jeans and a sky-blue shirt. His old jacket. Running shoes.

"Why didn't you tell Hugh where you were going?"

Hally shrugged. "Didn't feel like it."

Spark put his hand on the banister, his fingers leaving a trail of dust as he walked up the stairs. "Yeah, well, you gave us a scare . . . What the hell did you do to your hair?"

"I cut it."

"I can see that . . . Jesus, Hal . . ."

"You didn't like it. You made that clear. What do you care about my hair?"

"Yeah, well, you didn't need to take a hacksaw to it. How'd you get in here anyway? The front door—"

Hally held up a chain with a single key and the tiny tarnished figure of a fox terrier. "Gram," he said. "She gave it to me before she died—"

"That's Flory's keychain," Spark said, interrupting.

"—Said it had been my mother's. She said the house belonged to me now."

"Good old Gram. She never did worry about minor details like giving away a house she didn't own. You should have said something . . . What if Harkness is still hanging around, saw you, followed you? Trapped you in here alone?"

"I just needed to get out of the house before I went crazy."

"I wish you had told me about having the key all this time, about where you were going. What was Mom thinking? You were eight years old and she gives you the key to this house? Of all places? Why didn't you tell anyone?" Spark said, hesitating at the top of the stairs.

"We all have our little secrets."

"I guess." Spark's foot rocked, the floor creaking in agitation beneath him.

"What's wrong?" Hally asked him.

"It's freezing in here. Aren't you cold? It always was cold in this house. I haven't been here for a long time. It's just the same . . ."

"Not since . . ."

Spark nodded. "Yeah," he said.

"I guess that would make it hard to be here. I like being here . . . in her room. Makes me feel close to her. Makes me feel as if I know her." Hally started walking down the long corridor. He turned around. "Are you coming?" he asked Spark.

"I'll be along," Spark said.

Flory's room, elegantly monochromatic, was painted in a soft shade of celadon, the walls, the ceiling, the moldings. Even the furniture, simple and feminine, antique, was celadon green. The silk window coverings were the same shade and trailed onto the wooden floor. There was a framed poster of Phil Ochs on the wall. Pictures of Spark, on the wall, on her desk, looking young, tender, happy, full of fun. Not like the troublemaker he'd been made out to be by local legend. On her dresser, too, was a folk art statue of the Virgin Mary, primitive and carved from wood, South American maybe.

There was a miniature birdbath at the statue's feet, gray, made of stone, a red rosary visible within, two little birds on either side of the birdbath, flanking the overhanging beads, each bead the shape of a tiny rose. An atomizer containing Tweed perfume, half-full, sat next to it, along with a framed photograph of a Leonberger dog.

"Oscar," Spark said.

"What?" Hally said.

"Flory's dog. Oscar. She named him after Oscar Wilde. The Mac-Namaras imported him from Ireland. He came to live with us when we got married. The MacNamaras took him away after Flory died. I never saw him again . . . Anyway, what are you doing here? I still don't get how you could have kept all this a secret . . . why you haven't said anything?" Spark was sounding a little desperate.

"So you could tell me not to come anymore? So you could look at me the way you're looking at me now?"

"Hally, is this where you came, the night the Wrendle girl made up the story, after you took off?"

Hally nodded. "I like it here. It's quiet. It's calm. It helps me think."

"It does?" Spark said, appearing confused, listening but not listening, the house having the opposite turbulent effect on him.

"I come here a lot. Ever since Gram died. Why shouldn't I?"

"Since Gram died? You've been coming here that long? And no one knew?"

"What's wrong with that?"

"It doesn't seem healthy. A kid alone wandering around this house, with all its unhappy memories."

"What unhappy memories? I come here to get away from unhappy memories."

"Like what?"

"Like when Gram died."

"So you do remember." Hally suddenly had Spark's full attention.

"I'm sorry, Hally, I should never have left you alone with her. She was sick. You were just a little boy." Spark's sense of shame was like another presence in the room.

"Tell me the truth, Spark, did I do something to cause it?"

"What? No. Why would you ask me something like that?"

"Because she was fine and then we were playing cards and she kept winning and I said she was cheating."

"She always cheated."

"She got mad at me for accusing her of cheating and we got into a fight about it and then——"

"Hally, you had nothing to do with it."

"You say that but why does everything bad happen around me? My mom was fine until she had me. It seems like everything went wrong when I was born and it just keeps getting worse."

"Flory had a mental illness. Mom was dying of cancer. They were both ill. You had nothing to do with any of that. Nobody did. It's just what happened."

"You took off. You couldn't stand to look at me. I don't blame you."

"There is only one reason I took off. I took off because I was an asshole. I came back because I didn't want to be an asshole anymore."

"That's not what Hugh says. He says Gramp drove you away."

"I gave him the ammunition," Spark said. "Hally, you've got to forget all this stuff, and quit blaming yourself for things that had nothing to do with you. It's my fault. I should have stuck around. I should have talked to you about everything, told you the truth from the beginning . . . " Spark broke off. "Jesus, this place . . . Let's get out of here. I promise I'll tell you anything you want to know. Just not here, okay?"

Hally nodded. "All right."

Spark looked relieved. He smiled. "See why people keep things wrapped up inside? It's a hell of a lot easier— What?" he said, interrupting himself, surprised, catching unexpected sight of something on Flory's desk between two small piles of dusty books.

He walked over to the desk and picked up a small plastic squeeze bulb. "I don't believe it."

"What is that stuff?" Hally asked. "I found it in one of the drawers. I thought maybe it was perfume that had dried up. I sprayed it, but only these tiny yellow dust particles came out."

"Lycopedium spores," Spark said. "Little feet of the fox. Remember, I told you about it? They use it to make magic, to make firecrackers. Fire-breathers sometimes use it. I showed this to your mom when we first met. This was mine." He looked around. "Crazy. Everything's the same and nothing's the same."

He searched his pockets and pulled out a pack of matches. He set them down on the desk.

Hally gave him this look.

"You never know when you'll need to make a fire, kid. Hand me that candle, please," Spark said, sounding more like himself, pointing to a long white taper candle in its holder on the window seat.

Spark placed the candle on a small occasional table. He struck a match and lit the wick, then he squeezed the plastic bulb where the flame flickered highest. Nothing happened so he squeezed again, this time the lycopedium spores ignited, a fireball surging in theatrical exhalation, "breath of the dragon," Spark called it, the fire and its extinguishing occurring almost simultaneously, an instantaneous explosion of birth and death, side-by-side living and dying.

"My greatest and my only trick," Spark said in mock triumph. "It never ceased to amuse your mom. She said to me first time I showed her, 'That's it? That's all you've got?'"

Hally said she had a point. "It's over before it begins."

Spark sat down at the desk. "That's the magic of it," he said.

"No, that's you, Spark, over before you began," Hally said, the tension between them always ready to put in an appearance.

"You might be right," Spark said, letting the full effect of Hally's remark take hold.

"I shouldn't have said that," Hally said. "I keep saying things that I don't mean."

"Yeah, well . . ." Spark said, leaning forward. He looked down at the space between his feet. Focusing his attention on the large visible crack in the floor, he linked his hands, the way kids do when they use their fingers to make a steeple and a church filled with people. Glancing around the room, he paused to focus on the dresser housing the statue of the Virgin Mary, Flory's red rosary visible in the tiny birdbath. His forehead wrinkled.

"Hally, what really happened that day at Black Head?"

"Is that the first time you've ever asked me that question and meant it?" Hally said. He was standing next to the dresser. He picked up Flory's old rosary.

"I guess maybe I'm finally ready to listen." Spark was looking out at the ocean, clearly visible from Flory's bedroom window.

"I never thought I'd hear you say something like that," Hally said, seeming almost amused. He shrugged and shook his head. "Every day it gets harder to remember," Hally said, replacing the rosary.

"What do you mean?" Spark turned around to face him.

"The apparitions. The things she said. I have trouble remembering. You know how it is when you have a really vivid dream and then you wake up and you have all these intense feelings, you feel scared and upset and you know why but you can't quite get ahold of it and the memories of the dream are just beneath the surface and no matter how hard you try you can't retrieve them? They're always just out of reach."

"Yeah."

"That's how I feel all the time," Hally said. "It doesn't matter. It's too late now," he continued.

"I know it happened. I know I didn't make it up but I've lost the ability to see it or hear it or talk about it. I've grown 'forgetful of the cleansing of my old sins.'"

Spark looked at him, baffled, concerned even, as if Hally were suddenly speaking a foreign language in which he wasn't fluent. "What's that supposed to mean?"

"It's something from the Bible that Gramp told me about. I never used the grace I was given and now it's been taken from me. It means, I blew it."

"Hally . . . I don't know what to say. I give up." Spark seemed lost. He looked at the antique brass bed, white linen feather pillows visible beneath a satiny celadon cover. The flame from the candle burned away.

"Is that where they found her?" Hally said.

"Yup."

"What about you?"

"Kitchen."

"She shouldn't have killed herself. Suicide is the only sin God can't forgive," Hally said.

"Please. This from a guy who engineered his own son's crucifixion . . . She wasn't in her right mind. She died of a disease. She didn't kill herself. Flory didn't want to die." Spark covered his eyes with his hands in a thrust so forceful, for a second I thought he had been struck by something invisible. It was a gesture so unexpected, so uncharacteristic, it made me jump.

Hand to his forehead, Spark stood up, his other hand rubbing the back of his neck. He walked toward the window, and pushed aside the drape. "Let's get some air in here, some light," he said. "I can't breathe." Knees bent, he tried to raise the window but it was stuck. "Hal, give me a hand?"

"Are you all right?"

"I'm fine. I've got it. Never mind," Spark said, straightening up as Hally came up behind him, strong bracing breeze blowing through the room, the flame from the candle flickering, bending sideways.

"You don't seem fine," Hally said. "You're not fine. You can't admit it, can you? You never can just tell the truth. You say you'll tell me the truth. Nobody ever tells the truth."

"Hally, what's wrong with you?"

"Nothing's wrong with me. What's wrong with you?"

"Just so strange being back here in this room, in this house," Spark said, trying to control his agitation.

Hally's expression relaxed, letting go its edge. "I get it," he said, his naturally sympathetic nature showing through. "I'm sorry, Spark."

Spark's expression brightened. "Enough. What's wrong with us? Next thing we'll be saying 'I love you' to each other . . . When in doubt, blow something up," he joked, typical Spark, impulsively reaching for the lycopedium again. He squeezed hard, releasing a particulate cloud of combustible spores into the candle's restless flame and at the same time a gust of wind blew back the yellowed linen curtains.

This is how I remember it: There was a midair explosion of fire that should have lived and died in unison, but in a perfect simultaneous collision of the highly combustible with the highly flammable, the linen curtain, driven into the fireball by a gust of wind, erupted into flames. Shooting flames that immediately made their intentions clear.

There's no containing this, I thought, watching it elapse as if in slow motion.

The flames spread so fast and then the whole thing gave way, all of it, the ornate cream-colored iron rod and the curtains toppled to the floor, dust from the drapes spraying outward, particles of dust spinning and glittering in the sunlight, seeming to ignite the air.

It was as if the house, dusty and desiccated, despairing, had been waiting all these years for just such a moment, looking for the first opportunity to end itself. Smoke began to fill the small room, replacing the air, the air assuming cloudy physical form, growing thicker and grayer, burning my eyes, my throat, my nose.

I scrambled out of the way.

Spark, who had grabbed a pillow from the bed and used it to try to suffocate the flames, got caught beneath the drapes as they fell. Hally cried out and sprang forward as Spark tried to get free, the fire spreading to the bed, to the dresser, to the vanity, flames creeping up the walls, walls blackening and curling like parchment paper.

Hally grabbed the back of Spark's shirt and dragged him out from under the drapes. Once freed, Spark seemed fine but then I watched as his hands melted in front of me, palms filling with fluid, his hands transformed into transparent balloons of liquidized flesh. Hally looked on paralyzed. Spark gave Hally a sharp shove out into the hallway, the flames following behind us, the house filling with smoke, Hally snapping back to life as we ran down the stairs.

We reached the bottom and headed toward the front door, Spark leading the way, the house growing darker, light dimming. It was the smoke. All that smoke, but for the smoke I would have known he was there. I would have detected his scent. I would have recognized him and I would have warned them in time.

I am the chrysanthemum dog, the Chinese sleeve dog, the little lion. What dog am I when it matters?

It was something I sensed and felt more than I saw. It was big and shocking, a smash and a bang. It was small, too. Intimate. Something launched from the closet and into Spark, who collapsed, went down onto his knees, then flattened out onto the entryway floor. I didn't know what happened though I think I knew before Spark did. It wasn't until I looked down and saw the trail of bloody pawprints. That's when I knew.

Hally stumbled over Spark and fell, Harkness on top of him.

"Spark!" Hally called out as Harkness yanked him onto his feet and pulled him toward the door. I shot after them. He swung at me with the same knife he'd used on Spark. He swore as I swerved and yelped and bit him on the ankle.

Hally wrestled loose and we both ran back to Spark who made a single effort to crawl forward and then stopped motionless and silent against the floor. Hally put himself between Spark and Harkness, who was coming in for a second round. It was over. I crept onto Spark's chest and braced myself for what I was certain was to come. To hell with it. I made hasty plans to die well.

I never moved, my front paws on Spark's chest, my face at his neck. Sometimes I feel I will be forever in the present tense of that moment.

My father came to me as in a dream. How astonished he would have been to see me, keeping faith with all those who had gone before me, a dog prepared to face down eternity and the devil himself, to remain by his master's side.

Ignoring Spark's admonition to stay at the house, Hugh had decided to come to Tutela Heights to join Spark in the search for Hally, and was almost there when he smelled the smoke, saw it rising. He was so nearby that even amid the chaos, I heard him as he ran, wood chips and pine needles crunching underfoot. I heard his footsteps on the veranda, heard him exclaim, heard him curse, heard him shouting Spark's name.

"Hally!" he screamed, flinging open the front door.

"Hughie, help. It's him!" Hally pointed as Harkness, startled at this new presence, ran from the hallway and toward the kitchen, the door slamming behind him as he fled, blackness descending. Hugh pushed and felt his way through the haze of smoke and fear and certain ending, lifted me up and gave me to Hally, then gathered Spark into his arms, the floor burning beneath our feet, flames from the dining room now threatening the living room. We stumbled onto the veranda, Hugh coughing, faltering, falling and struggling back up again, half carrying half dragging Spark down the steps and away from the house, where, soaked in blood, he set Spark down on the frozen ground, light dusting of snow turning to red where Spark lay.

Hally sat on the ground beneath the crooked willow tree. His hands, the front of his shirt stained with Spark's blood.

"Hally, what in God's name?" Hugh said.

"It was the little feet of the fox, it was just this stupid magic trick Spark did. It was because of the fire . . . he was hiding downstairs . . . it was the smoke. We didn't see him until it was too late. Oh my God, Hugh, Spark is going to die, isn't he?"

"Spark's going to be fine. I'm going for help," Hugh said, his hands trembling.

Hally started to get up. "I can help him. I can heal him. I can."

Hugh pressed down on Hally's shoulders.

"No," he said. "No you can't."

Hally's hand went to his heart. "I'll pray for him," he said. Tears flowed down his cheeks.

"Hughie," he begged, "who will pray for me?"

Hugh, using both hands now, grabbed him by the shoulders. "Pray later. For now, pull yourself together."

"It's all my fault. I should never have come here . . . Why did I come here? Why didn't I just stay home?"

"Shut up, Hally." I'd never seen this version of Hugh before. "There's no room for this right now. Snap out of it. For once in your life, do as you're told."

We watched them load Spark onto a helicopter. By then a few strangers had gathered, drawn by the smoke and the sound of the propeller. Overhead the sky was mauve and purple and wavering, then it turned blue, every shade of blue, sapphire, indigo, cobalt, and turquoise and the sun was surrounded by a halo of magenta.

The next day around dawn, after a sleepless night at home—the Tick-Tock Girls in their bulky winter coats wailing songs of lamentation beneath the cold and moonless sky—we got the news. There was hope. Not a lot, maybe, but a glimmer. Spark had a chance, despite almost bleeding out before he reached the hospital. The knife had nicked an artery and just missed his remaining kidney. Flory had taken care of his other one. In addition, he suffered second-degree burns on both his hands.

"Some things resist ready explanation. I wouldn't have given you two cents for his life when they wheeled him in here," his surgeon said.

"A miracle. It's nothing short of a miracle." That's what everyone was saying, even some of the doctors and nurses expressed the same belief. Their comments and prognoses were in all the papers. They were interviewed on TV.

When I was growing up, on the street where we lived was a brindle bull terrier named Vera. One day, as I watched from the upstairs window, I saw Vera escape from her yard and run out onto the road and directly into the path of an oncoming car. The driver swerved to avoid her but the rear wheel of the car caught her shoulder, threw her in the air, and when she landed, the force spun her over several times on the asphalt.

The woman who owned her cried out helplessly as she watched. Madelyn and Martin, drawn by the commotion, reacted with shock, all of us, my parents included, certain Vera was finished.

The car pulled over just as Vera stood up on all fours, gave her head a shake, and, roaring with fury, charged at the car and attacked the offending rear wheel. Martin had to run out to help Vera's owner drag her away, so intent was she on murdering the car.

Everyone said it was a miracle. It wasn't a miracle. It was Vera. She was a bull terrier.

It was the way she was built.

Hally's followers descended on the hospital like an influx of migrating birds and like birds they perched and sang, hour after hour, through the day and through the night, nocturnal songbirds singing songs of joy for the miracle of his salvation, and for his deliverance from evil, and from the devil that pursued him.

Monhegan Monster, the media called him.

It seems to be true, what human beings believe, persistence does pay off. By his perseverance, Jonah Harkness had attained a kind of unwarranted mythology. No longer just a garden-variety bad man, he had been elevated to the status of monster. To me, it was a mistake, but then I don't romanticize evil by granting it any sort of mystique.

Meat gone bad, that's all he was.

Still, how different was what Harkness had done from what Flory did? How to distinguish between the madness that seemed to drive them both? It was a smoky business all right, though there were plenty of people who couldn't wait to make their own assessments, pass their own judgments, weigh in on the obvious ironies and tragic improbabilities, the eerie coincidences.

In every case, like a labyrinthine game whose every disparate path leads to the same place, the outcome was assured from the start, Spark lying on the cold floor of that grand old house, bleeding on to the tile.

One night shortly after the attack, after he had returned from visiting Spark at the hospital, I saw Pastor Ragnar sitting alone on the deck in the old rocking chair, the night sky black and cold, unyielding as slate. His worn blue jeans were rolled up to just above his shoes. He was wearing a heavy cable-knit powder-blue sweater under a gabardine jacket.

It was just the two of us awake. Hugh and Hally were in bed. I couldn't sleep.

From inside the house, behind the open crack of the kitchen window, the one so warped that it would never fully close, I could hear Pastor Ragnar murmuring to himself. It was a sound something between a hum and the kind of preliterate intonation of a baby's babble, after they've mastered the ebb and flow of human speech, but not the vocabulary.

I scratched one time on the door asking to be let out. Pastor Ragnar heard and got up from his chair. "Ned," he said, surprised. "You want to come outside with *me*?"

He held the door open as I walked outside and without looking up at him I sat down next to the empty rocking chair and stared out over the black ocean, the water indistinct from the horizon. Pastor Ragnar stayed standing, he bent down to pet my head and scratch behind my ears and then he sat back down in the rocking chair but this time he was silent, the only sound was the insistent lapping of water against stone.

A few moments elapsed and then turning around and facing Pastor Ragnar, I stood up on my hind legs and put my paws on his knees.

"You want up?" he said, reaching for me, lifting me up and onto his lap.

I curled into a circle, Pastor Ragnar's hand on my short neck. I had never before that night sought out Pastor Ragnar's lap. We stayed together that way for a long time, wind blowing, waves gently breaking. I didn't sleep but listened to the whir of the sand mixed with tiny shards of rock and stone, and pellets of ice, listened to the tiny individual thumps as they hit glass, heard the creak of the chair as it rocked on the old wooden boards and finally I listened to the soft sound of Pastor Ragnar as he wept.

"The world is full of unexpected bums and heroes. You never know who will fit into which category," my father used to say. I didn't agree with him. In those days, I was certain all things were obvious. People, like dogs, don't make secrets of themselves, that's what I thought, anyway.

I was wrong. More reliable is the idea that all of us are secrets even to ourselves.

The next morning, Hugh greeted Pastor Ragnar with a hug when he came into the kitchen. They clung to each other in a way I would not have previously thought possible, Hally looking on, eyes red and rimmed in black, coughing, his voice hoarse from smoke.

"I got up early," Hugh said, regaining his composure. "I made your favorite, French toast."

Pastor Ragnar sat down at the table. He unfolded a napkin and laid it on his lap.

"Is there any maple syrup?" he said.

I watched Pastor Ragnar quietly pour maple syrup on his French toast, sip his coffee, use his knife and fork to eat, pat the corners of his mouth with a napkin. I listened to him thank Hugh as he rose from the table, watched him scrape his plate and set his dishes on the counter, saw Hugh fill the sink and prepare to wash up.

Pastor Ragnar told Hugh he had some calls to make, arrangements to complete, people to see. Hugh said he was planning to go to the hospital to be with Spark.

How had I not known before then? Here was the miracle. Camouflaged in the rituals of ordinariness, the willingness to go on.

Three days had passed since the fire when news came that Spark was being transferred from intensive care to a high dependency unit. "He's still at risk," the doctor explained, "but we're short of beds and he's marginally better than the guy who is taking his spot."

Fred MacNamara, besotted with Hally and in deference to his plea, had Spark transferred to a private facility.

"I want to see Spark," Hally declared, standing in the middle of the living room, feet planted, set to do battle, confronting Pastor Ragnar and Hugh. "You can't stop me."

"Be reasonable, Hally," Pastor Ragnar said as Hugh looked on from the kitchen. "It's not safe for you, or Spark for that matter. Harkness is on the loose, obviously insane, driven by demons. Foolishly, we underestimated not only his capacity for evil but his talent for execution. I don't intend to repeat the mistake." Pastor Ragnar implored Hally. "What about the press? To say nothing of these mindless ghouls . . ." Pastor Ragnar checked himself even as Hugh and Hally failed to hide their shared amazement at his rare slipup. "Some of your followers can be . . . a little overzealous . . . They're camped out at the hospital just waiting for you to put in an appearance.

"Some of them even tried to get into Spark's room. Terrible. Lunacy. In his condition. My poor boy. Thank God Fred arranged for security for him. The whole thing's a bloody nightmare."

"I don't care about them. I don't care about any of that stuff," Hally said. "If you don't take me to see him then I'll figure out a way to see him on my own."

"Yeah, well, go for it, Hal. Good luck getting past those guys," Hugh said, pointing to the two men sitting out on the deck who had been hired by Fred MacNamara to protect Hally.

"Is that what it's come to? You taunting me about trying to get to my dad?" Hally asked, his voice breaking, as Hugh, chastened, quickly apologized. "I'm sorry, you're right . . . Hally, everyone's upset. We don't want anything to happen to you. This nutjob will be expecting you to show up at the hospital . . . the police are worried about a copycat . . . it's too dangerous."

Pastor Ragnar reminded Hally that his other grandfather was sending a plane for him, to take him to Virginia, where they could provide the kind of security he needed.

"I'm not leaving without first seeing Spark," Hally said. "So unless you guys want to tie me up and throw me into a cage, you can't stop me. If you send me to Virginia, I'll turn around and come back. I'll hitchhike, if I have to."

Hugh, defeat written in the downward slide of his shoulders, spoke to Pastor Ragnar as if Hally weren't in the room. "It's hopeless. He's not going to budge. I can't fight with him and worry about Spark, too. I'll take him," he said. "He can come with me. The security guys will be with us. Nothing is going to happen to him." He broke off and pointed at Hally. "Only if you agree that right afterward you'll go to the Mac-Namaras. Is it a deal?"

Hally nodded.

Pastor Ragnar threw up his hands. "Go get changed," he said to Hally, who was wearing torn track pants and a faded T-shirt and paused to give his grandfather a grateful hug. "You're not going to face the world looking like a common housefly."

"Not a common housefly," Hally said, bolting from the room, "an anointed housefly."

"You're just like Spark, you know that?" Hugh said.

"No I'm not," Hally said. "There's nobody like Spark."

In the car on the way to the hospital, Hugh, fingers tapping against his knee, tried to warn Hally about what to expect. Hally stared ahead, listening, then he turned his head and looked out at the passing cars. Hugh did the same. It was raining, big drops of slushy water drumming against the windshield, wipers unable to keep up with the deluge.

"Lousy day," Hugh said, peering at the darkening skies. "Maybe we'll get snow."

"Yeah," Hally said.

The first thing I noticed was the whiteness. Everything was white. The walls of the room, the bed linens, the nurses' uniforms, the linoleum floor, the cotton curtains on the window. There was a large bouquet, white flowers in a white vase from the MacNamaras, Madonna lilies, pure but glamorous, their worldly white fragrance at odds with the dull antiseptic air, hint of bleach at the edge of everything.

White bandages on his hands, white bandages covered in white gauze.

I wasn't prepared for the harm that had been done to him.

The first thing I had ever noticed about Spark was his white skin, his black hair, his blue eyes. His colors faded now, as if someone had applied a watery basecoat over top, his natural vibrancy was barely visible between a thin pale wash. Even his lips were pale. His eyes were gray and rimmed in black. Hugh reached out and clamped his wrist around Hally's forearm to steady him.

"Don't be alarmed by the tubes," a nurse had said before we entered the room.

I was ready for the tubes. The tubes were part of the mechanics of treatment. I wasn't ready for the stillness. We approached him tentatively. Was he breathing? His skin was almost translucent. For a moment I entertained the thought that even his blood had turned white in his veins.

"I've got a surprise for you," Hugh said, struggling for normalcy, lifting me out of a leather carryall and onto the bed next to Spark.

"Be careful, Ned," Hugh cautioned as I wagged the tip of my tail and lay down next to Spark, fearful of moving, afraid I might break him. Opening his eyes took all his strength.

"Hi, Spark," Hally said as Hugh shifted me to the bottom of the bed, away from Spark's burned hands. "Infection," he shrugged to Hally. "Sorry, Ned. Can't be too careful . . . Almost forgot, Beans sent you this," Hugh said, reaching back into the bag and retrieving a small stuffed lobster. Spark grimaced. "Don't make me laugh," he whispered, minus the whispering part. We read his lips. He seemed overwhelmed.

"How are you feeling?" Hally asked, not knowing what else to say.

"Hurts to breathe," Spark said. Even I had to lean in to hear him.

"I'm so sorry for what happened, Spark," Hally said, restraint giving way.

"Not your fault," Spark said, eyes closing, his body shaking with the effort to speak.

Hugh sat down in the chair next to the bed and looked down at his hands. No one spoke. Silence was all around us, seeming to fall in big steady meditative drops like the rain, but then Spark began noiselessly to cry.

"Holy shit, Hugh," he said, and Hugh, who in that moment seemed to shatter into a million pieces, quickly pieced himself together.

"Oh no," he said. "Don't. Please. What can I do? Spark, everything's going to be all right. You're going to be fine." He paused, hesitating, searching for the thing to say. "You're getting better every day . . . Oh my God, are you all right?" Hally ran for a nurse as Spark, shuddering suddenly and gagging, struggled to sit up.

Hugh and the nurse helped support him as Hally looked on helplessly while Spark retched repeatedly into a metal bowl. He gasped, coughing, as they lowered him back down.

"You're all right, sweetheart," the nurse said. "Hmm. You feel cold. Are you cold?" Without waiting for an answer she left the room and quickly returned with a warming blanket.

"He had a fever earlier. We're treating him for pneumonia," she said.

"Pneumonia," Hugh said. "What else can go wrong?"

"Plenty," she said, her response suggesting she thought he needed to grow up about what we were dealing with. Seeing the shock on Hally's face, she softened her tone a little. "Look, pneumonia's not unusual after surgery and the kind of trauma he's been through."

"What's he doing here?" the nurse said, glancing over at me as she covered Spark and fluffed his pillows. "Dogs aren't allowed in here. You should know better than this. He can't handle a dog right now. What are you thinking?"

"He's not a dog, not exactly," Hugh said. "They're inseparable. It will help him. If it's too much, I'll take him home. Let him stay, won't you, please?"

Grumbling a little, the nurse, seeing what a pitiable lot we were, agreed I could stay—on the floor—but she couldn't guarantee the next nurse would be so generous. "He needs sleep," she said, cautioning Hugh and Hally as she was leaving. "He's not out of the woods yet."

Hally, head bowed, stood for a long time at Spark's bedside, not speaking. He bent down to kiss Spark on the forehead.

"I'm going to go now, Hughie," he said.

Hugh stood up. "Wait a minute, Hal," he said, but Hally turned his back and headed toward the door. He held up his hand, back of his palm visible.

"Don't say goodbye," he said, and then he was gone.

"What do you think, Ned?" Hugh said later that afternoon. "What should we do?" He touched Spark's forehead and, satisfied he was neither too hot nor too cold, reaching over, he pulled a sketch pad from his bag and began to draw.

Spark slept on, seldom waking, and seeming only barely conscious when he was awake. Hugh, a fixture in the armchair next to him, filled several sketchbooks as he waited, day after day, for Spark to be all right. The nurses had long since stopped objecting to my presence and some even began to bring me treats.

Spark was asleep for three weeks, hovering in the mysterious place between life and death, until one morning, he woke up and stunned Hugh by asking him for pancakes. Hugh rushed out to a nearby restaurant and brought him back an enormous plate of buttermilk pancakes.

"Here, let me help you," Hugh said, eyeing Spark's hands.

"You forgot the brown sugar," Spark said.

"Sorry, I'll get some for you," Hugh said, still trying to understand Spark's sudden resurrection from the dead.

"Thanks," Spark said, looking at Hugh expectantly. "Uh, Hughie, they're getting cold."

"Oh yeah, sure," Hugh said grabbing his jacket. "I'll be right back."

After he left, Spark looked over at me, signaling for me to come closer. I was on the bed, the very place I wasn't supposed to be. I crept up along the inside of his arm and laid my head on his chest. I looked into his eyes, feeling so much lightness of being, it was as if I'd swallowed summer.

I was still thinking about the brown sugar. I thought about something my father used to say.

Where there's a yearning for sweetness, there's hope.

Twenty-six

~~~~~~

It was late March 1987, several months after the incident at Tutela Heights. Spark was driving. Pastor Ragnar was in the passenger seat. I was between them, my head resting on Spark's leg. We were heading for the airport. Pastor Ragnar was flying to Italy for a conference, where he was a keynote speaker. On his return, he had plans to move into a condo he'd bought on the mainland, but now he was having second thoughts about his decision. He wasn't sure Spark was sufficiently recovered to live on his own.

"Are you sure you can manage everything on your own?"

"Yeah, I'm fine."

"I don't think it's such a good idea for you to be alone."

"It's only for a few months. Hugh's coming back from New York for the summer. I'm a big boy, Pop, I can take care of myself. You need to be more centrally located. You can't continue to run things from the middle of nowhere."

"I know, but—"

"Ned and I are okay."

Spark checked his rearview mirror, signaled and swung into the left lane. "Don't worry," he said, glancing over at his father. "I'm not going to kill myself, if that's what you're afraid of."

"Jamie!"

"Come on, Pop, you and Hugh have been treating me as if I'm about to shatter at any moment."

We drove along for a few more miles in silence until finally Pastor Ragnar cleared his throat. "I was talking to Fred the other day."

Spark's leg tensed. "Oh yeah, what did he have to say?"

"Apparently Hally is doing well. He blamed himself for what happened to you, it had a very bad effect on him."

"What happened wasn't his fault. How was it his fault?"

"Of course not . . . but he feels guilty for sneaking off to the house with Harkness on the loose."

"That's just kid stuff. The rest was a convergence of factors out of our control. One of those factors being me," Spark said. "I'm responsible for the fire."

"There have been good things to emerge from all this, though. We really can't fault Fred. He never missed a beat. Sent the plane. Got him out of there quickly. Of course, Fred's brought in all the top people. Amazing the progress that's been made. These miracle pharmaceuticals . . ."

"Miracle pharmaceuticals?" Spark said. "Did I miss something? Whatever happened to healthy skepticism?"

"Are you all right to talk about this? It's hard to know sometimes what to say."

"Talk away," Spark said. "You don't need to censor yourself around me. He's my kid. I want know what's going on . . ."

"Good. Marvelous what can be done, so Fred assures me."

"Okay, well," Spark said. "I don't know . . ."

"What is it?"

"I'm not quite as convinced as the rest of you that Hally is mentally ill. Why the hell wouldn't he have a hard time with all that's happened? It seems like a pretty normal response to me."

"Oh, Jamie, given Flory's history, surely that's the case. He butchered his hair on that last day, for one thing. Who does such a thing? Mutilates themselves that way. You admitted yourself, you were concerned about him the night of the concert, what he might do. There were other increasing signs."

"Like what?" Spark looked over at him.

"Little things I'd begun to notice. Alarming things."

"So that's why you got MacNamara involved," Spark said. "You decided Hally was a mental case and you wanted the MacNamaras to take over. You drove him nuts with all the religion bullshit and then you let the MacNamaras pick up the pieces. Lucky for you I was out of the picture and couldn't do anything to prevent it.

"Is that what you think? You're right about only one thing. I had become concerned about Hally's mental state but you're wrong to say I wanted to dump him on the MacNamaras as if he were so much garbage. I reluctantly had to admit to myself that Hally's problems were beyond our pay grade. Also, he was in grave danger from this Harkness lunatic, or do you forget?

"Had you not shown up at the house that day, Hally would have been alone and God knows what Harkness would have done to him. The MacNamaras could provide the kind of security and life for him that no one else could. I can admit that, Spark, why can't you? I assure you, my motives were unselfish."

"Obviously he was kind of a mess . . . but Jesus, so was I when I wasn't much older than him. He'll pull out of it. I have a little experience with this stuff. I know. It's not like Flory. It's nothing like Flory. He's going to come through this and he's going to be okay."

"His psychiatrists say—"

"I gotta say, Pop, Hally falling into the hands of these guys, becoming a mental patient, is the last thing I wanted for him. Fred

MacNamara is someone with endless resources and no patience, who figures you assemble the 'best,' whatever the hell that means, and in short order you fix whatever's wrong. Hally would be better off spending time with Neddy than all these geniuses with no understanding of, I don't know—idiosyncrasy, imagination, hypercreativity, whatever you want to call it."

"I appreciate your reluctance to accept the facts, but truly, I think you're being naïve and indulging in wishful thinking."

"So does that mean you're okay with publicly declaring the apparitions a manifestation of Hally's mental illness? That's what his doctors think, right? It was just one big hallucination."

"Who am I to make such a claim when even the Catholic Church is taking the miracle on Monhegan Island seriously enough to launch its own investigation?"

Spark chuckled. "And I'm left to wonder how any of us decide who's crazy and who isn't."

"Best not to think about it. It does no good for you to keep going over it in your head. You've been through a hell of a time. You can't minimize the effects of trauma. You're still recovering." Pastor Ragnar waited for the response that wasn't forthcoming. "I only hope they catch that bastard Harkness . . ."

"Yeah," Spark agreed. "I'm running out of kidneys."

"Spark, you shouldn't paper over your feelings with punch lines."

"Is that what I'm doing?"

"Yes, it is—you've been doing it your whole life. I should know and I'm never wrong."

"One thing you were right about was Hally's disappearing only contributing to his mystique. People are more obsessed than ever—of course, the occasional fanning of the flames doesn't hurt." Spark gave his father a sly peripheral glance. "Never say die, right, Pop?"

Pastor Ragnar pulled a pair of sunglasses from the side pocket of the passenger door.

"Bright out today," he said, shielding his eyes from the glare. "So, then, what will you do to keep yourself occupied alone on Monhegan Island?" Without waiting for an answer he continued. "You know, Jamie, we may not be the MacNamaras but we have money now, for the moment anyway. You don't need to worry about anything."

"Thanks, Pop."

"Maybe you'd like to buy your own fishing boat?"

"Or maybe I'd like to work on my tan for a while longer."

Pastor Ragnar laughed.

"I've been thinking I might fix up the house," Spark said.

"That's a good idea," Pastor Ragnar said. "Good for you and good for the house."

We rode along in silence for a few miles when Spark spoke up. "What signs?"

"What do you mean?"

"You said you noticed other troubling signs about Hally's mental state. What signs?"

"His solitariness. His growing despondency. An uncharacteristic introversion. Not sleeping. Oversleeping. Odd things. He told me, for example, he had heard the lobsters on the boat crying. He said he heard them screaming when they were thrown into boiling water."

"Well, okay, it's a silent scream, then, but do you imagine they enjoy being boiled alive?"

"All right, it's hopeless. You're hopeless," Pastor Ragnar said. "Maybe it's a case of like father, like son."

"Don't let Hally hear you say that or he really will flip his lid."

Spark rolled down the car window and leaned over and turned up the radio, wind rushing into the car, ingenuous tenor of Phil Ochs singing bittersweetly about what it means to be gone.

Spark was carrying me around in a plastic basket. We were at an air-port kiosk watching Pastor Ragnar choose reading material for the long plane trip ahead. He grabbed *The New York Times* and *The Wall Street Journal* and then wandered over to check out the magazine rack. Spark picked up a chocolate bar and went to the cash register to pay for it, wincing a little as he walked, still feeling the effects of the attack.

The clerk was busy with another customer and as we waited, Spark looked back at his father, who was choosing among *Time*, *Newsweek*, *Esquire*, and *The New Yorker*, storing them in the crook of his elbow. Then, his manner brisk and purposeful, confidently oblivious, he reached out and picked up a current copy of *Playboy*, opening it up to the centerfold. He held it out and slightly away from himself, briefly looked at the April playmate, and then, closing up the magazine, he returned it to its spot on the shelf. He came up alongside Spark and took the chocolate bar from his hand.

"It's on me," he said as Spark smiled and said thanks and lifted me from the basket and as he tightened his hold I felt his heart break a little for in those few seconds he knew, as he had not known before, that his father was an ordinary man.

As we waited for boarding, someone in the business-class lounge approached Pastor Ragnar, politely, hesitantly, a woman who recognized him and seemed to want to engage him in a conversation about religion. She told him she was reading his book and agreed with many of his ideas.

"I was raised a Catholic," she said. "Catholics are accustomed to ignoring their beliefs. I believe in God, at least I think I do, I just don't want to do that much about it . . ."

Another woman, heartened by Pastor Ragnar's approachability, joined them. The two women were friends, on their way to France. Pastor Ragnar greeted the second woman warmly.

"Your friend was just telling me that she enjoys eating as long as she doesn't have to cook," he said. Everyone laughed, except Spark.

"That's all right," Pastor Ragnar said. "Believe in God. Don't believe in God. Some days I don't much believe in God. Always a struggle. Such duality is in the nature of man and the nature of God."

"Is He ever indifferent, though?" the first woman asked.

"Not that I've noticed," Pastor Ragnar said.

"Your grandson," the other woman, said. "I saw him a few weeks ago, walking with a couple of men, I assume they were bodyguards, they looked like bodyguards. Big. Serious. I was in Middleburg, visiting. I recognized him right away, something about him," she said. "It wasn't easily forgotten," she continued, "being in his presence. I didn't want to disturb him," she said, "and I was shocked to see him. He seemed lost in thought."

Spark, no longer distant, was listening attentively.

"Tell them," the first woman urged.

"You'll think I'm crazy," the second woman said, blushing.

"What is it?" Pastor Ragnar said. "I can assure you, we don't judge."

" Well," she said, beginning with a nervous laugh. After her brief meeting with Hally, she felt a strange peacefulness envelope her and a descending warmth, as if she were being held in an invisible embrace. "Colors were more vibrant. The sky seemed bluer. The sun shone brighter. I felt so happy and alive, as if all things were good. I felt such hope."

"I don't know what you were worried about. Nothing crazy about that story," Spark said as the women looked at him intently, trying to decipher his meaning.

True believers. Just like the ones who still made the pilgrimage to the house. Crazy, some of them, others simply wanting to scrub away the daily dullness in their search for the shimmering world, people seeking a bluer sky, a brighter sun, a tighter embrace.

Seeing Spark's face as he listened, he always had such sweetness of expression, and watching Pastor Ragnar be reborn in the moment, becoming ever more alive, while talking at great animated length with the two women, even as they were joined by other bystanders, until a small congregation of strangers had formed, drawn by Pastor Ragnar's ranging inclusiveness and the boldness of the conversation—"Nobody's perfect, not even God," he proclaimed, as if it were his motto—witnessing Spark's elegant estrangement and his father's clattering engagement, I had my own small epiphany.

If, as I suspected, Spark had always secretly believed Hally about the apparitions, I knew then Pastor Ragnar never had.

Twenty-seven

May 1991

Spark and I had been living alone at the house on Monhegan for four years, though Hugh came often, convinced that Spark needed someone to take care of him. And maybe he did. Hugh liked to paint on the island, too, especially during the summer months, something about the light, he explained. In his absence, we had our own comforting set of rituals and though Spark was never the same, in some ways, it's also true to say he was more the same in others.

Hally was living in Virginia with the MacNamaras. He had never been back home since that awful day at the hospital, but he kept in regular touch with everyone and Spark had visited him a few times, taking me with him each time. Hally was doing well, thriving even.

He had graduated from Georgetown Prep and was planning to go to Yale. He seemed in good shape mentally and emotionally, though, as his doctors reminded everyone, appearances aren't always reliable.

"What is reliable? I'd like to know," Spark asked them during one contentious meeting he attended.

"Your big mouth is reliable," Hally said.

He still had his followers, their numbers continuing to multiply, some driven as much by gossip as gospel, but they were kept contained, like a virus against which he had been effectively inoculated. The disease was still in circulation but was no longer the threat to him it had once been, or so it seemed.

"Never underestimate what money can do and what it can provide," Frederick MacNamara said.

Hally and Spark were on okay terms, affectionate with each other, though reserved, there was a persistent uneasiness, too, a longing of sorts, a melancholy that caused them to seem sometimes guarded when they were together, as if there was something going unexpressed between them.

Things were better when Hugh was with them.

"It's your cooking that makes all the difference," Spark told him, then more seriously: "Gotta face it, Hugh. I waited too long."

During one visit, I joined Hally—he was seventeen at the time—in his bedroom one late night, resuming our old habit of spending a few hours together before I retired with Spark. I took a long look around. Hally's room at the MacNamara estate bore little resemblance to his bedroom on Monhegan.

"I miss you, Neddy," he said. "I guess you'd never consider moving in here with me, would you?"

Not even if you got me my own pony, I thought.

I looked at him, my expression appealing to him for understanding.

"I know," he said. "I know you and Spark are a team. It's okay. I'm glad. He needs somebody. I'd never try to break you guys up."

He got out of bed and I followed him into the en suite.

"Time for my crazy pills," he said, reaching for a prescription vial. He popped open the lid, extracted a pill, turned on the faucet and watched as it dissolved down the sink drain.

"You're the only one who knows my little secret, Neddy. I've never taken any of this stuff. I may be nuts, but I'm not crazy."

It's seldom I think about my former life. I was supposed to take my place alongside my parents—one a Crufts winner, the other top dog at Westminster—a crooked incisor was all it took to keep me from shining on the world stage. A single wonky tooth conferred on me a defining ordinariness, destroyed my prospects, reduced me to the status of pet and eventually landed me in the back of an idling Mercedes in a convenience store parking lot on a lazy Saturday afternoon, instead of inside a show ring, showing off my daisy-cutting gait, my silky red coat skimming the ground.

My parents were admired by dogs and humans alike, all of whom viewed me as a disappointment, the mediocre progeny of an immaculate but underwhelming union, destined to become just another forgettable mutt snatched from the backseat of a car by an equally undistinguished human stray.

How then can it be I've led the most astonishing life?

Pray you, too, someday will experience the possibilities arising from a minor imperfection.

Hugh surprised Spark with a visit to Monhegan in early May 1991.

"What are you doing here?" Spark said when he walked through the door.

"Neddy!" Hugh bent down to greet me, even as I ran to welcome him.

"Hugh? Talk to me."

Hugh stood up. "I'm just here for a few days. Hey, you look good. The place looks great."

"Thanks, now quit stalling and tell me why you're here."

The police contacted Hugh because his painting, *Purveyor of Wonderment*, the portrait of me that had been stolen, was recovered when, acting on a tip, they broke into the apartment in New York City where Jonah Harkness had been living. The place was intact but abandoned and contained the predictable if no less disturbing shrine to Hally, complete with pictures, photographs, articles, and insane personal writing, hundreds of handwritten pages scattered throughout the apartment.

My portrait, a torn canvas, was taped onto the living room wall beneath a hand-painted slogan: ThiS is how it ends.

Hugh asked the police if he could notify the others first.

"I wanted to tell you in person."

"Sure. Thanks, Hughie. What about Harkness?" Spark asked, sitting across from Hugh at the kitchen table.

"Long gone. Nobody knows where. The police are still looking for him . . ."

Hugh fiddled with his coffee spoon. He stood up and headed toward the stove.

"Who is this guy?" Spark said. "Why can't they catch him?"

"I worry about you here alone . . . Plus, I know your health isn't that great, no matter how you try to pretend otherwise. You're not that strong, Spark."

"Hugh, come on . . ."

"All right. All right . . . How about some tea?" Hugh asked, reaching for the kettle, filling it with water. "Anyway, it's good Hally got away from here and from Pop, too, though it pains me to say it. The

MacNamaras have been able to give him some semblance of normalcy," Hugh said as Spark looked at him in disbelief. "You know what I mean . . . forget the dread privilege. Just think for a minute. He was able to go to school. Make friends. Have some stability in his life. Be a kid! Be protected. Feel safe. Live a life apart from this other life. Escape the intimacy and the wear and tear of the craziness. It was destroying him. Hell, Spark, it almost killed you."

"I can't argue with you about that."

"I'm surprised you've stayed on here, honestly. Aren't you lonely? Don't you get bored?"

"No. I like it here. I get into the big city now and then. What the hell? I don't have any career ambitions. I've got Beans. I've got Mrs. Houton to keep me humble. Do you know she cooks meals for me all the time and checks up on me, says she's got a duty to Mom to keep me out of trouble? You never know about people. What more can a man ask for? I figure I earned my pension from Cludo. What am I going to do?"

"It's never too late for dental school," Hugh kidded him.

Spark just kept shaking his head. "No," he said. "No. *That* is not how it ends."

Not long after Hugh's visit, there was a large gathering of the faithful at Black Head on May 13, the fifth anniversary of the apparitions. They came as they had been coming for the last five years. This year, unlike previous years, Spark made the pilgrimage to Black Head, too, standing apart from all the rest, listening to all those constancies, the wail of the wind, the lash of the waves, and the cries of the seabirds in concert with the rote singing of Marian hymns.

I looked around, the Tick-Tock Girls were there, older now but unchanged in all the ways that matter, wearing their matching dresses, their colliding harmonies intact. Pastor Ragnar was there. His voice rose above all the rest. He urged his followers to pray for Hally, for he had gone deep into the spiritual desert, he said, and was being tested sorely.

"Men forget that all deities reside in the human heart," he said, borrowing from Blake.

"Hallelujah!" someone shouted and soon others followed. All those Hallelujahs, resounding like trumpets, blowing out over the ocean, dispersing on the wind.

Spark stayed behind after the others had gone. He walked up to the edge of the cliff and looked out over the ocean. I sat at his feet. A scent I knew as well as I knew myself, crept up slowly behind me.

"Still not smoking, I see."

"Hally," Spark said, unable to conceal his shock. "You've come home."

"You did too, come back home, I mean," Hally said, giving his father a shy hug, breaking away to lift me up, holding me tightly against his chest.

"Yeah, well, we're not the same. I didn't have anyplace else to go."

Hally unzipped his jacket and shook his head free of its concealing hood, golden hair curling at his collar, amber highlights catching the sunlight.

"Hello, Joe College," Spark said.

Hally laughed. "You get like the people you live with."

"You look like Flory," Spark said. "Wow." He took a deep breath and lowered his head, exhaling loudly, overcome. "You're so much like her."

"I used to think so, too, but not anymore," Hally said. "I think I'm more like you."

In his own patently offhand way, Spark looked surprised. Hally set me down on the ground and he reached out and touched his father's hand. "You stole Neddy, didn't you, Spark?"

Spark sighed. "Yeah," he said. "I stole Neddy."

Hally smiled. Such a gentle sane moment. The sky was clear and blue and stretched out before us as if there were no beginning to it and no end either.

"Do you see what I see?" Hally said, looking out across the ocean.

Spark leaned over and picked me up, lifted me to his shoulder, top of my head at eye level.

"Yeah," he said. "I think maybe I do."

Acknowledgments

Thank you, Molly Friedrich, for your dauntless spirit and generosity, for the great gift of your representation and for letting me have what for. I needed that.

Thank you, Katie Adams, for being the real deal, and for single-handedly upending the modern myth that editors no longer edit. You make me a better writer. You make me tell a better story. I cut my favorite joke at your behest—that's not just respect, that's love.

Thank you, Lucy Carson, Molly Schulman, and Nichole LeFebvre, for your patience and your insights and for being so generous with your time and your suggestions.

Thank you, Peter Miller, Cordelia Calvert, and Amy Robbins. Thank you to the entire wonderful crew at Liveright, W. W. Norton. It's a privilege to belong to such an outstanding publishing house. Thank you, Robert Weil.

Thank you, Tara Hire of Monhegan Wellness, and Donna Cundy, for taking the time to help a stranger understand something about particular aspects of life on Monhegan Island. Your information was invaluable to me.

Thank you to the detailed historical accounts of Marian apparitions, especially at Fátima and Lourdes, which helped inform Hally's vision on Monhegan Island.

Thank you to the nuns of my childhood who so pulverized me with endless renditions of "Bring Flowers of the Rarest" that it is a permanent fixture of my daily brain activity, the ultimate earworm. I sing it involuntarily. I sing it *all the time*. It is like a form of musical breathing. I'm sure it will be the last thing about me to die.

Thank you to my husband, my children, my sisters, my beloved brother-in-law Andy. Yes, I have forgiven you for all those years of referring to my writing as "Liz's/Mum's futile efforts." Thanks for always keeping it real!

Finally, thank you, Ned, for being my inspiring companion in life and on the page. For a dog, you are one cool cat. May you live for a thousand years.